The Wars of Our Ancestors

▼ ▼ ▼ ▼ ▼ ▼ ▼ ▼ ▼ ▼ ▼ ▼ ▼ ▼

THE WARS OF OUR ANCESTORS

▲ ▲ ▲ ▲ ▲ ▲ ▲ ▲ **MIGUEL DELIBES**

Translated by Agnes Moncy

The University of Georgia Press

Athens and London

© 1992 by Miguel Delibes
All rights reserved
Published by the University of Georgia Press
Athens, Georgia 30602
Designed by Louise OFarrell
Set in 10/13 Ehrhardt by Tseng Information Systems, Inc.
Printed and bound by Braun-Brumfield, Inc.
The paper in this book meets the guidelines for permanence
and durability of the Committee on Production Guidelines
for Book Longevity of the Council on Library Resources.

Printed in the United States of America
96 95 94 93 92   C   5 4 3 2 1

Library of Congress Cataloging in Publication Data
Delibes, Miguel.
[Guerras de nuestros antepasados. English]
The wars of our ancestors / Miguel Delibes ; translated by
Agnes Moncy.
p.   cm.
ISBN 0-8203-1418-8 (alk. paper)
I. Title.
PQ6607.E45G813   1992
863'.64—dc20   91-32399
                                              CIP

British Library Cataloging in Publication Data available

This translation was supported by a grant from the Program for
Cultural Cooperation Between Spain's Ministry of Culture and
United States Universities.

To Christina

▲ ▲ ▲ ▲ ▲ ▲ ▲
Introduction

Two people talk in private for seven nights, an examining psychologist and an imprisoned criminal. Gradually, there is a story—the doctor's development of the case—and within it, another story—the patient's account of his life. For the reader of *The Wars of Our Ancestors*, it is a fascinating combination, a chance to explore two usually separate worlds.

Originally published in 1975 as *Las guerras de nuestros antepasados* (Barcelona: Destino), the novel scarcely shows a trace of its author, Miguel Delibes. So deftly have the parts been assembled that the story seems to tell itself. Yet clearly, the characters who speak, Dr. Burgueño López and Pacífico Pérez, have been created, and their encounters have been planned. Whoever has seen the theatrical production of the novel, which opened in Madrid at the Teatro de Bellas Artes in the fall of 1989 (and has enjoyed tremendous success) knows that the long dialogue stands the test of the stage. Written language becomes spoken, and the result is to remind one of the importance of voice, a character's voice, and the various kinds of imagination engaged in this piece of fiction: the author's, the reader's, the doctor's, and Pacífico's. Pacífico tells about his town in the relatively simple "real" space, the doctor's office, and thus the town becomes an imaginary space, populated by all who are made active in it. The contrast is stark and is emphasized by the austere set used in the play as well as the sparse description of the real space in the text.

Given the novel's technically simple form, one naturally wonders how the author manages to provide the richness a reader expects from fiction. Basically, Delibes relies on abundant indirect quotations. Pacífico, in telling his tale, dramatizes his world by allowing the doctor (his listener) and by extension us (his reader-listeners) to hear many other people speak; his parents, grandparents, great-grandfather, and uncle all contribute in their own styles, that is, their own speech, to his tale, permitting us to "hear" the whole family. The same technique allows the author to create the other significant characters, especially Pacífico's girlfriend, Candi, whose graphic speech and wild acts unsettle the physician somewhat.

Stylistically diverse, then, within its formal simplicity, *The Wars of Our Ancestors* is experimental as well as easy to follow. The chronological order and occasional clarifications identify each speaker, avoiding the blurriness of some contemporary novels that founder in the complexity they propose.

The technique is not new in Delibes's narrative work. In 1966, in *Cinco horas con Mario* (*Five Hours with Mario*), he had used it for a similar purpose: to facilitate the entry and exit of secondary characters from the main character's discourse. Interestingly enough, the 1990 winner of Spain's Premio Nadal, Juan José Millás, mixed various discourses for a similar effect in his novel *La soledad era esto*. In *Cinco horas*, one "listens" to a widow, who in her soliloquy, or "monodialogue," as it has been aptly termed by Gonzalo Sobejano, describes her life as Mario's wife. Her listener, unlike Pacífico's, is totally passive and has no part in shaping her story; he is her recently deceased husband, whose underlinings of passages in the Bible serve as stimulants to her thoughts. In both novels, spoken language takes precedence over an author's written language.

Framing the seven nights of conversation that constitute almost all of the book are two brief reports by the physician. The first precedes the taped medical interview and supplies enough information about the patient to establish for the reader the doctor's image of him. The second report acts as an epilogue.

Stylistic experimentation has been a constant in Delibes's work for a long time. Since shortly after the close of the Spanish Civil War, the productive author of *The Wars of Our Ancestors* has accustomed his audience to his versatility as a writer of fiction, notably in *Smoke on the Ground* (*Las ratas*, 1962) and *The Hedge* (*Parábola del náufrago*, 1969). Most would agree that he vies with Camilo José Cela as the greatest and most active writer his country has produced this century. His frequent journalistic essays express his ecological knowledge and concerns and define his political (moral) stance. His intense activity—both intellectual and physical—as hunter and sportsman make him a unique example of a contemporary Renaissance man.

Interested in marginal figures, Delibes captures the essence of their lives and of the society, urban or rural, that molds or sometimes disfigures them. In *The Wars of Our Ancestors*, these social realms are distant but complementary. Dr. Burgueño López, a well-educated, well-meaning man, probes the wily yet innocent mind and conduct of a Castilian peasant, allowing us to discover a Spanish town on the inside: in the values transmitted, in the customs described in amusing detail, and in its ways—brutal, amusing, or wise. One of the constant themes is ever-present violence: its force as a formative influence even on the most peaceful, "pacific" man. Indeed, the main purpose of the doctor's inquiry is to comprehend why his docile patient killed another man in cold blood without regrets. In order to understand Pacífico's conduct, the doctor must learn about his patient's world. He must learn to interpret not only individual violent acts, with their specific motivations, but also life and death themselves as experienced in a small town instead of a city. He must learn how his patient interprets the death of a loved one and, by extension, how he loves. His task is not a simple one: since his patient has always felt he was different from others, the doctor must gain a sense of the "norm" as he goes along and then, in that context, judge Pacífico's difference.

Is the doctor's inquiry guided by a method? Yes, he employs the analytical method. Elsewhere I have studied the medical aspect of this narrative, showing how the psychological theory adopted tends to shape the narrative material a certain way.* Suffice it to say that by uncovering early trauma, the doctor hopes to explain Pacífico's avoidance conduct; when the relevant facts about the patient's childhood are assembled, the doctor does in fact form a theory of Pacífico's personality. As this issue and the patient's physical illness constitute the clinically interesting aspects of the literary character, they deserve detailed treatment. Here I merely wish to indicate their presence and importance. In the doctor's reports, these aspects are naturally considered more central than others, such as Pacífico's knack for telling a story, his intuitive grasp of reality, his sexual preferences, and his honest instincts.

*See Chapter 6 of my book *La novela experimental de Miguel Delibes* (Madrid: Taurus, 1981).

Transference, another subject that looms large in discussing a therapist-patient relationship, is observable in the novel, although it is not a dramatic feature. Comfortable together, the doctor and his patient usually talk in trust, with a common interest of putting events into some kind of perspective. If not, the divergence is what one might expect: the patient needs to be reminded to stay on the subject, or he balks at being questioned too much or thinks the doctor is splitting hairs. Sometimes there is a slight miscommunication due to their different cultural and linguistic levels, which necessitates the analyst's "translating" his own terms, which are more sophisticated, into Pacífico's, which are simpler. Occasionally the doctor must ask his patient to elucidate certain particulars of rural life. Since Pacífico has been examined by various officials before these sessions with Dr. Burgueño López, he tends to see his therapist as another authority figure, comparable at times to the lawyer (when insistent), the priest (when judging his conduct), or another doctor (when diagnoses differ). No specific transference actually occurs, perhaps because Pacífico had already chosen a mentor in his Uncle Paco and because he does not suffer from an amorous conflict that might have led him toward a compensatory figure.

Another fictitious therapist-patient relationship was explored recently in Marie Cardinal's *Les Mots pour le dire*, in which transference is more important.* There the outcome is more satisfying in that the patient, seeking self-understanding and consequent liberation, achieves it, whereas no such clarity marks the ending of *The Wars*.

Finally, the only clear feeling that emerges at the end of the novel is that the doctor has tried to defend his patient, compromising his own ethics in the process as he advises Pacífico to lie at the trial about his lack of sympathy for his victim. So, oddly enough, therapist ends by asking patient to be less direct, not to deceive the judge willfully, but to give a version of his conduct that will guarantee the pardon that the therapist, knowing more, believes his patient deserves. That additional knowledge—of Pacífico's cooperative spirit in prison, his modesty about his gift for working with bees without getting stung, his normally unaggressive behavior in the town and later in the sanato-

---

*Cardinal's novel was translated from the French by Pat Goodheart, as *The Words to Say It* (Cambridge, Mass.: VanVector and Goodheart, 1983).

rium, and his generosity, charging his neighbors for his services only after his family nags him—uncovers heroic attributes in a man whose nature is unappreciated in a society obsessed with individual triumphs instead of being concerned about the moral fiber of those individuals' communities.

Basically, then, *The Wars of Our Ancestors* is social criticism, and in this it resembles other major novels by Delibes: it denounces most contemporary values—not overtly, but in the author's choice of protagonist and his sympathetic attitude toward him. His work leads us to reflect on several dichotomies we are used to perceiving as opposites: free versus jailed, normal versus abnormal, peaceful versus aggressive. In Pacífico Pérez the reader discovers a man who feels free in jail; whose "abnormal" avoidance of competitiveness and aggression may be a more "normal" course for humanity; whose struggle to remain peaceful in an environment bent on making war or, at least, bickering and fighting, is in itself a battle. As Delibes has said more than once, he writes not to entertain but to make his readers concerned about situations that can be remedied and about humankind's place on earth, threatened but still viable.

Recent events in Eastern Europe have prompted Miguel Delibes, who survived the forty-year Franco dictatorship, fighting it all the way, to speak on the new democratic system of government that his country has experienced for more than fifteen years. His assessment of its promise as well as its threat to the natural world remind us that social government and self-government are closely intertwined. As *The Wars* is a careful probing of an individual's conduct, the functional within the dysfunctional, it may be pertinent to hear what the author has to say about governmental systems in the real world. In his "Letter to Prague," addressed to his Czech translator Blanka Stárková ("Carta a Praga," *El País*, April 9, 1990), he recalls the revolution of 1968 and goes on to comment on the challenge awaiting Czechoslovakia in 1990:

> The way has been opened to freedom in your country.
> Czechoslovakia is preparing to create for itself a human, stable future. I would like to share this happy historic moment which we have been living in Spain for fifteen years. The awareness that it is we ourselves who are going to create our own fate en-

genders a comforting patriotic feeling, but at the same time, this feeling is not without its responsibilities. The joy of the moment should not prevent our thinking about them. To imagine that freedom itself is a panacea that solves everything could constitute an irreparable mistake. We must admit that the West also has its demons, which the new Czech society must try to correct. Take, for example, the enthroning of money, the maxim that you are what you're worth, popular in capitalistic societies today. Or competitiveness, confrontation, aggression as the only way to win in life, forgetting vastly superior ethical concepts such as cooperation and solidarity. The danger that unleashed capitalism, guided only by the notion of profit, might force out of the mainstream less audacious, weaker beings. The temptation to let industrial growth—which of course must occur in Czechoslovakia—get out of hand, sacrificing nature, as if she were not the basis of all our lives, the principle which man cannot override, is strong.

In this hour of hope I wish the Czech nation the best. But in outlining its future, I would hope that you not forget those rocks which capitalism has hit, some of which I mention above. It is true that freedom is going to prevent your becoming shipwrecked in the sense I gave this word,* but we should bear in mind that in the new seas there are other rocks, which could also make us sink one day.

Delibes's cautionary congratulations to the new Czechoslovak democracy remind us that in freedom, human nature is unchecked; we can stimulate peaceful as well as aggressive impulses in others. With

---

*The novel *Parábola del náufrago* (literally, "Parable of a Shipwrecked Man," although the English title is *The Hedge*) uses the image of a shipwrecked man to describe the plight of its protagonist, who is condemned to live without liberty in a totalitarian state. The novel was inspired by Delibes's pain, in Czechoslovakia, at seeing the failure of the independence movement in 1968. For this reason, his protagonist's name, Jacinto San José, was given in Russian in the dedication—Giacint Sviatoi Iosif—as a tribute to oppressed citizens in the Soviet Union.

the demise of the Communist party and the long-awaited liberation of the Baltic republics, the recovery of political freedom is a theme of our times, voiced recently by the former Soviet foreign minister Edouard Shevardnadze, at Emory University's 1991 commencement. "Long live democracy, long live freedom," he said, after expressing his belief that democracy would emerge victorious from current struggles.

Will the newly self-governed towns emerging in Eastern Europe resemble Pacífico's? The chance to improve exists, and if we listen to the words of Delibes's Castilian peasant, who is at peace with the world, we may learn how.

Agnes Moncy

The Wars of Our Ancestors

Violence is simple;
the alternatives to
violence are complex.
—Friedrich Hacker

*The patient Pacífico Pérez was admitted to Navafría Sanatorium on March
25, 1961. During the examination he appeared timid and reserved, answering
my questions in monosyllables. After an extensive exploration I discovered a
bilateral fibrosis with unhealed tubercular lesions in his lungs that had caused
his obvious propensity toward cardiorespiratory failure. I pitied him, as much
for his resigned disposition as for his serious condition. Several days later my
initial reaction turned into curiosity, for I noticed that his attitude toward
his companions was taciturn and somewhat distant, although still affable. It
was obvious that they came from different worlds; the boy responded to their
vulgarity and poor taste with a frank smile that was free of any hypocrisy or
reticence. Also, in the endless conversations that took place in the courtyard in
the mornings and in the lounge in the afternoons, conversations that inevitably
centered on the patients' pasts or futures, Pacífico Pérez kept a discreet silence.
It was clear that only the present existed for him; in that realm he did express
his agreement or disagreement, assenting or dissenting with a nod or a sketchy
phrase, trying as he did so to enhance his laconic words with disproportion-
ately cordial gestures and a generous expression on his face. He didn't want to
share his own world, but he didn't shrink from the forced cohabitation either.
The boy gave me the impression that he considered everything around him to
be alien, that he was only a drifting presence whose appearance in this world
had been purely accidental.*

*Pacífico Pérez, whose facial features were noble, was tall and extremely
thin. Because of his shyness and perhaps his illness too, he stooped slightly when
he walked. This, together with his prematurely receding hairline and the thick
glasses, which like a typically shy person he tried to keep in place by constantly
adjusting the earpiece on the right side, gave him an intellectual air belied by
his gestures and especially the tone of his voice and his language, which were
decidedly rural.*

3

   Two weeks after being admitted to the sanatorium, Pacífico Pérez began to grow a little garden in the northwest corner of the courtyard, an area shielded from the north wind by a high wall. He had very few seeds and tools, but thanks to his Benedictine patience he managed to convert that dry area into a vegetal oasis, which he watered at sundown every day by bringing water from the fountain basin (on the other side of the courtyard) in his aluminum plate. Obstacles seemed to stimulate him, and every morning he spent long periods contemplating the progress of his project, weeding, or explaining to his companions details about a particular flower or the needs of his miniscule seed plot. In truth, this was his only distraction, because Pacífico Pérez did not have any regular visitors. Only once, in mid-April, did a girl appear in the visiting room. She was quite graceful and was accompanied by a very young child. When she left, Pacífico's face didn't show the slightest emotion, and he carried under his arm, without any enthusiasm at all, half a dozen chocolate bars and in his right hand a string of sausages.

   Based on these indications, I reached the conclusion that Pacífico was a misfit, an unsheltered person who felt out of place, and this made my initial curiosity turn into a veritable obsession with helping him; his situation wasn't the least bit enviable. With this purpose and as a first measure, I scheduled his weekly examination as the last appointment of the day. In this way I could keep him for a while in my office, offer him a small glass of anisette—the only liqueur he liked—and chat with him in private. The process of obtaining a confidential connection was slow and difficult. Pacífico had a defensive attitude, due not so much to a sullen temperament as to a natural ambiguity and tendency toward circumlocutions. He spoke of the country as if he were referring to all the country in the world, and when he said "my town," he said it in an impersonal manner, as if no one lived there. One day I decided to face the situation squarely. I asked him if he had any family. His reply was laconic: "What can I say," he said. But it was impossible to get another word out of him. On another occasion, more inspired perhaps, I told him the story of my grandmother planting pumpkins and squashes in the garden, in lined squares, and when the seeds ripened, the bees fertilized both, and the pumpkins came out looking like squashes and the squashes like pumpkins. To my amazement, this story sparked his interest, and he talked on and on enthusiastically about bees and their peculiarities, eventually saying that he could cut the combs out of a beehive naked. This showed me that Pacífico Pérez had a talkative nature; undoubtedly, experience had taught him that being reserved was more advisable for getting along in life. I took advantage, though, of this crevice to open up a path, and for a long time, for half an hour, we talked about country things. The next day I went into town and bought some seeds— a carnation variety, some gilliflowers, and royal daisies—all of them seasonal flowers. When I gave them to Pacífico the next week for his garden, I noticed the impact of my gesture: it had dispelled most of his distrust. He must have realized that my intentions were good, that I meant well, because ever since then our conversations (although they were always on banal or general subjects) were fluent, and they filled up the consultation time comfortably. His first reference to a specific person was, if I remember correctly, during the first examination in May. The previous afternoon, Sopero, one of the bullies in the group, had viciously stomped on one of the bushes that Pacífico had been cultivating tenderly. The boy didn't recriminate, nor did he attempt to stop him; he merely looked at him as if the act were a natural, even anticipated one. When on the following afternoon I condemned Sopero's conduct, Pacífico smiled faintly and said: "It's not his fault; he just likes to pick fights, like Bisa." I immediately asked who Bisa was, and he answered: "So who else? My great-grandfather." The mention of Bisa was what really broke the ice in our relationship. From that day on, Pacífico no longer avoided referring to the particular people who had in one way or another influenced him, whether they were part of his family or not. As if they were irreconcilable beings, he spoke about "the bunch from Otero" and "the bunch from Humán," and he talked about Abue, Corina, his grandmother Benetilde, Señora Dictrinia, and, with easily noticeable frequency and warmth, about "my Uncle Paco." For my part, I talked too about my childhood in my own town, and he seemed to like to match my observations with his personal experiences. So our sessions had a natural, trusting atmosphere that led me one day to suggest the possibility of chatting openly about his past into a tape recorder that Agustín Parra, the pharmacist in Veguillas and an old school friend of mine, had just brought me from the Canary Islands. Pacífico had me use the machine several times, then remarked quite expressively: "That gadget's not bad—it coughs up everything." Nevertheless, he did not immediately decide to comply with my request, despite my assurance that unless he authorized me to, "that gadget" wouldn't say a word. At my beseeching, Pacífico agreed to consult his Uncle Paco, and a week later, he had scarcely come into the office when he declared without any preliminaries: "It's OK." "What's OK?" I asked. "About talking," he replied. "My uncle says it's OK." So this is how I was able to make the tapes I transcribe on the following pages. The texts are accurate and almost literal. I have suppressed only certain reiterations—just a few—and some tangled circumlocutions that detracted from the clarity of his tale. Also, I have trimmed off the banal wordiness of our farewells and successive greetings because they do not seem to add anything meaningful to Pacífico Pérez's confidences. So except for these items, the transcription is verbatim. I have even respected Pacífico's stammering and awkward phrases, which, even considering the loquacity he gradually acquired in the course of our evening sessions, are certainly not infrequent in his conversation. Phrases like "I mean," "now," "what else," "like," "on the whole," "wait," and others are included not only for textual fidelity but also as exponents of a life-style, a manifestation of the rural lexicon of Castille that, unfortunately, due to mimicry of urban language and television, is gradually disappearing. The sessions began on May 21, 1961, and ended on May 27. So there were seven consecutive nights of dialogue, the translation of which I offer forthwith to the reader, begging forgiveness beforehand for any errors that a defective recording may have caused.

Dr. Burgueño López

▲ ▲ ▲ ▲ ▲ ▲ ▲

First Night

Dr. Come in, Pacífico, sit down. Just make yourself comfortable, all right? Would you like a glass of liqueur, some anisette? Really. Just relax, and let's chat quietly. Nobody can hear us, and we can talk for as long as you'd like. Whenever you decide, we'll just stop and retire for the night. There's no rush. We'll pick up where we left off tomorrow, and if we can't tomorrow, then another day. There's plenty of time. The only thing I ask of you is that you make an effort to remember things, even little details that seem insignificant. I mean details about people and facts related to your childhood. And as for me, I'll try to help you. So now, to start with, if I'm not mistaken, you're from a small town in Castille, Humán del Otero, aren't you?

P.P. Yes sir, born and raised there.

Dr. Fine. And what is your first memory of the town?

P.P. Well, let's see. I mean, if I think about it, I remember Bisa, for instance, along with Grandma Benetilde and Mother and the house and everything. How could I forget?

Dr. Yes, of course, your home. You mentioned your house. What was your house like, Pacífico? Where was it located? Everything interests me.

P.P. Well, let's see. Well, actually, I don't know, Doctor. My house was like all the others, different, I mean.

Dr. In what way was your house different, Pacífico?

P.P. What a question, hey! Because everybody's house is his own, isn't it?

Dr. But what was special about it?

P.P. Well, like my house was made of limestone, you know? I mean, like all the houses, the ones in Humán and the ones in Otero.

7

But it had a glassed-in porch upstairs, a kind of long one, that the others didn't have.

Dr. And what else was there in your house?

P.P. Out back?

Dr. Out back or anywhere.

P.P. Well, look, out back the mill wheel was still there, and the watering trough, where every year around about St. Peter's Day we used to give Bisa his bath.* And next to the mill wheel was the fig tree, where they say communion wafers rained down the day Grandma Benetilde came of age.

Dr. Excuse me, Pacífico: you said Humán and Otero before. Were they different villages?

P.P. Well, yeah, that's right, Doctor. Otero was up above, at the top of the hill, right across from El Crestón, see? Up there with the cemetery and the parish, you know. Down below, next to the Embustes—the river, I mean—was Humán.

Dr. What was the town's economy based on? What did people live on?

P.P. Well, it depended.

Dr. On what?

P.P. Well, in the valley, on the whole, fruit trees, mainly apple trees.

Dr. And what else?

P.P. As for what there was, there were some plum trees and some pear trees, you know? And some beautiful walnut trees. But the nuts hardly ever ripened.

Dr. Why not, Pacífico?

P.P. The frosts, you see. If it iced over in the springtime, a cold northeaster would blow in between Las Puertas, and it was a lost cause. Everything got ruined by the cold overnight. Walnuts are a delicate fruit, you know.

Dr. And up above? What was up there?

P.P. Up on the mountaintops?

Dr. Yes, on the mountaintops.

P.P. Furze and moss for the wild boars.

Dr. Wasn't anything cultivated?

P.P. Let's see . . . well, at first, no. Nothing, sir. After a while, Father

---

*Translator's Note: St. Peter's Day is June 29.

took a tractor into the backlands, and he planted, too, about seven thousand acres, wheat and barley, you know. Cereal. The Otero bunch still haven't forgiven him for it. Father, I mean.

Dr.   What difference did it make to the Otero bunch whether your father sowed in the backlands or not?

P.P.   Because of the grazing. You see, breaking up new ground left the town without any pastureland. For the goats, see.

Dr.   Wasn't there any industry in your town—a distillery of applejack, for example—something to help you survive?

P.P.   No sir, nothing like that. I mean, all there was was the honey. In the streambeds of the deer country, and in the brambles, the heather grew good. And in there, protected by the dampness, the townspeople would put the beehives, you know? The ovens and stuff.

Dr.   Tell me, Pacífico, when you left the town, were there many people left?

P.P.   If I said a hundred, I guess I'd be off the mark. The young people were tired, you know. The land makes a slave of you.

Dr.   And was there ever a period when Humán del Otero, for whatever reason, attracted an unusual influx of people?

P.P.   What was that?

Dr.   In other words, Pacífico, did the town ever have more people than when you left?

P.P.   Well, a while back.

Dr.   When?

P.P.   Well, since I was a kid 'til I was a man. I mean, 'til I cleared out, half the people were gone.

Dr.   And before that? Were there ever more people?

P.P.   Let's see . . . well, or rather, according to what Bisa says, when he was a boy, with the business of the nuggets in the Alija streambed, up in Prádanos, the Aquilina Cliff, I mean, people came from all over the province.

Dr.   Gold nuggets?

P.P.   Yes sir, real gold. At least that's what they said. What's for sure is that up in Prádanos, the sheds and the placers are still there next to the rill. As a matter of fact, Doctor, it was there that Candi cheated on me, many years later. But that's another story.

Dr. We'll talk about that later, Pacífico. I wouldn't want us to forget it. So tell me about the gold fever you just mentioned. Did it last long?

P.P. You know how those things are, Doctor. Mainly, for about as long as the couple of nuggets they found would let it. That's all.

Dr. Since then, Humán del Otero hasn't been famous for anything again?

P.P. Wait a minute. Now that I think of it, more than the gold, it was what happened to Grandma Benetilde, you know? Her trances, I mean, 'cause according to Abue, they really made the town famous. Even foreigners came, all the way from Portugal. But it was the same old story: the bunch from Otero started in again, saying the mystic—Grandma Benetilde, I mean—was a fake, and it was all over with, like the gold.

Dr. Hmm. How about in your own life—do you remember anything extraordinary happening in the town?

P.P. Nothing, no sir. It was dead. Except for the Hibernater, you know. One of nature's whims. Just imagine—a pippin tree that blossomed in November and lost its leaves in April. A contradictor, Mother used to call it. On the whole, it *was* pretty shocking, I won't say it wasn't. But except for Don Patricio and a group of some learned people, you know? nobody paid much attention to the tree.

Dr. Tell me something, Pacífico: Why did it bother the bunch from Otero that your grandmother had visions and people came from the outside? They must have brought a little business to town, didn't they?

P.P. Listen, you just don't know what they're like. The Otero bunch, I mean. They never got along with the Humán bunch, never. Always fighting like cats and dogs, you know what I mean? They'd get in there and start a brawl over nothing. According to what Bisa says, it goes way back, that grudge they've got. From when the Moors were here, or even before that.

Dr. All this is very interesting, Pacífico, but I would like to keep things straight, start at the beginning, you know what I mean? Let's see if we can make some progress. When you left Humán, who was the head of your household?

P.P. The boss, you mean?

Dr. That's what I mean, yes.

P.P. Bisa, of course.

Dr. Bisa?

P.P. In other words, my great-grandfather.*

Dr. Fine. Do you think that your great-grandfather left a mark on you?

P.P. Who knows, Doctor. You can never tell.

Dr. Tell me, what was your great-grandfather like? How do you remember him?

P.P. Well, I remember Bisa in his wheelchair going this way and that. He never got out of the thing. And 'round about St. Peter's Day, too—in the watering trough, splashing around to his heart's content.

Dr. Of the people you lived with, is your memory of Bisa the most vivid?

P.P. It depends. I mean, I remember Abue, too, with his flat face, drinking out of a long-spouted wine bottle and looking sideways like a fish.

Dr. Who paid more attention to you, Bisa or Abue?

P.P. Oh, they were about the same. They both told me stories about their wars, you know? But they were so long I usually fell asleep. Bisa was always cursing all the time, and he'd say to Abue . . . I mean, he used to say something . . . that I shouldn't repeat.

Dr. What did he say? We're both men, Pacífico; it won't shock me.

P.P. Well, he said . . . he said we're going to be fucked, Vitálico. This boy doesn't have anything between his legs.

Dr. He said that?

P.P. Just what you heard.

Dr. Didn't you feel humiliated when you heard your great-grandfather say that about you?

P.P. Not really, no sir. It rolled right off my back. Bisa usually just talked about his war, and I wasn't much interested in that stuff.

Dr. What war was he talking about, son?

*Translator's Note: *Bisabuelo* means great-grandfather. *Abuelo* means grandfather.

P.P.   Listen, who knows? All I know for sure is that at home, starting with Bisa and straight down to Father, they all had their war, a war to talk about, see? And then there was my Uncle Teodoro, too. According to Bisa, as soon as the wars were over here, he took off for both Americas to find another one there. But I never met my Uncle Teodoro.

Dr.   And when they spoke about their wars, didn't your grandfathers mention any names—a general, or a battle, or something?

P.P.   Sure. Course they did, Doctor. With Bisa, for instance, it was General Moriones and Duke Torre. And as for Abue, well, it was Abd-el-Krim, and Fort Igueriben; always the same old story. If you want to know the truth, Doctor, at home, the only one who talked about the real war,* that is, about Brunete, Teruel, and all, was Father.

Dr.   Good. Now we're getting somewhere, Pacífico. How about the old fellow—what stories did he tell you? Your great-grandfather, I mean.

P.P.   Stories? Bisa just told me one, and hey, it was *always* the same one, ever since I was born. I remember that Mother, when she saw him going back and forth in his chair, making it sound like the shooting and the trumpet, she'd always say: With the way he gets, any day now he's going to give us something to be sorry about—that blasted war!

Dr.   Do you remember the story, Pacífico?

P.P.   How could I forget it? That's all he talked about for twenty years, so you can just imagine.

Dr.   Could you tell it to me?

P.P.   Yeah, I could, as far as that goes. But let me warn you, it's very long.

Dr.   Don't worry about that, Pacífico. I'm in no hurry.

P.P.   Well, let's see. The story actually starts with Captain Estévez, the night Captain Estévez said to Bisa that they had to take ahold of the railway outposts, do you follow? I mean, just to give you the background, the enemy had gotten entrenched in the sheltered

---

*Translator's Note: Pacífico means the Spanish Civil War, 1936–39.

part of the mountain, and since the train went up and came back without anybody giving them any trouble, it was a piece of cake. They weren't short on anything, like food, I mean.

Dr.   I get the picture. Go on, Pacífico.

P.P.   So the solution was to block the tracks, see. And one night, Duke Torre, who must've been in charge, said to General Moriones—Bisa was right next to him, and he says that he said: Morioncitos, you've got to show your balls. What do you need to knock that scum out of their stronghold? Then the general asked for some replacements. I mean he said: Give me five thousand men, two batteries, and a squadron on horseback, and next Thursday I'll be in Bilbao, got it? The Duke came through with them, and listen, from what Bisa says, the next day the replacements were at it, heading down the mountain to the river.

Dr.   Fine. What happened after that?

P.P.   Well, let's see. That same afternoon, according to Bisa, it started to pour, you know? So he and Sergeant Beitia and a party of soldiers went up to Ciérgola to get a room for the general. Bisa says it seems there wasn't a soul around except for a woman this big, stronger than Señora Dictrinia; and he went up to her—Bisa, I mean—and asked for a place where the general could stay, but she just stood there like a stone, as if he wasn't even talking to her. So Bisa went and repeated himself, but her—the woman—she just stood there, not a peep. That really ticked off Bisa, so he goes and points his machete at her belly and, Give me a room for the general! and she goes, OK, second door to the right. And what do you think was there, Doc, inside the second door to the right?

Dr.   How should I know, Pacífico?

P.P.   The john, that's what there was. Seems to me you've got to be pretty cold-blooded to give an answer like that.

Dr.   You certainly do, son. And what did your great-grandfather do?

P.P.   Look, what could the poor guy do? Shake his fist at her and go look for a room himself. But don't think she was fazed by it, the broad, I mean, 'cause when Sergeant Beitia asked her for some candles he got the same routine: that there were some in the church. So what could they do? They went into the church, and

Bisa says the sergeant wanted to set the town on fire, imagine! But luckily the general—a prudent one, he was—said to hold it, that he didn't want anybody going overboard, you know?

Dr.   When did that happen, Pacífico?

P.P.   Let's see, I think it happened—if Bisa was right—back in 1874, in April, maybe. A lot of water over the dam since then.

Dr.   There certainly has been. Go on.

P.P.   Well, they got up to the hermitage, they grabbed the candles, and Bisa carried off the alms boxes too, because, according to him, Bilbao was about to surrender, and he didn't have a cent.

Dr.   Bisa took the church's money?

P.P.   Hey, don't let it shock you. Bisa was kind of grabby. Personally, I think he hated churches. I was still a kid when he told me about going up to Prádanos, you know, where the gold nuggets were, to rob the statue of the Black Virgin. He said it was really mysterious.

Dr.   Excuse me, but let's not lose our way here, Pacífico. You were in Ciérgola, when Sergeant Beitia and Bisa took the candles. What did they do then?

P.P.   Gave them to the general. And they slept up above, in the hayloft. From what Bisa says, the hay is wonderful in those parts. So they'd almost gotten settled when a scratching, ruh-ruh-ruh, like rats, starts, and Bisa says, Is that you, Beitia? And Beitia says, Me? And then Bisa lights a match, and he sees him—just the scared eyes and the tip of his nose, the rest all covered up by the hay, you know? Well, anyway, Bisa didn't stop to think about it. He just grabbed his machete and ran it through him without even asking the guy what his name was, and it seems he was crying out, Mother! Mother! really weak, until he stopped. The next morning, as soon as God was up, Bisa opened the lookouts, and when he saw that the dead man didn't have enough hair for a beard, that he was only a kid, he said, says to Beitia: Beitia, he was only a kid. And the sergeant, who according to Bisa used to be in a foul mood when he got up in the morning, he didn't even blink, he just said: Let him be, Vendiano. You have to nip some things in the bud, you know what I mean?

Dr.   And so he had slashed him to death with the machete?

P.P.   That's right. With his machete. But don't hold it against Bisa, 'cause that's just how he was. He even said so himself: I've got this thing about bayonets. So now you know.

Dr.   He used to say that?

P.P.   Yes sir, he did. And he said it was really easy, you know? I mean just three fingers under the belly button, rrah! the bayonet goes in, and you give it a half twist to the right, and it's done. And me, I was just a kid at the time, I'd ask him: Then what, Bisa? And he'd explain that the guts just come gushing out of the buttonhole like water out of the Toba River when the floodgates are thrown open, you know?

Dr.   Oh yes, son, I do. Go on.

P.P.   So Bisa came down from the hayloft at dawn, and from how he tells it, the streets were full of soldiers sloshing around in the mud. It was still pouring. And they went down to take up their positions, and you could hear their boots in the puddles, juack-juack, juack-juack. And the general's horse's hooves too, the same thing; he says he was wrapped up in a big cape—the general, I mean—his mouth shut tight as a lock. But as soon as he got to the parapets he stood up in his stirrups and started yelling, Soldiers! Long live the queen! He gave them a real pep talk, you know? But according to Bisa not even five minutes had gone by when the show really got started, Doctor—the cannons and the guns—and rows of houses got blown all over the place by the shells, left and right. Hey, they didn't let up. But since Bisa had this thing about knives, well, he was like a chicken with its head cut off, shooting off his gun just to shoot, you know, to make a racket; but he couldn't hit anything. Says all he could think about was, When's this fucking fairy going to let us use our bayonets? But he never did. And between one thing and another his blood starts to boil, Bisa's, I mean, and he turns around and shouts at the soldier who played taps, Hey you, preemie! Are you going to wait 'til noon to play your music so we can get out our bayonets? But the soldier just ignored him, and I guess it made sense, don't you think? After all, he took his orders from up above.

Dr.   And what did Bisa do?

P.P.   Wait. The way he tells it, the cannonballs were flying, and Captain Estévez, with his sword in his hand, couldn't make up his mind. So meanwhile Sergeant Beitia yells: They're going to blow us out of our minds! When Bisa heard him he flew off the handle. He went over to the soldier and gave the order. I mean he just pointed his bayonet at his stomach and said: It's time to use your bayonets, you motherfucker! or I'll rip out your guts, right here and now, you hear? Bayonets were his thing, see. So the other guy, the soldier, grabbed the trumpet and started blowing for all he was worth.

Dr.   To get out the bayonets?

P.P.   What can you do in a spot like that? And Bisa, happier than a lark, jumped right out of the trench. He took off like a light.

Dr.   Was he the only one who jumped out?

P.P.   That I couldn't tell you. I guess the others went out after him. He says he just ran out and didn't look back, leaping like a lizard to keep clear of the bullets, you know? And as soon as he got to the enemy position, rrah! In went the bayonet, three fingers under the belly button, a half twist to the right, and it was done. Over and over. And he says some of them (the enemies, I mean) raised their arms when he stuck them, and others rolled their eyes, and there were even some that grabbed the cylinder of his gun and tried to pull it out, the bayonet, I mean, but that was dumb, 'cause the person on the outside can always push harder, right? So by the time Captain Estévez took over, Bisa had polished off a dozen of them. And the ones that were left took off up the hill, Bisa hard on their tails, there he was, 'cause from what he says, he had good legs then—you could hardly tell now, seeing him prostrate the way he is—and he knifed them in the back, but not just any old way. He had a method, he knew how to find their kidneys—either on the left or the right, 'cause the safest way according to him was to run it along their spine—you wouldn't want the weapon to boomerang and make a mess of yourself.

Dr.   Go on, Pacífico.

P.P.   Well, there really wasn't much else, Doctor. Except that the poor chumps he knifed would roll down the slope, and unless they got caught in the brambles they didn't stop 'til they reached the river, so naturally the water started running red, and the currents in the rapids looked the same. From what Bisa says it was a blessing. So he stuck one here, another one there—didn't stop 'til he got to the tracks near the tunnel. And once he got there he climbed up a little hill and yelled, Victory! and he lifted up his gun, all bloody and full of shit, you know?

Dr. And is that how the story ends?

P.P. Yes sir. The story ends there.

Dr. Is there anything else?

P.P. Well, let's see. Well, when I was a kid, Bisa used to tell me the same thing whenever he finished.

Dr. What was that? What did he tell you, Pacífico?

P.P. Well, he'd say . . . how did it go, now? . . . Oh, yes: My grandma had a cat with little ragged ears and a little paper ass, and d'you want to hear my tale again?

Dr. And what would you answer, Pacífico?

P.P. The truth. I mean, when I learned to talk. I'd say no, that it was scary.

Dr. Do you mean that before you'd learned to talk, Bisa was already telling you these stories?

P.P. Well, yeah, ever since I was born. And he didn't stop 'til Corina, my sister, put her foot down.

Dr. What was his purpose in telling those stories to a baby?

P.P. Actually, Doctor, Bisa—just like Abue and Father—what they wanted was for me to be a tough soldier when my war came along.

Dr. But did you necessarily have to fight a war?

P.P. Well, I guess so; yes sir, that's what they said. I can remember Abue saying: We each have a war just like we each have a wife, right? See, just so's you'll get the idea, every time we went past the telegraph office, where Señor Isauro was, Bisa always sang the same old song: Hey, Isauro! Has this one's war started yet? So Isauro, what could he say except there's no news yet, Señor Vendiano. I'll let you know if it does.

Dr. My goodness!

P.P. You want to hear something else? I'd hardly been born when Bisa and Abue were already feeling me between my legs, arguing about whether it was big enough or not.

Dr. Who told you these things?

P.P.   Told me? Nobody, sir. I remember it myself. Just like I remember the day I was born, or the afternoon that Grandma Benetilde took me out of the watering trough.

Dr.   Listen, Pacífico, I'd like to believe you, but it's not possible for you to remember the day you were born. Nobody remembers when he was born. It's a fantasy.

P.P.   There you go, just like Señora Dictrinia.

Dr.   Who was she, Pacífico?

P.P.   Who else? The one who helped me out, the midwife.

Dr.   And what did Señora Dictrinia tell you?

P.P.   Look, the same as you. In other words, kids don't know anything when they're born.

Dr.   You see, Pacífico?

P.P.   Well, I *did* realize what was going on, Doctor. I can practically see them now, Bisa and Abue playing soldiers next to my crib, driving me crazy with all that ruckus. Course I remember it. And I couldn't have been over two weeks old. So as you can see, I'm not saying it just to make conversation.

Dr.   Did Señora Dictrinia believe you?

P.P.   Well, no, she didn't. She said I was just dreaming. 'Til one day Mother let her have it. You sure are stubborn, Dictrinia. What do you mean, dreaming? And Señora Dictrinia hit her with she'd helped all the kids in town be born and none of them knew anything, 'cause when you're born your imagination doesn't work yet, see? And it went on like that 'til I swore I did remember, and Señora Dictrinia took it like a joke—isn't he cute!—and what did you see? Come on now, tell us what you saw, and me, I said, Well, you know, stuff, Señora Dictrinia, and her, Stuff, hmm? Let's see now, exactly what sort of stuff did you see? Oh, some sheets and water and a bright light . . . and bugs. This made Señora Dictrinia burst out laughing, and she nudged Mother, Did you hear that, Delgadina? God, what a creature! And weren't you scared, love? Was I ever, Doctor, so scared I wanted to go back in, and she—Señora Dictrinia, I mean—says, So why didn't you go back in, you whippersnapper? And me, I said I was wriggling around, but I couldn't, the current was pulling me out.

Dr.   The current! Hmm . . .

P.P.   After all, Doctor, these things happen, don't they? Aren't there calves born with two heads? And without going too far from home, there's the pippin tree, in Humán, on my Uncle Paco's farm. You want to hear some more? Well, there it is, an apple tree like all the others, right? But even so, when spring starts to come it wrinkles up and gets stiff. In other words, it does the opposite of what the others do.

Dr.   And did that tree bear fruit regularly?

P.P.   Why not? Yes sir, it did, every year. In other words, just so you'll follow me, the pippin tree's apple is smaller, about yea big, but it keeps its perfume for years, and it never rots.

Dr.   Where did the tree come from?

P.P.   Where else, hey, the capital, like all the saplings. The point is, my Uncle Paco planted them, he fertilized them, and one of them, the pippin tree, that is, started to blossom out of season, you follow me? In November, when the others shed their leaves.

Dr.   And its fruit?

P.P.   Well, in the winter, in January or February, to be exact, along with the frosts and the snow. You have no idea how people fight over that fruit. I mean, in town they used to say the pippin's apples were good for rheumatism and bone spurs because they didn't have any worms, see? You can't imagine how people lined up in the orchard: Give me six pounds! I want four! A real jubilee got going. It went on like that 'til one day a black car pulled up at the inn.

Dr.   Where was the car from?

P.P.   From Madrid. A black one, a nice-looking machine. Don Patricio—everybody said so—was a scholar from the university or somewhere. Usually he came alone, but sometimes he brought along three or four young people, students, you know.

Dr.   What did Don Patricio do in town?

P.P.   He never stopped. Hey, you have no idea what he was like. The tags he put on that tree! In the winter and the summer too, he never got tired of it. Either he was cutting it somewhere to get out some sap, or he was snapping off a blossom, or taking a sample from the branches. Or he was saving a handful of earth from around the roots. To analyze it, he said. The pippin tree sure kept Don Patricio busy! He even wanted to write a book about it!

Dr.   It does sound like an unusual case.

P.P.   And you still haven't heard the most surprising part, Doctor.

Dr.   What was that?

P.P.   The shakes I got.

Dr.   What shakes?

P.P.   The ones I got from the tree.

Dr.   It gave you the shakes?

P.P.   Listen, ever since I started thinking about how cold those apples must get, I mean, ever since the thought crossed my mind, every year, as soon as the real cold frosts started, I'd start shaking like the dickens. You may not believe this, Doctor, but Mother and Grandma Benetilde couldn't pile on enough blankets and quilts. They even had to stick a brazier in bed with me, imagine. And I wouldn't stop shaking for two days, and finally I'd get up and go to my Uncle Paco's orchard, and the pippin tree's buds had opened, you know? And every year it was the same story, so as soon as my shakes started I'd say to Mother: The pippin tree's buds are ready to come out. And the next morning I'd go up to the tree and bing, there they were!

Dr.   Just a minute, Pacífico. Are you insinuating that you felt what the tree felt? That you experienced the tree's chill?

P.P.   Wait a minute. I didn't say any such thing. I only wanted to explain what happened to me, right? Strange things happen in life, after all, to all of us, don't they? And since you seem to be taking an interest in me, I mean in the strange things that happen to me, well, I'm telling you about them.

Dr.   Right. Don't be annoyed, Pacífico. Well, how about Don Patricio? Didn't you ever tell Don Patricio about what happened to you that was related to the tree?

P.P.   Never, no sir. What good would it do? Except for Mother and Grandma Benetilde nobody ever knew about my shakes. I mean, this is the first time I've ever told anyone.

Dr.   All right, Pacífico. But you say strange things happened to you, and the business about the pippin tree, as remarkable as it is, is only one strange thing. Were there any others?

P.P.   How could there not be, Doctor?

Dr.   Would you mind telling me about them?

P.P.   Me? No, not at all. But you won't believe me.

Dr. What does that matter, Pacífico? I'm here to listen. Just talk, and don't worry about what I think.

P.P. Well, there was also what happened with the trout.

Dr. What was that?

P.P. Abue. He used to fish for them with a jackknife, the trout, I mean, 'cause ever since he'd been a soldier he was good with them. With knives, I mean.

Dr. So he was good at catching trout?

P.P. Oh yeah. Was he ever clever. He could get them between two stones, or next to a dried-up trunk, or through the underbrush. Wherever he pleased.

Dr. And what happened?

P.P. Well, one day when I was a kid he took me with him, see? Just seeing him scouting around in the ferns and the water lilies was a ball for me. Well, anyway, all of a sudden Abue turns and says to me, I've got him! And I saw the trout go white underwater, squirming and twisting. I had to bite my lips because they hurt, you know? And when Abue took it out and slashed its mouth to free the fishhook and said, Nice, isn't it? Me, I couldn't even look to see if it was nice or not, 'cause I couldn't stand the pain in my own mouth. So I went and said, Doesn't it hurt him, Abue? And he says, Hullaballoo! Hooks don't hurt a fish 'cause they're cold-blooded, see?

Dr. In other words, he ignored you.

P.P. Yeah, as if I hadn't asked him anything. But every time I caught one and I saw it bleed and twist, I had to bite my lips, you know? 'cause of the pain. So that night I went to bed with a fever, and the next morning all around my mouth it was swollen and out of shape. And Señora Dictrinia making jokes about it: Look at him, he looks like a Ubangi, and Mother all hasty saying, Let's go to Don Alfaro—to the doctor's, that is—saying, It's probably an allergy. So Grandma Benetilde gave me the juice from two apples from the pippin tree, and the next day there I was, fresh as a daisy, imagine.

Dr. Excuse me, Pacífico. And don't be upset by what I'm going to say. You and I are chatting here while people are sleeping. You're being sincere with me, and I appreciate it. But it is conceivable that because of the circumstances we're in—the solitude, the silence, my concentrated attention—you might be starting to fantasize, and your good intentions and your sincerity could fall into a trap. Do you understand? Listen, and don't be offended, now, please: Is what you're telling me true, or are you enhancing it with your imagination?

P.P.   If you're going to be that way, I guess I better shut up.

Dr.   That's not a solution, Pacífico. You won't be helping things at all by being quiet.

P.P.   So what do you want me to do, Doctor?

Dr.   It's very simple, Pacífico. Reflect on what you've told me, and tell me whether you've exaggerated a little or whether, on the other hand, it's the strict truth.

P.P.   What I've told you is as true as the fact that the earth will one day devour my eyes.

Dr.   Good, Pacífico. I don't doubt your words. The only thing I'm afraid of is that your imagination may play a dirty trick on you, you know?

P.P.   But if you don't believe me, what good would it be to tell you about the light bulb?

Dr.   What about the light bulb?

P.P.   Ah, it's probably silly anyway.

Dr.   Don't be childish, Pacífico. Talk about it.

P.P.   Well, look. You see, when I was a kid, back in the town, there were days when I got up that I felt like I had a bulb right here, in my chest.

Dr.   A bulb? You mean a glass light?

P.P.   Yeah, that's right. A bulb instead of my heart, you know?

Dr.   What gave you that impression?

P.P.   Hey, don't ask me. How should I know? But whenever I had the bulb in me everything made me flinch. I didn't even dare move 'cause I was scared of breaking it.

Dr.   The bulb?

P.P.   Yes, the bulb.

Dr.   And what did the bulb do?

P.P.   Nothing, really. But one day when I had it inside me, the bulb, that is, Bisa took me out to the fig tree, and he told me the story about Galdamés.

Dr. Hadn't he ever told it to you before?

P.P. Told it to me? Sure, hundreds of times. But never when I had the bulb in me, you see, and that's the point. So every time he talked about the knife, the bayonet I mean, I just winced. With the bulb in there it was murder, believe you me, I mean *everything* got to me, like a lightning rod, you know? I remember one day that I had it in there, the bulb, I mean, I caught Señor Bebel pruning the trees, and as soon as I got home, I dunked my hands in boiling water, just as if they'd cut off my fingers. I couldn't take the pain.

Dr. And lately, Pacífico, have you felt the bulb in your chest at all?

P.P. Why should I? No sir. I'm talking about when I was a kid, ages ago.

Dr. Right. Go on. I interrupted you. Your great-grandfather told you the story of his war, and you felt a stabbing, right?

P.P. And how! Every time he mentioned it, the bayonet, I mean, I'd jerk again. So Bisa got all annoyed. What's the matter with you? he'd ask. And me, Nothing, Bisa, 'cause after all, I never gave him any stories, and him, Bisa, I mean, he said, Then why the hell are you wincing like that? And me, I don't know, Bisa, it must be lice. But that night, right about when I was going to bed, I felt a stinging around my parts. I went to the toilet, and I urinated blood. What do you make of that?

Dr. Didn't you tell the doctor about it?

P.P. Not the doctor, no sir. I told Don Prócoro, the priest.

Dr. The priest? In your town?

P.P. In my town, yes sir.

Dr. Was the priest in your town young or old?

P.P. Hard to say. He must've been about your age, I guess.

Dr. Was he an understanding man?

P.P. Well, who knows. I'd say he was, yes. Except his eyes.

Dr. What about his eyes?

P.P. Hey, who knows! Like the nerves were broken or something. Anyway, his eyelids kind of drooped down, like window blinds. In other words, to look at you, Don Prócoro, I mean, he had to throw back his head 'til it almost broke his neck, or he had to hold them up with his fingers. It was one thing or the other, and to tell you the truth, it made you feel pretty comfortable, you know, that he wasn't looking at you; and you should've seen how people

lined up at Don Prócoro's to make their confessions to him, at
mission time.

Dr. Was Don Prócoro an educated man?

P.P. He read a lot. He was very learned, yes sir.

Dr. And what did he tell you?

P.P. Well, at first he—Don Prócoro I mean—he listened, his mouth
hanging open, you know? And what I say, Doctor, is, just the way
they say the blind see with their fingers, he must've seen with his
mouth, and that's why he let it hang open, but who knows, it just
seems to me that that may be it. But as soon as I finished, hey,
he really cut me off. He goes and says, That business of yours,
Pacífico, it sounds like a clear case of a sympathetic reaction—
imagine, what a thing to come out with.

Dr. The diagnosis doesn't strike me as farfetched, Pacífico. Everything seems to point to an extreme case of hypersensitivity. And
after Bisa's stories, did you ever urinate blood again?

P.P. Never, no sir. But as I recall, Bisa never told me the Galdamés
episode again when I had the bulb in me.

Dr. Changing the subject now, Pacífico: If your great-grandfather
fought in the Carlist war, he must've been pretty ancient,
wasn't he?

P.P. Look, I'm not the one to say. At home, except for Corina knowing
my age and me hers, nobody knew anybody else's age, see? But
come to think of it, I did hear my Uncle Paco say that Bisa was
the same age as General Prim. I don't know who that guy was,
but I can tell you one thing, I've never seen such a wrinkled face
in my whole life, that's for sure. And I wouldn't want to tell you
about the times we gave him his bath, around St. Peter's Day, in
the watering trough, wow! I probably shouldn't say it, but he even
had wrinkles on his ass. What I think, Doctor, is that some old
men start to fall apart while they're still alive. You should've seen
Bisa's face—like he didn't have any blood in him. The color of
cement, and if it hadn't have been for that red slash of a mouth,
you'd have thought he was a real mummy, that's what.

Dr. But his temper, Pacífico, wasn't exactly the kind a mummy has,
was it?

P.P. No, not in a million years. When it came to laughing or scolding,
Bisa was like a kid, I wish you could've seen him. He had a long

yellow tooth, you know? right about here, on the lower part, just one, and whenever he burst out laughing, it showed, the tooth, I mean, and it would go hee-hee-hee, like the seagulls laughing over La Charca. And when he started to curse, wow, he'd come out with all kinds of stuff 'til his tongue got stuck on the roof of his mouth, and he'd come out with all kinds of crazy stuff, I couldn't begin to tell you, Doctor. I don't know, it must've been that in his rush to say everything at once his brain got all mixed up, and nobody on earth could make any sense of him.

Dr.   From what you say, your great-grandfather must have been quite a character.

P.P.   You can say that again. If I could only tell you. Wait. Now I remember when he had a hernia, Bisa, I mean, right next to his belly button. Don Alfaro—the doctor—said it was only natural that when you got to that age, you know, it's all coughing and wheezing, and even moving your bowels—the tissues can't take it, I guess. Well, with Bisa, he was always putting his hand on his girdle and blowing on his hand, without letting the air out, you know? And meanwhile he'd start to laugh like a baby, heh heh heh, It's like a balloon! he'd shout. And if he caught me near him he made me feel it, and you have no idea what an ugly thing it was, and Mother, she'd say, Don't play with those things, Grandpa. Don't do something he'll be sorry about, and him, Bisa, You be quiet, Delgadina. And if Señora Dictrinia was around, Touch it, Dictrinia, and her, It sure is true what they say, the older they are, the tougher they get, and you know they'd start laughing and teasing each other 'til Bisa would sit her down with him in his chair and start feeling her up, saying, You're better than bread out of the oven, Dictrinia, and her, Señora Dictrinia, I mean, she'd laugh and start shouting, Stop it, Señor Vendiano! Are you still getting like that with me? Listen, they had a ball, I'll tell you.

Dr.   Some old man! Tell me, Pacífico, that Señora Dictrinia, the one you mention so much: Was she part of the family?

P.P.   No sir. She was the midwife, I already told you.

Dr.   What was she doing at your house?

P.P.   A little of everything. In the afternoon she used to push Bisa's chair over to the inn so he could have his game there, you know? Or if somebody needed a laxative, a poultice, or an injection, well,

there was Señora Dictrinia. And if not, well, she was there anyway, to talk to Mother and Grandma Benetilde, you know? To
give you some idea, let's say she was a friend of the family, but
like one of us.

Dr. Was she married? Did she have children?

P.P. No sir. I mean yes.

Dr. Which is it, Pacífico?

P.P. It's like this: Señora Dictrinia had a family, two kids, when she
was young. And it was like she said, it wasn't perverse, it's just
that she wanted to learn.

Dr. Learn what?

P.P. She was the midwife. In other words, she took kids out.

Dr. Oh, I see.

P.P. Señora Dictrinia said that it was the poor man's university, do
you get it?

Dr. Tell me something, Pacífico. Isn't it possible that your great-
grandfather was the father of those children?

P.P. Was it possible? Yeah, sure it was, 'cause they were involved. I remember once, Señora Dictrinia was so strong, Bisa sat her down
in his chair, and the brake got loose, and the two of them rolled
all the way down to the river. You should've seen them! Like
soup, hey!

Dr. The river that went past your house—was it the same one where
your grandfather went fishing?

P.P. The very same one, yes sir, the Embustes. And it was the same
one where I ran into Teotista when I was talking to his sister, you
know? But that river, just to give you an idea, starts out right in
town, that is, next to the Humán Mill.

Dr. Further up, there's no river?

P.P. No sir, there isn't. That is, there're three brooks up there: the
Matayeguas, the Lirón, and the Salud.

Dr. Why is it called the Salud?*

P.P. It's female, see. And up there where it starts, the water is real
good. There isn't a stomach in town that hasn't been cured by
the water from that spring.

Dr. Do all three brooks come from a spring?

*Translator's Note: *Salud* means health.

P.P.　No sir. The Matayeguas is mainly from currents, from the thaws, you know? But all three are from the mountains, and each one runs through its own little valley, and they meet up near the Humán Mill. So that's why up above the town there are two crags they call El Crestón and La Peña. And up above, near El Crestón, there's Otero, and down below, Humán, and it's got real good trout. They're small, but they're tasty.

Dr.　The Embustes must be a deep river.

P.P.　It's a mighty one, yes sir. And where the river flows in, the valley opens up, of course. And on both sides you can see the rows of apple trees, and next to it, on the craggy ground—it's full of briers—is where the townspeople put the ovens and stuff. For the two treasures we've got, the fruit and the honey. Do you follow me?

Dr.　Yes, it's clear, Pacífico. And where was your house?

P.P.　My house? Well, more or less two hundred meters down the river, from the mill, I mean, in Humán.

Dr.　And which has got more people? Humán or Otero?

P.P.　They're about neck and neck. Like if Humán has fifty, say, then Otero's got forty. That's why they call my town Humán del Otero. But actually my town is two towns.

Dr.　In a word, there aren't many of you, and you don't get along, right?

P.P.　That's right, sir. That's the way it is, so whenever anybody from Humán talks about somebody from Otero, they always call them those bastards, and may the Lord forgive me. But if anybody from Otero talks about somebody from Humán, they say, Those sons of bitches, you know? There've never been two towns so close together and so mixed up.

Dr.　And how about your family, Pacífico: Where are they from, Humán or Otero?

P.P.　Well, in most respects, the Pérez side was from Humán, born and bred there. But to tell you the truth, Bisa was from Prádanos, the deserted town, the one with the gold nuggets, remember?

Dr.　When it was deserted, did the people from Prádanos go down to Humán?

P.P.　Most of them didn't, no sir. Mainly they went to the capital. But a couple were left. Like Bisa, or Señor Escolino, the carpenter.

Dr.　And the one you call Abue, the fisherman, he was your grandfather, of course; but was he Bisa's son, or was he from your mother's side of the family?

P.P.   Wait a minute, Doctor. Let's see if we can keep this straight. Look, to start at the beginning, the first one of all, the one we could call the head of the house, was Bisa. After him came three children, all of them boys, OK? There was Uncle Teodoro, who went off to America, to the Chaco War, and he never came back 'cause he said there was more land to be had over there. Then there's Uncle Paco, who owns the pippin tree, the one I get along with, and then there's Abue, that is, my grandfather, who was Grandma Benetilde's husband. She was the mystic, the one who lived with us. And collected snakes.

Dr.   Did your grandmother stuff them?

P.P.   Wait, I said it wrong. It wasn't Grandma. It was Abue who collected snakes. And he didn't stuff them, no. They were live. But that's a different story.

Dr.   Your grandfather kept live snakes?

P.P.   Yeah. From what people in Humán said, Abue was big on snakes ever since he was a boy. Seems he grabbed them with his bare hands, just imagine, and put them in his pockets. And he could tell them apart just by looking at them, the poisonous ones from the others. And he could take out the poison sac from those vipers without even hurting them. And the water snakes, the ones they call the dumb kind, he used to let them run loose on the moss in the trough where we gave Bisa his bath on St. Peter's Day. And if they were from inland, he'd take them in, and wow, you should've seen it! We had to put up shields and everything so they wouldn't slither under the doors.

Dr.   What did your grandfather want so many snakes for?

P.P.   Nothing, I guess. He just liked them. They were his hobby, the same way Don Prócoro collected stamps, you know? To pass the time. You have no idea how he pampered those creatures. Even gave them grasshoppers to eat, you know? And hen feed, just like they were hens. There were some pretty big ones, believe me, almost a meter and a half. And the animals thanked him, of course. They'd get up on their tails, or they'd coil around his legs, whatever, just so's they could get the stuff out of his hand.

And you want to know what I think, Doctor? I think that catching so many trout and snakes made Abue start to look like a fish himself—his face was all flattened out, his little yellow eyes looked off to each side—he couldn't look straight ahead.

Dr. And was this grandfather the one who told you all about the war in Africa?

P.P. Africa?

Dr. Wasn't he the one who told you about Abd-el-Krim and Fort Igueriben?

P.P. Oh. That's right, yes sir.

Dr. Well, then.

P.P. Excuse me. I didn't understand.

Dr. And how did your grandfather's story go?

P.P. The one about Fort Igueriben? That was some trek.

Dr. What do you mean? Would you like to tell me about it?

P.P. Well, let me warn you: If we start on that we'll be in here for quite a while.

Dr. Are you tired?

P.P. Tired? No sir. From what?

Dr. So?

P.P. Look, what must've happened there—and God knows what I'm talking about—is that things weren't planned right from the start.

Dr. There's no doubt about it, Pacífico.

P.P. What I mean is that, according to Abue, what made Abd-el-Krim curse is that two years before, General Silvestre had told him to get lost. Or at least that's how I heard it.

Dr. It's possible.

P.P. What's for sure is that Abd-el-Krim got to Gorgues, and the first thing he said was, We've got to finish 'em off. Abue, he meant, and the rest of the troop.

Dr. Hmm, yes. Go on.

P.P. But things must've been messed up from way back, you know. Just to give you an idea, they'd burned Commander Pino alive, in Chentafa. The way Abue tells it, the thing that got to them, to the Moors, was that they were getting friendly with their women, see? And what Flores said—he was a friend of Abue's—was: If they want to throw themselves at us, what can we do to stop them?

After all, we're Christians, but we're not made of stone. And when you think about it, he had a point, don't you agree? Anyway, Doctor, Abd-el-Krim just couldn't swallow all that scorn, from General Silvestre, I mean, and to make matters worse there was the problem with the women, you know, chasing the men. Abue says that one night, when they were up there bivouacking in the mountains, Lieutenant Garrido came up to him and said: We're in the same boat as Lyautey back in '14, the same boat. Seems a man called Rodrígues—according to Abue, that is—a man who was part Moorish and part something else, came up to him and said: Well, how do you suppose this'll turn out? He was really fucked, poor sucker. Everybody knew it. And that night, right after that day, just before God got up, there he was playing the trumpet, 'cause the general—but wait a minute, I'm getting things all mixed up, Doctor.

Dr.   Not at all, Pacífico. It's perfectly clear.

P.P.   Well, excuse me if I don't express myself right. The point is, like I told you, the general, as soon as the troop was all set to go, well, he goes and splits it in half, just like that, and, Everybody on this side goes to Igueriben, to the fort, OK? And the others come with me. So anyway, Abue and Flores were in the Igueriben group, and they find out from the grapevine that Abd-el-Krim's scouting the mountain with some guerrillas. So hup-two-three-four, all the way to Igueriben, to the fort.

Dr.   Did they make it?

P.P.   Yeah, they moved right in. But Abue says it was hotter than Hades in there, that they couldn't even breathe. They had to suffocate. So the whole darned day they were just lying around, couldn't move a finger, 'cause you know even though he's pretty lean Abue sweats a lot—he didn't even wear shoes at home 'cause of that. So he ran through his clothes, rotted them out with sweat. Had to wear tires instead. But one night, round about twilight, God knows how many days they'd been shut up in that fort, he got this bright idea: he stood up, see, grabbed hold of the lens, and he spotted them—one, two, three, a whole cloud of 'em, of Moors I mean—down the mountain. Well, you can just imagine the yelling and shouting: Sergeant, Sergeant, the Riffians are coming!

And Commander Benítez asks: How many? And Abue: Hundreds . . . thousands! And the other guy, the commander, I mean: Play the trumpet! You can imagine what a mess it was, everybody running around like crazy trying to get to their posts. And from what Abue says, the night before, before all the commotion, he felt something strange around his parts, sort of like he had to urinate. It's not that he was afraid, believe me; it was his nerves, he thinks, or else he was just anxious to get into action, who knows.

Dr. Did the Riffians attack right away?

P.P. No sir, not them. They were going about their own business. And Abue says the stars were just coming out, but the evening dew was so bright on the desert that you could see the Moors coming like it was daytime—some of them walking, others on horseback. So anyway, Commander Benítez, next to the machine gun, didn't take his eyes off of them, and he kept saying, Don't shoot 'til I give the order. And down below, in the look-holes, it was the same with the officers: Nobody shoot 'til the commander gives the order, just keep waiting. And there were the Moors, hup-two-three-four, heading for the fort like a bunch of thieves, getting it all set up for a surprise attack. They were covering themselves up with the sand dunes, but Abue—he was already onto their desert tricks, how *they* played the game. You think there's nobody there, and it turns out there are thousands of them, hey, all ready to trap you, and you don't even realize what's happening.

Dr. It certainly must have been a very precarious situation.

P.P. You can say that again. I sure wouldn't want to have been in his shoes.

Dr. Well, did the Moors attack that night?

P.P. They sure did. Abue says once they surrounded the fort they let loose—bang-bang, bang-bang! Looked more like a bunch of crazies than a fight. He was standing still, just watching them come, with some artillery on his parts, couldn't even breathe.

Dr. Didn't the commander give the order to fire?

P.P. Wait a minute. Don't go so fast. He let them come in close, see? and then when they were close enough, Open fire! Long live Spain! You should've seen it, Doctor, all hell breaking loose out there, ratta-tat-tat, the machine gun and the rifles going at them.

Abue says there were men and horses hitting the dust and rolling over in the sand, a real massacre. Abue was in his element, all right, giving it to the Moors: Burn up those rubberheads!—just to keep up everybody's morale. He says the shots made it bright, that they'd shake in the light from those shots, and that it went on and on, just like fireworks. And they kept at it for more than three hours. It may not sound like much, but it was. And Abue says he knocked them down by the dozen, the Moors, I mean, like bowling pins, just like you do at a fair: ping! ping! ping! And then suddenly, he says he got this cold feeling, and he said to himself, Could they be playing dead just to take us by surprise from behind, like the sneaks they are? You follow me? And then, he says, he took aim at the ones who were crawling on the ground, and he let 'em have it: ratta-tat-tat, ratta-tat-tat, and then he gave 'em another round, just to be on the safe side. Finished 'em off. He says that two and a half hours later his gun was hot, so hot he couldn't hold onto it, he had to keep shouting, Rodrígues, you son of a bitch! Get over here and relieve me! From the shooting, you know. He couldn't cool his own gun anymore, it was too overheated. Just imagine, three hours straight, Doctor. So by the time the enemy backed off, his hands were covered with blisters, burning up on him.

Dr.   So they fought them off.

P.P.   Yes sir, they did.

Dr.   What did they do then?

P.P.   Well, according to Abue, Commander Benítez, who was as smart as a fox, doubled the guard at the picket line, just in case, to be ready. And the guys who weren't off—he had 'em make straw men, you know, to trick Abd-el-Krim into thinking there were more of us. The dummies were great—all dressed up in the dead men's uniforms, the caps and everything, standing up against the embrasures, you couldn't tell they weren't real. It looked as if we didn't have any casualties.

Dr.   An ingenious stratagem.

P.P.   Yeah, it was. But the bad part was up there in the fort. I mean, it was the supplies: there wasn't enough food. Water for only forty-eight hours, three sacks of flour, a cluster of dates, about forty kilos of salted meat, and that was it. The only thing we had lots of was sugar—forty sacks! But what I wonder is, what could they do with all that sugar if they didn't have anything to drink?

Dr. Yes, you're right, son.

P.P. So Abue, just thinking about it, he said it turned his stomach. At least the Moors didn't even give them time to think about it. They'd barely finished setting up the dummies when Abd-el-Krim was at it again. He'd even dug some trenches and pushed a mortar to the side of a pit. So Abue, who had his eye out, grabbed the machine gun and blew the artillery to bits before Abd-el-Krim even had a chance to fire the first shot. He may not have been sharp for other stuff, but nobody had a quicker eye than Abue. I wish you could've seen him in the river with a spoon. Well, anyway, you can imagine how that went, all hell breaking loose for two whole days. They couldn't even stop to wet their whistles; they just kept firing away. It was the wounded men that emptied the canteens; when you lose blood, it seems it makes you real thirsty. But by nighttime they were all pooped. And Commander Benítez would give them the pep talk: Come on men, we'll have them licked by tomorrow, or at the latest the day after tomorrow, when Navarro or Silvestre will break through their lines and relieve us.

Dr. But wasn't the water all gone?

P.P. Like I say, yeah, we finished it. With the wounded and all. And so Commander Benítez stood up and said: Men, everybody who can stand up will have urine with sugar. Imagine how awful it was, ugh. The remedy wasn't much good, because the body keeps part of what you have, the water I mean, well, actually, the urine. So the time would come when there wouldn't be anything left, and that would be it.

Dr. That sounds feasible.

P.P. What?

Dr. I mean you're right, Pacífico. It makes sense.

P.P. Well, anyway, with all that, Commander Benítez making objections and suggestions, he consulted the troops, and Abue was the first to say everybody should have his own. Since he always had trouble with that—he had to go every half hour—he thought it'd be easier for him. But Commander Benítez said no, that they had to share and share alike, that they should all piss into the same container, and every time they went they'd get a glass of sugar to add nutrition and get rid of the ammonia. It seems the commander was very strict, and when the questions were over, he told Sergeant Blecua to organize groups to hunt for rats and watch the canteens. So by morning they were all eating rats and drinking urine, imagine, Doctor.

Dr.   How awful. And tell me: How did your grandfather come out of it?

P.P.   Well, it was like this. He says at sundown they started to hear some shooting off in the distance. First one shot, then a couple, then a lot. So when they heard them, Commander Benítez had them line up in the courtyard and said to them: Soldiers, General Silvestre's coming to join us. We've been saved! Long live Spain! You know? Abue says the men were crying. And some of them started to jump up and down shouting, Viva! Sergeant Blecua even made them use the urine to toast to it, if you can believe it, they were so happy. But just when they were starting to celebrate, the shooting started to die down, just a little, then more, 'til it was so quiet you could've heard a pin drop. That's when the bad part came. Abue says the stench from the dead was horrible— it reached way out around them—and as if that wasn't enough, there were those green flies, the kind garbage attracts, you know? that kind. And since there were carcasses lying all over the place, it didn't matter which way the wind blew—and if it didn't blow it was worse, it stank. So Abue was holding a handkerchief over his nose and telling Rodrígues—you know, the one who's half gay— Hey, aren't you a sexy Moor, and pinching him, the whole bit. The last thing they wanted was to lose their sense of humor. And it was about then that the telegraph delivery boy came, saying to surrender, imagine. Seems Commander Benítez looked as if he'd been hit by a rock. Never, he said, Take note, boy: Igueriben's soldiers die, but they don't give up, you hear? But life's got its own designs. Abue says when he woke up the next morning he saw Commander Benítez lying on his back with a bullet in his head—his brains blown out and the flies buzzing around him. So

Lieutenant Canseco took command. He was a funny one. Had a raspy voice, like he had a cold or something, always telling jokes. And the first thing he did when he took over was to abandon the fort—get out of there. The fort didn't have anything, and they didn't know if Annual could last, so anything except surrender. They were desperate. Know what I mean, Doctor?

Dr.   But I gather that that battle ended in a bloodbath, Pacífico. How in blazes did your grandfather escape being slaughtered?

P.P.   It was like this. According to Abue, Lieutenant Canseco took twenty men about nightfall and left the fort from the main door, see, while Sergeant Blecua with Abue and another group went down a rope in back just like we did at Góyar. And that saved them. Lieutenant Canseco's men got it from the Moors; they shot them like rats. And while the Moors were after them, thinking there weren't any more men, Sergeant Blecua and his gang were already at the Kert Hills heading for Annual, where General Silvestre was.

Dr.   Wasn't it a long way off, though?

P.P.   Well, I can't tell you exactly how far, but yes, it must've been pretty far, because it took them a long time. But according to Abue they traveled at night and slept during the day—like lizards, digging a hole near a dune, so they hardly showed. So as you can see, when it came to tricks, they knew more than the Moors.

Dr.   Did they spend many days that way?

P.P.   Oh, about five or six. But Abue says the hike was a party compared with what was in store for them. Some confusion!

Dr.   What happened?

P.P.   Well, they'd just gotten to Annual; they hadn't even seen the general yet. And the Moors start firing away at them, an ambush. Abue says his shoulder splintered on him from shooting that many Moors. But there was no way around it. Pandemonium breaking loose—the cannons, and the rifles, and the dead and the wounded—nobody could make sense of it. With the way things were, everybody was out for himself; it was only natural. So Abue decided to flip a coin. He said to Flores, Heads I'm in charge, tails you're in charge. And heads won, and before picking up the coin he was already giving orders: Flores, hurry up!

Inside, they're going to hunt them like rabbits. And he went, and not one person was left to tell the tale. On the other hand, Abue and Flores, after a week of hardships, sleeping in the daytime and marching at night, saw Melilla come into view. And once they got to Melilla it was scarier than a black hole. Silvestre has died! Abd-el-Krim's coming! You can imagine all the shouting and running.

Dr.   But no Moors got into Melilla, son.

P.P.   Course not, Doctor, but that was the next day. They were heading down a street, and he says an old woman screamed from a roof-top: Ships! I see ships coming! You follow? And she was right, there were some ships—it was the Legionnaires—so it was all kissing and drinking and cigars. They couldn't give them enough. So that's how Abue saved his skin.

Dr.   Tell me something, Pacífico: Didn't Abue's feats make Bisa—as you call him—feel a little jealous?

P.P.   Jealous? Why should he feel jealous? It was the other way around. Bisa's thing was bayonets; he always said so. Abue's was his good aim. They were two different things. Each man had his own thing.

Dr.   And didn't they talk about their respective doings? I mean, wasn't there some discussion about which way of making war was better?

P.P.   Excuse me, I don't understand you, Doctor.

Dr.   Listen, didn't Bisa scorn Abue for shooting when he could have used a bayonet?

P.P.   Not really, no sir.

Dr.   Didn't they argue?

P.P.   Now that you mention it, I do remember that one afternoon they got heated up over it—over which was worth more, a death by bullet or a death by the knife.

Dr.   What did they say?

P.P.   Well, Bisa said that Abue had killed more people with a machine gun than he had with a knife, that was for sure, and he wasn't quarreling with that, right? But he said that killing with a knife was a different sort of thing, and that one death from a knife was worth a hundred of the others.

Dr.   Did they reach an agreement?

P.P.   No sir. They argued so much we went down to the barracks where Sergeant Metodio was.

Dr.   So he'd be the judge?

P.P.   Exactly.

Dr.   And what was the sergeant's verdict?

P.P.   Well, he said that even though you shouldn't make comparisons with wars, that a death by knife was worth more, especially because of the moral side. You understand? So, for example, a death by knife would get a cross, whereas a death from a bullet doesn't count, in a war. Nobody notices it. Isn't that so?

Dr.   Undoubtedly. And what did your grandfather say, Pacífico?

P.P.   He didn't press the point, Abuc, I mean, about how many deaths by bullet equaled a death by the knife. Said that what Sergeant Metodio said was hard to judge offhand, that he'd have to figure it out on paper and study the situation and give it some time.

Dr.   Fine, Pacífico. You seem tired now.

P.P.   No sir, I'm not tired. I'm just getting a little sleepy.

Dr.   All right. Would you like for us to stop now and get some rest, and continue tomorrow night?

P.P.   It's OK with me.

Dr.   So tomorrow I'll expect you at the same time, right?

P.P.   Whatever you say, Doctor. That's why I'm here.

▲ ▲ ▲ ▲ ▲ ▲ ▲

Second Night

Dr.   Last night you cleared up several things for me, Pacífico. But I'd like to know more, to get to the bottom of certain matters. One thing is plain: your great-grandfather and your grandfather were born soldiers. I don't think we have to say anything more about that. Both of them and, from what you say, your Uncle Teodoro, were all born to fight. Their aggressiveness exhibits some manifestations that are basic, yet also conclusive. Now I'd like to determine whether or not your father fit into the picture. In other words, was your father a born soldier too, or did other things concern him more? Did your father find liberation in violence? What do you think, Pacífico?

P.P.   Well, let's see, Father had his war too, if that's what you mean. But later on he got involved with his work, and he worried more about his business interests than other things.

Dr.   And did he tell you stories about his war, too?

P.P.   Of course he did. When I was a boy.

Dr.   Later on he didn't?

P.P.   Not really, no sir.

Dr.   Why not?

P.P.   Because of his work, the business I mentioned.

Dr.   What kind of business did he have?

P.P.   Tractors and harvesters—he sold mortgages for them. Father just loved to sell a mortgage. I remember Agatángelo telling me: You can be sure your father's got a knack for it.

Dr.   Who was Agatángelo?

P.P.   Señor Escolino the carpenter's son.

Dr.   Was he from Humán?

P.P.   He sure was. Saying his name to anybody from Otero was like invoking the devil.

Dr.   Do you remember any of your father's war stories?

P.P.   Father didn't talk much. He didn't tell stories like Bisa's and Abue's.

Dr.   Then how did he tell them?

P.P.   Well, I don't know. His way. Sort of little by little. He'd tell you some one day, then none the next, you know what I mean?

Dr.   Whom did he feel closest to, your grandfather or your great-grandfather?

P.P.   What's that?

Dr.   Your father, I mean. Did he prefer bayonets or machine guns?

P.P.   Father? Neither one. Father's thing was "Laffites," hand grenades. He went after tanks. He says he used to dig shallow trenches in a zigzag line, you know? And when the enemy got close, the tank I mean, bang! He'd throw a bottle of gasoline at it and then right away throw the Laffite. He says he never missed, and that the tank would blow up in a flash.

Dr.   Didn't the men inside shoot at him?

P.P.   That's the funny part. Father would hang in there and let them get so close that the machine gun couldn't be lowered. It couldn't point at him, you see what I mean? He had it all figured out. He really did.

Dr.   And how did your father's story go?

P.P.   He didn't have a story. Didn't I tell you already? Father just told little bits and pieces. Except for once in Brunete, he blew up four tanks all by himself, and they gave him a medal.

Dr.   He got them all with the bottle technique?

P.P.   Yep, every one of them. With the bottle and a Laffite. He didn't know how to do it any other way. But that time he almost got fried.

Dr.   What happened?

P.P.   A howitzer blew up between his legs while he was waiting for the tank to come. Father's got over twenty-five metal splinters behind his right knee, and it's easy to say, but just imagine all that metal. Some of it got into his bone. That's why he had to spend five years traipsing around from one hospital to another. To weld that bone—this one, in his calf—it took six months in the north, in Bilbao, with a five-kilo weight hanging from his leg. And the wound wouldn't heal on the outside. They even talked about cutting off his leg to get it over with. They were considering it when he came home one day—they'd given him permission—and one afternoon when he was out for a walk along the Salud, the brook, he slipped and fell in, crutches and all. And what do you suppose happened? Well, that very same night the wound started to look better, so the next morning Father squatted in the brook on purpose, in a kind of metal sieve, and he sat there for about an hour just letting the water soak his bandages. And the next day he did the same thing, and the day after that, and the next and the next, and after two weeks his wound healed. What do you think of that?

Dr.   It's quite possible. It's true that some waters have healing properties. But tell me something: Did your father also think that it wouldn't be long until your war came?

P.P.   Sort of, yes sir.

Dr.   Did you ever tell any of them that maybe there wouldn't be any more wars?

P.P.   Once, yeah. I told Bisa, and you should've seen him. He said we had war in our balls, and that as long as men had balls—and may God forgive me for this—well, as long as we did, there'd be war. That's how he saw it.

Dr.   What kind of war did they expect for you? A civil war or a cold war? Where did they think your war would come from, anyway?

P.P.   Aw, it was all the same. They were just waiting for it, no matter where it started, you know? They didn't know anything about politics—never even read the paper. It's not that they were illiterate, get me straight now; it's just that that part didn't matter to them.

Dr.   So?

P.P.   Look, how should I put it. Whenever spring came, Bisa started watching the hills to the west. He said summer started wars, and he'd just stand there by the grove as if the war would come from down there. And he'd say to me: Your war won't be long now, Pacífico. There'd never been such a long time without a war. And when I said I didn't see why it should, Bisa burst out laughing and said, Some fix we'd be in if there had to be a reason for one. You couldn't get him to see it any other way.

Dr. I don't understand very well, son.

P.P. But it's as plain as day, isn't it? For example, I'd ask him: What are wars like, Bisa? He'd get all excited, gesturing and pushing his wheelchair around, saying, Wars aren't something you can describe, they just happen, see? And I'd ask him, Who starts them, Bisa? and him, he'd say, Nobody organizes them, Pacífico; they just flare up. So to put it in a nutshell, Doctor, a war starts like a cloud in the sky, just because it does, and we don't know where or how. Do you follow me?

Dr. Sort of. According to you, your grandfathers would just look at the hills to the west and ask the telegraph man if your war had come yet. Is that it?

P.P. Yes and no. Bisa, Abue, and Father were all waiting for my war. I mean, they were really looking forward to it, you know? Other than that, they did what they could to start it. Like when Father got to Gibraltar and went over to the Rock just to call the Englishmen bastards.

Dr. Your father did that?

P.P. Why would I say it if it wasn't true?

Dr. How was that? Tell me slowly, with some details.

P.P. Well, that's how it was, Doctor. I mean one day Father got greedy all of a sudden and went over to the Union office. He put his medals on the table and said, A farming loan. And two weeks later they gave it to him, and he went over and got himself a red harvester. Then he said: I'm going down to the southern tip, and I'm going to thresh all of Spain on my way up. And he did just that: took off, and we didn't see him for three months. He claims he offered himself to the highest bidder, sleeping in roadside ditches and surviving on crusts of bread, almost starved to death. And you could tell—he came back all withered and skinny, must've lost almost ten kilos on that escapade. So Bisa looked him over and said, Well? And Father emptied his sack in the mill wheel—it was full of green bills—and all Grandma Benetilde could do was say, That's bad, pointing at the money. But come to think of it, ever since her silver anniversary, after the trance, she didn't say anything else. Father only said, Now I've got enough to pay off the equipment. Between you and me, Doctor, I think that's when he started to like the idea of mortgages. But let's get back to what I was telling you. Bisa and Abue and Father started to take swigs from the wine bottle with a long side spout, one after another, and Father's tongue started to loosen up, and he said that when he got to Gibraltar it hit him: Why not go over to the Rock and provoke the English? And off he went. He got into his harvester, went down to the shore, and, Bastards, you yellow-bellied bastards! You should've seen the others while he told it, Doctor: Abue's yellow eye was shining like a piece of glass, and Bisa, Did you really call the English bastards? Father got more and more into it, of course, and said he stared straight at the Rock. Bisa started to go back and forth in his chair—I thought he'd have a fit or something—saying wouldn't that start a war? Father said it wasn't up to him, that he did his share anyway. And Abue: Did you stick it out for a while, did you call them bastards for long? drooling to hear it all, and Father, 'Til there was a big crowd, and an officer came up and told me to move on, and had I gone crazy or what?

Dr.   But Pacífico, doesn't this mean that the men in your family excluded patriotism or heroism from war? From how you tell it, all they wanted was war for war's sake, satisfaction of their primary aggressive instincts. So your father went to Gibraltar and called the English bastards. Your Uncle Teodoro escaped to America because there were more opportunities there. But he could have gone to Oceania just as easily, couldn't he?

P.P.   Well, I guess so. Yes, he could have.

Dr.   What was your reaction to the gratuitousness of their aims? I suppose that you were a total disappointment to them.

P.P.   I can't quite follow you.

Dr.   I mean, your passivity . . . well, the fact that you weren't enthusiastic about their feats and their plans: Didn't that disappoint them?

P.P.   Well, sure. And I knew I was different from them, ever since I was a kid.

Dr.   You were not naturally aggressive.

P.P.   It's not a question of that, Doctor.

Dr. What was it, then?

P.P. Wait. Bisa, Abue, and Father were left-handed, and I was right-handed, like my Uncle Paco.

Dr. Your grandfathers were left-handed?

P.P. Yes, and so was Father.

Dr. What did that have to do with it?

P.P. A lot. You think kind of funny sometimes. If they were left-handed and I was right-handed, it means I was different, doesn't it? So if they liked something, it was only natural that I'd like the opposite, don't you think? Each person's different, Doctor. We're all marked when we're born, there's no changing that.

Dr. But let's get something straight, Pacífico. When you were little and told them their wars scared you, and when you were an adolescent and told them you didn't see why you should have to fight a war, how about them, your grandfathers: Were they resigned to it, or did they insist on making you into a real soldier?

P.P. Well, to tell you the truth, Doctor, I went through lots of scenes at home on account of that.

Dr. Because you didn't like their wars?

P.P. That didn't hardly matter. What they really couldn't take was to see me upset about the trees being pruned or mad if somebody stole the honey from the bees.

Dr. You seemed somewhat feminine, wasn't that it?

P.P. Feminine! Are you kidding? More like gay, or queer, and may God forgive me—the worst there was, you understand? I can remember the night I could hear the fig tree crying, the first vacation I went home.

Dr. So the fig tree cried, did it, Pacífico?

P.P. How can I help it? Yes it did, like a baby. Abue had pruned it that morning, and he didn't even bandage it up.

Dr. What did you do?

P.P. Go down, secretly of course. And as I was bandaging the stumps, Mother appeared in her housecoat, and what was I up to? Taking care of the fig tree 'cause it was crying, and she said, The fig tree's crying, child? Well, you know how women are, Doctor. Mother took me back to bed and didn't say anything about it. So as for her, for Mother, I mean, I didn't have to worry.

Dr. Your grandfathers must have been the worst ones.

P.P. You can say that again. The next morning they set up a trial next to the mill wheel; the courthouse was nothing compared with that. The mildest thing I got from Bisa was swear words. And Abue: God, what a boy! Do you mind telling us what's going to happen the day your war comes? Father said I'd be the first one in the family to miss mine. When Bisa heard that, he flew off the handle—grabbed me by the arm and shook me and you sonofabitchfairy I'm gonna—a real mess, you know?

Dr.   That means that they didn't accept your sensitivity.

P.P. Why would they accept it? They were born fighters, they never stopped, they were always at it. You want to hear something else? When I was still in diapers, I must've been about two years old, Bisa was already egging him on, Abue, I mean, to make me do exercises. I was always a little on the puny side, you know? Or else he'd get him to fire the shotgun next to my crib to get me used to it, or he'd put a snake up next to me to see how I reacted. Mean stuff, that's all they knew how to do.

Dr.   How did you react, Pacífico?

P.P. You're going to laugh, but the first time Abue put a snake up to me, I got the shakes, my eyes rolled out of place, I got stiff, and Mother had to send for Señora Dictrinia to snap me out of it. It was like life and death. Things are funny, though, Doctor. Corina, who was born to the same father and the same mother, she could take the snakes and stroke their sides, just like that, you know? I mean they liked it. Ever since she was a little girl. And on St. Peter's Day when we gave Bisa his bath she couldn't wait to grab the sieve and get the stupid things out of the watering trough. I can hear Bisa now: if he was like *her*, it'd be a different story in this family. And Abue would calm him down with, Be patient, Father, everything'll be OK.

Dr.   From what I can see, your grandfather was more understanding than optimistic—toward you, I mean.

P.P. Yeah, I guess so. Abue didn't give up on me. He always had faith in everything.

Dr.   What do you mean?

P.P. Just what I'm saying. I mean Abue could take anything that was dished out and still keep his chin up. And was he ever restless!

I wish you could meet him. Would you believe that ever since I was born, I never once saw him sitting in a chair or on a stool the way you'd expect? Not him, no sir. He was always out doing something—up there or in the bed of the fig tree if we were over at the mill wheel. Just to give you an idea: he'd beaten a path out there, you could recognize it was his—always on the go.

Dr.   And he probably wasn't as stubborn as Bisa.

P.P.   Well, yes, as a matter of fact he wasn't as stubborn as Bisa.

Dr.   But Bisa was the one who ran things, wasn't he?

P.P.   Course. After all, head of the house, remember that. So if he said, for instance, that I should be taken to the doctor, nobody said different.

Dr.   Why should you have to go to the doctor?

P.P.   Huh! You're still wondering about that? Because of the fig tree and the bees and the rest. I can remember Don Alfaro now, saying to us when we came in: So where's the Pérez battalion off to? We had a reputation in town, see.

Dr.   And what did they tell Don Alfaro?

P.P.   Oh, Bisa spelled it out to him without beating around the bush. He said, Frankly, Doctor, is it possible to be a man if you haven't got anything between your legs? Just like that. And Don Alfaro said, Let's see now. And he took down my pants, had me lie down on the table, looked me over and, Fine: as for that we didn't have to worry.

Dr.   What did Bisa say?

P.P.   He looked at Abue, you know? Personally I think they'd talked it over beforehand anyway. So Abue says, Look, Doctor, this boy's too soft. And the doctor agreed I wasn't strong, but that's not a sickness. And Abue: More than anything else, the trouble with him is that he's strange, Don Alfaro. Starts shaking if he sees us prune a tree, or he starts swearing if we cut the combs out of a beehive. Do you think that's normal? You should've seen Don Alfaro's face. He didn't know what to make of it. Finally he just said it was a case of sensitivity, and nobody died of that.

Dr.   How about Bisa?

P.P.   Just imagine! He got all mad and said what the hell could they expect from a creature like me the day my war came, you know?

They'd fought theirs, he said, not that he wanted to brag about it. But would Don Alfaro please tell them what I would do when it was my turn to fight if I spent the day watching smoke come out of chimneys or feeling sorry for trout when they got caught.

Dr.   How did Don Alfaro take that?

P.P. Badly. You can just imagine. Said that if they wanted to make a man of me, give me some skills, and let me have a chance in life, they shouldn't put me down. Life would be hard enough.

Dr.   He was a reasonable man, Don Alfaro.

P.P. A country doctor.

Dr.   How about your grandfathers—did they come away satisfied?

P.P. Not really, no sir. How could they? But deep down, I think that with the Krim business, the shooting I mean, Don Alfaro was to blame.

Dr.   Excuse me, Pacífico. We'll get to that later. Before I forget, what was that about your spending the day watching smoke rise from the rooftops? Is it true, or did the old man make it up?

P.P. Well, as a matter of fact, I did like to see the smoke coming out of chimneys on a calm day: it's true, Doctor. Is there anything wrong with that?

Dr.   That's not the point, Pacífico. But tell me, why did you look at it?

P.P. Just to see it. Huh! I mean, I liked to. Don't think I had any ulterior motives or anything.

Dr.   Did you go out for precisely that reason: to see the smoke?

P.P. Sure. My Uncle Paco, ever since I was a kid, he used to take me up to El Crestón, in the hills, just for the pleasure of watching the smoke rise from the chimneys, you know? And I remember that on some afternoons my Uncle Paco would point his walking stick toward the smoke, and he'd say to me: Life is just that, Pacífico. Don't expect anything else.

Dr.   And would you always go up to El Crestón? What was it like up there?

P.P. You're asking me again? A big rock, huge, twenty times the size of the town hall that's on the main square. Looks as if it's about to fall, but it doesn't. Up at El Crestón the three brooks meet: the Matayeguas, the Lirón, and the Salud, you know? And it was from there, from El Crestón, I mean, that the boar committed suicide in 1957, the night before the thing with Grandma Benetilde.

Dr.   Goodness! A boar really committed suicide?

P.P. I wouldn't say so otherwise. And besides, it wasn't just a couple of
      people that saw it, I mean it was fruit-picking season, and every-
      body from Humán was at the square. And all of a sudden, thud!
      No growling or anything, just a loud thud! when the animal hit
      the pavement, you know? You should've seen how bloody we got,
      and shitty too.

Dr.   What did you do? Because that must not have been a very com-
      mon occurrence in your town.

P.P. You have no idea what bedlam broke loose because of that wild
      boar. Right off, Agatángelo wanted to go up to Otero. I mean he
      thought they'd played a joke on us—the kids, you know—and he
      wanted to get back at them. But Abue came out with, Why the
      hell would those bastards give us such a beautiful animal? And
      they were trying to figure it out when Señor Escolino got there.
      He was a real mountaineer—used to spend his free time up in the
      Cieza area—and he said none of that, that it was a well-known
      fact that when cattle got old, if they didn't have toothaches, they
      got rabies or something worse, you know? And since the animal,
      the boar, I mean, already had gray hair and cavities, we figured it
      was a good explanation, see?

Dr.   Fine. Let's turn to something else, now, Pacífico. Several times
      you've mentioned your Uncle Paco, right? I gather he was a re-
      flective man, a kind of model of common sense. All right now.
      You've said that your Uncle Paco was your grandfather's brother,
      but that your grandfather was left-handed and Uncle Paco was
      right-handed, and that they didn't get along, isn't that so?

P.P. Yes, that's right, Doctor. If Abue said black, Uncle Paco said
      white. Fought like cats and dogs. But you know, just between you
      and me, the worst of it is that they didn't have enough heart.

Dr.   Heart?

P.P. Well, call it what you want. What I mean is, they didn't love each
      other enough. And you know what they say. It's worse to be un-
      loving brothers than strangers.

Dr.   But you were partial to your Uncle Paco, weren't you? It seems
      that you got along better with him than with anyone else in the
      family, except maybe your mother.

P.P. And Grandma Benetilde.

Dr. Did you love her very much too, Pacífico?

P.P. How could I help but love her, Doctor? She was the best person I knew. Her thing was to sew and keep quiet, you know? Ever since the silver anniversary of her trance, she never opened her mouth. The only thing she'd say was He's good, or He's not—depending on how somebody struck her, like in the Last Judgment. And as if that wasn't enough, Grandma Benetilde had a crown.

Dr. What do you mean, a crown?

P.P. Just what I'm saying. She had a crown, like saints in holy pictures.*

Dr. Do you mean your grandmother went around town wearing a crown, just like the men wore berets?

P.P. Wait a minute. Not exactly. Don't get it backward. Grandma Benetilde had a crown on some days, in certain places, see? In the stables, for instance, in the late afternoon, when she was feeding the animals.

Dr. Listen. Pacífico, was there by any chance a window in the stables that opened to the west, where the sun shone in at sunset?

P.P. Yeah. How did you guess?

Dr. I just figured there might be. But let's forget this for a minute. Tell me more about your grandmother. How did her trances start? What were they like?

P.P. Well, I only have secondhand knowledge, Doctor. Because her trances started when she came of age, see. She wasn't even married yet, or anything; I mean Father hadn't even been born yet. But according to Señor Isauro they were really something. I mean he swears up and down that he saw the communion wafers come raining down around her, around the fig tree, and Don Salvador, who was the parish priest then (and he was all excited about the trances), well, he gave everybody communion with those wafers, imagine. I mean, according to Señor Isauro there was a crowd: there must've been a thousand souls there that morning, you know. And that was just one time. He says on other days the wafers would come out of the flowers or right out of the mystic's pockets—always in strange places, see.

---

*Translator's Note: Pacífico's imprecision causes the Doctor to misunderstand him. Pacífico means that his grandmother's head was surrounded by an aureole.

Dr. The mystic was your grandmother, right?

P.P. Yes sir, she was. They called her the mystic 'cause she was so devoted. She never got tired or had any pain—nothing. I mean, for instance, she'd go into a trance early in the morning, and she'd stay on her knees all day long, and it wouldn't hurt, you know? And she'd just stare at the fig tree, where the Holy Virgin was. According to Señor Isauro, during the trance she'd speak to people in their own language; like, for example, she spoke French to the French, and Portuguese to the Portuguese. So Don Salvador wanted to test her, and one day he asked her something in Greek, and don't think Grandma Benetilde shied away. I mean, she answered him.

Dr. Your grandmother answered in Greek?

P.P. That's right. Or at least that's what they say. I wasn't around. But according to everybody in Humán, as soon as my grandmother went into a trance she could speak any language she wanted.

Dr. And in that state of ecstasy what did she see?

P.P. It depended. The Virgin Mary or Our Lord. Always in the treetop, in the fig tree, you know? It never changed. And according to Señor Isauro, if Our Lord came out, Grandma Benetilde's eyes—they were black—would turn green, and if it was the Virgin Mary, they'd turn sky blue.

Dr. Did she always go to the same fig tree?

P.P. Oh sure, the fig tree near the mill wheel, the only one in town. It's still there, and it wasn't just yesterday—it happened almost sixty years ago.

Dr. Were the visions very frequent?

P.P. From what I gather, the mystic allowed people to come only on Saturdays. But on those days there were real pilgrimages, like a party town, tons of people everywhere. Señor Isauro says that the day she took people, in the morning with the dew you could already tell who would appear to her because of the smell. I mean if it was going to be the Virgin Mary, well, it smelled like roses, and if it was Our Lord, then it was jasmine, see? All over the valley, you know? And as the time came it got stronger, and one day it seems the scent of the flowers went all the way to Madrid.

Dr. Where did all the people stay?

P.P. That's the funny part, Doctor. There wasn't room enough for them to eat, and there was even less to sleep. So they slept in the ditches along the road, or in the haylofts, wherever they could just find a spot, the thing was not to lose the message.

Dr. And was there a message?

P.P. Sure, there had to be one, Doctor. One afternoon the Holy Virgin said to Grandma Benetilde: Tell men not to destroy themselves, not to get carried away by greed, not to forget me.

Dr. Was that all?

P.P. That I know of, yes . . . But don't think it did much good. Hey, four days later they almost killed her.

Dr. Your grandmother? Who?

P.P. Who else? The ones with the grudge, the Otero gang. It was always the same. Señor Isauro says they'd been after her ever since she started. I mean they just couldn't take it—seeing all those people come to town. Even though some of the money they brought in went to them. Even with that and everything they claimed that the mystic, my grandmother, I mean, was a fake, a witch. And one night they set fire to her house, and wounded her; then they left her for dead. Thank goodness the next morning the bishop sent a car for her, and they took her to the capital, and the bishop put her in a convent for a year. And as soon as she came back to town, Abue noticed her, and a couple of months later he took her to the altar.

Dr. And your grandmother never had any more of those experiences?

P.P. No, not really. Except that twenty-five years after the trance Grandma Benetilde lost her speech. Either it was He's good, or He's a bad one, that's all you could get her to say. Seems to me that something must've happened to that head for it to get mixed up like that.

Dr. Hmm, it does sound strange.

P.P. Yeah.

Dr. Your grandmother said your Uncle Paco was good, didn't she?

P.P. Yes, she did. But don't think other people agreed with her.

Dr. Other people? What did they think of him?

P.P. Well, depends on who you mean. Like Abue, for instance, thought he was lazy, whereas Don Prócoro swore he was a poet. Like, I can remember one day I said to him, My uncle's never written a line of poetry in his life, and he says, What difference does that make? Imagine. What an answer.

Dr.   Your Uncle Paco interests me, Pacífico. Would you please tell me a little bit about him?

P.P.   What do you want to know, Doctor? I guess I remember him walking down the road ahead of me wearing his checked visor. I don't think he ever took it off, not even when he went to bed. Always all dressed up, with his walking stick. You know, my Uncle Paco was never in a hurry. And he never had a whole lot of things he had to do.

Dr.   Did he ever live with Bisa?

P.P.   With Bisa? He wouldn't dream of it. Well, when he was a boy, maybe, 'cause after all he was his son, but ever since I was born, ever since I can remember, no. My Uncle Paco lived by himself, in his own house, you know? About half a kilometer from town, next to the Embustes, in the apple orchards. With two goats, a half-dozen hens, and two white pigeons. And people said he used to send messages with them, with the pigeons, I mean, to a woman in Córdoba, to his girlfriend. But you know, he never said anything to me about any of that.

Dr.   How old was your uncle when you left?

P.P.   Look, Doctor, counting years and ages in my family is very hard. But my Uncle Paco can't be seventy-five, that's for sure!

Dr.   It's not likely he'll get married now.

P.P.   Oh, but not 'cause of his age. In my town they wait 'til late for that stuff—you know, weddings and dying. Look at Bisa.

Dr.   What kind of work did your uncle do? Was he a farmer too?

P.P.   He was a farmer, yes. In my town just about everybody is, except for Señor Del, Señor Edito, Señor Isauro, and Señor Escolino. I mean he had a little farm next to the Embustes, and it was enough for his needs. But you wouldn't want to suggest he pick his fruit: he couldn't, it was like taking an animal's critters away. He saw it that way, you see. I mean every year he'd make a deal with a couple of fruit pickers. And as for the pippin tree, well, I offered to do it myself, Doctor, 'cause I'd be more careful. You know, it seems to me that my Uncle Paco was a little weird. I mean, he never ate meat, for example, just vegetables and apples and honey.

Then every morning, when it was nice and fresh, he'd set out for La Peña for a mouthful of water first thing, before breakfast. He'd drink from the Salud fountain—and I mean every single day, through hell or high water. It was his routine. After that he'd take a walk around the orchards and the pigeons' cote in Cieza, and 'round about midday he'd show up at the house on some errand or other: Look, Vitálico—that's Abue—there're two apple trees around Fuentefierro that need propping up. Or else: Next to Las Puertas I've seen a little swarm of gold bees that look like the ones we keep at home. And Abue of course goes, Sure, 'cause the beehives we kept at home were undivided. I mean, each one was everybody's property—they weren't separate. So Abue, as you can imagine, as soon as he heard him, he said, Well, grab a straw hamper, Paco, and catch it, he said. So my Uncle Paco says, You know I can't make a prisoner out of anybody—he meant the bees, of course—and Abue started to call him lazy and got mad at him, but Uncle Paco didn't give an inch: Look Vitálico, if we're all so busy who's going to notice what still has to be done?

Dr. As for your devotion to him, Pacífico, could you tell me when you first started to feel it? Why were you so attached to him?

P.P. Who knows? I just was. He was different. My Uncle Paco, I mean. The others played war next to my cradle, or they told me stories that scared me, but he—well, he just never did, you know? I'm talking about when I was a kid, when Uncle Paco would show up with some white gravel or a fossil. There are lots of them around La Torca, hundreds of them, snails and shells, you know? Tons of fossils. Well, it must've been my instinct, Doctor; just seeing him made me start gurgling and kicking my legs. And Mother, when she saw me making such a fuss, she'd say, Virgin above! Paco, what is it about you that makes this boy act like that?

Dr. And as you started to grow up you didn't lose any of the admiration or rapport you felt with him?

P.P. Oh no, it was the other way around: I liked him more. Like, for instance, on winter evenings, he'd come and take me by the hand and off to El Crestón, to see the chimneys' smoke. And when the pippin tree blossomed, there he was, to see how Don Patricio worked on the tree. And when spring was about to come, during vacation, we'd be off to La Torca Palomera after fossils, all the way down—and it was really deep, Doctor. They took a long time to get to the water. I liked to go out with him, even if he didn't say anything—he usually didn't. But I liked to see him with his visor and his black walking stick. He'd use it for everything—to brush off a horsefly or to stamp down a bunch of nettles. And as I got older, you know, I used to think to myself that carrying a stick gives you some authority. Otherwise how could you explain that my Uncle Paco was able to make peace between the people in Humán and Otero, or the business about Señor Nestorio, or anything—they were all impossible. Even though Bisa would say different, I think my Uncle Paco knew how to value things; he knew how to know them. It was thanks to him that I realized that trees suffer and rivers speak and chimney smoke is like life, because it is, you know. For instance, Doctor, some afternoons, on the way to La Torca, my Uncle Paco would go and sit on the Peñacarrubia Cliffs, and he'd teach me how to distinguish the voices of the three brooks, you know? The Matayeguas, the Lirón, and the Salud. And he'd say, the Matayeguas calls out, can you hear it? It sort of does somersaults. And I'd say, Yes Uncle. And you won't believe this, Doctor, but when we shut our mouths I could hear the Matayeguas calling out, or the Lirón singing, or the Salud grumbling. Just like people talking.

Dr.   What else did your uncle tell you, Pacífico?

P.P.   Right there, on the Peñacarrubia Cliffs my Uncle Paco taught me that rivers break up the clouds—you know, make the sky clear. And that's as true as the blessed light. I mean, you could see it: a cloud would come up from the Embustes valley, from the northeast part, and when it got up to El Crestón, you could count on it: there'd be three smaller ones, one going up the Matayeguas, another toward the Lirón's valley, and the third along the Salud. There'd be three clouds.

Dr.   So you learned more from your Uncle Paco than you did at school, from what I gather. Is that right?

P.P.   Wait a minute. It was a different kind of knowledge. 'Cause books are one thing, and life is another, isn't it? Like, for example, in school you don't learn how to look at things—aren't I right about that? Well, my Uncle Paco taught me to look; 'cause, you know, there are things you've got in front of your nose, and for some reason or other you just don't see them. Well, like I was saying, Doctor, my Uncle Paco taught me how to look. It was 'cause of him that I knew our town was beautiful. From up on the top of El Crestón I could see the rooftops of Humán and all around them the ring of apple trees. And down below in the valley there was the Embustes shining like a mirror, you know? And the two oak trees leaning to both sides. And on top of everything, the walnut trees, like watchtowers. And then just about this far over to the right, on the top of the hill, there were all the Otero houses. They were made of stone. Off to one side was the parish church, blind as a castle, and next to it the cemetery walls—the ones Teotista climbed over one day. And inside, four black cypress trees, and if the north wind was blowing they'd sway like stems. Anyway, Doctor, that's what I learned to see. I don't know if you'll believe me or not—you're free to think what you want—but just seeing it made me feel like a different person. There were days I even felt like crying and all.

Dr.   Yes, Pacífico. Go on. What else did you learn from your Uncle Paco?

P.P. Oh, I learned so much from him, from my uncle I mean, that I could keep telling you about it for years and you still wouldn't know half of it.

Dr.   Was your uncle a sensitive man?

P.P. Well, it's easy to see that. But you know, if he was ever sad about something he just kept quiet. Kept his mouth shut and hung onto his walking stick with both hands like he was dizzy. That's what he did the afternoon he came and told me about the hole at La Torca Palomera being full of dead men.

Dr.   Was it true?

P.P. Look. Maybe he had other faults, but my Uncle Paco didn't know how to lie. I mean if he said it, that's how it must've been. I can remember I was throwing stones next to the ditch and listening to them bounce down to the water, and I asked him, Who made La Torca, Uncle? And he said, God, and I said, To go down to hell? And he said, Even lower. But I can tell you, Doctor, that black hole was awesome. It was even scary. And I told him so. He just said that the land around our town was like that, full of caverns, and that someday when I grew up he'd take me up to the Aquilina Cliff to see the Cangueta grotto. It was all full of stalactites and stalagmites, 'cause the water had been dripping in there for almost a million years, imagine.

Dr.   You were going to tell me about the dead men in the hole, remember, Pacífico?

P.P.   Oh yeah. That's right. I go from one thing to another without realizing it. Well, anyway, that hole, La Torca: it really got to me, you know? So I said to my uncle once: Uncle, use your watch to time how long it takes this stone to get to the water. So he timed it, see, and it took fifty seconds, and I go, Is that long, Uncle? And he goes, Depends on what you mean by long; in other words, if we weigh the stone, considering the force of gravity, how much the earth's pulling it down, I mean, we could guess the depth. That's how he explained it. I was just a kid, couldn't even follow him, and who knows why, but this crossed my mind: And if they throw a man down? Oh, Doctor, you should've seen his face. He turned white as a sheet, my uncle, I mean. He grabbed onto the handle of his walking stick, and he closed his mouth. And me— you know how kids are—well, I kept at him: And if they threw a man down, Uncle? Then his voice got kind of cloudy, as if he had some mucus in his throat, and he said, They did. And I had to sit down next to the elm so's I wouldn't fall over, it was such a shock. But after a while, you know, it was funny. I liked it, and it scared me all at once, you know what I mean? And I kept going: When was it, Uncle? and him, In the war, and me, In Bisa's? and him, In your father's, the big one, and me, Did they throw a lot of men down, Uncle? And him, Over a hundred. And me, What did they do? And him, he coughed a little as if he was clearing his throat, getting that mucus out, you know? And it took him a while to answer, believe me. He just stared at the Aquilina Cliff, and after a while he said, What did you expect? Cry, and shake, and kick their legs like they were being thrown into the pit of hell. And then both of us shut our traps, we were so scared. And I didn't ask him anything again for two years, 'til when Mother took me up to La Torca to see the souls in purgatory flying.

Dr.   Did souls fly out of the hole, Pacífico?

P.P. Oh yeah, every year on November 2. They never missed. You could've seen all of us filing up there, and you couldn't tell us apart—Humán and Otero, I mean.

Dr. And what did you see, Pacífico? Tell me about it.

P.P. It was kind of weird. I remember it was snappy that night, some frost, you know, but there was this deep silence. It was so quiet you could hear them get caught in the dry branches of the elm tree. So anyway, there we all were waiting next to the hole 'til midnight, Doctor. Then all of a sudden you heard the chains dragging and the splashing. And in the meantime, and you couldn't tell where it came from or why, there was this dusty light in the bottom of the hole—like if somebody was making a fire down there—and the women started blessing themselves and praying out loud, can you imagine? And after a while that dusty light started rising up and up 'til it was on top of the elm tree—this huge thing, I can still remember it—and Señor Edito, the butcher, was saying next to me, What'll come out this year? And when all the radiance had shone out, it started to take a shape. I mean, it started to taper off at the top and get wider down below, and it got more and more vivid, you know? Mother was trembling, and Señor Edito was saying, It's a cathedral. And then we were all quiet again. Nobody opened his mouth; we just stared up with our jaws hanging open, 'til the dusty light disappeared. But don't think it went back down into the hole or anything. It didn't. It just left, but I couldn't tell you where it went. I mean, just so you'll understand me, it was like when the mist clears.

Dr. It sounds incredible, Pacífico. Was it always a cathedral?

P.P. Oh no. Stuff you could recognize, though. Each year it was something different. I mean, once it was a castle, another time it was the Holy Virgin, another time it was a walnut tree, and I remember the last time I went up to La Torca: it was a gigantic angel, really huge, playing a trumpet.

Dr. This took place on the night of All Souls' Day?

P.P. That's right. It was the second of November.

Dr. And did you ever see the dusty light from the hole any other time?

P.P. Me? Never. Except for that date I never went up to La Torca at night. Or anybody else in town, far as I know.

Dr. Out of fear?

P.P. Call it what you want. Yeah, I guess so.

Dr.   How about the priest, Pacífico? What did he say?

P.P. Don Prócoro? What could he say? That it was only natural, that why all the fuss, that it was the will-o'-the-wisp.

Dr.   The will-o'-the-wisp?

P.P. Yes sir, that's just what he said: the will-o'-the-wisp.

Dr.   After that experience did you ever go back to La Torca Palomera with your Uncle Paco?

P.P. Oh sure, hundreds of times. But I didn't throw stones anymore. It was kind of revolting, you know, to see them break up the heads on the corpses.

Dr.   Something else, Pacífico. Did you ever talk over the spectacle of All Souls' Day with your Uncle Paco?

P.P. Never, no sir. I know it impressed him 'cause he never said a word. Anything that bothered him or upset him made him do just that—close his mouth. For instance, if Bisa or Abue mentioned their wars, he'd just grab his cane and stare at them. But he never said a word.

Dr.   How about your grandfathers, Pacífico—did they mind your getting together with him? With your Uncle Paco, I mean.

P.P. Not on your life. And you can be sure of this: If they sent me to the city to be educated, I owe it to him.

Dr.   Tell me this: Before going to the city, hadn't you ever been to school?

P.P. Well, sure. Five years I went, to Don Angel's school.

Dr.   How old were you when you left?

P.P. Thirteen going on fourteen. I'd just turned fourteen.

Dr.   And how was it you decided that you'd leave?

P.P. That's another story, Doctor. If you ask me, I think it was all three of them that decided it—Bisa, Abue, and Father, I mean— at those evening sessions they'd have, when I went to bed. Lots of times Corina would come and say: The old guys are meeting again, and I could hear the murmur their talk made through the bedstead 'til I finally fell asleep. Well, anyway, one morning after one of those meetings, just after I got up, Mother said that on Monday I'd be off for school, in Sinclético's car. So I didn't even have time to think about it.

Dr.   Did the prospect please you?

P.P.   How's that?

Dr.   Did you like the idea of going away to school?

P.P.   I don't know. I suppose so. It was all the same to me. I had to tell Uncle Paco, though. But since we were spreading out the apples on the ground those days, it wasn't any problem.

Dr.   Did you find him there?

P.P.   Course I did. He never missed a day, you know. He didn't actually pick the fruit, but he was very strict about setting it out. You should've seen how orderly he was. Like when I was a kid he'd say, Line them up on the shelves without crowding them together, Pacífico. Otherwise they get bruised, and until they rot apples suffer, you understand? And me, I'd be real careful. And he'd explain them to me: The ones with the leaves on them are shinier, and these yellow ones with the heart-shaped bottoms are pippins, Pacífico. You can tell an apple by its top and bottom— they're its face and rump, just like with people—and you tell them apart the same way. And so the afternoons went by like that, Doctor—putting the apples on the shelves and chatting. You should've smelled it, too. It was wonderful, from the apples. You could almost taste it, it was so strong. And you know, for me, now that I'm far away from there, my town is that smell, that smell of the apples. Like if I'm feeling bad some days, I close my eyes and try to imagine that smell, and then it seems I start to pick up and feel better, you know?

Dr.   Good, Pacífico. And how did you tell your uncle that you were leaving for the city?

P.P.   It was like this. As soon as Mother told me that Bisa and Abue had decided on it—that same afternoon, it seems—well, I went over where he was, my Uncle Paco, I mean, and I said to him, I said: Uncle, on Monday I'm leaving for school; Sinclético's taking me. See? And him, he was surprised of course. To the city? And me: Yep, the city, Uncle; my grandfathers figured that this way I wouldn't be with you. So he first of all just closed his mouth. I mean he didn't really say anything. But when I was saying good-bye, it was that darned habit of his. I mean, he put his walking stick between my feet, and I've caught a rabbit. And me, Come on, Uncle! I cursed myself, and he comes out with, You won't get beyond that, Pacífico, mark my words. Just like that, in his usual tone.

Dr.   But . . . did your uncle put his walking stick between your feet very often?

P.P.   Well, no, not really. Just sometimes. And when I was cursing, he took up the same old theme: You won't get beyond that, Pacífico, mark my words. What can I say, Doctor? I didn't understand him either, not any of it, not 'til the afternoon when the business with Teotista happened.

Dr.   And once you were in school, didn't you go to see your Uncle Paco? Didn't you see him on vacations?

P.P.   Yeah, I did, behind my grandfathers' backs. I can still remember when I went home for Christmas. Some excitement! There was Bisa going back and forth in his chair, and Abue on his stool, both of them watching me like hawks. I'd hardly got home, hadn't even kissed Mother yet, when Bisa goes, So? I just stood there, didn't make a move, and all of them were waiting. So just to get out of a tight spot, to make as if nothing had happened, I said, Is it true what Sinclético says, that Elio has had pups? Father said, Turo, Miaja, and Krim—they gave their dogs names from their wars, see. And then everybody was quiet again and stared at me. I guess it was to see if I'd made any progress in the city. I couldn't figure out for the life of me what to say to them, 'til suddenly I got this idea, I don't know why I should've, and I said, Bisa, did you know there was a war once that lasted a hundred years? You should've seen him: He coughed, almost choked to death, and, That's impossible. And me: I swear it's true, Bisa. I read it in a book. So he turns to Abue and says, Did you hear that, Vitálico? And Abue turns to look at me, just relishing the thought, you know? A hundred years of pure shooting! And me, I said to him, There weren't any guns then, Abue; so Bisa starts shouting, With knives! Just my style! And during all this Mother and Grandma Benetilde blessing themselves, Heavens above! and Bisa starts screaming and wheeling around in his chair, Now that's a school for you! Looked like a loony bin, Doctor.

Dr.   Yes. I imagine no other news could have pleased your grand-fathers more, could it?

P.P.   No, I guess not. They looked at me like I'd just come back from fighting in that war. But I've got to confess that I liked showing off, too. Then they left for their game, and I was on my way to Uncle Paco's.

Dr.   To surprise him?

P.P.   Exactly. That's what I wanted to do.

Dr.   And did you surprise him?

P.P.   Nah. He already had the news. I mean, when I said to him, Did you know, Uncle, that once there was a war that lasted a hundred years? he said to me, That was a long, long time ago, Pacífico. Weapons weren't as deadly then, so you had to spend more time to do your quota, understand? And then I was the one that was dumbfounded: Your quota, Uncle? And he goes, Sure. Wars where you don't kill your quota of men don't even get mentioned in history books. That's what he told me.

Dr.   And in that first encounter, after your experience in the city, weren't you able to talk with your Uncle Paco anymore, the way you used to?

P.P.   No, of course I could. I mean, he asked me if that was all I'd learned, and so I told him about Chinese handball and stilts and the arguments we had in class, you know, some of us ganging up on others to catch somebody in a mistake. My Uncle Paco nodded, and when I finished he said, I see you didn't waste any time. And then I told him the other stuff, I mean, something I'd had on my mind a long time, Doctor, so I asked him point blank: Uncle, do we always have to be against somebody in life? Don't think he whipped out an answer right away. Oh, no sir. Uncle liked to think before he opened his mouth. So he tapped his walking stick on the floor a few times, and after a while he said, That's called competition. And he just stared into the fire, you know? And you may not believe me, Doctor, but even with that I didn't get the picture; but since I'm as hardheaded as they come, I mean 'cause that's how I am, I asked him, And can't we live without competing, Uncle? Can't we all be *together* for a change? He looked worried, and he grabbed onto his stick and said, That hasn't been figured out yet, see? And you probably won't believe this, but that same afternoon, just as I was starting to walk out, he put his cane between my feet—my Uncle Paco, I mean—and I caught another rabbit.

Dr. Your uncle certainly made use of singular pedagogical techniques! Tell me something: Did you stay in school long?

P.P. Yes. Well, actually, no. Between three and four years. But I didn't get much out of it, to tell you the truth. First it was my glasses, and then with square roots and all, I lost out on a lot.

Dr. What's the story on your glasses?

P.P. Wearing them. I couldn't see the blackboard, so Don Alfaro said, This boy needs glasses.

Dr. That's common enough. I've worn them since I was a boy, too, but it didn't make anything tough for me.

P.P. I don't mean to say it does, Doctor. It's just that you don't know what a scene there was at home because of my glasses. All Bisa could say was: Did you ever see a soldier wearing glasses in a war? And Abue and Father naturally said they hadn't. Only the guys in the dispensary, or with the desk jobs, wore them.

Dr. So did they finally give you glasses?

P.P. What else could they do? But not 'til six months later. By then I couldn't see a priest in the snow, as they say. And in school they were already reviewing square roots, and they're something I could never get, Doctor.

Dr. Weren't you good at math?

P.P. Wait a minute. I don't have any trouble with history or grammar. Or even with arithmetic, Doctor—you know, adding, subtracting, multiplying, and dividing. I used apples to count, and one way or another I could figure it out. But apples just don't go with square roots, you know? Where do you put them? Anyway, little by little I started to slough off, and I got lazy, and when Mother died, shortly after Grandma Benetilde committed suicide, I was seventeen and in my third year. I was behind. But let's keep that between you and me, OK? Because I told Candi—the girl I was seeing—that I'd finished up and gotten my degree.

Dr. You didn't tell your girlfriend the truth?

P.P. On that, no. Nobody would've. She was the kind that wants to change the world, and she cared a lot about how much everybody knew. I can still remember that a little while after we met, she said hicks always had a kind of a dumb, startled look, but that my eyes were different. So I agreed with her—what else could I do?—but what I really thought was that it was probably because of my glasses.

Dr.   Something else, Pacífico. Once you started wearing glasses, did your grandfathers give up on trying to make a fighter out of you? Did they admit that if your war came, you could be in the dispensary or have a desk job?

P.P.   Well, I never really asked about it, Doctor. But I'm afraid they'd have said no. My grandfathers . . . well, they probably would've thought: He'll be the first fighter in glasses. Or at least that's what I think they'd say; I'm just guessing. You know what they're like.

Dr.   But you could infer it from their attitude, from their conversations, from their conduct with you.

P.P.   I don't really remember, to tell you the truth. Except for the rock fight.

Dr.   What rock fight?

P.P.   The only one I know about, Doctor, the big one with the gang from Otero, when water was being channeled into town.

Dr.   What happened?

P.P.   Well, you know. When the Otero bunch found out that the water couldn't go up the mountain, they came to watch when it was brought. They couldn't stand the idea that we were getting it and they weren't, so there had to be a rock fight. As if that could fix things. Anyway, Teotista up there, and Agatángelo down below— you should've seen how badly they took it. And Señor Del was scared to death, of course, putting up cardboard in the glass panels and giving me a hard time, saying, Pacífico, couldn't you speak to your uncle? We shouldn't have to pay for this, should we?

Dr.   Was your Uncle Paco the referee in those fights?

P.P.   Not exactly. It's just that I can't tell you everything at once. I mean, the stuff about Señor Del and Señor Nestorio is another story. Señor Nestorio, for example, he had his business about halfway between Humán and Otero, right on the borderline. And both sides claimed he was on their side. But he couldn't take sides or be on both either; he was looking out for himself, naturally. Like he said, I'm with everybody, OK? Business doesn't fight. But he didn't get very far with that. Teotista and Agatángelo wouldn't listen to him, though. Come on, they said. Take sides, damn it. Nobody's going to butter their bread on both sides around here. They kept forcing him to take a stand, see. But he wouldn't give an inch, of course, because with tiles and broken glass, it was like an earthquake. And they'd go to his place to make peace again, so of course he made a bundle off them from their drinks and all, celebrating.

Dr. So Señor Nestorio was a neutral party, then.

P.P. Yeah. That's exactly what Bisa said. He put it in those same words. But then when he heard that they hadn't left a single pane unbroken, he'd burst out laughing and, The blows have always been for neutral parties; it's their own fault for not taking a stand. But Señor Nestorio still didn't let them twist his arm.

Dr. Was the dispute resolved?

P.P. I was just coming to that, Doctor. One afternoon when Agatángelo and Teotista were at it again, both of them claiming he was on their side, along comes my Uncle Paco. So Teotista says to him, You sure picked a good time to show up, Señor Paco, and Uncle says, What's going on here? Well, to make a long story short, Teotista and Agatángelo filled him in, and the first thing my Uncle Paco did was close his mouth. And after a little bit he picked up his walking stick and pointed first to El Crestón and then down to the valley, down to Humán, and after a while he said: Nestorio shouldn't have to be mixed up in this; he's not from Humán or Otero. So Teotista laughs and says, Hmph! I like that. So where's he from, then? And my Uncle Paco, just to bully him a little, says, From Del, and it's in between. Just as sure of himself as can be.

Dr. A Solomonic solution, hmm.

P.P. Excuse me, what?

Dr. Don't mind me, Pacífico. Did your uncle's verdict do any good?

P.P. Course it did. You know people respected my uncle in that town, even if they did go around saying nasty stuff behind his back.

Dr. But did Teotista and Agatángelo accept what he said?

P.P. Well, at first they went along with it: He's got a point. Meaning my uncle. After that Señor Nestorio was left with Señor Del, and the tavern was a neutral zone, no-man's-land, like they say. And anyway, every time there was a rock fight, he got something out of it.

Dr.   He must have been grateful to your uncle, no?

P.P.   You can just imagine. Bear in mind that Señor Del's tavern is the place where everybody hangs out. I mean, there's not a wedding or a christening that people don't celebrate there. And it's funny, but you know, except for the main square, Señor Del's was the only place in town where the girls from Otero would agree to dance with the guys from Humán. And vice versa. And it was there that, just by chance, I got to know Candi. At Parmenio Marrero's wedding, during the reception. He's dead now.

Dr.   I'm afraid we're getting off the track, Pacífico. Please understand that it's not that I'm not interested in what you're saying; it's just that I'd like to keep things in order. If I'm not mistaken, we were talking about the rock fight with the Otero bunch, over the water conduction, and somehow we've gotten into talking about Señor Nestorio, who must be an interesting character, I have no doubt of it; but for the moment he's not relevant. Do you understand?

P.P.   Sure, I understand, Doctor. But what do you expect? If I start talking about one thing, and you come out with something else, I mean, you interrupt me, I get off the track. It's only natural, isn't it?

Dr.   I think you're getting a bit nervous, Pacífico.

P.P.   Me, nervous?

Dr.   Well, impatient, I mean. It's the same thing. Why don't we leave off here for today?

P.P.   Look, far as I'm concerned—

Dr.   Do you mind?

P.P.   No. Why should I mind?

Dr.   Well then, fine, Pacífico. We'll meet here tomorrow after dinner. But don't forget about the rock fight, now. And bear in mind that if we talk about the rock fight, it's in relation to your grandfathers and the dispute over your glasses, OK?

P.P.   Sure, Doctor. I guess I understand.

Dr.   Well, then, 'til tomorrow, Pacífico. Have a good rest, now.

P.P.   'Til tomorrow. Good night, Doctor.

▲ ▲ ▲ ▲ ▲ ▲ ▲
Third Night

Dr. Well, Pacífico, if I'm not mistaken, we interrupted our conversation last night when we were discussing how the water supply to your town worked. The fact that the water wouldn't flow to Otero started a rock fight with Humán, right?

P.P. That's right, sir.

Dr. Fine. Tell me more about it.

P.P. About the rock fight?

Dr. Yes, the rock fight.

P.P. Well, let's see. I heard about it from Señor Del.

Dr. Señor Del told you about the rock fight?

P.P. That's how it was, yes, Doctor. I was just going by, by the tavern, I mean, and he told me about it. Asked me to explain it to my Uncle Paco. He said that the rock fight that afternoon was something we wouldn't forget.

Dr. So did you go back down?

P.P. Yeah, I went back, but I didn't go to my uncle's. I went home.

Dr. Why didn't you go over to your uncle's?

P.P. Look, with things that messed up it would've been silly.

Dr. Well, I guess you know about that. So what did you do at home?

P.P. Same as always. Went out to the mill wheel, and there was Abue and Bisa under the fig tree.

Dr. Did you say anything?

P.P. Me? No sir. They spoke to me.

Dr. What did they say, Pacífico?

P.P. Asked if I was going to the rock fight that afternoon. I just played dumb. A rock fight? And Abue goes, Damn it! Of course there's one. You haven't gotten the picture yet?

Dr. Why are you laughing, Pacífico?

P.P.   Oh, nothing, never mind. Well, actually, 'cause it was fun to egg them on. I went and said I didn't much care about rock fights. You should've seen Abue! If you don't care about them at *your* age, would you mind telling me what you're going to do the day you become a soldier? And me, I just made light of it. It's 'cause of my glasses, Abue; they could get broken. Then Bisa starts going back and forth in his chair and screaming at me: It'd be worse if they smashed your head, you fool! You're going to that fight whether you like it or not, and you're not going to make us hang our heads in shame around here.

Dr.   That is to say, you showed your peaceful spirit to them for the first time. Isn't that right?

P.P.   I guess so. Call it what you want.

Dr.   And what was your answer to Bisa?

P.P.   OK, I said. OK, Bisa, I'll go, just so you won't look bad. Get me right on this, though, Doctor: I preferred the rock fight in the grove to the war at home.

Dr.   I understand perfectly, Pacífico. And how did the fight turn out?

P.P.   Well, they usually turned out bad for us in Humán. That's the way they went.

Dr.   Were you perhaps less aggressive as a group?

P.P.   It wasn't a question of that. We fought like anybody else. It's just that the Otero gang was up above, and we were down below. And to make matters worse, the ice broke up El Crestón, the rock, you know? So they had lots of ammunition, whereas we didn't have hardly any, not counting the old mine near the Matayeguas. And besides, they had the church's buttresses and the cemetery walls, see? And if they moved in on us, they also had the nursery plants and the side slope of Don Alfaro's house. And if they were really bad off, if things weren't working out for them, they could always just push some big rocks from up high and let them roll down the hill. It was awful; they'd knock everything over by the time they got down to the square.

Dr.   The topography was favorable to them, I see.

P.P.   It sure was. But that day, Agatángelo had learned his lesson, you see. That morning he'd ordered them to pile up some gravel along the way, you know? So as soon as we started, the rocks started flying. It was Teotista with the Otero gang; they were crouched down, moving in on us, and they didn't stop 'til they got to the cemetery.

Dr. How about you, Pacífico? Did you take part in an active way?

P.P. I'll get to that, Doctor. I'll tell you, I wish you could've seen Agatángelo with a slingshot. He was letting them have it with rocks as big as a hen's eggs, so fast you couldn't even see them fly by in the air. Next to him, I did what I could, but the truth is I was never much good at it. And Agatángelo, when he saw how I was doing, said to me: You haven't thrown many rocks in your life, have you, Pacífico? And me, I said, It's the first time, and him, Agatángelo, I mean, he said, You can tell. Why don't you hand them to me? We'll be better off that way.

Dr. So you stopped throwing rocks and hunted for rocks for Agatángelo instead?

P.P. Right. I'd pass him the polished ones for his slingshot, and I covered myself with the nursery shrubs. And he was yelling, Surrender, you bastards! Really yelling. The Otero gang gave it right back to him, though: Come on up if you dare, you sons of bitches! Teotista especially, you know? And we were. We were climbing up so fast that I had to jump from one pine to the next not to fall behind. And the Otero gang didn't hardly have time to pick up rocks. That's when they started to use the cemetery walls—started to take the stones right out of them. And Agatángelo was beside himself: Are you going to leave the dead exposed? They just ignored him; they grabbed the biggest stones and set them rolling down the hill, and you had to watch yourself, with those rocks coming down and uprooting the little nursery shrubs. So it got like that, Doctor. It was impossible to make any headway. And just because we didn't want to give up, we kept at it for another long hour, 'til finally Teotista and Agatángelo got tired and took out a white handkerchief and gave the signal for peace. They were getting ready to agree on it when I hit the road to go home. And I can remember thinking to myself: So we've had three people wounded and all this damage just for this?

Dr.   Bisa must have been waiting for you, wasn't he?

P.P. Oh yeah. Right there at the door.

Dr.   He must have been proud.

P.P. Proud? That's a laugh! As soon as he saw me, right off, Had I been in the fight? And me, Sure, course I had. But then he started in about the cemetery walls, saying how they hadn't even respected the dead, and me, That's right Bisa, and him, Did you throw lots of rocks? and me, well, the truth: I threw some, Bisa, but my aim was off. And Bisa started swearing, and when I said I'd helped more than others, that I'd passed rocks to Agatángelo that were as big as McIntosh apples so he could shoot them with his slingshot, he flew off the handle. You should've seen him.

Dr.   Didn't your behavior please him?

P.P. Please him, you say? You don't want to know about it! The scene he made! Vitálico, Felicísimo! he screamed, moving all around in his chair. Abue and Father were sort of scared, and Bisa turned white as a sheet and started pointing at me. Look at him!—meaning me—he goes to a rock fight to be a supplier! And then his mouth got twisted, and he started gibbering like crazy—it's this coirmoaguelarrasinhersamagarneelsilfow—the same old stuff he always came out with.

Dr.   His disappointment indicates that despite your wearing glasses, he still thought of you as a future hero.

P.P. Who knows what he thought. The only thing that's for sure is that he held it against me. As soon as he had a chance, he got his revenge. Do you want to know what the old man took it into his head to do, Doctor?

Dr.   What, Pacífico?

P.P. He held a cigarette to a bunch of fireworks I was holding on the day of the festival.

Dr.   And they blew up in your hands?

P.P. You'd better believe it.

Dr.   How horrible!

P.P. That's what I say. It was mean. Don Alfaro was real worried. He said with burns it wasn't so much what they were, but how much of a burn you had, and the boy's critical. And I had to spend a month in bed. It's easy enough to say, and at the beginning it wasn't so bad, but then the sores got infected, and it took a long time.

Dr. What did Bisa do in the meantime?

P.P. Gave me a hard time. Wouldn't get out of my room. I even thought once that maybe he wanted me out of order just so as to keep me at his side so he could bore me talking about his wars.

Dr. He talked about his wars again?

P.P. Did he ever! He never stopped.

Dr. And what did he say?

P.P. Nothing new, just the usual. This time it was about scars. Like he'd say, What you've got is nothing, Pacífico. Then he'd roll up his pants and show me the wound in his calf: Look, he'd say, the knife wound from Murrieta. Then he'd unbutton his shirt and, The bullet from Sodupe. And he'd go on and on. Me, I didn't feel like hearing it or anything. My sores were stinging, and I already knew Bisa's scars by heart—from giving him his bath every year in the watering trough.

Dr. Did he ever mention the rock fight again?

P.P. No, not really. He didn't mention it. Not directly, anyway.

Dr. Indirectly?

P.P. Well, sort of. He was trying to make me get over being afraid. I could tell what he was up to a mile off, and what he wanted this time was to make me see that bayonets weren't so bad.

Dr. So bad? You mean so cruel, don't you?

P.P. It's all the same, Doctor. At least that's what I think. Bisa wanted to get the fear out of my body. He'd say, for instance, Don't get the idea that bayonets are just for slaughter, Pacífico. The opposite of what he'd said before, get it?

Dr. New tactics, maybe?

P.P. Call it what you want. The point is, Bisa made light of them now. He'd say to me, A bayonet's not much more than an injection from Señora Dictrinia, Pacífico, you hear? A little buttonhole. But if something else strikes your fancy instead, you can still make the shit fly. Do you understand what I'm telling you?

Dr. To each his own, in other words.

P.P.   More or less, Doctor.

Dr.   And you, what would you answer?

P.P.   Well, you can just imagine, Doctor: Yes, Bisa. I didn't go beyond
       that, just so he'd be quiet. I had enough with the fever. But one
       afternoon while he was talking I got this pain right here in my
       parts, and then it came again, so Mother put a girdle on me. You
       can imagine how they laughed at me in the army when they saw it.

Dr.   Your pain, Pacífico—did it have any relation to Bisa's mention-
       ing the bayonet? I mean, could it have been a sympathetic pain,
       as the priest had said, or was it something else, perhaps?

P.P.   No, it wasn't. My hunch is that it was from a draft, but who
       knows? The only thing I know for sure is that since then, every
       time I get a chill, it comes back. You have no idea how much I
       suffered because of it, when the girl I was going out with took me
       up to Prádanos to get rid of my prejudices.

Dr.   Your girlfriend tried to rid you of your prejudices?

P.P.   Listen, let me tell you, that's all she did. Well, just so you'll under-
       stand me. Candi said we'd inherited a hypocritical world, and
       we had to change it. That's what she said. But that was later.
       Back then Grandma Benetilde had already hanged herself, and
       Corina, my sister, was running the household.

Dr.   That's a point I'd like to go over with you, Pacífico. How was it
       that your grandmother hanged herself? Wasn't she a very reli-
       gious woman who had even had a mystical experience?

P.P.   Who knows? Life, I guess. But something *did* go wrong in her
       head, I think. Or at least that's how it appears to me. Not even
       Don Prócoro, the priest, denied her a burial in holy ground.

Dr.   But tell me something, Pacífico: Didn't your grandmother say
       something to justify her decision?

P.P.   Well, I'll tell you. Ever since the anniversary of the trance there
       wasn't a peep out of her, Doctor. Just He's good or He isn't, that
       was it. And in Otero they all really ran her down. Not a single
       one of them showed up for the funeral. Not a single soul.

Dr.   Would you mind repeating what they said about her?

P.P.   Well, the mildest words they had for her were that she was a
       witch and that somebody ought to fuck the mystic. May God
       forgive me.

Dr.   How about the priest? Didn't he defend her from those obscenities?

P.P.   Oh sure. You can't blame Don Prócoro. You should've seen him at the funeral, saying the flesh was weak and that we'd all been killing Sister Benetilde little by little for fifty years. And if that was a sample of Christian brotherhood, then maybe the Lord should step down here and have another look at us.

Dr.   He said that?

P.P.   Yep.

Dr.   How about her, your grandmother—didn't she leave a suicide note explaining things herself?

P.P.   No. Well, I mean yes, sort of, in her own way. Personally, I think Grandma Benetilde did it on purpose, and late, so we wouldn't be able to stop her, you know? Nobody can get it out of my head that she got the idea from the wild boar. And even Don Alfaro himself once said that suicide was contagious.

Dr.   What boar are you talking about, Pacífico?

P.P.   Which one do you think? The one that threw himself from El Crestón because his teeth hurt him—that one, of course. Abue himself even said that Grandma never would've gotten the idea if it hadn't been for the boar.

Dr.   But your grandmother wasn't right in the head, from what you say.

P.P.   Look, it wasn't like that, Doctor. I mean, Grandma Benetilde might be OK some days and not others. For instance, ever since the trance she went about her business and did everything as usual. The only thing was, she kept quiet, and just by looking at her I could tell: She's brooding again.

Dr.   Do you mean that your grandmother gave the impression that she was brooding?

P.P.   Oh yeah. She was brooding, or thinking. No question about it, Doctor.

Dr.   Why don't you tell me this episode carefully, Pacífico. It might help us.

P.P.   Which one? About Grandma?

Dr.   Yes. About her suicide.

P.P.   Well look, Doctor. Just so you'll get the picture, one fine night the boar hurled himself from El Crestón, OK? And one fine morning Grandma Benetilde up and left home—just plain disappeared. Now you tell me if the first story doesn't match the second.

Dr.   Did she have an argument with her husband, or with Bisa, or somebody else?

P.P.   No, nothing like that. You don't have to worry on that score. The only thing was that that day Krim ate raw eggs for the first time.

Dr.   Krim was a dog, right?

P.P.   Abue's, yeah. Elio's pup. Miaja's brother, in other words.

Dr.   Fine. Go on, Pacífico.

P.P.   Well, anyway, it got to be four o'clock in the afternoon, and Grandma didn't show up. So Corina, my sister, says, Gee, a little while ago she was out near the mill wheel looking at the water flow past. So we check out the orchard, but there's no trace of her. Then Father sent word through Martín, the mailman, who announced it in Otero and Humán—her disappearance, see. As for Sergeant Metodio, he was a man with a lot of experience. He said it was strange, really strange. So Father goes, I'll tell you, Sergeant, ever since the anniversary of the trance, Mother's been acting kind of funny. And Sergeant Metodio just kept repeating, Strange, really strange. But he was ready with a search party in less than an hour. He didn't fool around. Got three groups together. Señor Escolino would lead the first. He's good at mountains, so he was supposed to go through the brush from the Aquilina Cliff on down—the whole Peñacarrubia area, Las Puertas, and Fuentefierro, even Prádanos and the place where they washed. The next would go with Agatángelo, and they'd follow the four rivers, past the Páramo basin, where the laughing seagulls are. And the last one, Sergeant Metodio's, would search along the narrow roads and the cliff, see?

Dr.   And is that what they did?

P.P.   Exactly that. They didn't leave a stone unturned. But a week went by, and nobody came up with anything, and that's when the Otero gang started saying, Oh, fuck the mystic! So after the eighth day was up, Sergeant Metodio went over to Abue, looked him straight in the face, and said, My sympathies, Señor Vitálico, but give her up for dead.

Dr. How did they know it was suicide?

P.P. From a letter. From a letter from America. Uncle Teodoro sent it, and inside the envelope there was another envelope that was smaller and a sheet of paper, see? And on the paper Uncle Teodoro said, This is the letter that Benetilde left for you. That's all it said.

Dr. So what did your grandmother say in her letter?

P.P. She explained it. I mean it said: "I'm dropping you a line to let you know that I'm going to hang myself from La Torca elm tree because you're a bad lot, all of you. And I'm going to hang myself by my feet because I'm afraid of strangling if I do it by my neck." That's what it said.

Dr. Who was the envelope addressed to, Pacífico?

P.P. To Abue, of course. He was her husband.

Dr. And how did the rest of you react?

P.P. Well, each person was different. Take Mother, for instance: she had a fit, and Corina had to slap her a couple of times to bring her to. As for Abue, well, he said, We'll have to go get her. And Father said, Without reporting it? And Bisa got pissed off and said, Who the hell are we going to report it to? So that afternoon we got ourselves together and headed up there.

Dr. Did you go up, too?

P.P. Me? I was up front. 'Cause Bisa had said to me, Come on, you lazy bum, push! So I grabbed his chair and started pushing. But by the time we got to La Cantera—it's a really steep hill—I was out of breath. Bisa weighed a ton, 'cause as everybody knows, old age makes you heavier. And around La Puntilla I could hardly keep it up—the wheels were getting stuck in the gravel. Thank goodness Father came and gave me a hand. And I still remember, just imagine, that the western side was all lit up, and just as we were topping the hill I could see it hanging over the pit, the corpse, I mean. And there were vultures buzzing around—they call 'em *baribañuelas*—circling around.* They could hardly fly, 'cause they'd gorged themselves on her.

Dr. So did you recover the body?

*Translator's Note: Local usage.

P.P.   What can I tell you? Calling it "the body" is a little too good. All that was left of Grandma Benetilde was her skeleton and a few hairs, you know? And what a stench! It was horrible. I can remember Abue knotted a handkerchief over his face and said, you know what he said?

Dr.   What, Pacífico?

P.P.   That Flores was right. Flores, you know, the guy who was in his war. He used to say that a woman rots worse than a man.

Dr.   And how did you get back?

P.P.   Oh, we managed. Abue and Father made a stretcher with some branches of the elm tree, and they put the deceased there. But between one thing and another it got late on us, and I can remember that it was on the Trocha shortcut that night fell, and we had to walk by the light from the lightning. Then we got home, and we put Grandma Benetilde out by the mill wheel, in the dew, and Bisa asked for a wine spout. He lifted it up and drank to the deceased: The only woman I ever knew that had something between her legs. And he emptied the thing in one gulp, without even stopping to breathe.

Dr.   So your grandfather drank to the deceased?

P.P.   No, Bisa. Hey, don't get things mixed up.

Dr.   Excuse me, Pacífico, that's not what I meant. Tell me, how old were you when these things were happening?

P.P.   Look, I can tell you for sure: sixteen or eighteen. And that's got to be right, 'cause Mother was only four months apart, and the day Mother died—well, the night before, I mean—I turned eighteen, and I didn't go back to the capital until I was in the service.

Dr.   What did your Mother die of, Pacífico?

P.P.   Don't ask me. Must've been something bad, Doctor. Don Alfaro didn't make any mention of it, but every now and then he'd whisper to Señora Dictrinia about the injections, you know? I have a feeling Mother was all gone inside.

Dr.   What symptoms did she have?

P.P.   How's that?

Dr.   What did it look like? What hurt her?

P.P.   Well, she started out with some gas, then stomach problems. The vomiting came later. And since she had no meat on her bones, well, she had to take to her bed, of course. Not even four days after the thing with Grandma Benetilde. Señora Dictrinia said it was the tragedy that got her sick.

Dr. What did Don Alfaro say?

P.P. Nothing, really. But the first day I went out behind him and saw him give the stuff for the injections to Señora Dictrinia, and she hid it right away, then, in her bosom, you hear? And that if she had any bad pain, to give her *that*, that it was better to avoid butchering her. Those were his words.

Dr. Did your mother suffer much pain?

P.P. Well, no, she didn't. That's the funny part. I mean you already know my fucking habits—and may God forgive me. Well, as soon as I heard Don Alfaro mention the pain, I was expecting it to come. I felt like I was waiting for a person at the door, Doctor, it was so weird. Anyway, I'd made up my mind that Mother would have to die in pain, and I kept asking her, Mother, does it hurt? And she'd always give me the same answer: I'm fine, Pacífico. Tomorrow I'll get up.

Dr. Did your mother's agony last long?

P.P. In bed, yes. She was there a long time. But she didn't lose her faculties or anything, you know? And Corina, just to entertain her, would give her a rundown every night. Like, for example, she'd say, Krim ate the eggs again, Mother. You know? Stuff like that.

Dr. I can see there was never a dull moment with Krim around.

P.P. That animal was something else, Doctor, I'll tell you. You'd have to see him to believe it. Don't think he went after the eggs straight out. As soon as he heard the hen start to cluck, his ears would perk up. But on the sly, see. I kept an eye on him, and I saw how he'd lift up his leg near the fig tree and then go moseying around as if he wasn't up to anything. And when he thought nobody was watching, he'd sneak into the barnyard and jump into the trough and eat the eggs. Then when he'd gobbled them up, he'd go over to the watering trough and make believe he was drinking, you know? But actually, what he was doing was getting the stuff off his nose.

Dr. And your mother would be upset, naturally.

P.P. No, not really. Mother didn't have much left in her. But she would ask: How did he get that bad habit? She was just saying it to make conversation, though. I mean when you think about it, Krim eating up the eggs couldn't have mattered much to her in the state *she* was in.

Dr. Meanwhile, what were your grandfathers doing?

P.P. Well, you can just imagine. There wasn't anything they could do to cure her, right? So every time Mother said to me, I'll be getting up tomorrow, Bisa would shake his head no to me. And as for Abue, he did just what you'd expect: he'd curl up on his bench like a little kid. And at night he'd say to Bisa: Why is it that women have to go and die, all of them? That's how he took it.

Dr. So they watched over her in her illness?

P.P. Oh, yes sir. In that sense you can't praise them enough. I can remember the day my poor mother died, I mean, the night before. She lost her sight and said: One more day, Señor Vendiano, and it's almost nighttime already. And Bisa burst out laughing so suddenly I thought he'd lose his tooth: Are you in your right mind, Delgadina? It's not getting dark; it's just that you're going through the days so fast. He was really tender with her. He didn't say it to be mean. And life's funny, Doctor. That same night, around about dawn, Mother died, and all she said was, I'm tired. I'm going to join Benetilde, hear? And she passed away.

Dr. How did you react, Pacífico?

P.P. To tell you the truth, Doctor, it made me uneasy, I mean, that she should have died without any pain coming to warn us. So I went up to Señora Dictrinia, and I put it to her. And I got into an argument with her and Don Alfaro, because I thought they were trying to fool me.

Dr. There was no such thing, Pacífico. The doctor did his duty. He didn't tell you, It'll be thus and so. In fact, he couldn't tell you anything. He simply foresaw a possibility.

P.P. Don Alfaro, I'll have you know, gave Señora Dictrinia the stuff for injections for the pain, and she tucked it in her bosom, see? But then the pain didn't come, and Mother died without any warning.

Dr. Please listen, Pacífico. In the case of a tumor, which is undoubtedly what your mother had, there may be pain, or there may not be. Medicine isn't an exact science, son. And the diagnostician can't determine for sure whether or not there'll be pain. The doctor prescribed a very sensible thing, a tranquilizer. If it wasn't necessary, as it turned out, better yet for everyone.

P.P.   All depends on how you look at it, Doctor. I don't see it that way.

Dr.   Well, I think it would be better to drop the subject, Pacífico. Tell me something else: The consecutive deaths of your grandmother and your mother must have been devastating for you. With your hypersensitivity, they must have plunged you into great bitterness. Didn't they?

P.P.   Well, actually no, Doctor. You could say I already knew what to expect.

Dr.   Are you asking me to believe that you didn't feel any grief upon the death of your mother?

P.P.   Well, let's put it this way: Grief? Sure, of course I felt grief. I mean I missed one as much as the other.

Dr.   But didn't you experience something like emptiness in the world?

P.P.   Well, no, not really. I mean I grieved for them, naturally, but it wasn't like a huge deep sorrow or anything.

Dr.   Was it more or less than what you felt when you saw a tree pruned?

P.P.   Hey! Those are two different things. The stuff about the trees is something I experienced when I was a kid. My fingers would sting and everything, you know? Just as if mine were being cut off.

Dr.   Do you mean that by the time you were eighteen you had gotten over it? Didn't you still feel the light bulb in your chest?

P.P.   No sir. By then I'd forgotten about the light bulb.

Dr.   And you didn't get chilled when the pippin tree started to bloom?

P.P.   No, not that, either. I already told you: All that was when I was a boy.

Dr.   And when do you think the change came about?

P.P.   I guess it must've been when I became a man, but I couldn't put my finger on the exact moment.

Dr.   But Pacífico, do you think that becoming a man means not experiencing grief when your mother dies?

P.P.   Now wait a minute. It's not a question of that, either. Let's keep things straight. I *did* grieve over my mother's death; it was only natural. But more than her death, you see, it really got to me that Don Alfaro and Señora Dictrinia had pulled the wool over my eyes.

Dr.   All right, Pacífico. Let's go on to something else. The disappearance—and it was almost simultaneous—of the women in the house must have caused a deep change in your family's life, didn't it? Could you tell me what happened in your house the first few weeks after your mother died?

P.P. Ooh! It was war.

Dr.   What do you mean, war?

P.P. Well, something like that anyway. Remember that even when Mother's body was still around, Bisa was already giving orders. Like, Corina—you! You take charge of the house. You're old enough now. You, Pacífico, go to work. You've had enough schooling. See what I mean? Then he told us to get everybody ready to bury Mother, but don't think he went. He'd always say, The only way I'll go to Otero is if they carry me up there.

Dr.   How is it possible that your great-grandfather could take things so far? Didn't he ever go up to Otero, not even once?

P.P. Well, let's see. That I know of, Doctor, not counting the night we shot Krim, never once did I see Bisa in Otero. But don't think he was the only one with that idea.

Dr.   Did the others do the same?

P.P. Look, Doctor, just so you'll understand me: the gang from Otero and the gang in Humán couldn't stand the sight of each other. I mean they looked as if they'd sworn to kill each other. And on top of that, even Don Prócoro had to say two masses so they both wouldn't miss Sunday Mass. And it was the same with the sermons—they couldn't care less when he said we ought to love one another. I remember the time Don Prócoro had the bright idea of broadcasting it from the pulpit that we were all brothers, that we were all children of the same Father. Teotista, who was up in the choir, suddenly goes, Except anybody from Humán! Can you imagine? And on the way out he grabbed the priest, Teotista, I mean, and he said, you know what he said?

Dr.   What, Pacífico?

P.P. That if he ever said the others were his brothers again, that he'd let him have it so hard he'd remember it for the rest of his life. Do you think that's any way to treat a person, especially a priest?

Dr.   And wasn't Don Prócoro able to lessen the tension?

P.P. How could he, Doctor? Being a cripple and all, what could he do?

Dr.   You say he was a cripple?

P.P. Of course. Don't be surprised, Doctor. He had the problem with his eyes. Like if he looked, he had to stop his hands because he had to hold them down. And if he moved his hands, he didn't look. It was either one or the other. And to convince people in my town of anything you need to use both, and even then . . .

Dr.   Going back to something else, Pacífico, your grandfathers—did they stand firm on their word? Did they refuse to go up to Otero to bury your mother?

P.P. Well, Abue did go. But Bisa—he didn't go up, no sir. Like I said, the only time I ever saw Bisa up there was with Krim. And that was when there wasn't a soul around.

Dr.   And what happened afterward?

P.P. After? After what?

Dr.   After the burial.

P.P. Well, like I said, it was war. When we got back from the Castro, the cemetery, we found Bisa out back in a uniform playing a trumpet.

Dr.   Where'd he get the uniform and the trumpet?

P.P. Where else? From his wars. They belonged to him. So anyway, in the time we were gone, Bisa messed up the whole place.

Dr.   What was he up to?

P.P. Who knows? He said that now that we'd been left alone we should lead a man's life.

Dr.   And what did that imply?

P.P. Well, mainly having drills every morning out in the orchard. He'd get up before the cock crowed and start playing reveille, and we'd—quick—get into the old rags left over from his wars. Like his blue cassock, for example, it fits me pretty good—I'd always been pretty puny, ever since I was a boy my chest was weak. So I'd put it on, what else could I do, and you should've seen us out there—Abue, Father, and me—like we were ready to have our portrait painted—carrying shotguns over our shoulders and everything. And he'd stand next to the mill wheel giving orders and blowing on his trumpet 'til he got red in the face, and I can remember Father saying, Your hernia, Abue, and he'd say, To hell with my hernia! Bayonets! And each one of us would creep toward the apple trees with our shotguns like we were going to ambush the enemy. And Bisa would get into the spirit of it and, Over the shoulder! Half turn to the right! Give 'em hell! You should've seen him! We'd spend hours that way, and listen, after a while I'd practically collapse. After about an hour Bisa would shout, Fall out! And Abue and Father would go back in the house, but I had to sit there with him at the mill wheel for lessons in strategy.

Dr.   What a character! And did that situation last long?

P.P.   If it had been up to him it would've lasted a lifetime. Luckily Corina got her courage up and told him off one day.

Dr.   Your sister stood up to the old man?

P.P.   How else can I put it? But don't be surprised. Corina has always been pretty tough, ever since she was a kid. It's just that she kept it a secret as long as Grandma Benetilde and Mother were around. But one day she was fed up with all that trumpet playing. I guess that was what ticked her off. Well, anyway, she stood at the window and screamed at him: Bisa! You stop playing that trumpet right now, or else I'll fix you!

Dr.   Just like that?

P.P.   Just like that, cool as can be. Just like you're hearing it.

Dr.   What did he answer?

P.P.   Oh, the old guy couldn't figure out what was going on. After a whole life of nobody ever dishing it out to him. So he said, Hey! What did you say, you little tramp? To my sister, see. And she says, You heard me: put that trumpet down. There's no war going on, and you're driving us all crazy. So Bisa's eyes roll, and he grabs his trumpet and plays three sharp notes and yells, Arrest her! But Abue and Father just stood there, didn't blink an eye; they just cringed. And then Bisa went dumb in the head, and his tongue got all twisted, and he started coming out with his nonsense: Shitouronbastallfuckifor!

Dr.   So that was the end of the patriarchy.

P.P.   Huh?

Dr.   I mean, from that moment on the situation must have changed. Bisa was no longer the head of the house, and your sister took the reins, didn't she?

P.P.   Well, yes. But no, not really. To tell you the truth, they went at each other's throats to see who was the strongest. The next morning, as soon as Bisa started his reveille, Corina grabbed the chair and put it on the rampart, next to the trough, facing the river. She stuck a stick through the wheels and said to him: If it moves, you'll pay for it, so take your choice. And the filth that came out of his mouth! Bisa's, I mean. But he learned to get the stick out without rolling into the river—because you can figure anything out after a while—and he went back to his trumpet and his bad habits. And that was when Corina set up a pulley in the fig tree, and she'd hang the chair with the old man inside for as long as she had to. Worked like a charm.

Dr.   Hmm. Your sister had a real temper.

P.P.   You have no idea! She was a tough one, all right.

Dr.   So it can be said that the fight with your sister and that nostalgic return to military warfare was your great-grandfather's last bellicose manifestation, can it not, Pacífico?

P.P.   I'm sorry, I don't exactly follow you, Doctor.

Dr.   In other words, after your mother's death, the old man didn't raise his voice anymore? Or did he?

P.P.   Well, he got scared of my sister, you know? But he didn't really change. Look how he ordered Krim to be shot.

Dr.   But was that before your mother died or after your sister hanged him from the fig tree?

P.P.   In between, Doctor.

Dr.   Tell me about it, will you?

P.P.   Well, as a matter of fact, there isn't much to tell. I think it happened because of the trumpet and the uniforms. Bisa and Abue and Father got all worked up, and that's why what happened happened.

Dr.   You may be right. But tell me: What was it with the dog?

P.P.   The same as usual. I mean, one morning Corina came out to the mill wheel saying she couldn't stand that dog anymore—that he'd eaten the eggs again and we had to do something about it. That was when it came to Bisa like a flash that, in his battalion, anybody who stole something was executed on the spot. And I remembered his story about the hermitage in Galdamés, the business about the stocks, you know? But I kept my mouth shut, not to make any waves. But Abue caught on right away—he was so into it, anyway—and he said, Why don't we shoot him? And Father piped up, I'm at your command. It was all so silly, but that's how we passed judgment on the animal.

Dr. Did you shoot him soon after that?

P.P. Before daybreak, soon as we could.

Dr. How did you do it?

P.P. Well, let's see. Bisa, Abue, and Father got into their war clothes, medals and everything. And I was watching them, when Bisa comes up to me and says: Come on, Pacífico. Call the dog, and let's get started. So I called him. You should've seen the little critter, so docile. How could he guess? And Bisa, Let's get going, and me, To Otero, Bisa? and him, To Otero—that's all it's good for: shooting dogs. So up we went, the four of us, I mean the five of us. The moon was as big as a mill wheel, and I recall that Krim, who was tied to Bisa's chair, kept yelping, and Abue and Father were flanking him, like he was a real person. And when we got to the cemetery, Abue said, Tie the dog to the iron grating, and you should've seen the little critter, howling like a soul in pain. They have an instinct, I guess. And when I went to bandage his eyes, he kept trying to pull it off with his paw, so I told Bisa: Bisa, he won't sit still. And Bisa just laughed—heh, heh, heh—let him be: it means he's got a good pair on him.

Dr. A terrible scene, son.

P.P. It was something, let me tell you. The moon up high, the animal next to the wall, the four cypress trees behind, and on this side, about ten steps away, there they were all lined up: Bisa, Abue, and Father with their shotguns, taking aim. So as soon as I moved away the animal started crying and tugging at the rope; he was trying to get close to me. And that was when Abue said to Bisa that he was in command, and Bisa said he wouldn't give the order because he wanted to shoot, and they said they wanted to, too, and then it suddenly occurred to Bisa: Well, let the boy give the command—meaning me, see—'cause when you think about it, I wasn't doing anything.

Dr. Did you resist?

P.P. Sure I resisted. I tried to. But he said, Look, it's easy: first you say Ready, then Aim, and then after a bit, Fire. You hear? But I swore I couldn't do it right, and why didn't they handle it themselves? But oh, no. Bisa asked me, Why should you do it wrong? This creature sure is a doubter. So whether I liked it or not, they put me next to them, and Bisa gave me my cue, and I said, Ready, but my voice wouldn't hardly come out of my body. It was awful. And there they were, the three of them with their guns raised. Then they cocked them. And Bisa goes, Yeah! And me, Aim! And Bisa goes, Come on! And me, Fire! And I closed my eyes and covered my ears, but even with that I heard a horrible crack.

Dr. Did the dog die?

P.P. Wait a minute. When I opened my eyes I saw the animal lying on his side, all full of blood, his head was stiff—you know what I mean?—and it was drooling. And those eyes . . . those eyes! Oh, Doctor, it was like they were asking why was he being punished like that? But Bisa didn't let me stop. He gave me the shotgun and, Finish him off! And me, Me? And Bisa, Yes, you—it's up to you. And I was shaking like a leaf, and Abue saying, Be a man, now; and Father, Get it over with! They were egging me on, and I was in a stupor, seeing the little animal's pleading eyes—it took away my willpower. And don't think they let up, Doctor: Come on, finish him off, do your duty. The moonlight made them yellow, and they looked like ghosts. I was even afraid of them. So I grabbed the shotgun, I aimed it at Krim's chest, I closed my eyes and shot both barrels at once, and it recoiled so hard it threw me back on the stones. And they said Good, Pacífico! You're a man now! But to tell you the truth, I hardly heard them. I was vomiting over by the cemetery wall.

Dr. And what did you do with Krim?

P.P. We buried him. But later, when we were heading back down the path, at the bend, the couple stopped us.* So Bisa said, We're from the town. And Metodio, the sergeant, asked, Is that you,

---

*Translator's Note: Civil guards, patrolling in pairs, are sometimes called "the couple."

Señor Vendiano? And Bisa, None other. So the sergeant asks him: What kind of racket were you making up there? We heard gunfire. And Bisa: It was only a dog, Sergeant: we were putting him to sleep. And the sergeant got all serious and, Next time, do it a kilometer away from town; it's the law. And Bisa, At your service, Sergeant; I won't quarrel with that.

Dr. Didn't they punish him?

P.P. Oh no. Like Abue said to Father, Mark my words, Felicísimo: money talks.

Dr. Had your father already made money by then?

P.P. Well, he said he had enough to get along on. He had saved everything he could.

Dr. A lot?

P.P. Well, to give you an idea, Father hadn't gone down to Gibraltar for five years, 'cause the last time he called them bastards—the English, that is—they put him in a cell on bread and water for three days. But by then Father had the red harvester, and the yellow one; and the Fordson—the tractor, I mean—had broken ground on the Cieza plains. And he was paying off the blue harvester.

Dr. The highlands—were they his?

P.P. They were common land, actually, but he made a deal with the town hall.

Dr. And didn't they give him any trouble about the goats?

P.P. Look, down there they were in favor of leaving the highlands for grazing, but Father contended that there was plenty of pastureland on the slopes, and growing potatoes and cereal was the best thing for up there. And to tell you the truth, I don't know how he wangled it, but he got his way.

Dr. The plains had never been plowed before, had they?

P.P. Never, no sir. But he worked them, you know. The hours Father spent up there! Between clearing stones, and weeding, and then using the Rototiller.

Dr. Just between us, what do you think your father really wanted, Pacífico?

P.P. You've got me. We certainly had enough to live on. But Father didn't usually talk about that. Truth is he didn't talk much about anything. With paying off his mortgages he even forgot about his war. I don't know if I've made it clear, Doctor: the mortgages were a vice with him. I mean, if he didn't have one going he wasn't happy. So as you can see, first it was the red harvester. Then the Fordson, then the yellow harvester, and on and on—Father worked like a dog. And the more he had the more he wanted. That's how it was with him, believe me.

Dr. Well, what do you think about it, Pacífico? Was your Father motivated by the vanity of social status, or did he want to make a fortune, or was he tempted by greed?

P.P. Who knows, Doctor? It's hard to tell. But if you want to know my opinion, I'd say that Father liked mortgages the way other men like wine or tobacco. They were his weakness.

Dr. Tell me something, Pacífico: When your mother died, you started to work, didn't you? Did you work for your father, or did you try something on your own?

P.P. Well, it depends. Since you ask, I was a honey taster in beehives.

Dr. A honey taster?

P.P. Yes sir. I checked the beehives and tasted the honey. Haven't you ever heard of such a thing?

Dr. And how did you become a honey taster?

P.P. Well, it started out as a hobby, imagine. I mean ever since I was a kid it made me furious when the gang in town robbed the bees.

Dr. You mean they robbed the bees in your town?

P.P. In my town and everybody else's. Don't act surprised. Or did you have the idea that bees anywhere work for the neighborhood? Well, they don't. Bees work for themselves. But people come and take their honey and let them go hungry. Then people complain about getting stung. Course they get stung: the little creatures are just defending what belongs to them.

Dr. Now I understand. What I don't understand, though, is how you could be a honey taster without robbing the bees.

P.P. Wait a minute. There are various ways to go about it, you know. I mean, between just going in there and taking it all and, well, being more careful. There's quite a difference, you know; you can show some respect.

Dr. Right, Pacífico. And how was it that you got into doing it?

P.P.   To be straight with you, Doctor, it just worked itself out. See, the year my poor mother died, the time came to check the bees, and the beekeeper mask and the bellows weren't anywhere in sight. And Abue was saying, Hey, it'll be too late soon. 'Cause as you know, if you want honey, it's got to be on Saint Andrew's, and if you want the honeycomb, it's Las Candelas.* 'Cause every day, there's a certain task. Anyway, around about then I liked bees: my Uncle Paco had taught me about them since I was a kid. Like about the swarms, and generations, and how the queen bee enslaves the drones with her sex; none of it was new to me. And you know, it burned me up that the neighbors would attack the beehives. 'Cause that's what they did: attack them, I mean with masks and everything. And like I say, somebody who's not committing a crime shouldn't have to hide his face. Well, anyway, seeing all that made me think that if I did it, I'd be different. So the year my poor mother died, when I saw Corina in such a state—when the masks and the bellows weren't anywhere around—I went up to Abue and said to him, I said, Never mind the tools, I'll go up. And he said, Barefaced? and me, Yeah, barefaced. They won't eat me alive. So I went up barefaced, and I got to the Cieza, where the beehives in the hollows and our fabricated ones were, and I rolled up my sleeves, and Abue asked, Is he really going to try it? From a distance, of course. And before I lifted the lid of the first one—the first beehive, I mean—I was already talking to them, to the bees.

Dr.   What did you say to them?

P.P.   Whatever, Doctor.

Dr.   So what did you say, Pacífico? Tell me.

P.P.   Well, it depended. That was the least of it. Just stuff. Like it doesn't matter what you say. What matters is your tone; they've got to understand from your tone that you'll take care of them, and you're not there to ransack them.

Dr.   Did it work?

---

*Translator's Note: St. Andrew's Day is November 30. "Las Candelas" is the popular expression for another holy day, La Candelaria, which designates the solemn blessing of the candles, on February 2.

P.P. Yeah, sure. You should've seen Bisa out in the road. They're gonna make you look like you've been crucified. But nah, it wasn't anything like that. I just stuck to my business. This one's for you, this one's for me. And if there were three honeycombs, I'd cart off one, but only one, hear? And since it was a nice afternoon, 'cause the fall was always quiet and sunny in my town, word went around that I was taking out the honey without wearing a mask or gloves. You should see how many people crowded around: Señora Dictrinia, and Don Alfaro, and Señor Escolino, and Don Prócoro, and Teotista, and my Uncle Paco. Lord knows how many people gathered around there! And they were all asking the same thing: Barefaced? Without a mask or gloves? And Bisa was bursting with pride, Doctor. I think it was the first time I ever gave him something to be happy about—and look how easy it was. Down below they were all making the sign of the cross, and after a while, I went down to where they were, proud as can be. Bisa just stared at my eyes, and my hands, and my neck: They aren't even swollen, he said, and me, They didn't sting me, Bisa. And Abue, I don't believe it; bees are the most treacherous beasts there are. And me, It's not like that; you've got the proof right in front of your eyes. Then my Uncle Paco picked up his walking stick and said: Bees respect whoever respects them, understand? And they shrugged their shoulders as if to say, There he goes philosophizing again.

Dr. So that was how you became a honey taster?

P.P. Wait a minute. Don't go so fast, Doctor. That's how it started, anyway. But you know how people are in towns. Word went around I'd gone in barefaced, and that got them going. That's impossible. No, it's not. A real argument, the same old story, and more and more people started calling on me. Some of them claimed I had diabetes, that the bees didn't sting me because your blood tastes bad then, and others came to smell my arms to see if I'd sprayed them with DDT, and the gang from Humán said it wasn't true, and the Otero bunch said it was too, that I swore it was. And personally, Doctor, I think if Don Prócoro hadn't stepped in to settle matters, it would've ended up in another rock fight. You know, everybody always envying everybody else in a small town.

Dr.   But they were finally convinced, weren't they?

P.P.   Well, sort of. One afternoon, before going up, I had to scrub myself in the river with soap and a brush because between the two
of them, they'd made a bet—Humán against Otero.

Dr.   And?

P.P.   And? Well Humán won, of course. And Teotista got really pissed
off. Said *he* could do it, too.

Dr.   And did he?

P.P.   No such thing! He did get us up there, all of us from the Horni-
llera La Peña area; made us sweat like pigs, and it was all for
nothing. 'Cause Teotista had the unfortunate idea of taking his
donkey up, and you can't imagine what they did to her.

Dr.   The bees?

P.P.   Who else?

Dr.   How about him?

P.P.   He got it too, of course. But the donkey—she was a young one—
it was awful. She was wobbling with the pain.

Dr.   And Teotista probably held it against you.

P.P.   Well, he was burned up about it, that's for sure. But I guess he
figured it was better to keep his mouth shut.

Dr.   So they must have realized then that you had a special gift.

P.P.   I won't say they didn't. And after the argument, I had work every
day 'til it started to snow. What a fall that was! Pacífico, be a
friend: Do you mind taking a look at our hives over at Punta Puntilla? Hey, Pacífico, it's been almost two years since I checked the
hives over at Peñacarrubia. Would you mind stopping by there
some morning? They'd ask me from both sides, Humán and
Otero. I never stopped.

Dr.   So did you take care of them?

P.P.   Look. If I could do them as well as the bees a favor, why not?
And it went on like that 'til I was getting calls from people from
other towns. There's somebody from Humán who goes in barefaced, they'd say. And they'd come looking for me—even from
Pozuelo and Quintana Ortega. You won't believe this, but there
were more and more of them. Good thing they didn't all bite at
once! And there I was going this way and that, like a rag doll
being tossed around.

Dr. Did anybody else try to imitate you?

P.P. Here and there, a few. Like Emigdio, for example, the vet from Quintana. He was starting to get interested in my sister, Corina. Well, he comes up to me one day and says: Is it true you talk to bees? And me, Sure. And him, Do you mind telling me what you say to them? And me, Well, it really doesn't matter; just be affectionate. So next Sunday, when he came down to see my sister, he tried it out with Señor Del's hives. And believe me, just as he was moving into the first one, they made his face look like a road map. Lord, what a face!

Dr. So you were the only one, eh, Pacífico? Some business!

P.P. There you go, just like Father, "Some business!" Can't you people ever think about anything except money?

Dr. I didn't express myself right, Pacífico. Excuse me. I was referring to your lack of competition and the advantage there was in its being a seasonal activity—only during the fall, if I understood correctly.

P.P. That's what you think. From the outside it all looks very pretty. But the honey business, if you do it right, makes a slave of you. In the summer, around St. Peter's Day, you have to go around with your hamper looking for new swarms. Then in the winter you've got to be careful the badgers and treepeckers don't eat them, see.

Dr. The treepecker?

P.P. Yeah, the treepecker, the bird that bores holes in trees. Haven't you ever seen one?

Dr. A woodpecker, you mean?

P.P. Yeah, that's it. I mean, I guess it's the same one. Well, anyway, that bird, there isn't a bird with a bigger sweet tooth than that one. Well, when winter starts to come and the bees slow down, it bores holes in their colonies of hives and eats them both: the bees and the honey. Those birds are smart, believe you me. Have you ever seen how they make holes halfway down?

Dr. Is the honey in the top?

P.P. And the bees, too. And that bird knows it.

Dr. Tell me, Pacífico: Did they call on you to get new swarms, too?

P.P. On the whole, after the argument. And even though I shouldn't say so, nobody dared step into the beehives without me. You know, Let Pacífico take a look, or Let's see what Pacífico says. And that's how it was. Most of the time it was routine stuff. Like with the small swarms. Everybody knows young bees don't sting. Well . . .

Dr.   They don't? Why not?

P.P.   Why not, you say. Well, why should they sting if they haven't been corrupted yet? What happens is that they're scared of getting mixed with the bugs in a pile all buzzing around and excited— and it's true, it's really a sight. But it's all very simple. All you have to do is pile them up, the bees, I mean, a hand's length away from the holes, and they go in on their own.

Dr.   Changing the subject, Pacífico: Before, when I mentioned the business, you said I was being like your father. Did he try to exploit your talent professionally?

P.P.   That's right.

Dr.   And how did he see it? What did he suggest?

P.P.   Well, mainly, Father said one day: How much are you asking per beehive? And per honeycomb? 'Cause as everyone knows, the beehives don't yield much, and they're not very good, whereas the colony yields a lot, and it's good. But it caught me off guard. Since when have we been charging to do a favor in Humán? I said. And him: Are you working for nothing, Pacífico? You've gotta have your price. And I came back with, Don't make me laugh, Father. Get it out of your head. And then he went and gave it to me, left me speechless.

Dr.   Well, what did he say, Pacífico?

P.P.   Oh, he started out with, Kick or you'll get kicked—it's the only way. And I said, But Father, I just keep busy this way. And he really flew off the handle at that. Isn't that nice! Your Father working his tail off all day and you coming in to sit down to dinner like company. What do you think?

Dr.   He was harsh on you. You're right, Pacífico. And was that the first time your father reproached you for not bringing home any money?

P.P.   If I'm not mistaken . . . the first . . . yes sir. That was the first.

Dr.   Did this make you want to set your fees as a honey taster or do something else?

P.P.   Well, so as not to lie, I wanted to do both.

Dr.   And what was your second job?

P.P.   Being a chicken farmer. I asked Father to set me up with a modern henhouse, the kind with automatic egg layers and all.

Dr.   Do you like hens?

P.P.   I didn't exactly *like* them the way you like stuff. But they were pretty interesting little critters.

Dr.   In what sense did they interest you? Because with your nature, the economic side was out, wasn't it?

P.P.   They just interested me. Who knows why? Have you ever noticed that there's not an animal in the world that's sadder or more bored than a hen?

Dr.   Well, no, as a matter of fact, I never did. But come to think of it, you're right. And did your father give you the henhouse?

P.P.   Soon as I asked for it. Just three months later, Quinidio, the guy from Quintana who does these jobs, was putting the roof on.

Dr.   And as for the henhouse, was it big? I mean, did you have it as a business or just for fun?

P.P.   Oh, it was big. You could fit two thousand hens in there. You should've seen it, all whitewashed with green windows and green doors, right next to the Matayeguas. It turned out real nice. Emigdio wanted to start right away, but I told Father that since I was just getting started, it'd be better to leave it 'til after I'd been in the army.

Dr.   Emigdio was your sister's boyfriend, wasn't he? What did he have to do with the henhouse?

P.P.   Well, he was a vet, right? So one day he said to me: Hey, you'll let me in on this, won't you? Hens are my specialty. And me, well, realizing his intentions, just to test him I asked him if he was planning on marrying my sister. And he took a tack that gave me a start. He goes and says, Hey, your daddy's rich and your sister's good-looking. What more do I want? Some way to think.

Dr.   So he out-and-out confessed to you that he planned to put away his tools, hmm?

P.P.   That's right, Doctor. But at least he was up front about it, not like some people I know.

Dr.   How about your sister—did she make eyes at him?

P.P. Did she ever! She looked dumbstruck when he was around. I mean, every time he came down from Quintana she'd come home in a daze or something. So one day I said to her: Do you like him that much? And she just stood there glassy-eyed and said: I like him so much that if he asks me to become a mother someday, I don't see how I can refuse him.

Dr.   So much for your sister. But getting back to where we left off: Did you start with the henhouse right away?

P.P. That winter, I didn't do anything. We let it dry out. Because like I told you, I had to do my stint.

Dr.   So you went into the army, then?

P.P. Well, I presented myself at headquarters.

Dr.   Your grandfathers must have been satisfied.

P.P. Oh, they were overjoyed, like a couple of castanets. That's all they talked about at home.

Dr.   How about your father, Pacífico—did he share their enthusiasm?

P.P. Well, actually, no, he didn't, to tell you the truth. Father was getting a little strange by then. Like if he was in a hurry. He didn't care about his war, and I don't think he cared about mine, either. He was involved in his own stuff—the mortgages and tilling new ground. And then the henhouse, too—it was all part of the same thing. So he said to me, You won't be gone long, will you now? And of course me, I told him that if I had my druthers, I'd be on my way home already, and him, he said, It'll be good for you, but it's going to be hard on me with your taking off now. But he said this when Bisa and Abue weren't in earshot, see.

Dr.   And didn't things go well for you in the army?

P.P. Well, as a matter of fact, it wasn't a ball, but then again it was no hardship, either. But it sure was a case of being pegged on the spot.

Dr.   What happened?

P.P. What had to, I guess: they said I didn't qualify. That's what happened. The minute they set eyes on me. Didn't take them over five minutes to decide.

Dr.   You never mentioned that before, Pacífico. How did they disqualify you?

P.P. Easy, Doctor. It was the easiest thing in the world. When I saw myself in that mob—there were even guys from Bilbao—I didn't know what to do. But the sergeant came and lined us up to look us over. You can't imagine the scene they made over my girdle. So I went past them one by one; they must've been doctors. And every one of them, I mean every single one of them, as soon as I got there: Turn your head! And I wondered what the heck it was—was I rotten inside or what? So I moved from one line to the next. And about then the sergeant had us line up in the court-yard to turn in our clothes, or at least that's what they said. And the sergeant comes up to me and yells, Pacífico Pérez! And me, At your command, sir! And him, Boy, we're finished with you: you're blind as a bat, a skinny chest, and lesions in your lungs. Can that be? And the sergeant, he made this funny face, and he says to me: You know what you're good for? To pick you up with some tweezers and throw you very carefully into the trash can. The fun they had on my account! So I figured, why should I hang around there anymore? I grabbed my card and went out the door. And that same day, Father and I went back to town in Sinclético's car.

Dr.   Goodness! That must have come as a real blow to your family.

P.P.   No, it wasn't that bad. I mean, I'd planned to meet Father at the Ciromarino, in the bar, you know? Where everybody from our town goes. And as soon as I showed up and said they'd disquali-fied me, that I had three strikes against me, the first thing it did was to wound his pride. That can't be, he said. But then he just looked at me real hard and said, he said: You know what I say, Pacífico? That there are worse things. And the day your war does come, nobody can stop you from going as a volunteer. That's what he said.

Dr.   But how about your grandfathers?

P.P.   That's what I was worried about, too. But Father knew how to handle them. Bisa was waiting for us, and, Well? Then Father, cool as a cucumber, goes and says, Forget it. The general said the boy already knows enough. And Bisa was like the cat that swallowed the canary.

Dr.   So did you take advantage of the opportunity to cure yourself?

P.P.   Cure myself? Cure myself of what, Doctor?

Dr. Your chest, I mean.

P.P. How could I? Father never even asked me what the three reasons were.

Dr. All right, Pacífico. So you started work right away. You started as a chicken farmer, didn't you?

P.P. That's right, yes sir.

Dr. And how did it go?

P.P. Well, the hens were fun. All white, and they laid a lot of eggs. I didn't have any complaints to speak of.

Dr. How about your brother-in-law?

P.P. Emigdio, you mean? Well, you can just imagine. He got into things right off. But don't think he was content to throw them their feed and collect the eggs, no sir. Emigdio was a learned man. So one day when I said hens were very sad creatures, he had the brainstorm about the wine, putting wine in their feed.

Dr. Wine, table wine?

P.P. Yes sir, barrel wine, the kind that only costs five pesetas a liter, from Señor Del's. And he kept saying, If you're happy you work better.

Dr. So did you put the wine in?

P.P. Oh yeah. But not all at once. We tried it out with one group. And we found they were laying 20 percent more. What do you think of that? You should've heard my future brother-in-law: This is going to be a revolution in chicken farming! And what a laugh: the hens ran around clucking all day, and they couldn't walk in a straight line. But no drunks, Doctor. Hardly any of them ever tied one on.

Dr. In view of your success, did you give wine to the others, too?

P.P. Sure. Wine and other stuff. Emigdio was always concocting some new formula. And one day he said to me, You know what I think, Pacífico? And I said, What? 'Cause he'd read books, and he knew about these things. He said, Well, if we used bran instead of feed and added some enzymes for their digestion, we'd save money.

Dr. Did he get around to trying it?

P.P. Did he ever! And it worked, too. That Emigdio had brains, I'll tell you. A little crazy, sometimes, but he had a good head on his shoulders. 'Cause you have to hand it to him: he does a good job. On the one hand, he watched his pennies, and on the other, turned us a profit. It was solid, either way you looked at it.

Dr.   And what did your father have to say about all this?

P.P.   Father had his mind on his own stuff, Doctor. He checked the balance at the end of the month and never so much as made a remark. What could he say? Sometimes I think Emigdio and I would've gone pretty far if I hadn't have stopped him. He had enough ideas to stop a train—just seething with them. You had to control him. Like after the enzymes. He comes up to me one afternoon and says to me, Why don't you convince your father to put up a sheepcote next to the henhouse? And what do you suppose he was thinking? Breed them on hen dung! Just imagine. He said there was a guy in another country who fed his cows wine, and since hen dung is rich in nitrogen, it was the same principle. What do you think of that?

Dr.   I don't know how you let him get away, Pacífico.

P.P.   I didn't. It had to be.

Dr.   Why?

P.P.   'Cause of Candi. She came to town that summer. And I don't know what it was about her, but I fell for her the minute I saw her.

Dr.   This episode in your life sounds very important.

P.P.   Oh yeah. You can be sure of that.

Dr.   So I'd like for you to tell me all about it, in detail.

P.P.   Look, if that's what you want, it might be better to leave it for tomorrow. It was a real mess.

Dr.   I think that's a sensible decision, Pacífico. So unless something should come up, let's meet again tomorrow. Here, at the usual time, OK?

P.P.   OK sir.

▲ ▲ ▲ ▲ ▲ ▲ ▲

Fourth Night

Dr.   Good evening, Pacífico. Make yourself comfortable. There's the anisette. I've already poured it for you. If I remember correctly, last night we interrupted your story at the point where Candi came into it, didn't we? I know very little about the girl, Pacífico. Actually, I don't know anything about her, except that you had an intimate relationship for four months, and that it indirectly brought on your misfortune. To start with, I don't know why she suddenly came to your town. Would you care to explain it to me?

P.P. Very simple, Doctor. Candi was Señor Bebel's daughter. He was from Otero, remember? In other words, she was Teotista's sister.

Dr.   I already know that she was his sister. But that's all the more reason that she should have lived in town, and not shown up suddenly. Just where was she before you met her?

P.P. In the capital. Living with some aunts.

Dr.   But her father . . . I mean, didn't the girl ever go to town to see Señor . . . what was his name?

P.P. Bebel.

Dr.   Oh yes, Señor Bebel.

P.P. Listen, Doctor, Señor Bebel, her father, that is, forgot about her when he became a widower. That's when some of her aunts on her mother's side took her in. But Señor Bebel did go to the capital to see the girl. Once in a while, anyway.

Dr.   Fine. So does that mean that you were twenty-one when you met Candi, when she came to town for the first time?

P.P. Well, yes. I mean, no. I already knew her when she was little, in school. But you know how it is when you're still a boy. Girls were like creatures from another planet; we just ignored them.

Dr.   At what age did she leave, then?

P.P.   Let's see, now. She left town to start junior high school. So she must've been ten.

Dr.   And wasn't that when you went to the city too?

P.P.   Not really, no sir. Bear in mind that I took off when I was thirteen, and Candi's older than me.

Dr.   Candi is older than you?

P.P.   Sure, of course, by two years and three months. She was born in January, and I was born in April.

Dr.   So when she came back to town, she was twenty-three, and you were twenty-one.

P.P.   Yes sir. That's right.

Dr.   And in the capital, what had she done there?

P.P.   Study. Candi was a student.

Dr.   What did she major in?

P.P.   That I couldn't tell you. I don't know. Wow, when she talked, though! It was like a book opening up.

Dr.   And how did you start to get on intimate terms with her?

P.P.   Actually, Doctor, she just caught my eye, soon as she came to town.

Dr.   She was that pretty?

P.P.   It wasn't exactly that. I mean, how can I put it? You just noticed her, you know what I mean? Just picture her: she was wearing pants, her hair was bobbed like a boy's, and she was wearing a scarf that hung down to her calves. Caused a real commotion in town. And then she never let go of her cigarette—always had one in her hand.

Dr.   And what did she do in town?

P.P.   Oh, she just hung out. All day long, just killing time. You'd run into her sitting on the tavern bench waiting for the bus, or under a walnut tree reading a book. There were no rules with her.

Dr.   And when you ran into each other, what would you say?

P.P.   At first, nothing. Like hi, or I'll see you around. But Doctor, let me tell you, Candi had a way of making eyes: she was real bold, you know? Like I say, she was the opposite of Don Prócoro, who wouldn't have fluttered his eyelashes if his life depended on it.

Dr.   She had a steady gaze, you mean.

P.P.   Did she ever! I remember thinking to myself, She'll let me. And she did. If I hang around with her, she'll start it for sure.

Dr.   You realized right away that she was fast?

P.P.   To tell you the truth, yeah, the second I laid eyes on her.

Dr.   And going out together—when did that start?

P.P.   It must've been nearly two weeks later, if I've got it right. She came to town May 28, and by June 9 we were already involved. During Parmenio Marrero's wedding, to be precise. During the refreshments.

Dr.   How did it happen, Pacífico?

P.P.   Well, you know how they are in small towns. Weddings, I mean: the party goes on and on. Well, anyway, we were having something to drink, and anybody that danced with her, with Candi, I mean, had something to say about it. You know, that she rubbed against you, that she didn't have anything on under her blouse, that she wasn't wearing a bra—stuff like that. But since Candi was sexy—'cause nobody would deny that—well, they just lined up for it. But nobody got what he wanted, though. She was a stubborn one; she was the boss all right. Didn't let anybody lead her.

Dr.   So you danced with her.

P.P.   Nah. It didn't get started that way. I've always been too shy for dancing and stuff.

Dr.   Well?

P.P.   Well, I was just sitting next to Agatángelo, in Señor Del's back room, enjoying my vermouth, and along comes Candi. She rubs against me and grabs my arm and says: Hey, take me for a walk. All this sweat and music give me a pain in my balls.

Dr.   She said a pain in her balls? Are you sure, Pacífico?

P.P.   Just like you heard, Doctor. Those were her very words. It shocked me, too, when I first heard it. I even wondered, Did I hear right? But after hearing it a lot I got used to it, of course.

Dr.   Did she say it as a rule?

P.P.   She was always saying it. And other stuff that was worse. Some tongue she had! You can just imagine. When Agatángelo says that next to her Teotista sounded like a missionary—well, that should give you some idea.

Dr.   Does that mean she had a bad temper?

P.P.   No, not at all. That's just the way she was. She had a hot tongue, that's all. Even when she got affectionate, it was the same story: every other word was crazy.

Dr.   Yes. Go on.

P.P.   Well, anyway, she said, Take me for a walk. And the other stuff, you know. I was a coward. I didn't know what I was doing. If she'd said, Let's throw ourselves off El Crestón, I would've jumped off. I don't know what it was that that girl had; it just got to you. I mean, she'd make you feel fucked just by looking at you. That's all there is to it. Well, anyway, we got onto the highway and went as far as the battlement on the Salud. It was pitch black.

Dr.   What was the first thing you talked about, Pacífico?

P.P.   You mean *her*, Doctor. 'Cause she did all the talking, see.

Dr.   Well, what did she say? How did the conversation get started? This is what interests me.

P.P.   Well, she talked about the townspeople. She said people in small towns had a kind of flat, startled look and had I ever noticed it. I said sure, it was only natural. All they ever saw was fields. But she said my eyes were different. I guess it must be because of my glasses. It couldn't be anything else, could it, Doctor?

Dr.   And that flattered you, naturally.

P.P.   Well, I kind of liked hearing it, yeah. Why should I deny it? And she'd go on and on, about anything. I couldn't get a word in edgewise, Doctor. I was sort of dazed. But just so she wouldn't think I was too dumb, I worked it in—that I have a degree, you know? And Candi said, Hey, you don't have to prove anything.

Dr.   Hmm. I see she knew how to wind you around her little finger. Go on, Pacífico, please.

P.P.   Well, once we were like that we got to talking. What did I do, she asked. So I let her know I was a honey taster and a chicken farmer, and she said I must be proud to be in a productive line of work, or something like that. A little sarcastic, though. And between one thing and another we got to the banks of the Salud, and Candi goes, Let's sit down. So we stretched out on the bank, and then she clammed up. And to get us out of the rut, I asked if she'd ever noticed that brooks talked like people: that the Matayeguas cried

out, and the Salud muttered, and the Lirón sang like a woman.
She thought that was very poetic, and me, Doctor, to talk myself
up, you know, I told her that Don Prócoro said that my Uncle
Paco was a poet. And she said, Imagine that, 'cause all Don Prócoro and priests in general said was stupid nonsense, and that
ever since psychiatrists had come along priests might as well go
into hiding. I don't see what one thing has to do with the other.

Dr.   And how did it end?

P.P.   End? You're too fast for me, Doctor.

Dr.   I mean that afternoon.

P.P.   Wait a minute, you'll see. We'd been like that for a while, sitting
next to each other, and then Candi goes and puts her arm behind
me, on my shoulders, and she gives me this explosive kiss.

Dr.   She kissed you?

P.P.   That's right. I'm not making anything up. Just as brassy as could
be. Wouldn't let go of me; it was such a desperate kiss. And me,
I don't know if it's 'cause I had a cold, or she caught me off
guard, or what, but I couldn't breathe through my nose, and she
wouldn't let me through my mouth. I was choking, let me tell you,
and I wasn't even enjoying it, and I said to myself, You're in for it,
Pacífico. Thought I'd die. And on top of it, my glasses, Lord, did
they hurt, grinding into me here, on top of my nose. So I wanted
her to back off, but it's as if we were stuck together. There was
no way out of it. And when she backed off, You were practically
starved, weren't you? I swear to you, that's what she said. And
she even asked me if I'd liked it.

Dr.   You told her the truth, didn't you?

P.P.   Well, no, I didn't. That's the funny part. I mean, as soon as I reacted I said, Yes, I did. And I think that's where I went wrong,
Doctor.

Dr.   What makes you say that?

P.P.   'Cause of everything that happened afterward. I mean, if I'd told
her no right then: that no, I didn't like it, there would've been
peace. That would've finished it, right there on the spot.

Dr.   What else, Pacífico?

P.P.   Well, since we're talking confidentially, there was something else.
Candi asked me if it was the first time a woman had kissed me
like that.

Dr.   And did you lie again?

P.P. No sir. This time I told her the truth. I said yes, it was the first time.

Dr.   What else did she ask you?

P.P. Well, she asked me what I thought about the woman making the first move. If I thought she was a slut because of that, and may God forgive my language.

Dr.   What did you reply?

P.P. The truth, of course: that some women are, and some aren't born that way. But she was like a broken record. She just kept talking about the same subject.

Dr.   And what did she talk about, Pacífico?

P.P. Oh, she talked about everything—I couldn't follow her for the life of me. The only thing I can remember is her talking about her Oedipus complex—that's what it's called, isn't it? Well, anyway, it was the Oedipus complex this and the Oedipus complex that, just the way somebody or other had proved. Said it was what happened when you lived in a patriarchal society. And I thought of Moses, to have some idea in my head. And that we had to overthrow those societies.

Dr.   Could it have been Freud who proved it?

P.P. That's it! That was the name. How did you guess?

Dr.   Has anyone told you that you have an enviable memory, Pacífico?

P.P. Well, I don't have any complaints about what it can store. Don Angel agreed. The thing that gives me trouble is figuring things out.

Dr.   Why don't you finish school now that you have time?

P.P. That's a thought. But we'd have to talk it over carefully, don't you think? Let's forget it for now.

Dr.   Whatever you'd like, Pacífico. Let's see now, where were we? Oh yes. So the first time you were together Candi talked about Freud and the Oedipus complex, right?

P.P. Yes sir, she did. Right off the bat. And she did other times, too. Come to think of it, she never did stop talking about them and other people I can't remember now. And me, at the beginning, just so's I wouldn't sound like a fool, I kept my trap shut. But then I went and checked it out, in the encyclopedia they've got in the town hall, and I said to her, I says, As far as I know, we haven't

got any of that here in Humán. So Candi bursts out laughing—
you should've seen her, Doctor—split her sides laughing, and
she said to me, You're so cute, Pacífico: if something doesn't exist
in your town you think it doesn't exist period.

Dr.   She said that to you?

P.P.   That's right, sir. And more stuff, except I don't remember it anymore. Candi was a very smart girl, like I said.

Dr.   But did those conversations interest you, Pacífico?

P.P.   On the whole, Doctor, I didn't understand her, that's the real
truth of it. I mean what I wanted to get out of her was the other
stuff, see? The stuff I could manage. 'Cause you know going out
with her appealed to me and scared me at the same time. Am
I making myself clear? It was both those things. I mean if she
appealed to me it was 'cause she was sexy, and I liked to see
her smoke strong black cigarettes, and her blue fingernails—they
were a real shocker. But then I got cold feet when I heard her say
all that stuff from books; it was like she was making fun of me.
Well, anyway, it just took about a week for us to get involved, and
then I didn't even notice that.

Dr.   To get involved? You mean to initiate carnal relations?

P.P.   That's right, yes sir.

Dr.   There, in your town?

P.P.   Well yeah, sort of.

Dr.   Which is it: *Did* you meet in town or *didn't* you?

P.P.   Yes, we did. I mean no, we didn't.

Dr.   Which is it, Pacífico? Did you perhaps meet in the henhouse?

P.P.   No, not in a million years. I'd never meet there.

Dr.   Well, where, then?

P.P.   In Prádanos, since you ask. At first, in Prádanos.

Dr.   In the abandoned town?

P.P.   That's exactly right, yes sir, near the washing place, in Bisa's
town. So after Parmenio Marrero's wedding I told Candi about
Prádanos. I mean I told her the truth—that it was a deserted
town, but that important people must've lived there some time
ago, of course. I mean it had palaces with coats of arms and arch-
ways over the doors and a special hermitage, too.

Dr.   Is there an interesting church in Prádanos?

P.P.   Is there ever! It's a national monument. But the bad part is that there's nothing like a path to get up there. 'Cause the bishop and those Americans came digging to see what they could get out of it. But they went away, and it's just sitting there. Since they didn't have a way to bring it down.

Dr.   Fine. Tell me something. Did Candi like the idea of your getting together up in Prádanos?

P.P.   Oh, sure. She'd even tried to go up herself. Lots of times, when she was a kid, but she never did manage to get up there. So that afternoon we took the Fuentefierro path, we went across the mountain, and two hours later we were walking around the town.

Dr.   What sort of impression did it make on her?

P.P.   On Candi? Well, at first she was speechless, everything struck her—the empty houses with the coats of arms, the paths covered with honeysuckle, the hermitage and the cemetery. Wow, with all those brambles you couldn't see a cross. But 'specially the silence, Doctor; except for the horseflies and the mosquitoes buzzing, and a blackbird every now and then, you couldn't hear a sound there. I'll tell you, Doctor, walking in those oxcart paths through ruins was just like being in church, the respect you felt, you know?

Dr.   Yes. But tell me, once you were there, what did you do?

P.P.   Hold your horses. Not so fast, Doctor. We looked around, up and down, and then we went over to the square with the watering trough, the cattle's spot, and we sat down under the shade of an acacia tree, right across from the palace, 'cause Candi wouldn't take her eyes off it. She'd look at the three coats of arms and the iron balconies, and then of all things some joker had stuck two beehives in the window, imagine—what a notion, as if it wasn't worth anything unless you made something from it. Well, anyway, sitting there next to the cattle's watering trough in that scorching sun, we were just letting the time go by when a cricket comes along, stops right by our feet. And thanks to him we realized how silent it was; you know, for me a town's not a town without kids yelling and dogs barking.

Dr.   A good point, Pacífico.

P.P.   Well, anyway, there was just this cricket, that's all. You couldn't even hear the blackbird anymore. And Candi just looking to her heart's content—that palace had her in a daze. On one of its corners the stones were crumbling, you know? You could see a narrow staircase, the kind they call spiral staircases, and she started to rub her eyes like she was dreaming or something. Then she stood up and went over to it, and then she came back to where I was, and she says to me, Wow, it's fucking beautiful!

Dr.   So she swore, that way too?

P.P.   Oh yeah. She'd say anything she felt like saying. A tongue like a truck driver, let me tell you. When you think about it, there wasn't a swear word she didn't use. And since she'd belt 'em out like that—with the cigarette in her mouth and squinting her eyes—well, it hit you. It really did. You might think it's 'cause she got angry, but no, it wasn't that. She couldn't get those words out of her system, not even when she was being affectionate!

Dr.   What words, Pacífico?

P.P.   Which ones do you think? The swear words, Doctor.

Dr.   Why are you laughing, Pacífico? Do you mind telling me what your thoughts are?

P.P.   Nah. Just silly stuff, Doctor. Don't pay any attention to me.

Dr.   But you *were* thinking about something, weren't you?

P.P.   Well, I was just remembering that while we were, well, you know, fooling around, she called me all these names: Hey, little prick, and my tiny baby goat—a whole rash of 'em.

Dr.   Good Lord! What did you *do*?

P.P.   In that situation, what could I? Laugh, make the best of it. I mean if what you want to know is whether or not I stopped her—no, I didn't. I knew what I was after, right? And she was playing her cards straight. She didn't make any bones about it. The way she saw it, anybody who got involved with her knew he'd be fucked, and may God forgive me for saying it.

Dr.   And how *did* she see it, if you don't mind telling me?

P.P.   No, why should I? Candi was set on building this community of country people and founding a school, see. The community was supposed to be made up of young men and women, but without any prejudices, see. I mean without any scruples. So each girl could make it with all the guys and vice versa—try all the combinations, and nobody would have the right to get pissed off about it. And as for the rest, well, everybody would pitch in, and they'd live off the land. I don't know if I'm making it clear.

Dr. It's clear, Pacífico. Where did she intend to start the community?

P.P. That I couldn't tell you. She never told me. But getting back to what I was saying, Doctor: If Candi thought like that, well, anybody that got involved with her, sooner or later, would be fucked, right? So that community of hers, or whatever it was, was a kind of cuckold factory: either she wasn't cheating on anybody or she was cheating on everybody, depends on how you look at it. But as far as I'm concerned, hey, she wasn't offending me when she called me those names. Don't you understand?

Dr. Yes, I understand your rationale, Pacífico. But tell me something: Before, you said Candi thought like that "at first." Do you mean to say she changed her mind later?

P.P. Well, she was kind of iffy on that subject. And since she'd say one thing one day and another the next, you couldn't trust her on that score. Like, for example, on some days, when we really had the hots for each other, she'd say: You and me, screwer, we'll go far in this business of making a purer society. 'Cause she had this fixation, see, that progress was messing up the world.

Dr. Did Candi ever say where she planned to take you?

P.P. She didn't, no sir. You know, she was kind of changeable—it could be Asia or Africa, whichever suited her at the moment. But as for settling on one thing, no, she never did.

Dr. Fine. Excuse me, Pacífico. We were in Prádanos looking at the spiral staircase, remember? And Candi had come up to you and said, It's fucking beautiful! What happened next?

P.P. She said it over and over.

Dr. She said It's fucking beautiful more times?

P.P. Lots of times, Doctor. All the time. She'd look at the little gardens overrun with blackberries and osiers, and she'd say it. Or she'd put her hands in the trough up to her wrists, and she'd say it. Or she'd look at the sign where it said Calle Mayor, and she'd say it.* Or she'd just keep quiet a while, listening to the silence,

*Translator's Note: "Calle Mayor" means Main Street.

and it was the same thing, Doctor: Wow, it's fucking beautiful! Everything was beautiful to her, in general.

Dr. But from what you say, she sounds like a sensitive girl, Pacífico, in spite of her language.

P.P. Hmph! Did I ever claim it was the other way around?

Dr. No, of course not. Excuse me. Go on.

P.P. Well, the point is, it was sweltering that afternoon up in Prádanos, you know? And the sun sure was shining hard. And while she was going this way and that, all of a sudden clear out of the blue she stops and takes off her blouse. Then her pants. And there she was in her birthday suit—well, except for her sneakers. What a body, the kind of firm, white flesh you find on a MacIntosh apple. So of course I lost my head; it was only natural. You should've seen her there on her tiptoes in the ruins, her arms crossed, like she was ready for a picture, and she goes and says, This is how we should live again, Pacífico, like Adam and Eve in paradise. Take off your clothes!

Dr. What a fiery one! Just like that, with nothing leading up to it?

P.P. Nothing, not a thing. Sure as could be, in control of everything. That's the way she was. And when I got behind a blackberry bush, embarrassed, you know, she, well, she shouts out: A slave to social conventions, that's what you are, screwer! See?

Dr. But you obeyed.

P.P. How can I put it? But you have no idea what a disaster my girdle was. Kept slipping around me, that darned girdle! And then I had to hide it in the blackberry bushes.

Dr. And were you bare then?

P.P. Wait a second. I took off my pants and my shirt, 'cause me, you've probably noticed already, I've always been a little puny in the chest, and my spine sticks out, between my shoulder blades. So I took off the elastic thing and my underpants. You should've seen Candi, wow! Soon as she sees me she says, You'll never be free of your rigid mental structures, you big dick. Kidding me, see. But I was already hot, Doctor, so I took off after her, and just as we were getting to the trough she jumps in, and she starts splashing me and laughing, and the water was running down between her breasts. It was driving me crazy, of course: but as soon as I tried to move in she up and jumps over a wall, me running behind her. I didn't even get my hands on her. So then she jumps over the wall on the other side of the orchard and starts running down the hill and laughing. She kept laughing, and the echo in the mountains repeated it, and it was worse, Doctor. And me, I go, Wait up, Candi! And she laughs at me, You're inhibited, inhibited, inhibited! Yelling it out and laughing so much I lost control. I didn't know what I was doing anymore. I was blind, just running after her without even seeing her, I think. And we kept it up like that, jumping over walls and running around the ruins. I don't know how long it was, and me shouting, Wait, Candi! It didn't even sound like my voice, it was so hoarse, and her, Inhibited, inhibited, inhibited! And laughing, with that echo, it was enough to drive you crazy, Doctor, like a bad dream, I mean a good one, the kind you have but you know you'll never get to live it for real. And then I see Candi up on top of a wall holding an ash tree branch, stark naked, so alive in the middle of all those dead things, and I called out to her, Candi, wait. I was almost crying. And we started to run again, on the gravel paths, or in the square, around the acacias. Inhibited, inhibited, inhibited! Like hide and seek. But she was panting by then, and as for me, well, I could hardly keep up. And then Candi jumped over the ruins of the palace and ran up the spiral staircase with me after her, and when we got to the great hall, that had the balcony with the beehives, you should've seen her, Doctor, all exhausted, when a wild pigeon—the gray kind, with a white neck—started flapping its wings like crazy, and she was startled. I mean she turned around, and then I caught her. She was laughing and breathing heavily. She couldn't even talk, and right there, with the pigeon dung and the cobwebs, Doctor . . . well, it happened right there.

Dr.   Goodness! It certainly was a laborious conquest.

P.P.   You can just imagine.

Dr.   And did things change somewhat after you'd made love to her?

P.P.   What was that?

Dr.   I mean did things go on the same way after the great hall?

P.P.   More or less, Doctor. Candi was like that. She always said we have to go back to simple pleasures.

Dr. They weren't *that* simple, it seems to me.

P.P. Well, depends on how you look at it, doesn't it?

Dr. Yes, I guess it does. And tell me, after she'd put out your fire, didn't you consider the problem more serenely?

P.P. Well, it was like this. After we finished we stood on the balcony together, leaning on the railing, facing the hill that's called Las Lástimas—it's at the foot of the Aquilina Cliff—remember? And she looked at the blue mountains, or at the swift, swirling around the church tower, or at the yellow plots of cultivated land spotted with beech trees, or at the ruins down below us, and after a while she nudged me with her elbow and she said: This is peace, screwer. The rest is shit.

Dr. I'm constantly surprised by Candi's sensitivity to beauty and her gross way of expressing it. Do you think that maybe Candi was falsifying herself? I mean, trying to seem different from what she really was?

P.P. Who knows, Doctor?

Dr. Fine, Pacífico. What was your reply?

P.P. To tell you the truth, I wasn't in the mood to see peace or anything, 'cause the open window and the stairwell made this horrible draft, and I was starting to feel it in my stomach, and I missed having my girdle on, you know? But I kept my mouth shut. What are you going to say at a time like that? So anyway, we walked around there in the evening dew, 'til the sun set. And then later, when we went back down, I couldn't bear those prickly bushes; it was awful. I mean, I couldn't even walk. And meanwhile, we were going along the path, between two lights you could see, and she goes and says, Just a second. And just like that, Doctor, she stopped and squatted down right next to me and started to pee. Course I didn't say a word, but I must've frowned, 'cause as she was getting up she said: Hiding to satisfy your bodily needs is a repulsive petty bourgeois prejudice. So whenever she felt the urge, she'd just squat and fire away, as if I wasn't even there, you know?

Dr. And it bothered you, naturally.

P.P. Well, you know, you're taught different.

Dr.   Yes, Pacífico. I assume that after that initial experience, the two of you went back to Prádanos frequently.

P.P. Every afternoon, Doctor. Right after lunch. And we'd stay up there 'til late.

Dr.   And did you play the same game you'd played the first day?

P.P. Oh no. It changed. There was never a dull moment with Candi. Either we'd sunbathe, or we'd search the schoolhouse or the chests in the palace—it depended. And for example, if we went into the schoolhouse it'd be a long session. She'd inspect the kids' notebooks and read the letters they wrote to their parents, must've been years and years ago. They'd gone off to the capital or Bilbao or Germany, wherever. And if we were in the palace, it was the same story: she wouldn't leave a stone unturned. She had to see it all, as they say.

Dr.   Did you force open the doors?

P.P. No sir. Up there, since about ten years ago, it's been wide open. There are no thieves in Prádanos. Even the church, it's wide open. I remember one afternoon, under the church bell tower, where the clock is, do you know what we came across?

Dr.   What, Pacífico?

P.P. The bier.

Dr.   What bier?

P.P. What bier do you expect? The one they use for coffins. For burying the dead the way they do in small towns.

Dr.   Do you mean to say that they use the same coffin to bury everyone?

P.P. Wait a minute, no. They take the corpse to the cemetery in that coffin, see? And once they get it to the cemetery, they take it out and throw it in the common pit, and that's that.

Dr.   Do you mean to say that they buried the dead without coffins?

P.P. Well, sure. After all, what do you think life's like in a small town?

Dr.   Fine. Go on, son, go on.

P.P. So anyway, we came across the bier in a room full of cobwebs and swallows' nests. You should've seen Candi asking me, Hey! You don't suppose there's a body inside? And me, Nah, look. And I opened it up, see, and off to the side I said, And here ends the pleasure of the unjust. And Candi bursts out laughing and says, And of the just, too. So I ask her, Don't you believe in the afterlife? And she giggles, Hey, screwer, all I believe in is what I can see.

Dr.   That fits in perfectly with her way of being, Pacífico.

P.P.   It may, Doctor. But that's beyond me.

Dr.   But tell me something. After the first day, was the purpose of your visits to Prádanos exclusively, say, archaeological?

P.P.   How am I supposed to handle those subjects?

Dr.   Listen, Pacífico. What I'm asking is, did you spend your afternoons discovering relics, or did you do something else too?

P.P.   What a question, hey! Of course we did, naturally. That's why we went up there. It's just that in that sense, Candi was always thinking up something.

Dr.   Thinking up what?

P.P.   Oh, it depended. She was pretty wild. Like she might grab a reaper's hat or some coarse leather sandles and suddenly show up in them, bare, on a balcony. Or she might do something else. I'll never forget the afternoon she got a cloak out of the palace. It was black on one side and red on the other, all moth-eaten, and she broke into a run down the path, the cloak over her shoulders, and as she ran she showed her legs, just one, then the other, you know? And Doctor, let me tell you, those stunts drove me crazy with desire. I don't know if it's 'cause they were new to me or what, but they did.

Dr.   And did you always get together in the great hall, in the palace?

P.P.   Not on your life. A fine one she was for that! Every day, it was a different place. Candi was really free-living. Said you had to experience new sensations.

Dr.   She did? And did she experience them?

P.P.   How can I put it? I bet you can't guess what occurred to her one afternoon when she saw I was hotter than usual.

Dr.   What, Pacífico?

P.P.   To lie down in a bed of brambles. Yep, you heard right. She was twisting around like a snake, from the sting. And, Come on, screwer, don't let me down, she'd say. And me, of course, I was out of my mind. I think I would've gone down to hell itself.

Dr.   What a barbarous thing to do!

P.P. Oh, she was always like that. Not just once or twice. Another day, in the blackberry bushes, we came out of there covered with wounds. Me, at least I was wearing my elastic contraption, but her, she was stark naked, and with that tender flesh of hers.

Dr.   The woman sounds like a masochist, Pacífico.

P.P. Who knows what she was! She was anxious, anyway, on that score. And she said she had the moral obligation to liberate me.

Dr.   Is it actually possible that she spoke of moral obligations?

P.P. Well, what do *you* think? Of course! According to her, she did these things to liberate me, see. But that didn't fool me any. She did it 'cause she relished doing it, same way you like eating with your fingers. And the point is, I thought to myself, she'll get tired of inventing stuff. But not on your life! I mean after the brambles, and the blackberries, the grouse in the grove, and everything else she dreamed up, what do you suppose she came up with next?

Dr.   Well, what, Pacífico?

P.P. Doing it in the coffin on the bier, imagine.

Dr.   Is it actually possible?

P.P. It sure is. It's as possible as daylight, Doctor. And what a hardship that was! A real punishment, it was so narrow in there. And Candi saying, Come on, screwer, let's enjoy the pleasure the unjust get. We made it, after a fashion.

Dr.   But I find it unacceptable, Pacífico, that you gave in, just to please her, on all of her whims, irreverent as they were.

P.P. Well, what could *I* do? That woman had me by the balls, Doctor. That's the long and short of it.

Dr.   And how about you—didn't you experience any fear or regrets about such disorder?

P.P. Sometimes, yes. Afterward, when we went back down.

Dr.   That is to say, you were conscious of the excess.

P.P. Yes sir. We were overdoing it.

Dr.   Did you by any chance feel disgusted at any point?

P.P. Well, let's put it this way. As I was going back down, I felt sort of broken, you know? As if I had slime on me. And it was always the same. I'd say to myself: I'm not going back to her. One night I even went to Don Prócoro to confess, you know? And I started telling him about it right there in the rectory. And you know, as I started to get it off my chest I felt better. And Don Prócoro was so scared that he even raised his hand to his eyes to get a better look at me, and I said to him, If you open your eyes I'll sew my lips. And he was very prudent then. He kept his eyes closed 'til the end.

Dr. And did you leave Candi after that?

P.P. I couldn't. I saw her the next day, and we went to Prádanos again. I was out of control.

Dr. Did you go back to see Don Prócoro again?

P.P. Three days later, Doctor, in the evening.

Dr. And?

P.P. As I recall, he said to me that my repentance was worthless if I didn't plan to mend my ways.

Dr. Didn't you plan to?

P.P. Mend my ways, you mean? Of course I did! Every night, Doctor. But the next morning I'd see Candi, and I'd be lost again.

Dr. But then after being with her you experienced the awareness of your sin again. Is that it?

P.P. That's right. That's exactly how it was.

Dr. And how about Candi—did you tell Candi anything about your sessions with Don Prócoro?

P.P. Not a word. She wasn't one for that! Just imagine the scene she'd have made if I went and told her: Don Prócoro's liberating me more than you are. I couldn't tell her anything like that. She would've torn out my eyes.

Dr. I realize that, son, but let's get back to the point. Aside from look- ing through old chests and so on, what did you do in Prádanos, a deserted town, day after day?

P.P. I don't know. Stuff. There was always something to do. She was in favor of simple pleasures. So we'd look at nests, or we'd pick flowers or lavender. She used to put a twig of it in her hair, of lavender, I mean. And if we'd gotten carried away she'd put them in her underarms, and another twig between her breasts, right here. I don't know! We kept ourselves entertained. Sometimes Candi would bring a ball, and we'd play *tepeté* at one end of the church, inside.

Dr.   What's *tepeté*, Pacífico?
P.P.   Just a silly game kids play.
Dr.   What does it consist of?
P.P.   Well, nothing, really. I mean, you grab the ball, and you throw it against the wall, see. And when it bounces, you catch it, and you say:

> When it's one
> you don't talk,
> you don't laugh,
> you don't move,
> with your foot and
> the other foot,
> with your hand.
> *Tepeté, tepeté,*
> in behind and in front,
> in a circle all around,
> and my granny too!

It's just nonsense, to kill time, and it goes like this: when the ball bounces, against the wall, that is, you keep quiet if it's "you don't talk," or you look serious if it's "you don't laugh," or you hobble if it's "with your foot," and if you don't follow the rules, you lose, get it? Just nonsense, you know.

Dr.   And did you always play the same game?
P.P.   Nah! No sir. Other days we played *tanga*, or we played jump rope. But mainly we ate toasted pine nuts, lying in the sun, on the meadow, while we chatted. We'd open them with a jackknife.
Dr.   What did you chat about, Pacífico?
P.P.   I don't know, stuff—life and everything.
Dr.   But what exactly were the topics of your conversation?
P.P.   I don't know. I do recall we talked about prejudices pretty often. They bugged her. She was always saying to me: I don't know two more bigoted people than my father and my brother Teotista.
Dr.   So she accused her family of being backward.
P.P.   I didn't say that. But it *is* true that she couldn't stand the sight of Teotista.
Dr.   What did she say about Teotista?

P.P.   She said, let's see now, she said: That Teotista's such an animal that if he ever caught us together like this he'd kill you.

Dr.   Wait a minute, wait a minute, Pacífico. This is very important. Candi stated that her brother might kill you if he caught you with her?

P.P.   State it? Well, don't put it that way. She said that the same as she said other stuff, the same as she said, for example, that even the best men over forty should be hanged.

Dr.   She distrusted maturity, you mean.

P.P.   Oh, for her that was the worst of the worst. Candi said that as long as old farts were around—and may God forgive me—there was no remedy for this world.

Dr.   And old farts were men over forty?

P.P.   From there on up, yes sir.

Dr.   Some fix we're in, then . . . And tell me, how did Candi think she could change the world? What do you think about it?

P.P.   Oh, in every way possible—everything. She'd start with fucking. That was first, see. And she cursed the day she was born as a woman. But don't get me wrong: it's not that she minded being a woman, but it ticked her off that women were dirt, "a zero to the left of one," as we say. Do you understand?

Dr.   Perfectly, Pacífico.

P.P.   Well, that was part of it. And then she said that for thousands and millions of years nobody had paid any attention to women. That they'd been slaves to men. That a man could just sign a paper and bingo! he had a slave. And that men take advantage of women, not just when they stick their hand up your skirt, 'cause that's really nothing. It's when men feed women, and then in exchange for that they get a mother, a lover, and a maid all in one piece, understand?

Dr.   So that's what she thought, eh? And to whom did she attribute the situation?

P.P.   Well, to men over forty, to priests, to society. To everybody.

Dr.   Candi undoubtedly referred to woman as object, didn't she?

P.P.   Yeah, that was it. Woman as object and . . . wait a minute, now, how did it go? Her thingify . . . thingify . . . it's on the tip of my tongue.

Dr.   Thingification?

P.P. That's it—thingification.

Dr.   Good, Pacífico. And did you counter her argument? Did you make any observations?

P.P. Basically no, sir. What could a chump like me say to her? Except for when she talked about women being objects. I'd look at her nails, painted blue, and I thought to myself, Well, she paints herself like an object. But I didn't say anything, no sir. She took pride in being different from everybody else.

Dr.   In how she thought?

P.P. In how she thought and in what she said. I can recall one morning walking along the bank of the Embustes, she stopped and stood staring at the pippin tree, all shrunk up when the other apple trees were full of fruit, and she said to me, I want to be like that tree: the opposite of everybody else. Plain as day, Doctor. She made it plain as day.

Dr.   There's one point that interests me particularly, Pacífico. During your relationship with Candi, except for the sexual aspect, I observe that your activity was purely receptive, submissive. You didn't get mad at her, you didn't challenge her word, you didn't show any initiative. You kept quiet. Didn't you ever feel like liberating yourself from her tutelage? Did it please you to feel dominated? Or did you ever try to establish your relation with Candi on equal footing?

P.P. How could I, Doctor? She had me by the balls, I already told you.

Dr.   You're right, Pacífico. I know that, and it's evident. But I'm talking now about theoretical or dialectical grounds, or something of that nature. Take, for instance, this: Didn't it ever occur to you, in view of her foul tongue, to come out with even filthier language yourself, just to one-up her, you know, put her in her place?

P.P. Well, frankly, Doctor, I don't think there *is* any language dirtier than hers. So there's that, first of all. But come to think of it, I do remember that soon after we met I did let out a swear word, you know? But I can't say them with any gusto—I guess it takes practice—it just kind of limped out of my mouth. I didn't even say the whole expression, and she was already laughing at me, Hey, you'd better not say those things, screwer. You don't know how, and besides they sound funny coming from you. So that was it, Doctor, just the one time. And after that I kept my mouth shut— I was better off that way.

Dr.   Forgetting words for a minute, didn't you ever give her a show of your strength, or your skills, to dazzle her, to assert your personality, to say, in effect, Hey, this is Pacífico?

P.P.   On the whole I can't recall that I did. Except maybe with the beehives in the palace.

Dr.   What happened there?

P.P.   Nothing special. I don't know. One day I got the urge to look at them, so I grabbed a ladder and went up in my bare skin—the way I was—to check one out. But it wasn't to show off. I was just curious—it'd been almost ten years since anybody had looked in there.

Dr.   And how did Candi react?

P.P.   Well, come to think of it, she was a little jealous, you're right. I mean, when I came down with the honeycomb, she asked, Hey, don't those things bite? And I told her what I'd learned from experience: No, the more defenseless you are the better, Candi. So she went up to the other beehive, totally naked, eh? except for some green garters she'd gotten from the schoolteacher's next to the schoolhouse. I don't know what she did, Doctor, but the fact is that she'd hardly stuck her hand in when two of them had already stung her, one on each teat, what a coincidence, eh? almost like they'd planned it.

Dr.   Well, that must have filled her with respect, or admiration, for you, didn't it?

P.P.   Are you kidding? All it did was tick her off. You should've heard her swear and curse! Calling me every name in the book, she gave it to me, hard! She didn't put me up on any pedestal. Oh no. It was the other way around. And then I tried to help her and talk it over with her, but it was worse.

Dr.   Frankly, I don't understand your attitude, Pacífico.

P.P.   Well, try to. I didn't want Candi to get all upset. That was the last thing I needed. 'Cause remember, that woman—and I don't know how she managed to but she did—she had me by the balls, Doctor, and I was nothing without her. And it's common knowledge that if one person needs another, the other takes advantage of it, that's just how it works. And you couldn't get it out of Candi's head that she'd liberated me and that that's how I was paying her for it, with the bees.

Dr. So she maintained that she had liberated you through sex?

P.P. Through sex, that's right, that's what she said. So me, of course, I was grateful to her.

Dr. And do you really think she liberated you?

P.P. Look, that's another story. 'Cause ever since Parmenio Marrero's wedding, I couldn't keep my mind on anything. All I thought about was when we'd be together again, and doing it. That's the truth of it. I mean, I forgot all about the beehives and the hen-house—everything.

Dr. That's true, hmm. And meanwhile, who took care of the hen-house?

P.P. Emigdio. Who else? He was my future brother-in-law. By then he and Corina had gotten serious, and he'd come down from Quin-tana every afternoon. He was a good kid, Emigdio. 'Cause with Corina as hot as she was, it could've turned out bad—just a big stomach on her—that's for sure. But Emigdio respected her, you know why?

Dr. Why?

P.P. Well, first of all, 'cause he was a decent person. And second of all, 'cause he had his head in the right place.

Dr. Did he report directly to your father on the henhouse?

P.P. Nah, he passed all the stuff to me. Then I'd go and make the report to Father. But since Father was all concerned about break-ing ground in the uplands, he didn't even register what I told him. He just put away the bills. And since the bills were in order, Father was happy as a lark. Except for his greed. He'd say to me every so often, Pacífico, smarten up: this henhouse thing could be a gold mine.

Dr. His greed got the better of him, you mean.

P.P. The way it would anybody, Doctor, 'cause it seems to me as far as that goes we're all pretty much alike. Take Candi, for example: different from everybody else, right? Not right! What happens when we go up to where they separate the gold from the sand?

Dr.   I don't know. What, Pacífico?

P.P.   I mean up next to the Aquilina Cliff.

Dr.   I know, I know. Well, what happened?

P.P.   Same old story! One afternoon I told Candi about the place. I told her how the waterwheel hollows up at the Aquilina Cliff dragged the water from the thaws, and how they made the Alija Stream form in Mesa del Brezo, right? Well, I explained to her how in the stream, in the part that's in Mesa, some gold nuggets turned up ages ago, when Bisa was a kid, and how the washing places and the troughs were still in working order, see. Candi couldn't get up there fast enough. So there we went, up the mountain. It was in July, about five o'clock in the afternoon. Your brains could've fried it was so hot. Well, anyway, Doctor, when Candi started to look over the troughs where they used to sift the stuff—and you can just imagine the condition they were in, from the rust, I mean—well, I got my feet into the stream and started to lift up the stones. To see if I could catch a crayfish. And I was busy with that when I see this shiny thing—real tiny, it couldn't have been bigger than a lentil—and, A nugget! I cried. You should've seen Candi, did she ever jump! And me, It's mine! and her, I didn't say it wasn't! So she lunges at me like crazy and starts shaking me, and I'm thinking it's a game or something. So I clenched it in my fist, the nugget I mean, and, I won't give it to you! And she goes, It's mine, it's mine! Wouldn't even let me speak. She couldn't have been taking it to heart; it must've been her nerves. Otherwise how could you explain such a thing. But she said, Give it to me, or I'll slap you one, hard! And she said it twice, so me, I said, OK, here: take it, keep it. What difference did it make to me? I gave it to her, of course. But I'll be honest with you, Doctor. I didn't expect something like that from Candi. And do you believe that because of that nugget there wasn't a single afternoon that we missed going up to that place?

Dr.   To hunt for gold?

P.P.   Why would we do that? All there was was pebbles.

Dr.   What did you do, then?

P.P.   She would look. She'd stir up the whole gravel pit. You should've seen her go at it. From the end of the Aquilina Cliff all the way to the washing place, she didn't leave a stone unturned. So me, with *that* being the order of the day, I'd just lay down under a shelter and wait 'til she got tired.

Dr.   Did she ever find anything?

P.P.   How could she? There was nothing to find.

Dr.   Was Candi bothered by her failure?

P.P.   Listen, Doctor, around about then Candi wasn't up to her usual tricks. I don't know. She was kind of strange, saying those herbs must not be good for her.

Dr.   What herbs?

P.P.   The stuff she smoked.

Dr.   You mean Candi smoked grass?

P.P.   Halfway through the summer, yeah, she took it into her head to try it.

Dr.   Exactly what kind of grass was it?

P.P.   Oh, some wild stuff that grew near the Parallones Islands of La Peña. In the cracks, right in the humus. But don't think she was the one that discovered them. In my town people had used that grass, or herbs, for ages, since I was a kid, for toothaches, you know? Señora Dictrinia would prepare a concoction, and she'd tell us to gargle, but she'd always warn us: Don't swallow it, now, dear, 'cause it can harm you. Spit it out. See?

Dr.   And how did Candi start smoking the herbs?

P.P.   Well, Candi already knew what they were for. And one day, going up to the islands, she gathered an armful of them and laid them out to dry in the schoolhouse window, up in Prádanos. And a week later I saw her rolling a cigarette, easy as pie, and I asked her, Hey, what are you smoking? 'Cause usually, see, she smoked dark tobacco, already rolled; there were days when two packs didn't satisfy her. Well, anyway, she looks at me and says, It's the grass from La Peña; it's just to try it. Me, I said to her, It might be harmful, you know, and her, she just laughed: Don't be such a worrywart, Pacífico! And that's how she started, just experimenting. But after that hardly a day went by without her smoking one up there in Prádanos, after fooling around for a little while.

Dr.   And what effect did it have on her? Did you notice any changes in her, while she was smoking the grass or when she finished the cigarette?

P.P.   Yeah, sure. But get me straight on this: She didn't start jumping for joy or dance on one foot. No, it wasn't like that. At first she'd just look sort of dazed. But then her eyes got funny, and she'd start smiling for all she was worth, you know? Like babies, when they've just finished nursing and let the nipple go. I even got the feeling she was drooling a little. And then she'd lay down in the meadow and start rubbing her back against the ground, and laugh, and I'd ask her, What do you see, Candi? And her eyeballs would roll, but real drowsy, and, It's not what I see, screwer, it's what I *don't* see that makes me do it. Imagine, Doctor. And I asked her if the stuff blinded her, and she broke into those smiles again—they made me sick—and after a while she comes out with, They don't blind me, screwer. They just keep me from seeing what I don't want to see—this filthy world, garbage, old decrepit people—that's what.

Dr.   Did she ever tell you what she saw?

P.P.   Basically, no. She didn't explain much, Doctor.

Dr.   Did she smoke these herbs frequently?

P.P.   Well, like I told you, after that first time, 'til we broke up. I don't rightly know if she gave them up later on.

Dr.   Didn't she try to get you to share her vice?

P.P.   Oh no. She wasn't one to persist. Except that one day I did take a few drags. I remember it very well, 'cause it was the afternoon they came back.

Dr.   Who came back, Pacífico?

P.P.   Oh, didn't I say? The townspeople, from that neighborhood.

Dr.   They came back to Prádanos, to their homes?

P.P.   That's how it was, yes sir.

Dr.   You mean they *all* came back?

P.P.   I don't know if *all* of them did, but there were quite a few. You should've heard them laughing and teasing each other. What a racket!

Dr.   I don't understand a word you're saying, Pacífico.

P.P.   Well, there's not much to understand, Doctor. I was after Candi as usual, fooling around, you know. And I caught her at the plaza. And we were just starting to get cozy, when suddenly the windows and the streets and the doors were filled with people, and they were all laughing and kidding around.

Dr.   But where did they come from? Wasn't the town deserted when you got there?

P.P.   When we got there, yes. It was empty, as usual. But then it wasn't, and if you ask me, I think they were getting ready, inside the houses, I mean.

Dr.   Getting ready?

P.P.   Yeah. The women—they were wearing their black dresses and a scarf on their head. The men—they were in their berets and corduroy suits and white shirts—all dressed up for a party. And then the kids—you should've seen them: they crowded around us and made little digs. They had a ball.

Dr.   At your expense?

P.P.   Oh yeah, at our expense. There was Candi in her birthday suit and yours truly in his underpants—they got an eyeful all right!

Dr.   Are you sure you're not imagining things, Pacífico? Couldn't this be an effect from smoking that grass?

P.P.   What does one thing have to do with another? The smoking left me with a bad aftertaste, just in case you want to know; but that's another story. And if you want to hear more, on the palace's balcony there was an older man leaning on the railing. He was all dressed, except his red and black cape was moth-eaten, and he had a goatee and a moustache.

Dr.   What was he doing there? Did he say anything?

P.P.   Mainly he lowered and raised his head as if to convince himself that he had to bear it. And right at the corner, you know? right next to the spiral staircase, there was a pair of civil guards. But we didn't faze them a bit. They just elbowed each other and laughed, like everybody else.

Dr.   Well, if you say so, Pacífico, I guess I'll have to believe you. What was your reaction to a situation like that? What did you do?

P.P.   What *could* I do? I started running and didn't stop 'til I got to the Peralta Fountain.

Dr.   And Candi?

P.P.   Candi turned up later, with her clothes, about a half hour later. Fresh as a daisy. And I gave it to her, Doctor. I said I couldn't be dragged back to this town, never again. She just laughed and said, Well, they're not going to eat us alive.

Dr.   And tell me: Did Candi see what you saw?

P.P.   I couldn't say for sure, Doctor, and I didn't ask her, either. But if she said they weren't going to eat us alive, it must be because she saw somebody, don't you think?

Dr.   I don't know, Pacífico. It doesn't strike me as a convincing argument. And is it true that you never went back to Prádanos?

P.P.   Since that afternoon, I've never set foot in that town again.

Dr.   What did the two of you do? Where would you meet?

P.P.   Oh, we'd go for walks. To La Torca on some afternoons, other times to La Charca—it depended. But usually we'd go to the poplar grove at the Embustes, at the edge of the river.

Dr.   It was the middle of summer by then, wasn't it?

P.P.   Oh, we were practically into September. I mean the trees were studded with apples, with that wonderful aroma. It was really glorious out in the country about that time, Doctor.

Dr.   And did you change your ways with each other?

P.P.   Hmm? What do you mean?

Dr.   I mean, did you lead the same kind of life as before?

P.P.   The same, yeah, so's not to change.

Dr.   But the riverbanks—didn't you find more people there than in Prádanos?

P.P.   Well, sort of.

Dr.   And weren't you afraid of getting caught?

P.P.   Look, Candi was very determined, you know? And in the poplar grove, in the osiers, in the cattle shelter, there was a really nice little place.

Dr.   But didn't you risk running into somebody who was out there fishing, like your grandfather, for example?

P.P.   No sir, that wouldn't have happened. The trout season closes in my town on the day of the Virgin of the Assumption, middle of August. And after that the Embustes runs real cold, with troubled waters—which is why it's not good for crayfish. So there wouldn't have been any chance of that.

Dr.   And how about Candi—didn't she say she wanted to leave town?

P.P.   She always said it'd be in October.

Dr.   And did you still plan to go off with her?

P.P.   Well, I don't rightly know what to tell you. 'Round about then she was talking about the community again.

Dr.   And wasn't she counting on you for that?

P.P.   No sir. As far as the community was concerned, she wasn't counting on me.

Dr.   Weren't you planning a future in common, for both of you?

P.P.   Not really, no sir. I mean until she got pregnant she didn't even mention it.

Dr.   When did Candi find out she was pregnant?

P.P.   If I'm not mistaken, it was a week before the episode with Teotista. On September 3, to be exact.

Dr.   What did she say?

P.P.   At first she wanted to get rid of the creature, the fruit, you know? Said a kid would wreck her plans, and did Señora Dictrinia know anything about these matters.

Dr.   About performing an abortion?

P.P.   That's right. That's exactly what I mean. 'Cause she didn't trust Don Alfaro. Said he would rat on her to the priest.

Dr.   Then she changed her mind, right?

P.P.   The very next day.

Dr.   What did she decide then?

P.P.   That she wanted to marry me and have the baby.

Dr.   And what was your reply?

P.P.   To sit on it for a while. That I had to think it over.

Dr.   How did she take it?

P.P.   Pretty bad. She acted like an animal. Hit me twice and scratched my face. Left me covered with wounds.

Dr.   This took place a little before the incident with Teotista, right?

P.P.   Six days before, yes sir.

Dr.   May I ask why you didn't accept her proposition, Pacífico? Did the responsibility for a child seem overwhelming?

P.P.   Oh no, it wasn't because of the kid. But there was the other thing, see, that she'd cheated on me, and it wasn't just a joke. She even warned me about it.

Dr.   Yes, I see.

P.P.   As for the rest, it seems to me that everybody's responsible for the consequences of what he does. It's only natural.

Dr.   Fine, Pacífico. And tell me: Is there any other point about Candi that's relevant and you may have left out?

P.P.   Excuse me? I don't follow you.

Dr.   I mean, is there anything else about Candi you haven't told me yet?

P.P.   Well, as for anything big, no, I guess not, Doctor. I mean there's the bit about the visit, OK? But by then I was already in Góyar, and everything had happened already.

Dr.   We'll get to that later, Pacífico. For now, all I'd like to know is whether during those days, the last days especially, once Candi decided to respect the baby's life, anything happened that would lead me to believe that she wanted to pressure you into accepting marriage as a solution. Do you follow me?

P.P.   Oh yeah, sure.

Dr.   Do you remember anything?

P.P.   About that, no, nothing, sir.

Dr.   Fine. Go on.

P.P.   Well, one afternoon when we were sitting like this—like you and me right now—well, Teotista showed up. You already know the story.

Dr.   Don't trust my memory, Pacífico. I'd like for you to tell me everything, even what I already know, with as many details as possible.

P.P.   Well, Teotista showed up.

Dr.   Where were you and Candi?

P.P.   In the summer pasture, sitting, just like you and me right now. Except we were sitting on the grass, as usual.

Dr.   And were you naked?

P.P.   Well, she was. Candi, I mean. She was walking around naked. As for yours truly, I was in my jock strap and shorts.

Dr.   Forgive my indiscretion, Pacífico, but what were you doing at that moment?

P.P.   Nothing. And hey, I really mean nothing. Just sitting quietly in the sun shelling pine nuts.

Dr.   Roasted pine nuts, wasn't it?

P.P.   Roasted, yes sir. The kind that have a little slit down the middle, that you open with a jackknife.

Dr.   That is, you had the jackknife in your hand.

P.P.   Yes sir, in my hand. And Candi was just sitting there.

Dr.   I have a question, Pacífico: Did you notice whether Candi was surprised to see her brother appear?

P.P.   Course she was! She covered her teats with her arm like this, and with her other hand, you know?

Dr.   Didn't she say anything? Please, Pacífico, try to remember her precise words.

P.P.   OK. She said: What are *you* doing here, Teo? That's what she said.

Dr.   That's all?

P.P.   All's I can remember. Nothing else, Doctor.

Dr.   And do you think her surprised reaction was sincere? I mean, do you think it really surprised her to see him?

P.P.   Why shouldn't it, Doctor?

Dr.   How do you know it wasn't put on?

P.P.   Hey, she covered herself up right away. Oh, I get it! You're wondering if Candi and Teotista . . . if they were in cahoots. Is that it?

Dr.   Look, Pacífico, what I think doesn't matter right now. The main thing is to discover the truth. Do you think Candi was sincere when she acted surprised?

P.P.   Well, yes I do, Doctor.

Dr.   Let's move on to something else. Tell me about Teotista. What did his face look like when he got there?

P.P.   Well, let's see . . . Well, he *did* look annoyed.

Dr.   Furious, even?

P.P.   Yeah, I'd say he did, Doctor.

Dr.   Let's forget about the situation for a second, Pacífico. And try to forget what Teotista's usual character was like. Was he really beside himself that afternoon?

P.P.   Well, my guess is that he was. But you make it kind of hard.

Dr.   And how did he suddenly appear? Did you hear any noise?

P.P.   No, no noise. He crept into the pasture real foxy-like, making his way through the osiers with a stick. And then we saw him.

Dr.   So he was carrying a stick in his hand?

P.P.   Yes. A sort of javelin, in his right hand.

Dr.   And what did he say?

P.P.   At first he didn't say anything.

Dr.   You mean to say Candi spoke first?

P.P.   That's right. Candi said first, What are *you* doing here, Teo?

Dr.   And how about him? What did he answer? Be very careful, now. Try to recall exactly what he said and did.

P.P.   Well, he said: I already had a hunch about this, you little tramp, mixed up with the seven-monther from Humán. That's all he said, not another word.

Dr.   You're sure that was all?

P.P.   Yep. That's all he said.

Dr.   Did he get his javelin ready then?

P.P.   No sir. He mainly just stared at us—first at her and then at me. But he kept his mouth shut.

Dr.   And how about you—what were you doing in the meantime?

P.P.   Shelling pine nuts.

Dr.   Without even looking at him?

P.P.   That's right. Well, no, actually I'd look at him, and then I'd turn away for a while.

Dr.   Seated on the ground?

P.P.   Yeah, I just sat there.

Dr.   And when did you get up?

P.P.   When Teotista came over.

Dr.   To you, or to his sister?

P.P.   To me. Well actually to both of us. We were sitting next to each other.

Dr.   And once you got up, Pacífico, didn't Teotista pick up the stick as if he were going to hit you?

P.P.   Hey, you're starting to sound like the lawyer.

Dr.   Answer me, please. Did he pick it up, or didn't he?

P.P.   No sir. Teotista just stood there staring at me.

Dr.   And you, what did you feel at that moment, Pacífico?

P.P.   Cold. Between one thing and another, the night dew had come, and I'd hidden my girdle under the bushes.

Dr.   Fine, but let's leave that aside for now. Tell me, Pacífico: Deep down inside, what did you feel? Hatred, anger, confusion, shame? What was it?

P.P.   Not shame, sir. After four months I was used to walking around the countryside in my underpants.

Dr.   What did you feel, then?

P.P.   Nothing, as far as I know, Doctor.

Dr.   But you must have been upset, it seems to me.

P.P.   No sir, like I'm telling you: I wasn't confused or upset. I just missed not having my girdle on.

Dr.   Fine, all right. What did you do then?

P.P.   Well, as soon as I stood up, I had my knife in my right hand, and I threw it. At Teotista, I mean.

Dr.   What did Teotista do after your aggression?

P.P.   Nothing. He didn't have time. I mean he dropped the javelin and put his hands on his belly, where I'd wounded him, and he said: He's killed me. Then he fell to the ground, he curled up, his legs trembled a little, and he was still.

Dr.   Listen, Pacífico, wasn't your knife a toy—I mean just an instrument to open pine nuts and so on?

P.P.   Well, yeah. The blade was just five centimeters long.

Dr.   So how do you explain that only one throw was enough to kill a strong young man like Teotista?

P.P.   Look, Doctor, it's hard to tell with things like this. It's a question of luck.

Dr.   But in attacking him with such an innocent weapon, it's clear that you weren't planning to kill him. I mean, the fact that he died was fate, pure fate. The harm caused didn't go with the means used, don't you agree?

P.P.   Maybe that's how it was, Doctor, if you say so. But when I threw it at Teotista, I was out to get him. No doubt about that, Doctor. I've got to tell it like it was.

Dr.   And couldn't it have been your wish to dazzle Candi, to overcome those humiliations, that pushed you to homicide?

P.P.   No, it wasn't like that, Doctor. I got what I wanted out of Candi. I didn't need anything else.

Dr.   But in any case, Pacífico, I imagine that after you lost your temper you rushed over to help Teotista, didn't you?

P.P.   You're wrong on that, Doctor. I didn't lose my temper, and I already explained it all to the lawyer.

Dr.   Well, whatever you say, Pacífico. Did you or didn't you go to Teotista's aid after you knifed him?

P.P.   Me? No sir.

Dr.   What did you do, then?

P.P. Well, I recall that I pushed Candi away. She was all over me screaming that I'd killed him, see. So I went over to the bushes and slowly put on my girdle. Then I got dressed and went down to the barracks, where Sergeant Metodio was, and I told him. I mean I said, Sergeant, I killed Teotista, and I'm turning myself in. You understand?

Dr.   I understand, Pacífico. But is it really possible that you walked away from there without even looking at your victim's body?

P.P. Not exactly, no, Doctor. As for that, I *did* look at him. Candi had loosened his pants, see, and you could see a little black line on the right side of his belly. It wasn't even bleeding or anything.

Dr.   And did you do anything to help Candi then?

P.P. No sir.

Dr.   Well, what was *she* doing?

P.P. She was crying.

Dr.   She was crying, eh? Didn't she accuse you?

P.P. Yes and no. I mean she said, You killed him, Pacífico.

Dr.   Didn't she call you any of those names she used to call you— screwer, or bastard?

P.P. Not then, sir. She called me Pacífico.

Dr.   What do you attribute that to?

P.P. Well, if you ask me, Doctor, getting pregnant turned Candi into a different woman.

Dr.   You mean to say she even forgot about changing the world?

P.P. More or less, Doctor. She wanted to get married! I already told you.

Dr.   All right, Pacífico. I think we've reached a point where you need some serenity and clear judgment more than ever. I even think this final questioning has been hasty, and that we need to stop to think over your answers. We mustn't rush things. Go and rest now, and tomorrow we'll talk some more. Until tomorrow, son.

▲ ▲ ▲ ▲ ▲ ▲ ▲

Fifth Night

Dr. Hi, Pacífico. Make yourself comfortable. How are you? You know, I haven't done anything except turn over in my mind the events you told me about last night. I can't help it. Everything strikes me as very odd, to tell you the truth. I'd like to think that toward the end of our talk you were very tired, because no matter how hard I try, I can't fit together the pieces of this puzzle. How is it possible, for example, that when Bisa gave you a graphic account of the Galdamés story you urinated blood, and yet you were able to kill a man in cold blood, without batting an eye? It's just not acceptable, Pacífico. You've got to agree. The fact that you urinated blood indicated a strong shock, the kind that a hypersensitive person would have. Nevertheless, you insist that you just plain killed Teotista, without any motive. I mean, without his provoking you or threatening you, and that even after knifing him, you didn't go to his aid. I just can't assimilate it, son. I'd like to think that you were tired last night, that you were answering me without weighing your words, or that for some reason or other you were hiding part of the truth. Let's see now, Pacífico—and please, don't answer lightly—is it true that when you attacked Teotista, he hadn't provoked you?

P.P. Yes sir, it's true.

Dr. Are you prepared to swear to it?

P.P. As sure as it's night right now. Hey, I'm not fooling you.

Dr. Listen, Pacífico—and bear in mind that this question is extremely delicate—your girlfriend once told you up in Prádanos that if Teotista ever caught the two of you the way he did, that he might kill you. This much is true, right? Well, can you state categorically that in the instant you attacked him, the fear of this threat didn't affect you, even if only subconsciously?

P.P.   If you want to know the truth, Doctor, by then I didn't even remember that Teotista had sworn to kill me.

Dr.   All right, fine. But somewhere in the back of your mind, couldn't there have been an automatic defense mechanism?

P.P.   Who knows? I don't understand that stuff.

Dr.   But what did you feel when you wounded Teotista?

P.P.   That it was easy, hey.

Dr.   Nothing else?

P.P.   Well, and that he was soft. Softer than I expected.

Dr.   We're back to square one again. How do you expect me to believe that when you killed a man, your only thoughts were that he was soft and it was easy?

P.P.   Well, I'm not forcing you to. You can think what you like. I'm just telling you how it was.

Dr.   But, please, Pacífico. I'd like to understand how the idea of killing him entered your head.

P.P.   Well, if I really stop to think about it, I never said I took it into my head to do it. I mean, I did it, that's for sure, and it wasn't hard, understand?

Dr.   Well, no, I don't understand. I simply don't understand that you can wound another human being just like that. And I don't understand how you can wound him and then not help him. Much less in your case, you being a person whose pathological sensitivity makes you throw up because a dog's been shot, or makes your fingers sore when a tree's pruned?

P.P.   Wait a minute. By then, it didn't matter to me whether or not they were getting the olives off the trees. And the other stuff was when I was a kid.

Dr.   Tell me something, Pacífico: Even though you didn't give him a hand, you must've felt some repentance afterward, didn't you?

P.P.   I can't rightly say I did.

Dr.   Teotista was that bad a person?

P.P.   Well, as for being harmful, yeah, he was. Why deny it? But that doesn't have any bearing on this. I mean it would've been the same with anybody else.

Dr. And when you went down to the barracks and confessed your crime to Sergeant Metodio, didn't you regret it then, either?

P.P. Nope, I didn't sir.

Dr. Does this mean that you weren't aware of having sinned?

P.P. Well, not exactly. I mean I wasn't sorry, and that's the truth.

Dr. But how do you explain that you felt you *had* sinned several weeks before, with your physical excesses, and yet you didn't feel you'd sinned after killing a man?

P.P. I don't know. I guess that's how things are.

Dr. Listen, Pacífico, isn't Thou shall not kill a Commandment just like Thou shall not fornicate?

P.P. Well, yes sir. I guess you're right.

Dr. Well then?

P.P. They're two separate things.

Dr. What do you mean, separate?

P.P. Hey, you're starting to sound like the lawyer—just as stubborn. It's as if I'm supposed to say that I was scared and I helped him and then I repented, even though it's not true.

Dr. It's not that, Pacífico. Don't misinterpret me. There are things in your conduct that don't fit; I mean, they even clash. And that's what I'd like to clear up. That's why I'd like for you to tell me the truth.

P.P. That's what I'm doing, hey, but you're trying to take over.

Dr. Excuse me, Pacífico, if I get excited. Sometimes I'm set on my desires fitting in with reality, and if it doesn't work, I get upset, you understand? But I don't mean any harm. You believe me, don't you?

P.P. If you say so.

Dr. Good. Well, let's sum it up now: You went to see the sergeant, and you confessed your crime. What happened next?

P.P. Well, at first Sergeant Metodio made light of it. I mean, he wouldn't believe it.

Dr. Did he have a good impression of you?

P.P. On the one hand, yes. And then there was my father and my grandfathers—they were his buddies.

Dr. And how did he come to believe that it was true?

P.P. 'Cause I swore it, see. And as soon as I'd sworn it, he sent a couple of men down to the river, and they found the corpse. And that same night, Don Lucio came over—he's the forensic pathologist from Quintana—and he did the autopsy. On Teotista, I mean.

Dr. What did the pathologist say?

P.P. That it was true, that he'd died from a knife wound; that I'd killed him, in other words. What did you expect?

Dr. And they locked you up?

P.P. Oh, Sergeant Metodio took a couple of hours. It wasn't 'til dawn, the next day, that he sent me to jail. It was so Bisa and Abue and Father and everybody from home could say good-bye.

Dr. There, in the barracks?

P.P. Sure. Where else?

Dr. And did they come?

P.P. Why wouldn't they? But one by one, see. The sergeant said it had to be one at a time.

Dr. And who came first?

P.P. Bisa.

Dr. Was he affected by it?

P.P. Affected? Nah. He seemed happy.

Dr. Happy?

P.P. Yeah, he was happy.

Dr. Why do you suppose?

P.P. Look, ask him that.

Dr. Well, what did he say to you?

P.P. Well, at first he said that this would show the Otero gang. Then, 'cause of the symptoms, he said bayonets would be "my thing" too. And while he was saying this he started dancing around in his chair, and it was wiggling. Like a kid! You should've seen him!

Dr. And how about Abue? What did Abue say?

P.P. Too bad. I mean, that I'd done a good job of it. But that I should've waited 'til the season opened.

Dr. The season?

P.P. Yeah, the hunting season. In other words, that killing men was like killing wild boar: you have to do it when the time's right. 'Cause if you kill a boar in January, you get rewarded, but if you kill him in July you're sorry, see. Well, the same goes for men. You kill 'em in wartime and you get a medal, but you kill 'em when there's peace and off you go for a while.

Dr.   Who else came to see you?

P.P.   Everybody, Doctor. Everybody from home. The sergeant only allowed family, see.

Dr.   Not Candi?

P.P.   No, Candi wasn't allowed.

Dr.   Didn't she send you a letter or anything?

P.P.   Nothing, not a word. I didn't hear from her 'til I got sent to Góyar.

Dr.   And how about your father—how did he react?

P.P.   Oh, Father had ants in his pants. 'Cause of the henhouse, more than anything else. Well, anyway, Father told me to come back soon, that he needed me to run the business. He said these things don't do well if the owner doesn't keep his eye on them.

Dr.   Didn't he mention Emigdio?

P.P.   He couldn't help but mention him. He even said he was involved in crossbreeding partridges with guinea hens, you know? But don't go thinking Father cared much about that sort of stuff, about inventions, I mean.

Dr.   Didn't he say anything about paying for a lawyer?

P.P.   No sir. Didn't even bring it up.

Dr.   He didn't even mention your trial?

P.P.   Not once, no. The only person who looked out for me on that score was my Uncle Paco.

Dr.   What did your uncle say?

P.P.   Well, you know. That I could count on him for the lawyer and stuff.

Dr.   Did you accept?

P.P.   Look, I told him not to go to any trouble, but he said it wasn't any trouble, that it was the law. And then he came out with the other stuff.

Dr.   What other stuff?

P.P.   The usual—that not to worry, that it wouldn't get any worse. And while he was telling me that, I got this picture in my mind of the walking stick.

Dr.   Whose walking stick, Pacífico?

P.P.   Whose stick?! Well, his, of course. My Uncle Paco's walking stick.

The one he'd put between my legs when I was a kid. Don't you remember?

Dr. I don't recall. I don't know, son. I can't see the connection between one thing and another.

P.P. You can't see it? But it's as clear as day. He meant things wouldn't get any worse. In other words, that that was it. The limit, as they say.

Dr. But how about jail?

P.P. Jail?

Dr. Was your uncle suggesting that you couldn't sink any lower?

P.P. That's it exactly, Doctor.

Dr. And was he happy about it? Or do you think he suffered when he saw you in such a situation?

P.P. Well, the poor guy did have a long face.

Dr. But let's get something straight here, Pacífico: If your uncle said you couldn't sink any lower, he must have meant—it seems to me—that you were in an abject state, or something worse, right?

P.P. Well, not really, sir. I don't think he was driving at that.

Dr. What are you basing your hunch on?

P.P. Look, as soon as my Uncle Paco said I couldn't go any lower than jail, I caught his drift right away. I mean his walking stick came to me in a flash—what he used to do to me when I was a kid.

Dr. And how did you interpret it? What did you understand?

P.P. Well, just that—that I couldn't hurt myself anymore.

Dr. What do you mean, you couldn't hurt yourself anymore?

P.P. Let's see, how I can explain this? It's like what you know—nobody could take it away from me anymore, understand? He'd already given it to me. So all there was left was to live. It was that easy.

Dr. I'm sorry. My interpretation seems more correct.

P.P. Hey, you really are hardheaded. It goes to show what happens when somebody doesn't want to understand something. My Uncle Paco, in case you want to know, meant that I could rest my mind now.

Dr. In jail?

P.P. In jail, right, 'cause nothing else could happen.

Dr. But these are just your suppositions, Pacífico.

P.P.   No, they're not. He made it plain as day. I mean, as soon as he said, You can't go any lower, I asked him: Even if Bisa decides on something else? And he said: Even if Bisa decides on something else. And me: Even if Candi comes after me? And him: Even if Candi comes after you. And me: Even if there's a rock fight with the Otero gang? And him: Even if there's a rock fight with the Otero gang. And me: Even if my war comes, Uncle? And him, cool as a cucumber: Even if your war comes, Pacífico, it won't go beyond this.

Dr.   But your uncle's philosophy was kind of strange, wasn't it?

P.P.   What do you mean, strange?

Dr.   You tell *me*, Pacífico. According to his rules, jail was freedom.

P.P.   More or less, yeah, that's what he meant.

Dr.   Did he say that jail was freedom?

P.P.   Well, something of that nature.

Dr.   Be specific. What did he say, Pacífico?

P.P.   Oh, I can't recall exactly, Doctor.

Dr.   But with that theory, why would he be paying for a lawyer?

P.P.   To do me justice, hey.

Dr.   But with his ideas it didn't matter whether or not they did you justice, did it?

P.P.   No sir. For him, justice came first. Except that he didn't believe in justice.

Dr.   He didn't believe in justice, and he was paying for your lawyer?

P.P.   Don't cross the wires on me, Doctor. He said once while we were at La Torca that he'd rather die than judge a man. Those were his words.

Dr.   But somebody's got to do it, son. Don't you understand?

P.P.   That's why my uncle was paying for my lawyer, see.

Dr.   OK, Pacífico, you win. These Byzantine arguments aren't getting us anywhere anyway. Let's drop it. When the farewells were over, what did Sergeant Metodio do with you?

P.P.   He packed me up. And the next morning he sent me to the city with two numbers on me. To the judge. And from there they sent me to La Provincial.

Dr.   What kind of an impression did it make on you to see the iron bars clang down behind you?

P.P.   Oh, I don't know. I just said to myself: Well, now you can have a quiet life, Pacífico.

Dr.   Did the iron bars give you a sense of security?

P.P.   Yeah, they did.

Dr.   Didn't you think about your family? There are prisoners who say that being locked up feels like drowning. They say that in one minute all you've ever experienced your whole life flashes through your mind. Did something like that happen to you?

P.P.   No, not really, sir. Think about them? About my family, yeah, I thought about them. But not the other stuff.

Dr.   Did you feel sorry for them when you thought about them?

P.P.   I don't know. Well, I guess I do recall that I said to myself: Well, you're all out there now. But that was it.

Dr.   And did you feel content when you said, Well, you're all out there now, because you hadn't stayed out there too?

P.P.   Yeah, that's right.

Dr.   If somebody had said to you at that moment: Hey, Pacífico, you can go home, would you have been glad to go home?

P.P.   No sir.

Dr.   Out of fear, maybe?

P.P.   Out of fear, yes sir.

Dr.   But weren't the characters you met in there more dangerous?— in prison, I mean, as opposed to the outside world.

P.P.   Not on your life. They were a little ignorant, sure, but they weren't bad, those guys in prison. Not at all.

Dr.   OK. Well, now tell me about your first experience in jail.

P.P.   Well, what do you want to know?

Dr.   Oh, I don't know—what you did, whom you talked to, how the trial went—things like that.

P.P.   Look, first they stuck me in a cell. As you go in, it was on the left, next to the surveillance center. And they kept me in there for two weeks.

Dr.   Alone?

P.P.   At first, yes sir, although there was room for somebody else. And later on somebody was brought in.

Dr.   They put someone else in with you?

P.P.   Three days later. A blond kid. He was classy, you know? I remember his name was Bernardo, but the other guys, out in the courtyard, they called him Pocholo. And of course spending so many hours in there together, we ended up getting to know each other.

Dr. What did you talk about, Pacífico?

P.P. Bernardo taught me a lot. I mean, for example, how you could tell the guards' rank by their uniforms. Three rhombs, the director; two, the assistant director; and one, the chief of staff, see? And it was the same with the officers, except they wore angles. And the horn: how they played it—whether it was reveille or a war call, or fall out, or retreat. That stuff, you know. I mean, he taught me what I needed; 'cause if you stop to think about it, I was like a goat in a garage.

Dr. So your friendship with Bernardo was useful, you mean.

P.P. Oh yeah. I mean, like it was Bernardo who told me, when we came out of the meeting with the judges the first time: Don't waste your breath with the lawyers. It's all the same. The D.A. will stick you with ten, the lawyer with one, and in the end, the judge will give you five. That's how it goes. Doesn't matter whether you talk or not.

Dr. And was that how it turned out?

P.P. More or less, Doctor.

Dr. And what was that fellow Bernardo in for?

P.P. That I couldn't tell you, hey. According to him, they'd nailed him by mistake.

Dr. Hmm. And were you in there with him for long?

P.P. Oh, about eight or ten days. But toward the end we got into a fight.

Dr. Why did you fight?

P.P. What can I say? That guy Bernardo turned out to be gay, a little sissy. One night he starts saying he's cold, and would I get into bed with him. And when I said no, he jumped into mine. Anyway, since I didn't want to rat on him I ended up off my cot. I spent the whole night standing up with my back to the wall 'til reveille, and I could hardly stand up. That was the worst part about the clink—all those gay guys. I guess you have to understand it, so many men by themselves. But let me tell you this: If that little Pocholo had met up with Patita instead of me, his goose would've been cooked.

Dr. Who was Patita?

P.P.   Somebody from Góyar, a cellmate.

Dr.   OK, but wait. Don't go so fast, Pacífico. Let's take one thing at
       a time. Tell me about the lawyer. How did he handle your case?
       When did he come to see you?

P.P.   Roughly about a week after I was locked up. I can remember the
       guard announcing, Pacífico Pérez, to the judges! And me being
       new and all, I didn't even know what he meant. So he opens the
       door and walks me down to the visiting room. And in there, on
       the other side of the window, was the lawyer—and what a speci-
       men *he* was! Tall as a beanpole, but with wide shoulders, and
       wearing glasses like mine. And as soon as he saw me he had me
       sit down and listened, all ears; but after a while whatever he said
       was law, and you couldn't let out a peep.

Dr.   What do you mean?

P.P.   It's like I'm saying: He'd set things up his own way, and that's
       how it had to be. In other words, Teotista was a criminal who pro-
       voked me 'cause he didn't want me talking to his sister, see. And
       he chased after me with the javelin. And when he hit me, I was
       smart and grabbed him by the hand, and as Teotista was raising
       the javelin I stuck him with my jackknife. I got to him first . . .

Dr.   And didn't you tell the lawyer . . . ?

P.P.   Course I did. I tried. But don't think he let me. I'd open my
       mouth, and he'd say, Listen. You'd think he was the one that had
       given it to Teotista. Just so you'll understand: He'd already made
       up the story, and he wanted me to learn it by heart to spit it out
       just the way he wanted in the courtroom, to the judges.

Dr.   What did he base his defense on?

P.P.   Didn't I explain it? Teotista didn't like me talking to Candi. So
       he'd sworn to take my life, and he was after me with a stick behind
       my ears. So because of him Candi and I had to meet secretly.
       But one afternoon he caught us together down by the river. He
       tore me down in front of her, called me a seven-monther. And I
       asked him to apologize, but him, what he did was to light into her
       and call her a whore and all—and may God forgive my tongue.
       So, according to the lawyer, I tried to calm him down. Teotista, I
       mean. But as soon as I saw him go for the pole, I knew he was out
       to get me, see. And then things got blurry, and I lost my head, and

I stuck him. In other words, legitimate self-defense, and defense of my girlfriend. And by looking at the weapon, the jury—that's what he called the courtroom, the lawyer, I mean—or rather the judges, could see for themselves that I didn't mean to cause the huge harm that I did. In other words, if I killed Teotista, it was just by accident, understand? And I wanted to tell him that that's not how it was. But he didn't pay any attention to me. The lawyer, I mean. He just said, You: listen here. There were no buts about it. The only thing that counted was his version.

Dr.   What happened at the trial, Pacífico?

P.P.   Well, at first—in the morning, I mean—the guard warned me about it. He said to dress up nice, you know? And at five minutes to nine on the dot, the two escorts came to pick me up, and they took me over and sat me down on a low stool to wait. And when the judges arrived and the president called out, Ladies and gentlemen of the court! people started coming in, and pretty soon it was jammed. You couldn't squeeze in another soul. They were just the townspeople, though.

Dr.   How did you feel at that moment, Pacífico? Were you calm?

P.P.   Oh, yes sir. I was calm.

Dr.   And how did things get under way?

P.P.   Well, let's see. When it started, the president was very attentive: What was my first name, my mother's and father's last names, had I been on trial before . . . you know.

Dr.   And the prosecutor?

P.P.   Oh, that's another story! I mean, that man you're asking about: Well, he starts questioning me, OK? But as soon as I saw what he was after I sealed my lips. Where would I have gotten if I'd crossed him?

Dr.   But what stand did the prosecutor take?

P.P.   Well, if you read between the lines of what he was saying, what that man thought was that I'd sworn to take Teotista's life, and that I'd made up the part about the pine nuts just to have an excuse for having the knife on me, so I could be ready when the time came. He said I was a sly one—a bum without a job or anything to offer—and that I'd acted in a deceitful way, abusing people's trust in me.

Dr.   He said all that?

P.P.   More or less, yes sir.

Dr.   You must've been nervous.

P.P.   Nervous? No. Why should I be nervous?

Dr.   Tell me, how about the lawyer? What did he say?

P.P.   Well, you know. Like the others, except from his angle.

Dr.   What do you mean, from his angle?

P.P.   Well, I mean he asked me yes-and-no questions, so my answers would fit in.

Dr.   And what did you do?

P.P.   The opposite. I said no when he expected a yes. And vice versa.

Dr.   But you must have ruined his defense with that . . . ?

P.P.   Yeah. That's what he said later. The lawyer, I mean.

Dr.   And how about the judge?

P.P.   Once the lawyer got it all mixed up and started shuffling his papers, it seemed as if that piqued his curiosity. The judge's, I mean. And he said to let me speak, and he even cupped his ear to hear me better.

Dr.   And what did you say?

P.P.   The truth, of course. That neither the lame man that spoke at the beginning nor the other one, the one in glasses, was right. Well, you have no idea of the commotion *that* stirred! Over such a minor detail. The judge finally had to ring his bell.

Dr.   And once he called the court to order, you let the whole thing fall through.

P.P.   Fall through? What do you mean? I did not. What happened was that they got into a mess, the lawyer and the cripple. I mean, one of them shouted that since I had already confessed, there was nothing to go against, and the other one disagreed and said the sentence should be postponed 'til after a medical examination, because when I had opposed my own defense it was proof enough that I wasn't right in the head.

Dr.   Did the jury agree to interrupt the trial?

P.P.   Oh yeah, they looked all concerned and said we should.

Dr.   And how about the medical exam?

P.P.   That too.

Dr.   And how did it go?

P.P.   Well, I can't complain. They appointed two experts, Doctor Raimundo Peñuelas and Don Luis María Cárdenas, but I hardly got a glimpse of Dr. Peñuelas—he wasn't feeling so hot.

Dr.   Was he ill?

P.P.   Well, sort of, you know.

Dr.   How about Dr. Cárdenas?

P.P.   He wasn't. Don Luis María really took it to heart: he never left me alone for a second. He was out to prove that I was nuts. For my own good, of course. And I'm not blaming him—his intentions were good—but every single thing I'd do, he'd write it down. Like if I took off my glasses for a while, or if I laughed. 'Cause according to him, you can tell from those little things.

Dr.   Whether someone's disturbed?

P.P.   That's what he said.

Dr.   Well, it's true, it's a fact: a physical exam does give us data. But the conclusions come only after you've studied all the facts. They must have asked you a lot of questions, didn't they?

P.P.   Oh yeah, they got their fill. Don Luis María even asked me about my mother.

Dr.   Heredity has considerable importance, Pacífico. Didn't they make you tell your life's story to them?

P.P.   That was the first thing they asked, yeah.

Dr.   Were you sincere?

P.P.   Sure.

Dr.   Didn't you tell the expert that you could remember the day you were born?

P.P.   No, not that.

Dr.   Why did you leave it out?

P.P.   He wouldn't have believed me. Nobody does. Why should I waste my time?

Dr.   That was very wrong, Pacífico. Did you tell him that when you saw a tree pruned your fingers hurt so bad you could hardly stand it?

P.P.   No sir. I didn't tell him that either.

Dr.   And that you sometimes felt the fig tree crying?

P.P.   None of that, Doctor. 'Cause I figured that if I mentioned that stuff, Don Luis María would end up saying I was nuts.

Dr. Of course! That was the whole point, Pacífico! What kind of sincerity is it when you leave out everything that could give the report meaning?

P.P. Hey, don't get upset. I knew I wasn't nuts and . . .

Dr. You can't know if you're crazy or not.

P.P. Is that so, Doctor? Could I be nuts and not know it?

Dr. Listen, Pacífico. From the moment the jury decided to have you undergo a medical examination, you shouldn't have decided you'd tell one thing and keep another to yourself. You should tell everything, to facilitate a precise diagnosis, do you understand?

P.P. I'm getting to that. If I didn't tell Don Luis María certain things, it was because I didn't want any misunderstandings.

Dr. But listen, Pacífico. It's him, Don Luis María himself, who, in view of the facts that you provide, should determine your condition, not you. But for that he has to have handy the results of all his inquiries. Now if you go and keep things to yourself, or you omit something, you disorient him, and the conclusions aren't valid, do you see? Why are you staring at me? What's wrong?

P.P. Look, if there's one thing I regret, it's having said too much now.

Dr. No, it's not that. It shouldn't bother you, Pacífico. I promise that without your consent I won't say a word, and I'll stick to it. You can rest assured: I won't deceive you.

P.P. But do you really think I'm nuts, Doctor?

Dr. Listen, Pacífico, an emotional instability, no matter what provokes it, doesn't mean that you're nuts. There are millions of unstable people who adapt to daily life.

P.P. But I'm not nuts, Doctor. I swear it to you, on my mother's honor.

Dr. Of course not, Pacífico. Did I say otherwise?

P.P. You're thinking it, and that's enough for me.

Dr. Who says that I think that you're disturbed?

P.P. Well, I don't know. I mean, you think that if I tell Don Luis María what I've told you, that he would've said I was nuts.

Dr. I didn't say any such thing, Pacífico. All I'm saying is that in a medical exam there shouldn't be any reticence.

P.P. Look, Doctor, if I'd let the cat out of the bag they would've said I was nuts. And you know as well as I do that it's not true.

Dr.   And who's to say that being like you are, Pacífico, an apparently controlled man, that you don't suffer certain anomalies in your personality, or hallucinations, or delirious ideas, or some other suffering that weakens or annuls your sense of responsibility?

P.P.   I say so, and that's enough.

Dr.   In that case there's no more to be said, Pacífico. You're very stubborn. Frequently, those anomalies are covered up, so the patient is the last one to find out about them. For example, didn't the doctor ask you if you heard voices of strange or unfamiliar people?

P.P.   Sure. Of course he asked me.

Dr.   You see?

P.P.   Hey, yeah. Come to think of it, Don Luis María asked me some funny stuff. What do you suppose he asked me one day?

Dr.   What?

P.P.   If it was hard for me to urinate in front of other people. Imagine!

Dr.   What are you laughing about, Pacífico? What did you say?

P.P.   What was I supposed to say? If they were real close, like looking and all, you know, well, yes—I couldn't. Some conversation, that one!

Dr.   And could you please tell me this: What interested him most, of everything you told him?

P.P.   The part about Grandma Benetilde. Like, he wanted to know if there were any more cases in the family.

Dr.   Of suicide?

P.P.   Yes sir, of suicide.

Dr.   Did you tell him about the crown?

P.P.   No sir, I didn't hardly mention the crown.

Dr.   And about your great-grandfather making you all shoot a dog, and leading a drill every morning?

P.P.   Yes, I told him that.

Dr.   And didn't it shock him?

P.P.   At first, it sure did, like I told you. But once I told him that in Humán they said Bisa was at least a hundred, he didn't pay any attention to it.

Dr.   He didn't pay any attention to it?

P.P.   Well, you know. He said it was a sign he was senile.

Dr. Yes.

P.P. Old people, on the whole, they're, well, let's just say they're all cracked. That's what he meant, you know?

Dr. Yes. To sum it up, the report was negative: you weren't considered disturbed.

P.P. No, I wasn't, no sir.

Dr. And how did you find out?

P.P. On my own, understand? I mean one morning they called me in to court, and one of the employees said that the jury hadn't swallowed the part about me being crazy. And that therefore I'd have to stand trial again.

Dr. And what happened?

P.P. Oh, it was OK. It was all just like the first time. Except there weren't so many people, 'cause I guess everything gets boring after a while.

Dr. Did you support the lawyer this time?

P.P. Why should I support him? I told my version, see? But don't think he insisted too much. I mean after his disappointment, don't think he put himself into it anymore.

Dr. And they gave you twelve years and a day, right?

P.P. That's right, sir. Twelve years and a day.

Dr. Didn't the world come crashing down on you when you heard it?

P.P. Why in heaven's name should it? Of course not.

Dr. All right. Where did you start to serve your sentence?

P.P. Right there, in La Provincial. But the idea was to transfer me to a prison later.

Dr. And did they?

P.P. No sir. The vomiting happened first.

Dr. How was that?

P.P. The silliest thing, listen. I mean, one night when I was getting into my cot—no nausea or anything—I suddenly felt like I was going to throw up. And I felt it again. Then I did throw up and made an awful mess. Just like that, in a minute.

Dr. It was blood, wasn't it?

P.P. Blood, yes sir. The guard almost jumped out of his skin when he saw it.

Dr. And so you went back to the doctor?

P.P. Oh yeah. First I went to the jail doctor, but he couldn't treat me. Next morning we grabbed a car for the hospital.

Dr. A car? You must have liked riding in a car, didn't you, Pacífico?

P.P. Don't think I did, no sir. It made me dizzy.

Dr. Who went with you? Did you feel the urge to escape?

P.P. The things you come up with! Where else could I go that was better?

Dr. I don't know! To the town.

P.P. Well, some picture I would've made, showing my face around town.

Dr. By town, I only mean another place, Pacífico. What I want to know is whether you were tempted to escape from there and recover your freedom.

P.P. What freedom, Doctor?

Dr. What freedom? The only kind there is—what people in the street have, what normal people have.

P.P. And do you really believe they're freer than I am, Doctor?

Dr. All right, Pacífico, you win. So you checked in at the hospital. What did the doctor say?

P.P. Well, he took my temperature, he looked at my chest, he gave me some X rays—the works. So anyway, after all that he went and sent me to another doctor.

Dr. For more tests?

P.P. Yes sir. They took my blood, and they made me urinate into a test tube. It just wouldn't come out, hey! They had to turn on the faucet and leave me alone.

Dr. So to sum up, Pacífico: After the exploratory tests, they diagnosed you as ill, isn't that so?

P.P. Yeah, in my chest. They said I had something in my chest. I mean the doctor sent word to the director, and the guard told me; he said they'd be taking me to a penitentiary sanatorium. And that's how I got to Góyar.

Dr. From your admission to La Provincial until your transfer to the sanatorium, how much time elapsed?

P.P. Look, it's clear-cut, Doctor. I killed Teotista on the ninth of September, right? Well, by the night of the tenth I was already into La Provincial. And about August 17 the following year I left for Góyar. So there you have it.

Dr.   And during all that time, did you carry on any correspondence with your people? Did you receive any letters from your town?

P.P. Well, there was one from Don Prócoro and another from Señora Dictrinia. It was through them that I found out that Corina and Emigdio were engaged and that I'd become a father.

Dr.   Didn't anyone write you from home?

P.P. Look, it's easier for the whole town to be destroyed than to get Bisa or Father to pick up a pen. And it's not that they're illiterate, no. It's just that they don't write letters.

Dr.   Didn't they come to see you, either?

P.P. No sir. Except for my Uncle Paco, who came once.

Dr.   You must have liked that, didn't you?

P.P. Sure, it's always nice to have a visitor.

Dr.   And what did he have to say?

P.P. Well, as I recall, he told me that my future brother-in-law, Emigdio, I mean, had made the hens wear lenses.

Dr.   Lenses?

P.P. You heard me right. And that it was doing OK—the hen business, that is—and that Father was happy. And he also told me—I'd already gotten it from Señora Dictrinia—that Candi had given birth to a baby boy and she'd named him Pacífico. Imagine.

Dr.   What was your reaction when you found out you'd become a father?

P.P. OK. It was only natural, after all. Since I'd been expecting it for nine months, it wasn't any big deal.

Dr.   How about Candi? Didn't Candi come to see you?

P.P. Not 'til I got to Góyar, no sir. Once I was in Góyar, yes. They called me into the visiting room, and there she was—Candi with the kid. The way it should be.

Dr.   How old was your son then?

P.P. Oh, going on six months, Doctor. He could already say Papá, and he sucked his thumb.

Dr.   Your son could speak when he was five months old, Pacífico?

P.P.   Wait a minute. Don't go so fast. All the kid could say was Papá. And he sure said it—over and over.

Dr.   She probably taught him to.

P.P.   I guess so, yeah.

Dr.   Speaking frankly, Pacífico, weren't you moved by it?

P.P.   Not really, no sir. To tell you the truth, Doctor, I couldn't get that bit about "bastard" out of my head. I mean, I felt like it was nailed to my brain . . . bastard . . . may God forgive me. Do you understand?

Dr.   But how about her? Did you find her different?

P.P.   Oh yeah, she'd changed. She was sort of, like, stronger. And when I saw the kid hanging from her breast, she didn't look like herself, the way she'd been in Prádanos.

Dr.   I was referring to her personality, Pacífico. What did she say? What did she talk about?

P.P.   Well, you can just imagine, that the kid was all over her, nursing, that he did this and he did that, you know. And that Señor Bebel, her father, after the thing with Teotista, had wanted to make mincemeat of her, there at home with the kid and everything.

Dr.   And how about her plans? Didn't she speak of her plans?

P.P.   About getting married, you mean? What could we do? She said we ought to get married right there in jail. And I told her that the kid didn't deserve to have a prisoner for a father.

Dr.   What was her reply?

P.P.   That it was better to have a prisoner for a father than not to have one at all. And maybe she was right, I won't say she wasn't. But you see, I just couldn't forget about being called a bastard. I'm just telling you what I felt.

Dr.   So you told her no, then.

P.P.   More or less, yeah. I told her to wait. That I'd think it over.

Dr.   And what did she say?

P.P.   Well, what could she say, after all? I told her there were lots of ways to stay together without sticking.

Dr.   Did she accept this?

P.P.   To tell you the truth, she ended up in tears.

Dr.   She cried?

P.P.   Did she ever! Some case of the hiccups, too.

Dr.   Didn't it weaken your will?

P.P.   If you mean didn't I say yes to the wedding, no sir, I didn't.

Dr.   Didn't you soften up when you saw the baby? What did you feel when it said Papá?

P.P.   I felt sorry.

Dr.   Why did you feel sorry?

P.P.   Babies have always made me feel sorry for them, Doctor. Who knows why? And more so my own. With the situation I was in . . .

Dr.   What else did Candi say?

P.P.   Well, I don't rightly recall, Doctor. All I can remember is that she brought me some homemade sausages and rolls.

Dr.   Didn't she say anything about Bisa or Abue?

P.P.   She said they were OK, and that Emigdio lived with them now, at home, I mean. Oh yes! Come to think of it, she also told me that my brother-in-law's hens had died, and I said, The ones with the lenses? and she said, What do you mean, the ones with the lenses? The whole lot of them, from the epidemic.

Dr.   So you didn't resolve anything with her?

P.P.   We agreed to wait. That's all.

Dr.   Fine. We were talking about your transfer to Góyar. Who took you there?

P.P.   Two policemen.

Dr.   On the highway?

P.P.   No sir, we used the railroad.

Dr.   What impression did your new quarters make on you?

P.P.   It was OK. I mean, being as how I had something in my chest they were nicer to me. At first they put me in a room with four other men, all of them infected, you know? And since the prison, or the sanatorium, was like a castle, the room was sort of round, like a bucket, and the cots went around the outside. Well, anyway, from up there we could almost see the sky, you know? There was only one grilled window two meters up from the floor, but in the afternoons we could enjoy looking at the town and the mountain range, and according to my cellmates, Madrid was behind it. So we didn't have any complaints to speak of.

Dr.   Did you like it better than La Provincial?

P.P.   Sort of, yeah. At least we were in the country. And on days when the north wind blew, you could even hear the cowbells ringing.

Dr.   Did you get used to it right away?

P.P.   Sure. It was an easy life, you know? The afternoon I was admitted, with the business about the toilets, I said to myself: Some snake pit. But no, it wasn't.

Dr.   What was the business about the toilets, Pacífico?

P.P.   Sheer coincidence. I mean, the day I was admitted, they were pissed off—the inmates, I mean—about meals, see. And so they started banging the toilet seats up and down—making a real racket—it sounded like a metal shop or something. And the officials and the guard were going all over the place. They didn't know how to stop it. And there was Don Avelino saying, Cut it out, boys; cut it out. But it didn't do any good. He might just as well have been talking to the stones.

Dr.   The official called the inmates boys?

P.P.   That's right. You've never seen a more considerate or prudent man than Don Avelino. And don't go thinking he was a pipsqueak or anything. Oh no, he was big as a fortress. But that's how he was.

Dr.   Were those outbreaks frequent?

P.P.   Oh, no sir. Just by chance—I went in and walked right into it, the riot, I mean.

Dr.   Did they take you straight to your cell?

P.P.   Well, actually, they called them halls there. Mine was San José Hall.

Dr.   So they put you in San José Hall, then?

P.P.   That's right, yes sir. Don Avelino himself took me. And once we were there he made the introductions—to Don Santiago, see. Everybody called him Don Santiago. He was the only one they called Don. The others were Patita, Capullo, and Buque. And they called yours truly Seminarista. I still don't know who baptized me with that. Right from the start, eh?

Dr.   What did Don Santiago say?

P.P.   Well, for a starter he gave me a nice welcome, and after that he started talking to Don Avelino. About the riot, see. I mean Don Avelino asked him to step in, to speak to the inmates, you know?

And if he agreed, then he, Don Avelino, I mean, would take an interest in his case, and that it was better like that, 'cause if things got up to the next level, we'd all be in for it, especially the inmates. You should've seen them there talking—anybody would've thought Don Santiago was the boss. He had so much poise. You could tell from way off he was from a good family—by the way he carried himself. Tell you the truth, soon as I saw him I thought of my Uncle Paco.

Dr. Because of his authoritative presence?

P.P. Yeah, that was it. Don Avelino was asking him to step in like an equal, like one of them. And Don Santiago took it in stride. After Don Avelino persuaded him finally, he said yes, he'd speak to them, but that the food was awful and they had to improve it. So Don Avelino said OK, just to leave it to him, and he'd take care of it, see? But just so's to keep order in the house he'd have to lock up Capullo and a man called Morris, from San Vicente Hall, for a few days. The troublemakers. And I thought to myself, Don Santiago is going to give him a no; but he only said to Capullo: Go with him. And that was it. And Capullo didn't so much as blink. He was off with the guard in nothing flat.

Dr. And when Don Avelino left, did Don Santiago speak to you?

P.P. No sir. He stretched out on his cot and started reading a book, same as if he'd been by himself.

Dr. How about you—what did you do?

P.P. Well, I couldn't do much of anything. I just stayed there, quiet, you know, sitting on the cot, 'til Buque came up to me.

Dr. Who was Buque?

P.P. Another guy in San José Hall. One that had an eye like this— sort of cockeyed, so it was all white sometimes.

Dr. What did he say?

P.P. He asked me if I'd seen a carriage at the door.

Dr. A carriage?

P.P. Yeah. But that guy wasn't all there. Anyway, I said no at first, that I hadn't seen any carriage at the door. And he said it *had* to be there. We got into this thing about the carriage, and it went on and on. 'Til I finally figured out that when Buque said carriage he meant funeral. Let me explain myself: In the courtyard, next to the infirmary, there was the depository, and since all of us inmates were there 'cause we had something wrong with us, with our chests, I mean, well, scarcely a day went by without somebody passing on. So in the afternoon, when we were all in the gallery, the black cart might go by, and we'd kill time watching how they brought out the dead person and hearing the family sobbing, you know? But Buque was dead set on it—he said the carriage was for him, and it was waiting for him to come out. Every afternoon it was the same old story, so after a while, since everybody'd heard it over and over, nobody bothered to contradict him. So that's why when I got there, if there was a carriage at the door? Well, you can imagine me, I'd say, What? and him, he'd go on and on the whole blessed afternoon. He was a tough nut to crack, hardheaded and ignorant as they come, that Buque, the most ignorant one in the hall. It got to the point that—would you believe what he came out with one night?

Dr. What, Pacífico?

P.P. He asked who San José was. The one the hall was named after, mind you. Me, I said, He was the father of Christ. Just to shut him up, of course. But he was in a stupor or something. He goes and asks me, Is God San José? And so on, kept pestering me. I've never seen anybody so dumb, believe me. I swear to you.

Dr. And tell me, that fellow Buque: What sort of terms was he on with Don Santiago?

P.P. Oh, about like the rest. Some were closer to him than others, but all of us in the hall knew Don Santiago one way or another.

Dr. In what way?

P.P. Well, we served him.

Dr. And what kind of service did you perform for him?

P.P. Oh, we'd do one thing one day, and something else another. Like, for example, we'd brush his tabard and wash his clothes.* We'd even be his taxi.

Dr. His taxi?

P.P. Yes sir, his taxi. We'd take him down to the courtyard or out to the gallery. So when it was time, somebody—it could be anybody—

*Translator's Note: A tabard is a wide, loose worker's coat.

> would go up to him and say, The taxi's here, Don Santiago. And he'd either take it or he wouldn't, depending on what he felt like.

Dr.   But how did he "take" it? What sort of taxi is there in a prison?

P.P.   Wait a minute, Doctor. What we called a taxi was our rib cage. I mean we'd take Don Santiago down piggyback, like when we were kids. Don Santiago said he was very sick and couldn't tire himself, see. And sometimes he'd give us a nickel for our service and other times nothing.

Dr.   But did you do this out of fear?

P.P.   Oh, no sir. We waited on him with pleasure.

Dr.   Do you mind telling me what sort of person this Don Santiago was?

P.P.   I've already told you—he was a man with authority. Even Vegas, the guard, admitted that he was a competent man.

Dr.   Tell me about him, Pacífico.

P.P.   About Vegas?

Dr.   No, Don Santiago. What was he in for?

P.P.   He had a problem with his chest, too.

Dr.   I mean as a prisoner. What crime had he committed?

P.P.   Look, Don Santiago had money, like more than thirty million, in England. I heard it on the grapevine that Don Santiago embezzled somebody and then he took off for a foreign country to live the life of Riley. But one day they go and tell him that another guy is going to be sentenced on account of the embezzlement, an innocent guy, I mean, a patsy, like they say. And as soon as Don Santiago found out he grabbed a plane for Madrid: I'm the one that did it, they say he confessed. So the judge says, Well, hand over the money, but him, Don Santiago, he said, Not that. Understand? In other words he kept the dough stashed away, and if he came back, it was only so an innocent man wouldn't suffer on his account.

Dr.   Not even a child would fall for that story, Pacífico.

P.P.   Well, as for me . . . I'll keep my opinions to myself, but he sure was loaded.

Dr.   How did you notice that he was loaded? Because he paid a nickel for the taxi service?

P.P.   Oh, no, that was the least of it. To start with, he got his meals served from a bar in town. A waiter dressed in white would come, every day. Do you think that's free?

Dr.   But didn't he organize the toilet seat riot? What did Don Santiago care how it turned out?

P.P.   The things you say, Doctor! 'Cause he was humane, that's why. Humane.

Dr.   And when he rode piggyback on sick inmates, was that being humane, too?

P.P.   Look, Doctor, don't twist things. Don Santiago was in pretty bad shape. I mean he was always coughing, always. On a day he was better he didn't take a taxi. The man had a big heart, trust me. I mean, he looked out after others. Whether you were in the gallery or the courtyard, it was Don Santiago this, Don Santiago that. Everybody was hounding him, asking his advice. He was an engineer, you know. Don't think he was some nobody.

Dr.   How did he get along with the prison director and staff?

P.P.   Oh, he talked with them.

Dr.   What do you mean, he talked with them?

P.P.   Well, it was like they looked up to him, you know? So he could go have a cup of coffee where the director and the staff had theirs. Nobody told him he couldn't. Money talks, you know, Doctor.

Dr.   Did Don Santiago have many visitors?

P.P.   Mainly one woman—she came a lot.

Dr.   How do you know it was a woman?

P.P.   Some of the guys saw her. Like Capullo, for instance. And anyway, you didn't have to see her. He'd come back to the hall reeking of perfume. Don Santiago, I mean.

Dr.   Did they see each other in the visiting room?

P.P.   Oh, no sir. In the workshop, next to the commissary, out back, alone.

Dr.   I see, Pacífico. And how about the everyday treatment—was it different for Don Santiago than for the rest of you?

P.P.   Not especially, no sir. Orders were orders, understand? We all had the same schedule. Except for the tapestry, and his light, you know—that kind of stuff.

Dr.   What stuff are you referring to, Pacífico?

P.P.   Oh, you know. He had to have some advantages. Like, for example, Don Santiago's cot. It wasn't a cot, see. It was a regular bed, with a headboard and a footboard. And on top of it he had a red tapestry with flowers and birds, and according to Patita, the woman brought it to him. Then next to his bed there was a night table and a reading lamp. There wasn't a thing missing, oh, no sir. You could've called it luxury.

Dr.   How about the rest of you—didn't you have tapestries?

P.P.   No. All we had were the leaks from the dampness, on the stones.

Dr.   But you *were* all together, weren't you?

P.P.   Course we were. But since Don Santiago's bed was sort of in the middle, with the tapestry and all, we looked like God and all his saints.

Dr.   What kind of books did Don Santiago read?

P.P.   All kinds. But I didn't especially notice what.

Dr.   Where did he get them?

P.P.   Oh, some were from the library, and the others from the woman. He'd donate them to the prison after he was finished with them. And he was like a maestro. He'd say, This one's good, this one's not, depending. I mean he'd decide if we could read it or not.

Dr.   Tell me something else. How did your companions like you?

P.P.   Oh, you know how things are. The first night Buque put a rat in my bed—initiating me, I guess. They were running all over the place. And the next night he unlocked the legs of my cot, so that when I laid down, it collapsed on me. The usual stuff, you know. But on the whole, I didn't have any complaints about my cellmates.

Dr.   Tell me, what was your life like there?

P.P.   What can I say? Orderly, you know. I mean, since we had germs we got special treatment. Like, for example, if you didn't feel like it, you didn't have to get up to eat. Not much duty, understand? And as for formations, just for retreat, at nighttime, so they could count heads in the halls. Otherwise we came and went, and in the afternoon we'd go into the gallery, to the sun—ah!

Dr.   Do you mean to say that they didn't lock the hall?

P.P.   At night, yes, they did. I mean, they bolted the door. But during the day, with those slabs of wall around us, where could we go? It's like I say, hey, those old guys back then, they knew what they were doing when they built that castle. Nothing disturbed *their*

	sleep. Those walls were at least three meters thick. So who could go waltzing in and out? And if it rained, well, we'd just go out to the corridors. And if it cleared, we'd go out to the courtyard for a card game.
Dr.	But what you liked best was the rest period in the gallery, you say.
P.P.	Oh yeah, that's for sure. Me and everybody else.
Dr.	And what did you do there?
P.P.	Mainly just look, and chat.
Dr.	Look at what, Pacífico?
P.P.	At the townspeople, striving away. Some lookout we had! When there wasn't a funeral we'd look at the square, or at the flocks, or the pine groves, or the breweries. Don't think there was any lack of places. Oh no.
Dr.	And weren't you envious, Pacífico, when you saw people going about their business in the streets of the town?
P.P.	To tell you the truth, no sir, I wasn't. Every time I laid eyes on them, I'd say to myself: You sure got out of a mess, Pacífico.
Dr.	Were you thinking of your great-grandfather when you said that?
P.P.	Well, sort of. I was thinking of Bisa, and Abue too, and my war, and the Otero gang, and Candi, and Father, and everybody and his brother, understand?
Dr.	So outside prison you felt threatened?
P.P.	Sure, of course I did.
Dr.	You felt safer inside?
P.P.	Oh yeah. There was no comparison.
Dr.	But didn't Buque, and Capullo, and all that riffraff around you seem more dangerous?
P.P.	Not on your life!
Dr.	Did you by any chance think they were victims?
P.P.	That's exactly what I thought, yes sir.
Dr.	Even Don Santiago?
P.P.	Well now, he was a different breed of cat.
Dr.	What's your impression of him, Pacífico?
P.P.	Well, Don Santiago played his cards the way he'd been taught. It was all he knew how to do.
Dr.	And when you saw the pine trees, and the hillsides, and the people coming and going, didn't it remind you of your town?
P.P.	How could I help it? Yeah. I remembered El Crestón, and the

pippin tree, and La Torca, and the Embustes. I'd sort of gaze at the oak trees, and I'd imagine I was taking a walk in my town, and it was just as if I was there, you know? I mean, it was weird, it was so real. And another afternoon I'd say to myself, for instance, Today I'm going to climb up that cliff. And I'd go right up—in my imagination, I mean. I'd take a narrow path and stick to it 'til I got up there. With nobody to bother me, see? I mean, I'd stop here or there, in my imagination, naturally, and I'd have a drink, or I'd stop for a little snooze, or I'd listen to the cowbells, or whatever I enjoyed—it didn't matter what. So between going up and coming back down, Doctor, I'd spend two to three hours, and some afternoons it got really late. And you know, by night my legs were as tired as if I'd gone on a real trip. And I'd lay down in my cot and curl up under the blanket and sleep like a baby. It's like I say, Doctor: Whatever you imagine—it's like living it. It's silly to be so busy.

Dr.   So you slept soundly in prison?

P.P.   Like a log, yeah.

Dr.   Didn't you miss your friends' company?

P.P.   Well, no sir. Not the slightest bit. They said that Buque snored and Don Santiago coughed for all he was worth. Well, if they did, I never heard them. Except for Patita.

Dr.   What did Patita do?

P.P.   He'd bug us about whether he'd slept or not.

Dr.   What do you mean?

P.P.   Oh, it was this fixation he had. Because he was flaky. He'd ask us when night came, too. The same way he'd ask us afterward about when he'd fallen asleep.

Dr.   Couldn't he tell night from day?

P.P.   It wasn't a question of that. Let me put it this way so's to make it clear: As soon as the sun set, Patita would start in: It's day, day . . . In the gallery, see. And then suddenly, in a minute, he'd say, It's night, it's night now. When did it become night? That was his thing. Every evening, the same old story.

Dr.   Do you mean to say that Patita wanted to pinpoint the instant in which day turns into night?

P.P.   That's right, yes sir.

Dr. But that's impossible.

P.P. That's what I thought too, Doctor. But one afternoon he comes and says to me: Seminarista, I know when day turns into night now! And me: You do? Just to humor him, you know. And him: Yeah. And me: When? And him: When the infirmary lights go on, get it? In other words, when they turned them on downstairs, the courtyard got darker, right? Sure. Well, that was enough for him—for Patita, I mean. He'd say, Don Santiago, I know when night comes. All I need now is to find out when I fall asleep!

Dr. So Patita also wanted to separate waking from sleeping?

P.P. Well, he wanted to be aware of the instant he fell asleep. I'm not sure if I've expressed myself right. Have I?

Dr. In a word, he wanted to realize when he wasn't realizing anything anymore.

P.P. More or less, Doctor.

Dr. Some problem!

P.P. You can see for yourself.

Dr. And what would he do?

P.P. Wake us all up. Like, for example, at midnight he'd shout: I almost had it! So Don Santiago goes: Is something wrong, Patita? And Patita goes: I almost had it, Don Santiago, but I woke up. You should've heard Capullo: Can't you guys keep quiet? 'Cause, you see, Capullo was real nervous. He'd crack his knuckles all day, over and over, you know? And from what Patita says, he was worse when he got out of the cell.

Dr. The punishment cell?

P.P. The cell, yeah. After the riot.

Dr. Was it that bad in there?

P.P. That's not it, hey. The thing is, he was stuck in there for thirteen days with a dead man.

Dr. A dead man?

P.P. A dead man: Morris, from San Vicente Hall. Capullo himself says that Morris kicked the bucket two days after they confined him—that he just withered on the vine and dried up. But Capullo kept his trap shut.

Dr. Do you mean to say that he was in the cell for two weeks next to a corpse and he didn't say a word about it?

P.P.   That's right, sir.

Dr.   Well, what was his objective?

P.P.   Oh that's easy: to get double helpings of food.

Dr.   Were meals skimpy, Pacífico?

P.P.   Look, on that particular point I'm no judge, Doctor. I take whatever they give me. I've been a bad eater since I was a kid, and you know, it must've been a torture for my poor old mother.

Dr.   Well, how about the others?

P.P.   As for Don Santiago, there was no problem, as you know. 'Cause they brought his food up from town. But you couldn't fill up Capullo, Doctor. He was always out there at the stand to see what he could get. And he had a sweet tooth too, sir.

Dr.   At the stand?

P.P.   Yeah. The taxi stand, I mean.

Dr.   Oh yes, of course.

P.P.   So whenever a tip came, he'd rush over to the commissary to buy himself a package of cookies or a pound of chocolate. The thing was to fill his belly, like I say.

Dr.   And what did Capullo think? Did you ever talk about your past?

P.P.   Oh sure, lots of times. Being all cooped up like that, what else could we talk about?

Dr.   Why did they condemn Capullo, Pacífico?

P.P.   For the assassination.

Dr.   Would you mind telling me about it?

P.P.   No sir. Why should I mind? But let me warn you: It was Isabelita's fault.

Dr.   Isabelita who?

P.P.   His girlfriend—I mean, his lover. Capullo's.

Dr.   He had a girlfriend?

P.P.   Wait a minute. He was involved with a widow they called Isabelita, see?

Dr.   Yes.

P.P.   Well, in the meantime, Capullo started to have this problem in his chest, see, and they sent him to a sanatorium for poor people. For nine months, mind you. Not just two or three, but nine. So when he got out, he found out she'd married somebody else—a church wedding and everything. He was a peasant from around Lugo.

Dr.   And he couldn't accept it?

P.P. Right. He wasn't one for that. He was in love with Isabelita. He'd even cry whenever he talked about her. It was for real.

Dr.   Fine. Go on.

P.P. Well, anyway, he came back and found her married to the peasant. It was like he said: He didn't have anything against the peasant except that he'd taken his girl. So he went to see her and proposed to her. But Isabelita, she said no, that she was an honorable woman and what was past was past. Then Capullo swore at her, and Isabelita said to get out, that the peasant, her husband, you follow me? was very jealous, and she said he'd be back any minute. Told him it was better if he didn't find them together because otherwise she wasn't sure what he'd do, see?

Dr.   And he didn't leave.

P.P. Wait a minute. He did leave. What else could he do? Capullo, I mean. But then he started thinking about how he could get Isabelita back. So he took her pastries and candy, 'cause that's when there were a lot of people going hungry. Well, anyway, it seems that Isabelita for some reason or other—it's none of my business anyway—well, she didn't like him anymore. So Capullo did what you'd expect. He went crazy when he was dropped like that, and when you think about it, he had every right to, 'cause he'd been first, but the peasant got into the picture, and that's all there was to it.

Dr.   So he decided to get rid of him.

P.P. Exactly. He swore he'd take his life. I mean, he started to imagine the best way to do it, you know? And he says that about that time Miguel—the peasant, I mean—was down at the riverbank digging holes for a plantation. So the night before Capullo went down, before daybreak, to see if the holes had been dug, 'cause what occurred to him right off was to bury him in one of them. It was like he'd dug his own grave, as they say. The peasant, I mean. So that same day, after sunset, Capullo grabbed his bike, and a sack, and two ropes, a noose, and one of those big shawls you use to tie up a bundle of clothes, and he waited for him next to an abandoned mill, you know? On the road back. And he says that when he heard him coming along singing, so *out* of it—the peasant, I mean—he felt a lump in his throat. He could hardly breathe. And he got this tingling in his hands, something awful. So Capullo goes out into the road with the noose, and soon as the other guy comes along he shouts, Stop! And the peasant did, just so's not to walk into him, you know? And as soon as he had a grip on the handle and his foot on the ground, Capullo went and let him have it behind the ears with a stick 'til he knocked his brains out. And then according to him, he dragged him behind the mill, see, and then he hid his bike just in case anybody came by, naturally. But since he saw that the peasant was still stirring, he grabbed the noose and stuck the stick in his neck at least ten times, as if he'd been a pin cushion, hey. And all for Isabelita, imagine.

Dr. Go on, son, go on.

P.P. Well, anyway, according to him, since it was still light, Capullo went and hid the dead body in a woodpile next to the mill and went to take a nap in the silo. And then after it was dark he went back to the woodpile, pulled out the body, pushed the knees up against the stomach, and tied it up and pushed it into the sack. And even so, he couldn't manage it, you know, with one hand on his handlebar, so he had to carry it on his back and steady it by tying it to a bandana across his forehead. He says it weighed a ton. So with all this he had to get on his bike next, see, and he says it wobbled like crazy—like a scared bull in the ring—first this way, then that way. And he finally got to the shore where the pits were. It was pitch black by then, and when he came to an odd-numbered one he says he dumped the sack into it, all covered up, just like he'd prepared it, and he buried it, see?

Dr. And how did they find it?

P.P. She did. Isabelita, I mean. After he finished he went to see her. And, You'd better be on your way 'cause Miguel's going to show up any minute now, he says she said. But Capullo said, Oh, don't worry about *him*, and she goes, Get out of here, or I'll scream. Well, this really made him lose his head. He says he didn't know what he was doing—he grabbed Isabelita and forced her, and he left in a huff. But when she saw that the other guy wasn't coming, she went to the police and reported he was missing. So the next day the search got started, of course—where could Miguel be?—well, down at the shore. So everybody went down to the shore of the river, and the pit's all covered up. Well, to make a long story short, in five minutes they dug it up and found the body.

Dr. Did Capullo get sentenced?

P.P. That's another story, Doctor. Twenty-five years for what he did to the peasant. Article 406. Just like me. And he got six for Isabelita. And as if that wasn't enough, he got another punishment for illegal burial. Don't you think they went overboard?

Dr. The law's the law, Pacífico.

P.P. You can say that again. But it seems to me they should've gone lighter on him, seeing as how he buried the body.

Dr. The law applies to dead people too, son. You've got to follow certain procedures when you bury somebody.

P.P. Look, I was always taught that burying the dead was an act of mercy. Well, it didn't work that way for Capullo: they called it another crime. Depends on how you look at it.

Dr. Have it your way, Pacífico. This argument is pointless. Capullo didn't bury Miguel out of mercy; he did it to erase the traces of his crime. His purpose wasn't merciful; he was acting in contempt of the law. As you must see, there's a big difference. But let's forget this for now. Where did you have these conversations?

P.P. Wherever they came up. In the gallery, or the courtyard, or in the hall itself if we were feeling lazy and just hanging out, on our cots. It depended.

Dr. And did Patita and Buque tell their stories too?

P.P. Oh yeah. Everybody did.

Dr. Even Don Santiago?

P.P. Well, no. Don Santiago didn't usually talk about himself. I mean, what we knew about him came mainly from the outside. But he'd listen and give us advice, though. He knew the penal code by heart. Between you and me, we called him the Brain. But he didn't know. It was always Don Santiago this, Don Santiago that.

Dr. And why was there such a difference?

P.P. Out of respect. Nobody wanted it any other way.

Dr. How about you, Pacífico? Did you tell the Teotista thing?

P.P. Sure. What else could I do?

Dr. What did your cellmates say about it?

P.P. You want the truth?

Dr. Of course I do.

P.P. They said to skip it and tell them about Candi.

Dr. Did you tell them about your relationship with Candi?

P.P. One afternoon I just blurted it out. Didn't even realize I was doing it, and I told them about Prádanos, when she'd run around naked up there. And then when I wanted to stop, I'd gone too far. I couldn't.

Dr. Why not?

P.P. Because they couldn't get their fill, Doctor. There were days when Patita would make me tell the same story three times.

Dr. Was that fellow Patita the ladies' man in the bunch?

P.P. Well, as far as that goes, I'd say it was even stephen. I mean, they all liked skirts. You should've seen Buque when I told them about Prádanos—his eyes would roll, and he'd start braying like a donkey. But I've got to be straight with you, Doctor. If Patita was locked up, it was because he was a man, too much of a man, as he said.

Dr. Did he abuse a woman?

P.P. Tcch! No. A man tried to abuse *him*, which is a different story.

Dr. A man?

P.P. Yes sir, a man. Juan José Viñat, was the one.

Dr. Do you mind if we leave this for tomorrow? I'm catching a cold, I think, and I'm going to have to retire for the night.

P.P. Are you sick?

Dr. It's not that, Pacífico. I'm just a little feverish.

P.P. Hey—you should've told me. We could've stopped sooner.

Dr. Don't worry, son. With a little cognac and an aspirin, I'll be a new man tomorrow.

▲ ▲ ▲ ▲ ▲ ▲ ▲
Sixth Night

P.P. Good evening, Doctor. How do you feel?

Dr. Fine, Pacífico.

P.P. Are you over it?

Dr. Yes I am, thanks.

P.P. 'Cause if you're not we can leave it for tomorrow.

Dr. No, that won't be necessary. I'm perfectly all right. Come on in, sit down. Do you remember what we were talking about yesterday?

P.P. How can I help it?

Dr. You were starting to tell me about Patita, about his manhood.

P.P. Yes, that's right, sir.

Dr. You said another man tried to abuse him. Do you remember, Pacífico?

P.P. Yes sir, Juan José Viñat.

Dr. And who was he?

P.P. A friend. Of Patita's, I mean.

Dr. From where?

P.P. Cutting. Out in a pasture. In Extremadura.

Dr. What kind of work were they doing?

P.P. Like I say, cutting. They were day laborers.

Dr. Had they both been there a while?

P.P. Look, whether or not they'd been there, I couldn't tell you. All I know is, one night a cow was giving birth, and the two of them slept in the stable, one alongside the other, Patita and Juan José Viñat. And that's how the story I have starts.

Dr. To help the birthing?

P.P. I guess so. It must've been, Doctor. Otherwise what would they have been doing in there?

Dr. And what happened?

P.P. Well, according to Patita, he was out like a light as soon as he got settled in the hay.

Dr. Uh huh.

P.P. So anyway, when Patita woke up, he said to him, Hey, stop that, OK? But he says Juan José just stuck to him, and then Patita jumped to his feet.

Dr. Go on.

P.P. Well, it seems that Juan José Viñat wore these huge glasses, three times thicker than mine. They were like the bottom of a tavern glass, you know? In other words, he was as blind as a bat.

Dr. That's an insignificant detail. Go on.

P.P. Insignificant, you say? That's what you think! If Patita got twenty years thrown at him, it was because of those glasses.

Dr. He was condemned to serve twenty years because of the man's glasses?

P.P. You heard right. That's what did him in. Like, it was a question of was he or wasn't he wearing them. You know. Because according to the judges Juan José Viñat was lost without his glasses. In other words, he couldn't defend himself. You follow me?

Dr. Yes. So Patita got up. Go on.

P.P. Yeah. Well, like I was saying, he was going to wet his whistle. So he went into the kitchen, which was next to the barnyard. He says it must've been about three o'clock in the morning.

Dr. OK.

P.P. Well, Juan José stayed in the barnyard waiting for him. And meanwhile Patita grabs a plowshare and heads back toward the other guy, no big deal.

Dr. To the stable?

P.P. Yeah, the stable. Soon as Juan José Viñat saw him, he pulled his shirttails out of his pants, 'cause according to Patita he was hot for him. But life's too much. Between one thing and another Juan José Viñat had taken off his glasses and put them down next to a trough, see. And that's what did Patita in.

Dr. He attacked him without his glasses?

P.P. Right. He whacked him on the head with the plowshare. And when he fell down he kept on prodding him with it, but there was no fight. According to the judges he died of a traumatic brain hemorrhage.

Dr.   Good Lord!

P.P.   And once he finished with him, he went out next to the stairs and called to the owner. It seems he shouted, Don Félix, come down! And as soon as Don Félix came down, they went over to the barn, and he showed him the body and said to him, he says: Don Félix, I killed Juan José Viñat because he was a fairy. Report it to the police.

Dr.   He didn't try to get away?

P.P.   Oh no! Didn't I just tell you how it was with him—he asked the owner to send word to the station?

Dr.   And even so, he got twenty years, you say?

P.P.   Twenty, yep. Article 406. Homicide with premeditation—'cause of the glasses, of course. What I say, Doctor, is this: Wouldn't Patita have hit him just the same with his glasses on? But no, they call it premeditation. That's how things are. It's like what Don Santiago said, hey: You're no criminal, Patita. You take the law more seriously, that's all.

Dr.   That's what Don Santiago said?

P.P.   Yeah. According to Don Santiago, a man that kills another to defend his own manhood shouldn't be punished. It's the law that makes guys turn into gays.

Dr.   Do you really believe that, Pacífico?

P.P.   Look, I'm not saying that it's true. It was Don Santiago who said it. And in Buque's case it's the same story, Doctor. He said that Buque wasn't a criminal. Just that he took the law in his own hands, see.

Dr.   Do you mean to say that Buque almost got raped too?

P.P.   It's not that, sir. It didn't have to do with that. Buque's another story. Let's see if I can make this clear. You see, what Don Santiago said was that neither Buque nor Patita was guilty. But that doesn't mean that they couldn't have done different things.

Dr.   And what *did* Buque do, Pacífico?

P.P.   He didn't do anything at first, Doctor. Just kid stuff—you know, pranks.

Dr.   But what was it he did?

P.P.   Nobody's going to get it out of my head that Buque was suffering from what they call the "dead man's sickness," you know? If not, what was the carriage all about? The one that was waiting for him, for the burials? A real obsession of his.

Dr.   Do you mean to say he was a necrophiliac?

P.P.   Something like that, yes sir.

Dr.   Tell me: What exactly did Buque do?

P.P.   Well, you know. At first he used to get together with some bums, and at night they'd jump over the cemetery walls, and they'd steal the crosses and the chains from the graves, to sell them for scrap metal. Pranks of theirs.

Dr.   Do you think so?

P.P.   Yeah. It was like the other stuff. One thing led to another. I mean once they'd picked the place over, Buque got the bright idea of sending one of the gang to the mourning sessions to see the dead—the stuff that was put in the coffins, get it? So as you can imagine, sometimes it was a ring, or earrings, or even the shoes and the suit the dead man was wearing. And at nighttime they'd simply jump over the walls and make off with it. Buque doesn't have too much up here; he's always the dumbest one in the group. Well, anyway, one day went by and then another like that. They kept at it, 'til one night they finally got caught. These other guys tricked them with a fake pearl necklace. And they fell for it. They got caught red-handed.

Dr.   Was Buque very young when they arrested him?

P.P.   Oh, he was eighteen when he got into it—just a kid at first. But by the time the necklace thing happened he was twenty-three—he was even married and everything. The way Buque looks now, you'd never guess it; he was the opposite of sickly then. What a build! I was a runt next to him.

Dr.   So they locked him up?

P.P.   Yeah. He got fifteen years.

Dr.   And why do you suppose that Don Santiago thought this fellow who ransacked graves was a fair man?

P.P.   Wait a minute, that doesn't have anything to do with it. Buque redeemed himself, you see, and with amnesty and so on they let him off in six years. Then the other business happened—the big thing with Catalina.

Dr.   What do you mean?

P.P.   His wife. After he'd been locked up five years, she went to see him at the penitentiary, and she out and tells him she's pregnant.

Dr.   She confessed that another man had made her pregnant?

P.P.   Oh no. That's the funny part. She told him she was expecting his baby, Buque's, from before he was put away. And Buque was so dumb he believed her.

Dr.   Buque believed that after five years apart, his wife was pregnant by him?

P.P.   Yeah! You just don't know what he's like. That guy wasn't playing games or anything. He was just dumb, that's all. I know it's wrong for me to say so, but he didn't even know how to wipe his own nose.

Dr.   That's a little too much, Pacífico.

P.P.   Whatever you like, hey. I swear to you by the light of heaven that in Góyar he still thought the baby Catalina was expecting was his.

Dr.   Fine. Go on.

P.P.   So as soon as he got out of the penitentiary, he went to see her. And Catalina was real nice to him, saying how it was great he'd gotten there in time and all. I mean she fooled him. And she said that the man in the kitchen with her, Francisco Rincón, that is, was just staying there like a guest since he'd been away. What a dunce, the poor guy. That night, when he got to his sister's place, Had he seen his trashy wife? She came right out with it. At first he didn't want to listen, but after his sister swore to it he went home. And he says that high up on the bedroom door there was this glass pane, and he got up on a stool and saw them making love in bed—Catalina and her friend, see? And that's when Buque realized his sister was right. So he grabbed a switchblade, kicked open the door, and went in. He says Francisco Rincón started shaking when he saw him—it was only natural—and he ran out screaming into the street in his underpants, imagine. But it seems that Catalina stretched out at his feet, as tall as she was, and said to him, You're the only man I care about. That's what he says she said. A fine time to say *that*. But this time Buque didn't buy it. Why should he? He says he didn't notice her belly or anything with all the commotion. And big as he was he grabbed her by the hair and picked her up. Then he stuck her with the switchblade over and over 'til she was dead.

Dr.   How about the baby?

P.P.   I'm getting to that. They autopsied Catalina. And they found an eight-month fetus in her womb, a baby girl. And of course she was dead too. But like Buque said, he wished he could've saved the kid.

Dr.   There are provisions for that type of crime in the penal code, Pacífico.

P.P.   You can say that again! Parricide and abortion. Twenty-three years and eight months plus accessories, you know.

Dr.   So to sum it up, in San José Hall, yours was the shortest sentence.

P.P.   That's right. That's how it was. But it didn't much matter. Patita was finishing up by summer.

Dr.   When you started to tell one another your respective crimes, how long had you been in Góyar?

P.P.   The things you come out with, Doctor! Since I went in, every day, you understand? It could be said that we didn't talk about anything else.

Dr.   And how about Candi's visit: Was it soon after you got there?

P.P.   Well, let's see now. I went in the seventeenth of August. And Candi brought the kid in October, if I'm not mistaken. I recall that you could feel the damp from the dew.

Dr.   And you of course knew all about your friends' deeds by then.

P.P.   Yeah.

Dr.   And with all those atrocious things they told you, didn't you feel like going quietly back to your town with your son?

P.P.   Quietly? No, not really. In fact I felt less like it.

Dr.   Why less?

P.P.   Just because. How did I know I wouldn't run into Juan José Viñat, for example, or the peasant, or Catalina? And that they'd fry me?

Dr.   But Pacífico, it seems worse to run into Capullo or the likes of him. He'd bury you. Or somebody like Patita, who'd break your neck with a plowshare. Or Buque, who'd stab you to death. Don't you agree? At least that's how I see it.

P.P.   That's right. That's why I was fine in there. Don't think I was very tempted to leave.

Dr.   But if your thoughts were along those lines, would you please explain why you participated in the Góyar escape?

P.P.   Look, Doctor, we'd better not talk about that.

Dr.   Why not, Pacífico? I won't say a word. You know that.

P.P.   It's not that, Doctor.

Dr.   What is it, then?

P.P.   Well, my Uncle Paco always said in his letters that things shouldn't go past that.

Dr.   Your Uncle Paco was writing to you then?

P.P.   Yeah. Often. After I was admitted to Góyar, once a month. He never missed a month.

Dr.   Fine. Go on.

P.P.   What do you want me to say? My disappointment hit me like a rock. That's all.

Dr.   With your Uncle Paco?

P.P.   No, I mean from what Don Santiago said.

Dr.   Let's get this straight, now, Pacífico. What do you mean, from what Don Santiago said?

P.P.   Look, I don't want to do anybody any harm.

Dr.   Pacífico, you can trust me the way you would a friend. No one will find out anything that you don't want known.

P.P.   If you say so . . .

Dr.   That's our agreement, isn't it?

P.P.   Yes sir, that's exactly what you said.

Dr.   So?

P.P.   The truth first, Doctor. The last thing I wanted was to leave prison. It didn't even occur to me.

Dr.   Then why did you change your mind?

P.P.   Bad luck.

Dr.   What did it consist of?

P.P.   Well, the afternoon Candi came to Góyar, the other guys were in the gallery, see. And I was thinking to myself, What wonderful sun I'm missing. Well, anyway, Candi brought me some sausages and homemade rolls, and I went into the hall and put them aside for that night, see. Well, after taps, when the guard had bolted the door, I went over to Capullo's cot—he was the hungriest one—and I said to him, Get up, the supplies are here. To give him a sausage and some rolls, see. I mean, I didn't have any other motives. *That* was my intention. And I tugged at his blanket and uncovered him. But Capullo wasn't there!

Dr.   What do you mean?

P.P.   Just what you heard: he wasn't there. There was a pile of clothes and a box, that's all. But no Capullo. And everybody starts looking at me as if I'd cursed his mother. I can still see Buque's white eye. It makes me shiver to think of it.

Dr.   So why had they put the pile of clothes and the box there?

P.P.   To make a shape. So if the guard looked in he'd think we were asleep.

Dr.   What did you do?

P.P.   I just stayed there, Doctor. What could I do? And then Patita and Buque turned toward Don Santiago, who was reading a book, as usual. And then Don Santiago looked up and stared at me, just stared at me. And me, as long as Don Santiago was looking at me like that I didn't dare move a finger.

Dr.   Didn't he say anything?

P.P.   After I don't know how long.

Dr.   What did he say?

P.P.   Well, he said: Lie down and shut your trap, Seminarista. Capullo's digging. We'll talk tomorrow. That was all.

Dr.   He didn't explain anything?

P.P.   Not for the moment, no sir. So I covered up Capullo's cot right away, and I jumped into mine, and was I scared. I couldn't catch a wink all night.

Dr.   When did he finally talk to you?

P.P.   The next morning. He took me aside and said they were preparing an escape and did I want to substitute for the Honorable, because the Honorable had already gotten away.

Dr.   Who was the Honorable?

P.P.   The other guy. The one before me. The one I substituted for in the hall.

Dr.   Had he really escaped?

P.P.   No sir. It was a figure of speech. The Honorable had passed on.

Dr.   I see. So what did you reply to Don Santiago?

P.P.   Well, you can just imagine. It caught me by surprise. I said no, that I was happy there. It didn't mean I was scorning him or anything, though.

Dr.   And how about him?

P.P.   Uhh! Some tongue Don Santiago had! Nobody would force me to, if I didn't want to. But hadn't I thought about helping out others, and I thought back on my Uncle Paco, and said it wasn't a question of that, that if I had to lend a hand, I'd do so gladly. And Don Santiago took me at my word. Nobody will ask anything else of you, he said. And that's how we left it.

Dr.   That is to say, you agreed to help them.

P.P.   Wait a minute. To give them a hand, yes sir. But I'd stay in prison myself. That was the agreement. So then Don Santiago said to me, When do you want to start digging? And me, I said, Whenever you want, Don Santiago. So by that afternoon I was down in the hole.

Dr.   A hole? In the floor?

P.P.   No, not in the floor. The things you come out with! We would've ended up in the prison commissary. We made the hole through the wall, get it? All along it, in the part inside the tower. Off to the right were the toilets. And on the other side, as you go out into the corridor, between our hall and San Vicente, there was the guard's office, to keep watch on the stairs that led up to the castle courtyard. Do you follow me?

Dr.   More or less, Pacífico.

P.P.   I mean that between the hole and the guard, there was the hall, ours I mean, San José. So he couldn't hardly hear us.

Dr.   And how did you dig the tunnel? Along the width of the wall?

P.P.   What do you mean, along the width? Like I said, we did it alongside, the length. You see, between our hall and the toilets there was this huge wall, at least three meters thick, and it must've been eight or ten meters long. Well, Don Santiago's idea was to dig down those eight or ten meters, take a stone off the tower, and make an exit there. Do you understand?

Dr.   Not very well, no.

P.P.   It's easy. Do you have a pencil?

Dr.   Here.

P.P.   I can't draw, but it was sort of like this, with the tower over there. I mean, these are the toilets. And in between, sort of like this, there was the wall. Well, in the wall, in exactly the same direction it went, we were making a hole. What Don Santiago wanted was to get to this corner and take off the stone. Exactly where the tower starts, from the toilets.

Dr.   I've got the idea now, Pacífico. But how did you manage to pierce the stone?

P.P.   We didn't, sir. We removed it.

Dr.   And the wall?

P.P.   The wall wasn't solid stone. That would've knocked us out. You see, between the stones there was cement and mortar. That's where we dug.

Dr.   How did you start the tunnel? How did you do it so the opening wouldn't show in the hall?

P.P.   No problem. At first Patita and the other guys lifted a stone near Don Santiago's cot, under the tapestry. And when there was a hollow space inside, we pushed it, the stone, I mean, and then, whenever the dunce came in, we'd put it back, see? But even if you moved the tapestry aside, you still couldn't see it.

Dr.   But even so, cement is pretty hard to dig through.

P.P.   You can say that again! How long do you suppose it'd been the day Don Santiago spoke to me about it?

Dr.   How long had it been since what, son?

P.P.   Struggling in the tunnel, I mean.

Dr.   Who knows! Months?

P.P.   Over a year. They started it around St. Peter's Day, so give a day or take a day, they'd been at it for a year and four months when I joined them.

Dr.   And what tools did you use?

P.P.   Well, mainly the end of a spoon—we had a couple—and two knives. There weren't any other tools there.

Dr. Nothing else?

P.P. Well, we had an iron bar too, you know? But at nighttime we couldn't use it. We could only use it during the day. When they were making a racket out in the courtyard.

Dr. Where did you get an iron bar?

P.P. Don't ask me. I don't know, Doctor.

Dr. So when you joined them the tunnel was pretty far along.

P.P. Oh, it was over six meters long. Don Santiago estimated it was seven and a half, with the stone and everything. Don Santiago always said: Well, by New Year's we'll be moving on to somewhere else. And it turned out he was right.

Dr. The part I can't get into my head, Pacífico, is how you could live with your companions for two months without suspecting that they were planning an escape. Or did they stop work during that time?

P.P. Yes, they did. Don Santiago told me so afterward. They just chiseled by day. They'd stop at night. They didn't want to let it be known 'til they were sure I wouldn't rat on them. The night I discovered the clothes and the box in Capullo's cot was the second night they'd chiseled since I got there.

Dr. How did you organize the work? Did you take turns?

P.P. Yes sir, we took turns. Don Santiago had it all thought out. At eight o'clock, after breakfast, the first would go in. Then at one, after lunch, the second. And then at eight, after taps, the third. And the last one to go in, after taps, would have a twelve-hour stint in that hole.

Dr. Why didn't you rotate once more?

P.P. As a precautionary measure. The guard was on the other side, and he could've caught us. There were some guards that would look in on us every so often. You couldn't even take a leak.

Dr. Did you always put the mound of clothes and the box in the bed as a disguise?

P.P. Always, yes sir.

Dr. So from the moment you joined them, every fifth night was a sleepless one for you?

P.P. Well, to tell you the truth, it was every fourth night.

Dr. Weren't there five of you in the hall?

P.P. Yes, there *were* five of us, but Don Santiago didn't dig. He took care of supervising things.

Dr. Is that what he called it, supervising?

P.P. Yeah. Don't make fun of it. That's how it was. Don Santiago kept a map and a sheet with our work schedule, and he said when it was time to stop, and he'd set our relays, see. In other words, it was his responsibility. Among ourselves we called him the Brain.

Dr. How did he let you know the relay was ready?

P.P. With three taps. He'd tap three times, slowly, on the stone. You could hear it clearly inside. It must've been because of the echo.

Dr. I guess Don Santiago never got stiff, eh, Pacífico?

P.P. The things you say, Doctor! Don Santiago was in charge. That's what I'm trying to tell you. So, for example, if the guard was nearby, he'd tap four times in a row, fast, on the stone, and the guy inside waiting wouldn't get impatient.

Dr. How about during the daytime? Didn't Don Santiago help out then, either?

P.P. No sir. All he did was tell us what we had to do, see? Like if we were supposed to go up, or down, or sideways. He'd point the way.

Dr. I see. Tell me, Pacífico: Wasn't there a risk that the fellow working in the tunnel would be missed?

P.P. No, not really, 'cause you see we didn't line up except for taps, and there was no roll call during the day. And since each person was on his own—either over at the water basin, or in the courtyard, or in the library—well, it didn't matter. Except for meals and taps. That was all. And Don Santiago was on guard for that. So it was pretty hard for them to notice.

Dr. The first time you went into the tunnel, it must have impressed you.

P.P. Just imagine. I thought I'd suffocate.

Dr. Was it that narrow?

P.P. Well, not at the beginning, no, Doctor. There was a big hollow space for the stone. But then, hey, we had to walk like snakes, dragging ourselves. And as soon as the stone was back in place, it was really cramped. It felt like being buried alive, a real agony.

Dr.   Did you work in the dark?

P.P.   Course we did.

Dr.   But then you couldn't have known what you were doing.

P.P.   Why not? We had our hands to tell us.

Dr.   Did you let yourselves be led by your sense of touch?

P.P.   Yeah.

Dr.   The first time you went in, was it day or night?

P.P.   Nighttime. For the long shift.

Dr.   You called it the long one?

P.P.   Yeah, that's what we called it. After all, it was twelve hours non-stop.

Dr.   Could you take it without any problems?

P.P.   Without any problems? Well, let's just say I took it, OK? At the beginning, when I set the stone in place, I thought I'd scream. I even had to cover my mouth with my hands. I had this tightness in my chest.

Dr.   Did you get used to it pretty soon?

P.P.   To being cooped up? Yeah. The worst part was later, with the dust and the cold.

Dr.   Did you work without a tabard?

P.P.   A tabard? With a girdle and all, oh sure! Don Santiago was very strict on things like that. It'd just take a speck of dust to give us away, he said. So Buque and Patita had to work stark naked. And me, there were days when I'd come out of that hole half-dead, shaking like a leaf.

Dr.   Couldn't you wear something other than your uniforms to cover yourselves?

P.P.   Yes. I mean no, Doctor. They would've noticed at inspection on Saturdays. Don Santiago was very strict, as I said. He thought of everything, too. I'd come out after a long shift all numb, and there he was to rub me down before I went out to the courtyard. Thought of everything. Without him we wouldn't have been able to do things the way we did.

Dr.   What did you do with the dirt you scraped away?

P.P.   We'd take it out of there.

Dr.   How?

P.P.   In plastic bags we saved from candy and peanuts. And depending on how many we filled, Don Santiago could tell if we'd done our job or if we'd sloughed off.

Dr. How many bags did you average?

P.P. Oh, we usually got four from the morning shift, four from the afternoon, and six from the long one.

Dr. What would you do with them?

P.P. We'd spread them around. First we'd tie them to our waists, under the tabard, and then we'd empty them out in the courtyard. We'd scatter the dirt around, see.

Dr. But the courtyard must've gotten full of dirt, Pacífico.

P.P. Well, the ground was dirt anyway. So you didn't notice if there was a little more.

Dr. Wasn't the courtyard paved?

P.P. Wait a minute, Doctor. Don't get things mixed up. The castle courtyard, the inside one, *was* paved. But that one wasn't ours. Us San José guys were in the outer one, see? In the one that was next to the gallery, next to the infirmary.

Dr. I see.

P.P. So like I was saying, once we got out in the courtyard, we'd empty the bags and spread the dirt around.

Dr. Wasn't there a risk that you'd get caught?

P.P. Oh yeah. That was always possible. But hey, that's why we were careful. Like Buque, for example. He was never allowed to bring down any bags.

Dr. Buque didn't empty any bags?

P.P. No sir, never. Don Santiago said he dug better than anybody else so he should get off with less. So's not to humiliate him in front of the others, see. You couldn't really tell him it was 'cause he was ignorant.

Dr. Didn't the work in the tunnel affect your health?

P.P. It sure did, Doctor. In there the cement dust got into your bones. I mean, I had to tie a handkerchief over my nose and mouth. But believe me, even with that I still kept coughing. And I had to put up with it, you know? 'Cause at night, during the long shift, you could hear a cough from the toilets. You can just imagine what dirty work it was. One day the prison doctor discovered that something was wrong. I mean, one day he must've seen something funny in my lungs, 'cause he said: You've been smoking. And me, I said, No, Doctor, I swear to God I haven't. But he insisted on it: You've been smoking. At night, when it was time for taps, Don Avelino and Vegas came into the hall with the doctor who was on duty. To look me over, see.

Dr.   Did they find anything?

P.P.   Not from the tunnel, no sir.

Dr.   How about the maps and papers that Don Santiago kept?

P.P.   No. Why should they? That stuff was stored away, behind the stone. The worst part was when Don Avelino touched the tapestry. I was speechless, I swear to you, even though it shouldn't have made any difference to me.

Dr.   Did they leave, then?

P.P.   Oh, they stayed a bit to chat about the book Don Santiago was reading. Don Alberto, the doctor, liked that kind of thing.

Dr.   Did they find anything suspicious in your lungs?

P.P.   Not really, sir. Don Santiago took measures against that happening.

Dr.   What measures?

P.P.   Well, on the twenty-seventh of every month, three days before our physicals, we'd stop chiseling.

Dr.   All of you?

P.P.   Yes, all of us, sir. It was a general rule. Don Santiago did it so that Patita, Capullo, and Buque wouldn't think I was getting special treatment, you know? Don Santiago picked up on everything.

Dr.   Didn't the delays bother him?

P.P.   No, not really. I never saw him worry about being in a rush. In fact he always said, If you want to get somewhere on time, go slowly. And he had a point. The point was to do a good job of it. Not make anybody suspicious.

Dr.   Did he talk about what he planned to do once you got to the outside stone in the tower?

P.P.   On the whole, don't think that Don Santiago went overboard when he talked. He took things one at a time, see. Probably 'cause he was on his guard with Buque, who might spill the beans or get his orders mixed up. I've never seen anybody as stupid as that.

Dr.   So he didn't say anything.

P.P.   Wait a minute—yes, he did, little by little. And about halfway through December the woman came to see him, and she brought the rope.

Dr.   The woman with the perfume?

P.P.   The same as always. When he came back to the hall, hey, he would reek of that perfume she wore. Anyhow, as soon as he got back up, he said: We've got a rope now. And Capullo says, Where, Don Santiago? So he goes over to the corner—Don Santiago, I mean—behind the peephole, and he takes off his clothes. And there it was, wrapped around his body! A rope, not very thick, but strong, like twine or cord that could take a man's weight. So Patita says, Do you think that'll be enough? And Don Santiago says, We'll have the rest by the end of the month. Don Santiago could be pretty tight-lipped, it's true, but he did inform us of things as they happened.

Dr.   How about the place you were planning to hang from: Was it very high up?

P.P.   It was on the second story, but you know how uneven the heights are on castles. Down below was the batter, cut sharp, right into the rock, so the prison was sort of overhanging it, on a cliff. Between one thing and another, Don Santiago figured it was about a twenty-meter drop. On the rope, I mean.

Dr.   And how much did the woman bring him?

P.P.   Oh, about ten or twelve. No more than that.

Dr.   What did you do with it?

P.P.   Oh, we coiled it up carefully and stored it away.

Dr.   Where?

P.P.   Behind the stone, of course.

Dr.   I imagine, Pacífico, that as you advanced in your preparations for the escape, your companions must have talked less about the past and more about the future, about what they planned to do when they were free, didn't they?

P.P.   Oh, they'd been talking about that for some time, between themselves.

Dr.   What do you mean, for some time?

P.P.   To tell you the truth, ever since I started chiseling with them they were talking less about what they had done and more about what they were planning to do, long before the rope came.

Dr.   What *were* they planning to do? Buque, for example: What was he planning to do if the escape worked?

P.P. Holy smokes, Buque! He wanted to find Francisco Rincón. He didn't have any doubts on that score.

Dr.   The guy who took his wife away?

P.P. You've got it. He'd sworn to take his life, understand? He said that it was Francisco Rincón's fault that he'd lost his daughter. He said he wouldn't rest 'til he saw him in his grave. That guy Buque was as stubborn as they come, Doctor, let me tell you.

Dr.   And afterward? What did he plan on after that?

P.P. The stuff you come up with! For Buque there was no afterward. He couldn't keep two things in his head at the same time. As long as he could polish off Francisco Rincón, he was satisfied.

Dr.   How about Patita?

P.P. Well, Patita still had an obsession about being asleep or awake. For him the most important thing was to feel at what moment he fell asleep. It was a rare night that he didn't bother us with that.

Dr.   But what were his plans for the future?

P.P. Who knows, Doctor. All Patita thought about was the land. He couldn't understand life without working the land. So he'd talk about going someplace where there wasn't a soul. And about living off the land by himself. It was his dream. But it was just a dream, 'cause nowadays there aren't any places left without people. I don't know how, but men manage to get everywhere.

Dr.   Not really, Pacífico. Look at Prádanos.

P.P. A fine place to pick! Remember that when Candi and I were all alone up there people suddenly started popping out of the windows.

Dr.   Do you mean to tell me, Pacífico, that you believe that all those people came back to Prádanos just to laugh at you? Do you seriously believe that they stood in the windows in their party clothes just to watch you?

P.P. Let's not start in on that, Doctor. Why do you suppose I'd make up a story like that anyway?

Dr.   All right, Pacífico. Let's get on with Patita.

P.P. What else do you want to know?

Dr.   Well, for example, where did he expect to find a solitary place today?

P.P.	In Extremadura, I guess. But don't quote me on it.
Dr.	But last night, or maybe the night before, you told me that Patita's sentence was almost up.
P.P.	That's right, yes sir. In the summer. If he was right, it was for the end of July.
Dr.	How long had he been there?
P.P.	Patita? Locked up, you mean? Twelve years on the Day of the Holy Virgin, just imagine. Twelve years for killing a guy who was gay. That's punishment enough, don't you think?
Dr.	I don't understand, Pacífico.
P.P.	What don't you understand?
Dr.	What you're telling me. If Patita had been in for twelve years and he only had a few months left, why did he get involved in the adventure in the tunnel, with all the risks it entailed?
P.P.	Well, Doctor, Patita wasn't like Buque, but he didn't exactly invent the wheel, either.
Dr.	Was Patita forgetful too?
P.P.	Well, let's see now. On the whole, in that prison, except for Don Santiago, don't think they were like engineers or anything. Patita didn't take chances, but that doesn't mean . . .
Dr.	Could it be that Don Santiago roped him into it?
P.P.	You've got something against Don Santiago, don't you?
Dr.	No, it isn't that. But for some reason or other, I have the impression that Don Santiago used his intelligence to his own advantage.
P.P.	What for? He'd propose something, and we'd either accept it or not. As a majority, I mean.
Dr.	Very democratic, yes, but look how he snared you.
P.P.	No sir. You're wrong on that score. If I started to chisel it's because it, well, it appealed to me. I wanted to do something for the others.
Dr.	But if you weren't planning to escape, why should you let your lungs burst day after day in a tunnel?
P.P.	They wanted to get away, Doctor. And I gave them a hand. I volunteered, that's all. On the whole, it was like checking the honeycombs in my town. If it hadn't been for Father, I wouldn't have charged anything, you know. Suppose we all started charging for the favors we do—some life this would be!

Dr.   OK, whatever you say. How about Capullo? What were his plans?

P.P. To get together with Isabelita.

Dr.   After killing her husband?

P.P. Well, that's why he killed him, isn't it? You get the strangest notions!

Dr.   He loved her that much?

P.P. You have no idea how much he loved her. He carried her picture around with him. Never parted with it. And one day he said to Buque for him to tattoo his upper chest with her face, you know?

Dr.   And did he tattoo it for him?

P.P. Yeah. I mean, he painted a woman there.

Dr.   How did Buque do tattooing in jail?

P.P. Oh, it was easy. With a pin and a bottle of ink, that's all. He'd get the ink under your skin with a common pin. And it would last. Even if you scrubbed the place with soap and a sponge, Buque had a knack for it.

Dr.   And tell me, how about Don Santiago? Did Don Santiago talk about his plans for after the escape?

P.P. Well, no sir. Don Santiago didn't open his mouth on that subject.

Dr.   Didn't he mention the thirty million in London?

P.P. Well, that was the gossip.

Dr.   Didn't he ever refer to the money?

P.P. No sir, not that money or any money.

Dr.   Did all of you ask him?

P.P. Why would we do that? Nobody asked Don Santiago anything. That would've been the limit.

Dr.   How about you, Pacífico? What would you say when the others talked about their plans?

P.P. Oh, I'd keep my mouth shut and perk up my ears.

Dr.   Didn't your silence seem strange to them?

P.P. To Patita it did, once. I mean, one day, when they'd all told their plans, Patita comes up to me and says, Hey Seminarista! What are *you* planning to do? Me? I told him the truth, that I was happy there. So Patita goes: Did you guys hear that? And the other guys went wild, of course, hearing *that*, 'specially Capullo and Buque, 'til Don Santiago broke it up. Enough! he said. Nobody tells anybody else what to do around here.

Dr.   But later they did tell you, didn't they?

P.P.   When things got complicated, yeah.

Dr.   Yes, I see.

P.P.   Hey, what an obsession! You're not happy unless you pick at Don Santiago, are you?

Dr.   You simply don't understand me, Pacífico. But I trust that you'll open your eyes someday. Don Santiago was playing with you the same way a cat does with a mouse.

P.P.   Whatever you say, Doctor. Look, as for me . . .

Dr.   I'm sorry, Pacífico. Sometimes I get too carried away in our sessions. I admit it. Go on, now. When did Don Santiago explain the details of the escape itself?

P.P.   Once we got to the stone, in the tower.

Dr.   Who got to it?

P.P.   Me. In a long shift.

Dr.   It must have been exciting, wasn't it?

P.P.   You can just imagine. After all that effort. At first I couldn't believe it, though. I kept on scraping, but nothing was happening. And I thought to myself: Could it be the stone, already? And the next morning, I told Don Santiago about it. He didn't bat an eye, not even over that. He went up to Patita and said to him: It seems that Seminarista has reached the stone. Try to widen the hollow and find the joints.

Dr.   And did he do it?

P.P.   Did he do it! If everything didn't go to pot that day it was 'cause God was on our side.

Dr.   What happened?

P.P.   It was Patita. He blacked out in there.

Dr.   He lost consciousness?

P.P.   He was out like a light.

Dr.   Was it a fainting spell, or what?

P.P.   He could tell you. What's for sure is that he blacked out and it was time for the trumpet to be played. You can just imagine our panic. Don Santiago tapped three times, and there was no reply, nothing. Usually we'd answer his tap with one foot, 'cause of the posture. But nothing came from Patita. So Don Santiago gets all scared and says, Something's happened in there.

Dr.   What did you do?

P.P. You should've seen Don Santiago, hey, giving out orders like a general: You, Seminarista, to the corridor, and if the guard comes, distract him, even if you have to throw him headfirst into the courtyard. You, Capullo, stay at the door and don't let anybody by, like during reveille. 'Cause, you see, Buque, who was the strongest, and Don Santiago were going to try to get him out, see? Patita, I mean.

Dr.   And were they able to?

P.P. According to Don Santiago, there was no way of getting him out. He was stuck in there, and they couldn't push him forward or pull him back. Since they couldn't use their strength, it was hard; the opening was narrow, and they couldn't budge him. Don Santiago says he's never been in such a shitty spot, may God forgive me. And Buque with half his body in the hole, pulling at Patita by the legs, desperately. It was taking forever. And meanwhile, Vegas, the guard, came up, and I was thinking how could I stop him, see. So I charged downstairs and bumped into him. And I socked him one and left him cornered on the landing. And you should've seen how he reacted! Called me every name in the book. And me, I said, Excuse me, it's bugle call time. And I went and helped him to his feet. And I even shook out his pant legs and everything. But he claimed I'd done it on purpose, and like it or not, we go see the officer on duty. And in there it's the same story: that I was running out to bugle call and him—Vegas, I mean—saying I'd gone after him, that I'd done it on purpose. And so on. It got nasty. I was stalling, you know? Thinking about Patita. And after I don't know how long, he said I'd be put in the cell for three days, in solitary confinement. And that was all. Three days later I came back, and I saw Don Santiago, all attentive, congratulating me, and saying if it hadn't been for me, it would've been a fiasco, 'cause it seems it took Buque over a quarter of an hour to get Patita out of the hole, imagine.

Dr.   And what do you have to say about your new experience?

P.P. Which new one?

Dr.   The one in the cell.

P.P. The one in the cell?

Dr.   Yes.

P.P. OK. I mean, it was OK. Close quarters in there. And dark, hey. But after the tunnel it was like a rose garden.

Dr.   Didn't the loneliness bother you?

P.P. Why should it? I was better off like that.

Dr.   Do you like to be alone?

P.P. Sure. Who doesn't? I'd stretch out on my cot and let myself daydream. It was all the same to me what I saw—the pippin tree blossoming in the snow, or the chimneys smoking in Humán, from up at El Crestón. Whatever gave me pleasure. And for the rest I was pretty calm. I got out of chiseling for three days.

Dr.   And once you returned?

P.P. Hey, we celebrated it.

Dr.   Your return?

P.P. What do you mean, my return! The stone! Capullo gave me the word, said we'd finished the tunnel, imagine. And Don Santiago congratulated me about the Vegas thing, having stopped him, I mean. Then he sent Buque out for hot chocolate, tea cakes, and soda, and we celebrated it.

Dr.   Do you remember what day it was that you reached the stone, Pacífico?

P.P. It was the twenty-first of November. I recall it very well. But call it the twenty-second, 'cause it was early morning.

Dr.   Weren't your friends in a hurry to escape?

P.P. Don Santiago was never in a hurry, Doctor, I've already told you. He liked to do things right, tie up all the loose ends, as they say. So on the twenty-second we made it to the stone, but the escape wasn't 'til January 6. So you can judge for yourself. Don Santiago held off almost two months. Just between you and me.

Dr.   Don't worry, Pacífico.

P.P. And anyway, the stone was still there.

Dr.   But that must have been easy.

P.P. That's what you think! Moving that stone took us over two weeks.

Dr.   You had to move it?

P.P. Well, yeah. And you couldn't move it any old way, like just roll it down the slope, for example. We had to loosen it first, and then get it back inside, carefully, just like the other one, rotating it, like it was a door, understand?

Dr. How did you manage to do it?

P.P. With patience, the only way that works. At first we used the blade of a knife, then a wire. We just gnawed away at it, like rats.

Dr. With a wire?

P.P. A wire, yes sir. The blade didn't go beyond the handle, of course, 'cause the stone was twice as thick as the knife blade. So we'd stick the end of the wire into the crack and scrape, that's all. And with that wire, you couldn't last long. Don't think we got more than a bag from each session—of dirt, I mean. And to top it off, Patita defaulted after the problem.

Dr. Was he injured?

P.P. No, it wasn't that. As a matter of fact he was OK—just like you and me. Except that he took this dislike to it. Hated it all with a passion.

Dr. Hated what?

P.P. The tunnel, the hole. If you took him over to the tapestry he'd go crazy. We couldn't do anything with him, believe me.

Dr. So that left three of you, then, right?

P.P. Yeah. Buque, Capullo, and me.

Dr. Did you keep up the same pace?

P.P. Yes sir. Well actually, no. Every fourth night we'd take off. Patita's night.

Dr. It occurs to me that if there was an iron grating in the cell window, Pacífico, wouldn't it have been easier to file down the bars? Don Santiago's friend, or whatever she was, could have brought you as many nail files as you would've needed, couldn't she?

P.P. The hall window, you mean?

Dr. Whichever—the cell window or the hall window, whichever.

P.P. But remember that the guard was a few steps away, with a wall in between.

Dr. You could have done it in the daytime.

P.P. That's what you think! Mornings and evenings the guard checked the bars. In the window in our hall and in all the windows. Then he checked the width of every bar. If they weren't as thick as my arm, he'd be onto it. Don Santiago was no babe in the woods, remember. If he said to dig a tunnel it was because there was no other way.

Dr. All right, I see. So it took you two weeks to loosen the stone, right?

P.P. Give a day, take a day. What I can tell you is that when Capullo saw light for the first time we were well into December, the eve of the Immaculate Conception.*

Dr. It must have been a big event for him.

P.P. You can say that again. He says when he saw it—the light, I mean—he clenched his fist and burst out crying like a baby. And he was like that 'til reveille.

Dr. Did you follow him?

P.P. It was my turn, yes sir.

Dr. And then what?

P.P. What do you mean, then what? It was great to get your nose into the crack and breathe.

Dr. Breathe the air of freedom?

P.P. Freedom, my foot! Just fresh air. I'd been cooped up in that hole for ages. And seeing a ray of light made you go at it with new energy. But we had to be more careful, too. You should've seen what the last days were like.

Dr. What happened during the final days, Pacífico?

P.P. It wasn't so much that anything happened, Doctor. It was just that you had to be more careful. Don Santiago said, Don't let anything bigger than a fingernail fall out of there. We couldn't be careful enough.

Dr. Why so many precautions?

P.P. Because of the sentries.

Dr. Could they see you? Weren't they up in the merlons and crenels of the castle?

P.P. Not in Góyar. They kept watch outside.

Dr. It must be a unique case.

P.P. I won't say it wasn't. The lookout posts in Góyar were built into the outside part, circling around the prison and facing it, understand? One every sixty or seventy meters. In the afternoon, lots of times, from up in the gallery, since we didn't have anything

*Translator's Note: This holy day, also Mother's Day in Spain, has been officially celebrated on December 8 since 1854, when the Roman Catholic Church proclaimed the dogma of the Immaculate Conception.

better to do, we'd watch the changing of the guard. The corporal would march up with a new sentry and walk back the other. And he'd go one by one, from one sentry box to the next. We'd kill time that way.

Dr.   Do you mean to say that the sentry boxes went all around the castle, facing it?

P.P.   Yeah, like I said, facing it. Up in the tower all there was was the searchlight and the machine gun.

Dr.   They must have made the escape more difficult, didn't they?

P.P.   I guess so. That's why Don Santiago said it would be better to wait for a misty day, to slip through the sentries with the mist.

Dr.   But like that you might have walked right into one of them. The mist can be very deceptive, Pacífico.

P.P.   Yeah, it's false, and it'll trick you, you're right. I figured it'd be a good idea to take advantage of it.

Dr.   And escape on the holiday, of course.

P.P.   Oh, no sir. The opposite. Don Santiago said prisoners usually wait 'til Christmas Eve or Christmas Day to get away, when there's all the commotion, see. The guards are on the lookout around then; they even get special instructions. Don Santiago said we'd leave when they least expected it. For example, after a party, when the sentries weren't thinking too clearly after the eating and drinking.

Dr.   So once you moved the stone Don Santiago told you his plans?

P.P.   Wait a minute. After moving the stone, Buque and Capullo and me, that is, we were at it for two more weeks widening the exit of the tunnel, making its "living room" there at the end.

Dr.   At the end of the tunnel?

P.P.   Yes sir, next to the stone in the tower.

Dr.   For what purpose?

P.P.   Look, what Don Santiago wanted was for the four of us to be in the living room the day of the escape. And he pretty much got what he wanted. But you should've seen the work it gave us! We ran around like chickens with their heads cut off for days, always at it.

Dr.   But at least you must have had some air and light coming in through the cracks.

P.P. Some air, you say? At that time of the year Góyar is worse than the North Pole. Some frosts! And there I was, wearing only my girdle. I was freezing! As soon as I crawled in, my stomach would act up on me. It took me over a day to start to recover from those chills.

Dr.   How about Patita? Couldn't he help you out?

P.P. I already told you: He hated it. Patita didn't go back to the tunnel 'til the night of the escape. And then only 'cause we pushed him in. The one who did go in was Don Santiago.

Dr.   Don Santiago went in to work?

P.P. No, to inspect it. But he was pleased by what he saw. And then he ordered the ropes put into place—the espadrilles, the clothes, and everything that would come in handy, see. After that, except for one morning when Capullo went in, nobody went back in.

Dr.   Why did Capullo go in?

P.P. To set the stone up on a pole so we could move it easily. Capullo had experience with that in his town, and he knew what he was doing.

Dr.   How about the rest of the rope—did Don Santiago's lady friend bring it?

P.P. Oh, it had already been in the living room for two weeks by then. Just in case you want to know, Don Santiago's lady friend came one day before the holidays with the rope and all our outfits: the tabards, the blankets, overcoats, espadrilles. She brought everything. Didn't stint on anything, no sir.

Dr.   What did you need all those clothes for?

P.P. For our cots, to make bulky shapes, get it? The plan was to sneak away after the call for silence. 'Cause if the guard showed up, we had to make sure he'd see our cots were occupied, right?

Dr.   Didn't the guard in the visiting room suspect something when all those clothes were brought in?

P.P. Hey, why should he? It was the season for getting a package. Everybody got something, and if they didn't get it from home, they got charity, of course. And they knew that Buque and the others didn't have any means, whereas Don Santiago and his lady friend were people of high standing, for whatever reason. I won't get into that 'cause it's not my business. So anyway, she left word that the clothes were for Don Santiago and his friends. So when the guard felt the packages and checked out the clothes, he was satisfied.

Dr. When did Don Santiago tell you his plans?

P.P. Well, on a day like today, Capullo set the hinge in place. It was the big topic in the hall. And Don Santiago repeated things over and over and looked at Buque. If you want my opinion, he didn't trust him; he was scared of what he might do. And he was right to be—you've never seen anybody so stupid.

Dr. So to come to the point, Pacífico: What date did Don Santiago set for the escape?

P.P. The second of January, at first.

Dr. Did he change it later on?

P.P. Yes he did. He made it definite for the sixth, the Feast of the Magi.

Dr. Wasn't that night a holiday?

P.P. Not for us prisoners, no sir, it wasn't. But it was for the officials and the guards, although they celebrated it on their own time. And according to Don Santiago the staff was reduced that day, because just about everyone had some family waiting at home. Well, anyway, that night, with the hangovers from the partying those days, the staff would be kind of sluggish, and besides, there was no moon. So it was a piece of cake, right? Well, anyway, Buque wanted to know if there'd be any fog: Any fog that night? And Don Santiago—was he ever patient—says, Forget the fog, Buque, the fog doesn't matter.

Dr. Go on.

P.P. Well, the first thing to do according to Don Santiago was, as soon as we heard the signal for silence, to make the dummies in our cots. The stone—at the opening in the hall—would already be moved aside. After the evening retreat Capullo would roll it sideways, and the hole would be covered by the tapestry, see? And we'd all disappear in a flash, into the tunnel.

Dr. How about the watchman? Wasn't he right at the wall?

P.P. Wait a minute. After the guard gave the signal for silence he usually made his rounds in the gallery, all around the courtyard; he'd go from one hall to the next telling everybody to shut up.

And there were halls—like San Vicente, for example—with over twenty men where it never failed: some guy would be giving him a problem. So between one thing and another, the guard would take fifteen or twenty minutes to get to our hall, to the peephole, I mean, to make his rounds. By then, according to Don Santiago, we'd all be in the tunnel. But just in case, we'd go barefoot; he'd put the espadrilles in the living room. And Don Santiago was supposed to start coughing, and he wouldn't stop 'til they'd finished.

Dr. Did Don Santiago give you a special role to play?

P.P. Well, sort of. I was supposed to hang around the peephole while they made the dummies in their cots. To keep an eye on the guard, see. And as soon as the guard showed up I'd be standing up in the middle of the hall, on purpose, so he'd think the others had gone to bed when he saw the bulky shapes. And the guard was supposed to scold me as usual, and say, Come on, Seminarista, it's that time again. Well, anyway, I was supposed to play it cool, just amble over to my cot and go to bed right in front of him, and the guard was supposed to go out calmly and catch a few winks himself.

Dr. How about the guys in the tunnel?

P.P. They were supposed to wait in the living room 'til the changing of the guard.

Dr. The changing of the guard?

P.P. Yes sir. They changed on even hours, so, for example, if silence started at nine o'clock, they were supposed to wait in the living room 'til ten.

Dr. What would they do then?

P.P. Move the stone, stand it up so it wouldn't roll back into the hole. Then tie the rope and run.

Dr. Who was supposed to go first?

P.P. Don Santiago, of course.

Dr. Why Don Santiago?

P.P. He was running the show, wasn't he? Let's see if I can make it clear. Don Santiago was supposed to go down first, and once he was in the moat, he was supposed to tug at the rope three times. Then Patita, who was behind him, when he felt them, was supposed to go down. And once he got to the moat, Don Santiago would tug three times again, and Buque would go down. And Capullo would follow suit.

Dr. Meanwhile, how about you?

P.P. Oh, I'd just be resting on my cot.

Dr. Wasn't Don Santiago afraid that they'd make you confess the next day?

P.P. He couldn't have cared less. He even told me so. Whether I had to or not didn't really matter. It was water over the dam.

Dr. Are you sure that what you're saying is right?

P.P. Well, why would I tell you otherwise?

Dr. Then why do you suppose that afterward he did the opposite of what he'd planned or of what he'd told you?

P.P. The stuff you say! 'Cause he got mixed up. You know, if the guard hadn't shown his face, nothing would've happened. How could it? But for some reason or other he took it into his head to do something he never did: look in on us. And it screwed up the works.

Dr. I see. Well, once the four of them were in the moat down below, what did they plan to do?

P.P. Take off. Run down the ditch. The sentries could hardly see them down there. So the plan was to run around the tower and keep running to the infirmary, on the outside side. Don Santiago figured that all four men could be there by 10:30. So they still had an hour and a half 'til the next changing of the guard.

Dr. How did they plan to cross the sentry line?

P.P. That was the funny part. From the gallery, you see, you could see the infirmary. And on the outside there was a dry gully, a refuse dump, and four evergreens—or they might've been spruces, or juniper trees—you couldn't tell from that distance. Well, to give you an idea, those trees were halfway between the lookout posts. There must've been thirty meters either side of them. Don Santiago took Buque aside, and he taught him the route—spent hours at it—so he'd understand: first came the gully, then the dump, and then the spruces, see. He had a time of it at night, quizzing him on it. But Buque couldn't even repeat the words in the right order, he was *so* stupid.

Dr. And the others?

P.P. Learned it right off the bat.

Dr. Did Don Santiago ever get mad?

P.P. Not in the slightest. It was like he was teaching a child. Used a paper and pencil and drew it for him. Hours and hours, he spent. A really patient man.

Dr. But the gully and the dump must have been in sight, for the sentries, I mean, weren't they?

P.P. Yes sir, they were. That's why they had to crawl to the spruce trees on their elbows and knees, without ever standing up. Like snakes.

Dr. And did Buque know how to do that?

P.P. Oh yeah. Even at nighttime, without making any noise, I'd stand guard at the peephole, and they'd practice walking like snakes. You should've seen the knack Buque had for it! He could last the longest, by a long shot.

Dr. You mean to say that from the ditch to the spruces they had to crawl all the way, one after the other?

P.P. One by one, yes sir, just like you say.

Dr. And did they plan to meet again at the spruce trees?

P.P. No sir. Once they got out of the ditch each man was on his own and had to drag himself to the first oaks, see. Once they were there, about three hundred meters from the prison, they could get up and climb the hill, cross the waterway, climb up the other hill, cross the road and a little forest of beech trees 'til they reached the train tracks, understand? And once they got there it was duck soup, according to Don Santiago: all they'd have to do would be turn right 'til the tunnel. And they were supposed to meet up at the exit.

Dr. How did he get all that into Buque's head?

P.P. Well, Don Santiago sort of gradually got it across to him. He would've been satisfied just to see Buque going along the sentry posts. That's why he kept telling him: The gully, the dump, and the spruce trees, Buque. Got it? And Buque would say yeah, he got it, but it wasn't 'til the night before the escape that he could repeat it.

Dr.   That means that once the sentries had been tricked, Don Santiago would wash his hands of Buque.

P.P. No sir, don't get it twisted. Capullo was in charge of him. Capullo would be setting the pace, calling the shots, as they say. And once they got to the hill, next to the oaks, Capullo would take over. In other words, as soon as they could stand up, Capullo and Buque would take off together and run through the thicket 'til they got to the tunnel.

Dr.   How did Don Santiago get to know the terrain around the prison?

P.P. From a map.

Dr.   He had a map?

P.P. Oh yeah. He'd had one ever since I got there. The kind engineers use.

Dr.   A surveyor's map?

P.P. I think that's what they're called, yeah.

Dr.   But it would be hard to tell on a surveyor's map whether there were oaks or evergreens, or whether there was a beech tree forest behind, wouldn't you say?

P.P. Look, we could see the grove very clearly from the gallery. As for the beech trees and those things, I guess she must have explained it to him.

Dr.   The woman?

P.P. Who else?

Dr.   Tell me, Pacífico, once they were in the tunnel, what did they plan to do?

P.P. Grab the 1:05.

Dr.   There was a train at that hour?

P.P. Wait. Don Santiago said it was a train with both passenger cars and freight cars. Every night, at 1:05 more or less, we could hear it chugging by, you know? 'Cause the train would pass right through the tunnel, and they—Don Santiago and his troop, I mean—well, they'd hop onto one of the freight cars, and they'd be off on a nice ride to Madrid. See? According to them, the train was due in at 4:10, so they'd have plenty of time.

Dr.   Wasn't Don Santiago afraid the guards would discover the escape before it took place?

P.P.   Oh, no sir, that was impossible. There was no reason to discover it 'til morning reveille.

Dr.   But how about the watchmen?

P.P.   Well, the guard went off duty at one. He'd take a walk around the gallery then, and then again at four, see. But it was just a routine checkup. Lots of nights he didn't bother.

Dr.   He didn't go into the halls?

P.P.   You can be sure of it. Unless somebody got sick, of course. Their round was just a routine. Then Don Santiago asked me to switch beds for the one o'clock round, to stuff some clothes in mine and go and snore in somebody else's cot. What he wanted to avoid was the guards coming around and always finding the same person awake. So they wouldn't get suspicious.

Dr.   I see.

P.P.   It was pretty well thought out, don't think it wasn't. I'd bet you Don Santiago remembered what the grass they'd step on was like. He had it all up here in his head. Nothing got past him. Just to give you an idea, when it struck one, he'd wake up the three of them, so they could hear the train whistle.

Dr.   The passenger and freight train?

P.P.   Of course. The one they'd have to catch.

Dr.   Didn't he wake you up?

P.P.   No he didn't. Since I wasn't part of that plan.

Dr.   How do you know, then? Did you have trouble sleeping by then?

P.P.   Well, yes sir, I did. Ever since they got me involved in their scheme I couldn't sleep the way I used to. I was never calm. It must've been my nerves or something. I was always agitated. And then when the Christmas holidays came, you should've seen it around there, Don Santiago telling us to make more of a racket than anybody else. What more could they want? From morning to night there we were with our tambourines. Capullo never let up; he had a finger in every pie. And the son of a gun had quite a voice, too. So the guards were directing the choir, and it was all a big party. But don't think they took their eyes off us for a minute; they just pretended they weren't watching us. And Don Santiago was after Buque with the usual: You've got to keep it straight, now, Buque—the gully, the dump, and the spruce trees,

OK? And Buque'd say, Yeah, I've got it. But actually he didn't have the faintest idea. And to top it off, he goes and falls the night before and breaks a bone. That's all we needed.

Dr.   Buque fell down the night before the escape?

P.P.   Well, practically. It was five days before, on the thirty-first of December, the tail end of the year. Imagine. And it was so stupid: he fell down a flight of stairs, just like a parcel from the post office. Personally, I think he'd had a couple of drinks. If not, there's no explaining it. So four of the guys had to carry him to the infirmary. We went through hell with that.

Dr.   Because of having to postpone the escape?

P.P.   That was the least of it, Doctor. Don Santiago was never in a hurry. What he was afraid of—and he had every reason to be— was that Buque would let the cat out of the bag, understand? 'Cause Buque was very talkative, see.

Dr.   Did he take long to get back?

P.P.   Buque, to the hall?

Dr.   Yes.

P.P.   Three days. But it seemed like three years. Don Santiago didn't know what to invent. To keep us busy, I mean. You can imagine our nerves. That was when he got the brainstorm of making a pack of cards out of a shoebox. You have no idea what talent he had. All Capullo could say was: You made the gold knight perfect! He has the same jerky face. Meaning him—the guy on horseback. We had lots of laughs with it.

Dr.   So you played cards?

P.P.   How could we help it? Except in the afternoon, when we were in the gallery keeping cozy. All day long playing cards. Don Santiago said that the first to get a hundred *tutes* would get a free meal from the rest of us.* After the escape.

Dr.   That is to say, Don Santiago was already counting on you.

P.P.   No sir. You're the one who said that. Don Santiago wanted to amuse Patita and Capullo. He trusted me more.

Dr.   Who won the hundred *tutes*?

---

*Translator's Note: *Tute* (from the Italian *tutti*) is a Spanish card game, like *mus*. The object of the game is to win all the kings or all the horses.

P.P. We didn't even have time to finish. Buque got there first.

Dr.   What happened to him?

P.P. The worst. Broke his fibula bone, the right one.

Dr.   Couldn't he walk?

P.P. No way. I mean, they put his leg in a cast, from the knee down. It was hard as a rock. That cast must've weighed five kilos. But two days later he was using two crutches, and he was getting around with no trouble—ran around the courtyard like a hare. May God forgive me for saying so, Doctor, but that guy Buque was as dense as they come.

Dr.   So he was getting along pretty well?

P.P. Like you and me.

Dr.   What did Don Santiago say?

P.P. Well, at first he tried to draw it out of him, see if he'd gone off at the mouth.

Dr.   Had he?

P.P. According to Buque, he didn't open his mouth once, not for three days, except to eat. And then Don Santiago proposed that they postpone the escape 'til he was ready.

Dr.   What was Buque's reply?

P.P. That if the others didn't cut out, *he* would, by himself. Not exactly what you'd expect of him.

Dr.   And Don Santiago?

P.P. Just imagine. Wouldn't let him alone for a minute. Once he said that, he followed him around, trying to teach him how to walk on his own. And at nighttime, in the hall, he'd trail behind him. You won't believe this, Doctor, but even with the broken bone and the cast he could take more than the others.

Dr.   Did Don Santiago go ahead and confirm it then, that the escape would be on the sixth?

P.P. Sure, it was only natural.

Dr.   And as the day approached, did he decide on anything else that was new?

P.P. In general, no sir, or not that I know of, anyway. Except for Buque's cast. Since everybody wrote on it, Don Santiago drew the gully, the dump, and the spruces, so he'd study it. For the rest, according to Don Santiago, he planned to take down one of

Buque's crutches, and Capullo would carry the other. Outside of that, they'd do things just the way we'd planned.

Dr.   The days before must have been pretty restless ones, weren't they, Pacífico?

P.P.   No, don't think they were, Doctor. I mean, the night before, Don Santiago kept them all up 'til one o'clock, and once they heard the train whistle he said: Tomorrow we'll be on that train, hear? And that was all he said. But I know he was shaking in his boots, thinking about Buque.

Dr.   And the next day, what happened?

P.P.   It was like any other. Except that Don Santiago didn't budge from his cot. Although that wasn't strange in him.

Dr.   Yes. Well, let's get on with the escape.

P.P.   I believe they're calling you, Doctor.

Dr.   Me? They're calling me now?

P.P.   At the door, I mean. Somebody just tapped on it.

Dr.   What time is it?

P.P.   Who knows?

Dr.   Oh my goodness. It's after three, Pacífico. Do you mind if we leave this for tomorrow?

P.P.   It's fine by me. I'm in no rush.

▲ ▲ ▲ ▲ ▲ ▲ ▲

Seventh Night

P.P.   Was it anything serious yesterday, Doctor?

Dr.   The usual complaints. How did you sleep, Pacífico?

P.P.   So so. As usual.

Dr.   Did you have a nightmare?

P.P.   No sir. Why should I?

Dr.   About what we talked about.

P.P.   That's over with now.

Dr.   Do you remember where we left off in our conversation?

P.P.   Sort of, yeah.

Dr.   You were starting to tell me about the escape when we were interrupted. Isn't that so?

P.P.   Yes, that's right, sir.

Dr.   Fine. Go on.

P.P.   What do you want me to tell you about?

Dr.   Everything, Pacífico. Go back to the beginning. If I'm not mistaken, you had agreed to get under way when you heard the signal for silence, as soon as the watchman started on his rounds, right?

P.P.   That's right, yes sir.

Dr.   And did you do it?

P.P.   Sure.

Dr.   Just as you'd planned?

P.P.   Exactly.

Dr.   But tell me something: Your mission consisted of looking through the peephole and watching the watchman. Did you accomplish it?

P.P.   Well, yeah, I did, sir.

Dr.   And then what?

P.P.   Well, I warned them.

198

Dr.   Warned them of what?

P.P. Of what we're saying: that the guard was starting his rounds.

Dr.   How did you warn them?

P.P. By raising my right hand, the way we'd agreed.

Dr.   Had Capullo already moved the stone?

P.P. Oh yeah, during evening retreat.

Dr.   Speak up, now. So you raised your hand. What did they do?

P.P. They took off their shoes.

Dr.   And then?

P.P. They put their shoes in their cots and went over to the closets.

Dr.   To get their clothes?

P.P. Yes sir.

Dr.   You're not being very explicit tonight, Pacífico. Is something wrong?

P.P. With me? No sir, nothing.

Dr.   Fine. Go on. They stuffed the clothes under the blankets to pretend they were sleeping, right?

P.P. That's what they did. But first Don Santiago decided on something else: to escape in their shirts and underpants.

Dr.   Without anything to cover them?

P.P. Half-naked, yeah.

Dr.   But why?

P.P. Look, flurries started on the afternoon of the fourth, and it didn't let up for two days. So by the morning of the sixth the ground was whiter than the walls.

Dr.   And Don Santiago must have been afraid they'd stand out against the snow, right?

P.P. That's exactly it.

Dr.   Didn't anybody object?

P.P. What was that?

Dr.   I mean, didn't anybody protest?

P.P. Whatever he said went, so nobody piped up.

Dr.   Fine. Continue. They started making the dummies. Then what?

P.P. Nothing else. They didn't even have time to finish.

Dr.   What happened?

P.P. That's what I'd like to know. I mean, I don't know what got into him, but the guard turned around. And instead of going up the gallery like he did every night, he did a turn and came toward us. Why, I have no idea.

Dr.   Well, did you make any noise or do something that might have attracted his attention?

P.P.   No! We didn't make any noise at all. It was just one of those things, a hunch he had, I guess.

Dr.   Some fix! What did you do?

P.P.   You can just imagine: He's coming! I mumbled, Hey, he's coming. I even raised my voice.

Dr.   How about them?

P.P.   Them! They hopped into their cots as fast as they could. To save their necks.

Dr.   All of them?

P.P.   Will this stay between you and me, Doctor?

Dr.   Of course, Pacífico.

P.P.   You promise?

Dr.   Don't you trust me?

P.P.   OK. Well, Don Santiago didn't get into his cot.

Dr.   What did Don Santiago do?

P.P.   He grabbed the bar and crept over to the wall, right next to the door.

Dr.   Who was on duty?

P.P.   Vegas, of course.

Dr.   What do you mean, Vegas, of course?

P.P.   I don't know! We had an unlucky streak with that man. The day we banged on the toilet seats he was on duty. The day Patita got stuck in the tunnel, same thing. And the funny part is that that guy Vegas wasn't such a bad person, but for some reason or other he was always around when there was a jam.

Dr.   Tell me about the bar that Don Santiago picked up, Pacífico: Where was it from?

P.P.   Oh, I don't know. That bar had been lying around in the hall ever since I got there. But I recall that on that particular night Don Santiago had tied a muffler to the end of it.

Dr.   So the blows wouldn't be heard?

P.P.   I guess so. But don't quote me on it.

Dr.   OK. Well, what did the watchman do?

P.P.   He went up to the door and looked through the peephole, twice. Then he put the key in, and just when he'd put it in, Don Santiago let him have it with the bar. But that's strictly between you and me, Doctor.

Dr.   Don't worry, Pacífico. And why do you think the watchman decided to come in? Could it have been because there was no dummy in Don Santiago's cot?

P.P.   Maybe. Or maybe it wasn't made right. Or maybe Buque with his clothes in there looked too big. Who knows, Doctor? All I know is that the guard got an impulse to look in and that that did him in.

Dr.   Tell me about it.

P.P.   Well, he turned the key in the lock, see. You should've seen the lump I felt in my chest. I mean, as he was coming in, Vegas, that is, I couldn't even breathe. He hadn't set foot in the hall when Don Santiago whacked him one so hard he knocked him down. In a flash. It happened faster than it's taking me to tell you about it.

Dr.   The watchman died on the spot?

P.P.   Well, yeah. Me, when I grabbed him by the arm to hide him under my cot, I could still feel his pulse, that's for sure. So he must've died while we were moving him and covering him up with the blankets.

Dr.   So when you went into the tunnel he was already dead?

P.P.   Yes sir, that's a fact. You can be sure of it. Don Santiago looked at his eyes and listened to his heart and said, Well, he's a goner.

Dr.   Would you please explain to me why you put him under your cot and not somebody else's, Pacífico?

P.P.   Easy. It was the only free one. The others all had clothes under them.

Dr.   And couldn't you have moved them?

P.P.   Well, I guess we could've if we'd wanted to . . . But with all that commotion one cot was the same as another.

Dr.   Did Don Santiago lose his composure?

P.P.   Oh, no sir. Don Santiago was as cool as a cucumber, just like always. You don't know him. But everything changed, of course. Everybody was shaking like a leaf.

Dr.   Did the watchman make a loud noise when he fell?

P.P.   Noise? No. The noise a man makes when he falls onto a slab. And as for the blow, well, it was quieter, 'cause Don Santiago had the sense to hit him with the muffled end. So if you're wondering if that was a problem, it wasn't. It's just that things had gotten off to a bad start. We hadn't counted on it, you know?

Dr.   Where did Don Santiago expect you to go once the body was under your cot?

P.P.   He worked it out. While we were dragging the corpse over, he said: Hurry up, Seminarista. You're coming with us.

Dr.   In other words, he had you join the escape.

P.P.   Well yeah, he did.

Dr.   And you?

P.P.   I told him no.

Dr.   That you weren't going?

P.P.   That's what I said, yes sir. Said I was happy there, and that that was it.

Dr.   What did he answer to that?

P.P.   Don Santiago?

Dr.   Well, of course, Pacífico.

P.P.   Well, he said, he says: I'm sorry, Seminarista. You haven't got any choice. Those were his words.

Dr.   But you insisted, right?

P.P.   Yes sir, I insisted on staying.

Dr.   Did that make him furious?

P.P.   Furious? Oh, no sir. He didn't bat an eye. The only thing he did was grab the bar and say: Come on, Seminarista, make up your mind. If you don't come I'll have to hit you.

Dr.   With the bar? He threatened to hit you with the bar?

P.P.   Yeah. With the bar.

Dr.   In other words, either you escaped too or he'd kill you.

P.P.   Wait a second. He never said anything about killing me.

Dr.   You know better than I do.

P.P.   And hey, don't stick that in. All Don Santiago said was that I'd better get out of there or he'd let me have it.

Dr.   Didn't he explain himself, give you a reason?

P.P.   He did.

Dr.   What did he say?

P.P. Just that. That he didn't care to have me give it away, and if I stayed, they'd make me.

Dr. So what did you decide then?

P.P. Well, I kind of insisted a little. Not much, though. Once he threatened me with the bar I made up my mind fast.

Dr. What did you say to him?

P.P. That I agreed. That I'd take off with them.

Dr. And you all went into the tunnel.

P.P. Well, let's see. At first, Don Santiago bolted the door to the hall and hung up the keys. Then he lifted up the tapestry and went in. Into the hole, that is.

Dr. How about you? What place did you take?

P.P. Don Santiago said to stay in the middle. He didn't trust me, I guess. So I was supposed to go behind Patita and in front of Buque.

Dr. Did you leave the hall in order?

P.P. Yes sir, we tidied up. Vegas didn't bleed or anything. The worst part was when it was Patita's turn. Nobody had thought of it.

Dr. What happened?

P.P. He screamed. What do you think of that?

Dr. He screamed? Really loudly?

P.P. Loud as he could.

Dr. To warn the watchmen?

P.P. No, of course not. You see, ever since he was stuck in there he'd hated it, the tunnel. These things are like that. I remember Krim, our dog at home, when Abue built him a new doghouse. Krim hated it, just took a dislike to it for some reason or other. He wouldn't go in there for all the tea in China. And he'd spend nights next to it howling like a possessed soul. Well, the same thing happened with Patita.

Dr. Did you force him into the hole?

P.P. Capullo went up to him and slapped him a few times. And not just to bring him to his senses, either. Then he grabbed hold of his head and stuck it in, in the tunnel, that is. Well, anyway, between one thing and another we took longer than we expected, and I was thinking to myself, They're gonna catch us before we get down.

Dr. Did somebody come into the hall?

P.P. Apparently not, sir.

Dr. How is it possible, Pacífico, that Patita screamed the way you said and there was no alarm?

P.P. Oh, 'cause they were used to it. If a guy didn't talk in his sleep, he might snore or just scream, understand? Look at Patita. Well, everybody was like him. So if the guard didn't report it to the surveillance center, nobody paid any attention. Down there they relied on the guard in every gallery, and as long as the guard didn't talk, it was like nothing had happened.

Dr. I see. So you shut yourselves up and waited.

P.P. Sort of, yeah. But since the living room could only fit four, the last man—Capullo—had to stay in the tunnel. All he could do was look in, see.

Dr. What did Don Santiago say once you were all together?

P.P. To stay cool. That things had gotten complicated, but to stay cool. That we wouldn't get anywhere if we let our nerves get the best of us. You should've seen us packed in there like sardines, in the dark, our knees touching. We could hardly fit in there. And then there was Buque's cast.

Dr. Did Don Santiago mention that you'd joined them?

P.P. Sort of. He asked if I had any doubts.

Dr. And?

P.P. Well no, I didn't. After he'd repeated it all to Buque a thousand times, what doubts could I have?

Dr. Nothing else?

P.P. Not really, no sir. Well, actually, yes. He talked about the snow, said the snow was very treacherous. And to watch for the gully, the dump, and the spruces; to follow the tracks he'd leave us. In there in the darkness I couldn't even see Buque, you know? I could only hear him grunt. So anyway, after a while, when Don Santiago saw we'd calmed down, he said the most important thing was the guard's death. 'Cause with his death, the latest they'd discover our escape would be at one o'clock, when the new shift was on duty. And by then we'd be at the track catching the train, understand? Don Santiago said we had to change our plans, because they might search the train at any station, or when it got to

Madrid. So we were supposed to split up, every man for himself. Like, for example, one person could get off at a town, or somebody else might transfer to another train; but whoever wanted to go all the way to the capital should get off before the train got to the station. I couldn't get Buque out of my mind. I mean, how was he going to manage? But everybody said OK, they understood.

Dr.   How about Patita—wasn't he nervous?

P.P.   Once he got settled, no sir. Buque was the only one who kept on fussing. He couldn't sit still, had to move around.

Dr.   Did you calm him down?

P.P.   Sure. It was good for us, too, to keep him quiet. You should've seen Don Santiago: Calm down, Buque. Wait now, Buque, don't get excited. The way you'd talk to a dog, the same voice. But Buque's eyes were popping out of their sockets. They looked like cats' eyes in the dark.

Dr.   Hmm.

P.P.   But the worst part, hey, is when it occurred to Buque to ask What's a spruce? Imagine. After teaching him for a month.

Dr.   What did Don Santiago say?

P.P.   To forget about the spruces and just follow our tracks in the snow—his, Patita's, and mine.

Dr.   How about you—what were your thoughts during that tight situation?

P.P.   My thoughts? I didn't have any. What did you expect me to think?

Dr.   But what did you feel?

P.P.   Out of sorts.

Dr.   Because of the escape?

P.P.   Well, yeah. There I was all snug, and all of a sudden bang! I'm somewhere else: outside.

Dr.   You were annoyed that they'd forced you against your will?

P.P.   Something like that.

Dr.   But were you calm?

P.P.   That I was. After all, why shouldn't I be? Except for the cold. After we got over the scare with Vegas and all, we noticed we were freezing in that living room. And my stomach, it was killing me.

Dr.   Had you taken off your girdle?

P.P.   No sir, I had it on. But it was very cold and damp.

Dr.   But the wait didn't last long, did it?

P.P.   Oh, about half an hour. Afterward, Don Santiago ordered the stone put back and for us to shut up. And that's when Capullo started to crack his knuckles. He was nervous. Well, anyway, after a while we heard the corporal coming up with the new watchman to the sentry box next to the elm tree, right across from the tower. So it meant it was ten o'clock. So Don Santiago ordered the stone to be propped up and the rope tied. Then he said for us to put on our espadrilles, and that's when I realized that there weren't any for me, that Buque had even put one on his wounded foot. I had to go barefoot, imagine, and with all that snow falling— flakes as big as saucers. And we waited 'til the corporal passed with the new sentry near the spruces, at the last box. Just as soon as he turned around, Don Santiago jumped. Good luck! he called out. And he took down one of Buque's crutches, and he said we should wait for him to tug on the rope.

Dr.   Couldn't you hear him as he went down?

P.P.   No sir, not him or anybody else. What with the espadrilles. And least of all me, being barefoot.

Dr.   Did you wait for the tugs?

P.P.   Of course. Soon as he got down. But they were taking longer than we expected, and Buque was getting itchy, 'cause you know he was a real case. And everybody was going, Quiet down, Buque, hold your horses. But he just kept fussing. I don't know how we managed to hold him back, he was such a pain! Thank goodness Patita felt the tugging and went on down. Then I got into the hole and held onto the rope. 'Til I felt the tugs. What a spot to be in! That hole was very narrow, no more than this, understand? And you had to back out of it, your seat first, without letting go of the rope. Once you got your footing on the stone, you were OK. So anyway, I went down the tower and then the side slope, and suddenly there was no more rope! I was hanging there like a puppet, my feet dangling, and I didn't know which way I was going. Then I heard Don Santiago's voice, very low, see. Jump, Seminarista! And I jumped. Into the moat. It had half a meter of snow in it. I was OK, but I thought to myself, boy, a guy like Buque's going to hurt himself for sure. I mean, imagine a man as big as him making that jump, and with a broken bone besides.

Dr.   And how did you handle it?

P.P.   Well, at first Don Santiago took off his undershirt and asked us for ours, Patita and me, I mean. Then he climbed the slope, and we braced him from below, by the seat of his pants. And he tied the undershirts to the rope so Buque could get one more meter down, understand? Then he had us pile up some snow under the rope, so when Buque jumped there wasn't even half a meter. So he didn't hurt himself or anything.

Dr.   Did you leave the undershirts hanging there?

P.P.   No way! And it wasn't 'cause of the cold. It was 'cause of the snow. The sentry could notice them, see.

Dr.   Were you still cold, Pacífico?

P.P.   Frozen stiff. Couldn't even feel my feet.

Dr.   Continue. What did you do next?

P.P.   Once we were together, in the moat, that is, Don Santiago said to follow him and keep our mouths shut. Not a word, he said. And I was afraid 'cause of Buque, but he didn't let out a peep. So we went ahead, around the tower and up to the infirmary, see, on the outside.

Dr.   That's where you were supposed to leave the moat and trick the sentries, right?

P.P.   Right, Doctor.

Dr.   Didn't Don Santiago give you new instructions?

P.P.   No, not really. Wait a second. He did say, come to think of it, that I should go behind Patita. And that all Buque had to do was follow our tracks in the snow. That's what he said.

Dr.   Nothing else?

P.P.   Nothing else. Well, he greeted us. Shook our hands, one by one. Don Santiago was a very polite man.

Dr.   Go on.

P.P.   So he got out of the moat, and before he even showed his face he stretched out on the ground. After a while we couldn't see him. Then Patita went up, after him. Following suit.

Dr.   How much time did you allow between each man?

P.P. To get out of the moat?

Dr. Yes.

P.P. It seemed like a long time, you know? But say five minutes. Not more than that.

Dr. OK. So you went up. How did you manage?

P.P. Wait a minute. The dog came first.

Dr. A watchdog?

P.P. What do you mean, a watchdog! No sir, it was from the town; or at least I think it was. Patita had just taken off, and we heard a noise up above, and a dog, a stray dog, the kind you see sniffing around garbage cans, shows up. Anyway, Capullo says, Get out of here! And Buque was set on smacking him on the snout with his crutch, and the animal naturally started to growl. You can imagine what a spot *we* were in.

Dr. What did you do?

P.P. What my Uncle Paco taught me to do. Make as if I was unscrewing my head to hit him with it.

Dr. Throw it at the dog?

P.P. Yeah, at the dog.

Dr. But . . . your head?

P.P. Don't get me wrong, now. I was just threatening him, that's all. But it never fails. It scares a dog, and he doesn't come back. He cowers.

Dr. Did it leave?

P.P. Sure. That much we could count on.

Dr. Without barking?

P.P. Well, he did whine once. But it wasn't loud.

Dr. Did you get out of the moat then?

P.P. Yeah, I didn't waste any time. I'd already delayed enough.

Dr. And?

P.P. And what? Judge for yourself. Ever since I put my stomach to the snow I thought I was a goner. And then the storm. Did it ever snow! It made you numb, you know? And as if that wasn't enough, the snow covered the others' tracks. I was shaking, just thinking about Buque, Doctor. What would become of him? But I hit the ground and went on that way 'til I got to the reed grass near the gully.

Dr.   Couldn't you hear anything?

P.P.   I couldn't hear or see anything. It was like a cemetery. A real impressive silence, you know?

Dr.   Did you find the gully soon?

P.P.   Right away, yes sir, there it was. And in the reed grass you could see Don Santiago's and Patita's tracks better, their footprints, I mean.

Dr.   Did you follow them?

P.P.   As long as the gully lasted. Then I hunted for the dump for a while. And what do you suppose I started thinking about the whole time, ever since I got down the rope?

Dr.   What, Pacífico?

P.P.   About Abue. And I hadn't mentioned him for months. Well, I started thinking about him just then, about Igueriben and the fort, when they went down a rope to fool Abd-el-Krim. I couldn't get it out of my mind.

Dr.   Actually, it was a similar situation.

P.P.   Yeah. Except we had snow instead of sand.

Dr.   And tell me: Did you find the dump?

P.P.   That would've been the limit, not finding the dump! I was walking in it. But so's not to have any surprises, I checked: I stuck my hand in a heap and pulled out two pieces of rubbish.

Dr.   Didn't you see Don Santiago's and Patita's tracks?

P.P.   It was hard to tell. So I decided that once I got to the spruces I'd wait up for Buque.

Dr.   But that wasn't part of the plan.

P.P.   No sir, it wasn't. But neither was the blizzard, or me, right? Escaping, I mean. I just suddenly felt sorry for him, you know what I mean?

Dr.   Perfectly. Go on, Pacífico.

P.P.   Well, from the dump, straining your eyes a little, you could just barely make out the spruce trees. The wind was coming from the north, and since I was going along the west side, well, I could see them darkening. In fact, I could almost see the sentry box. And all I did was to tell myself, Watch out, Pacífico, don't blow it. I mean I talked to myself like old people do, you know? To be on the safe side.

Dr.   And how about the man ahead of you, and the one behind you—
      Patita and Buque—what did you know about their movements?

P.P. Nothing. I couldn't see them, and I couldn't hear them. It was
      as if the earth had swallowed them. But as I was getting to the
      dump, I did think that Don Santiago must be going up the hill
      by then, and that Buque must be in the snow and Capullo must
      be alone in the moat. I made my calculations, but as for seeing
      them, really seeing them, I mean, no sir. They were out of sight.

Dr.   Did you get to the spruce grove without any difficulties?

P.P. Difficulties, you say? All you can think of, and more. My hands
      and feet were freezing, with a tingling that was starting to burn.
      And my stomach, oh, you don't want to know about it. What I
      can't figure out is how I had the strength to go on.

Dr.   But you kept on.

P.P. What else could I do? Yes sir. But I hadn't gotten to the spruces
      when the voices started. At first, hey, I just stopped in my tracks.
      They were something else.

Dr.   What voices?

P.P. The only ones there were! The sentries'.

Dr.   Did they discover one of you?

P.P. No, I don't mean that. I'm talking about their shouting to each
      other. They did it to stay awake, see. The one in the elm box
      would shout, for example, Sentry! On the alert! And the other
      one, near the road, would answer the same way, and so on. All
      around the prison, you know? But at night like that, and with the
      snow, and the silence, it sounded louder.

Dr.   I see.

P.P. So anyway, I huddled up like a rabbit 'til the voices died out,
      'cause they'd gone around the tower. Then I went over to the
      spruce trees, and it turned out they weren't spruce trees after all.

Dr.   Then what were they, Pacífico?

P.P. Junipers, like I said before.

Dr.   Couldn't that disorient Buque?

P.P. Oh, junipers and spruces were all the same to him. Remember,
      he was a man who asked us what a spruce was. After we'd been
      talking about them for over a month, in the living room. He was
      just plain dumb.

Dr.   I see. Well, if I'm not mistaken, the spruce grove—or rather, those juniper trees—were in line with the sentry boxes, weren't they?

P.P.   Yes, Doctor, that's right. So if you headed straight out, you'd end up on the other side.

Dr.   And what did you do?

P.P.   I stopped a while, to catch my breath.

Dr.   To wait up for Buque?

P.P.   No sir, not yet. I waited 'cause of the tingling; it was starting to burn. And the tightness in my chest, because of that sentry being nearby. I could hear him move.

Dr.   You could hear the sentry stirring?

P.P.   Oh yeah. And rubbing his hands together, and humming. I guess he was cold.

Dr.   You must have had a bad time of it.

P.P.   I sure did. As soon as I started to recover a little, I went on ahead. I must've been trailing them by about forty meters; it couldn't have been more than that. In other words, I was about halfway between the junipers and the other trees. And I came to a pin oak and sheltered myself there, 'cause the storm was getting really fierce.

Dr.   Did Buque make it to there?

P.P.   That's what I was waiting for.

Dr.   And did he?

P.P.   Don't even dream of it. I didn't see the slightest trace of him, and I thought to myself: That animal's probably spending the night going 'round and 'round the prison. I didn't have any hopes for him.

Dr.   And what had happened?

P.P.   What I was afraid of. Who knows where he got held up? All I know is, after a while I heard a noise near the sentry box.

Dr.   Noise? What kind of noise?

P.P.   It sounded like snorting or bumping or something. Right next to the sentry box.

Dr.   And was there actually fighting going on?

P.P.   I don't know. What *I* think is that Buque mistook the sentry boxes for the spruces. He probably got out of the dump and bumped

	right into a sentry. I could hear the struggling and the blows. And even what they were saying to each other.
Dr.	You mean to say that they were talking?
P.P.	Listen. And excuse my language. It was stuff like You son of a bitch! I spit in your shit. But as for what you'd call talking, no. What did they have to talk about?
Dr.	Listen carefully now, Pacífico: I'd appreciate it very much if you would make every effort to give me an exact version of the facts from this moment on. And I'm as interested in your accuracy as in the order in which things happened, do you understand?
P.P.	Yeah, sure.
Dr.	Well then, tell me: The first thing you heard was the sounds of the fight—their struggling, the insults exchanged between Buque and the sentry. What did you hear next? I mean immediately afterward.
P.P.	The shot.
Dr.	What shot?
P.P.	Well, the sentry's, of course!
Dr.	Did the sentry who was fighting with Buque fire?
P.P.	Well, it couldn't have been anybody else. Because the blast came from there, right next to me. You should've seen the light and the echo. What a crack!
Dr.	It must have awakened the whole prison.
P.P.	You can just imagine the scene. Shouting, bell-clanging, the works! And meanwhile, Buque's trying to beat the daylights out of the sentry. He must not have hit him, with the first shot, I mean. And after a while I heard a crunch as if they were breaking something, you know? And that's when I think Buque must have smashed the guard's head open with his cast.
Dr.	Forgive me for interrupting you, Pacífico. This moment is crucial, and I'd appreciate it if you spoke in a more orderly way. Tell me the events one by one, as they happened. After the sentry's shot, what was the next thing you heard?
P.P.	How Buque smashed his head with the cast.
Dr.	And then?
P.P.	This will be between us, won't it, Doctor?

Dr.   Of course, Pacífico. Don't worry. Until you authorize me, whatever you say will remain secret.

P.P.   Won't that gadget give it away?

Dr.   That gadget, as you call it, won't say a word until I order it to. Tell me, what did you hear after Buque's blow?

P.P.   The siren in the tower and, a little later, an engine.

Dr.   You heard an engine start up?

P.P.   Yes sir. Up in the grove, on the other side.

Dr.   Are you sure?

P.P.   As sure as I'm sitting here.

Dr.   And after that?

P.P.   Well, it was like all hell breaking loose. Screaming, alarms, shots. You can't imagine what chaos! In a minute.

Dr.   But before all that commotion you heard the engine, right?

P.P.   That's right, sir, up in the grove.

Dr.   What did you think it was?

P.P.   A patrol. I thought to myself, We've been surrounded, there's no way out. It hadn't dawned on me.

Dr.   What hadn't, Pacífico?

P.P.   That there was a car up there. That there might be another patrol, behind the sentries, on the lookout.

Dr.   And didn't it occur to you that it might be Don Santiago?

P.P.   Who?

Dr.   The one in the car.

P.P.   Don Santiago?

Dr.   Naturally, Pacífico. The woman was waiting for him up high on the road with clothes and a car to escape in. It's very clear: Don Santiago never planned to take the train with the rest of you.

P.P.   Who told you so?

Dr.   Nobody. It's obvious. My common sense tells me that.

P.P.   Well, I don't believe it, no matter what.

Dr.   Have it your way, Pacífico. But why don't you try using your head? Where were the five of you going to go in your underwear? Do you think you can walk down the Gran Vía in Madrid in your underpants and not be noticed?

P.P.   No, but that's why there are scarecrows.

Dr.   Scarecrows in January?

P.P. In January, yes sir. In my town we'd put them near the beehives because of the woodpeckers.

Dr.   OK, fine. Let's go on, Pacífico. What did you do when you heard the first shots?

P.P. What do you expect? Crouch under the oak tree and wait. And after a while I started to whisper to Buque, but he didn't answer. Then I called.

Dr.   What did you say?

P.P. Buque! I called his name.

Dr.   And nothing happened?

P.P. Nothing. He was quiet as a tomb. And I thought to myself, Where has that blockhead gone?

Dr.   Didn't you insist?

P.P. No sir. If he'd been there he would've heard me. So why should I call him again?

Dr.   So you went off to the hills then?

P.P. Wait a minute. After a while the shots stopped, but they turned on the searchlight in the tower. And it started sweeping left to right, right to left, 'til there wasn't a bush left to search. And you should've seen it—how it snowed, I mean, with the searchlight lighting it up. Looked as if it had been snowing forever. God, what a sight!

Dr.   And you stayed still then?

P.P. Well, yeah. For as long as it took to pass the oak tree.

Dr.   The searchlight?

P.P. Yeah, of course, the searchlight. The light wouldn't stay put. It kept going from one side to the other, without stopping. And if it ran into something suspicious, a bump or something, it shone more, with the machine gun.

Dr.   They used the machine gun?

P.P. Sure. The whole time.

Dr.   OK, Pacífico. And once you got a feel for the searchlight's movement, did you decide to leave the pin oak tree?

P.P. Yep. I got up and ran. Then I crouched down again and ran again. Get the idea?

Dr. Toward where?

P.P. Toward the grove, to hide behind the oak trees.

Dr. What were your thoughts during this episode?

P.P. Thoughts? I was just running, Doctor, that's all, like a rabbit, so I wouldn't get shot at.

Dr. Weren't you thinking about catching the train anymore?

P.P. Hey! If I said I wasn't thinking about anything, it's because I wasn't. Except about not getting hit. It was only natural in those circumstances, if you ask me.

Dr. So you were moving to stay out of the light, right?

P.P. Exactly. As soon as the light came, me, boom! I'd hit the ground, see. And I mean hit it: I even stuck my head in the snow.

Dr. What distance would you say there was between the pin oak tree and the others?

P.P. Say about fifty meters. No more than that.

Dr. And how many races did it take you?

P.P. I think there were four, but don't pay much attention to me. The guards discovered me during the last one, and it was some shooting spree. You should've seen it!

Dr. What did you do?

P.P. Well, what *could* I do? I ran as fast as my legs would carry me. But not straight. Oh no. Making esses, all wobbly, you know? The point is, their aim was off, so I got to the first oak and huddled up under it.

Dr. And did they keep shooting?

P.P. Yeah, did they ever. Me, I was behind the trunk, hanging in there, just like when there was the rock fight in Humán, remember?

Dr. Yes I do. And tell me, did you stay there for long?

P.P. Yeah, a long time, and boy, did that splintering noise scare me, every time they shot. It was something, let me tell you. But finally I jumped out from there and made a dash for the oak tree that was in front, and from there I jumped from one to the next 'til I was under cover. Then the guys up in the tower stopped shooting, and there was screaming again, so instead of going straight up just like that to the road I turned left, without leaving the oak trees.

Dr.   Did you hear the engine on the road again?

P.P.   No sir, how would I? I didn't hear any engine again.

Dr.   So why didn't you head for the road then?

P.P.   'Cause I was scared. How did I know that the patrol wasn't crouching there just waiting to catch sight of me?

Dr.   In other words, you were afraid their cars were parked on the high road.

P.P.   That's right, I was.

Dr.   What direction were you heading in at that point?

P.P.   As for walking, I was walking toward town, but I wasn't taking a straight route. I was kind of circling around without leaving the area.

Dr.   Had you given up escaping?

P.P.   Escaping? You know very well that I never planned on escaping.

Dr.   Not even when Don Santiago said he'd have to hit you?

P.P.   Well, *then* I did. But not 'cause I wanted to. It was just to keep from getting hurt by that bar he had. But as it turned out, the best thing was to go home.

Dr.   Back to prison?

P.P.   Yeah, prison. Except I had to be careful not to show up at the wrong time, or else they'd do me in with a bullet.

Dr.   Well, it seems clear that you wanted to turn yourself in, Pacífico. Isn't that so?

P.P.   Yeah, I guess so. Since our plan was messed up, what was I doing standing there, half naked in the snow?

Dr.   Did you run?

P.P.   I'd run for a while, then I'd stop for a while, you know? Have you seen how hares run once they're discovered? The same way.

Dr.   Were you afraid a sentry might be stationed in the woods ready to ambush you?

P.P.   Sort of. I thought they were everywhere. I mean, I walked very cautiously. Then I'd run, then I'd stop still, to listen.

Dr.   And when you stopped, did you hear anything?

P.P.   You won't believe this, Doctor, but what I heard most was my heartbeats.

Dr.   Your heart was audible?

P.P. It sounded like a pump, with a drum and everything. I guess it must've been because of that tight feeling in my chest. I could hardly breathe.

Dr. And voices? Did you hear voices?

P.P. Lots of them, like orders or shouts. It was like the end of the world.

Dr. And did you get to town through the oak trees?

P.P. Wait a minute. First I came to the clearing. And I stopped there 'cause I couldn't make up my mind. So it was one of two choices: either I went back the way I'd come or I peeled out of there. I couldn't decide which was worse.

Dr. What did you decide?

P.P. What do you think? I hit the ground and crawled, just the way I had from the moat to the junipers.

Dr. Go on.

P.P. Well, once I got to the other side of the thicket, I could see the town's lights near me. Not the prison. The prison was on the other side by then. But that was neither here nor there. What I was concerned about was turning myself in before they fired a shot at me.

Dr. What did you do?

P.P. For the moment I just waited and made sure there were no sentries around. But as I was waiting, taking cover under an oak tree, what do you suppose I heard?

Dr. What, Pacífico?

P.P. The train whistle.

Dr. The passenger and freight train?

P.P. That's right, Doctor. It was our train coming through.

Dr. And?

P.P. Well, you can just imagine. I started thinking about my friends, and I even forgot my own name for a second.

Dr. Did you have an idea of where they were at that time?

P.P. Well, as for Don Santiago, and even Patita, I wasn't worried. I mean as regards the time. They were probably catching the train. But I *was* worried about Buque and Capullo, who were behind us.

Dr. Were you fearing the worst?

P.P.   Well, to tell you the truth, I wouldn't have bet anything on Buque.

Dr.   Why were you so scared, Pacífico?

P.P.   Well, if you call somebody by his name, and I mean shout it out—after the shooting, you know—and he doesn't answer, well, where could he be?

Dr.   It's not what you think, Pacífico. He could have escaped in the opposite direction from you.

P.P.   Without me hearing him?

Dr.   You may be right, Pacífico. Go on.

P.P.   There isn't much more to tell. When I heard the train whistle I kind of stopped to reflect, like I said. Then I came out from behind the oak tree. I grabbed a path and went as far as a pigeon house. From the pigeon house I went on to the electric transformer, and then I went down a dark street, groping my way, 'til I got into town.

Dr.   Did you turn yourself in?

P.P.   Did I turn myself in? Hmm. That's easy to say.

Dr.   What happened then?

P.P.   Well, that's what I'd planned to do, as you know, but I was beat. Between the exhaustion and the cold I could hardly drag myself around. So I took off my girdle, 'cause of what they say about a white flag, and I walked down the main street of the town, and I waved it up and down, so they'd see me. But nothing happened. Then, Look at him! somebody shouted, and no sooner had he said it than bang! a shot about twenty steps away—that close, eh? I could hear the bullet whiz right past my head. Well, after that I made for the side street again and took off so fast you couldn't hardly see me. I was flying. I went down that street like a flash: first right, then left, then right again. It was a maze. I didn't know where I was headed.

Dr.   Where did you end up?

P.P.   That's what I'd like to know, hey. The thing is, once I was on the main street again, there was a shed with a cart inside. And I climbed into it, past some rods, and in the back there was this pile of manure, see. And what do you suppose occurred to me then?

Dr.   What?

P.P. To jump into it. Up to my ears.

Dr. In the manure?

P.P. In the manure, yeah, in that stink that's always disgusted me. Up to my ears, like I'm telling you.

Dr. And how did you feel?

P.P. Relieved. I got into it, and from the legs up it was nice and warm. God above! If I hadn't thought of that I probably would've ended up flat on my back out in the street.

Dr. And stiff from the cold, too.

P.P. What could I have done?

Dr. Tell me about the shed, Pacífico. Was it dark in there?

P.P. Well, there was a lamp post on the corner, see, but other than that, the cart was mostly in the dark. I mean, I could see a little bit of the street, the corner, but it was hard for me, being covered by the manure like I was.

Dr. How long were you in there?

P.P. Well, I wasn't in any hurry. So I said to myself, Hey, Pacífico, just sit tight 'til your nerves calm down.

Dr. How did you notice your nervousness?

P.P. You're still wondering, Doctor? After the shot, which I felt whiz past my head, and then the running and shouting, you still ask me how I noticed my nerves? It was like a war!

Dr. Could you hear them?

P.P. How could I help it? Right there next to me was the official or whatever he was giving orders, right? There must've been an army there, with all that racket. And he goes, Close the windows! to the townspeople. They were curious, of course. And the official sent a patrol to the area—I could hear him—and another patrol to the transformer near the barnyards and sheds where I was watching from, see. So I wasn't exactly going to walk around waiting for them.

Dr. Didn't they search yours?

P.P. My what?

Dr. Your hiding place, the shed.

P.P. Not mine, no sir, but the official put a civil guard on every corner. What he ordered them to search was the street, the block where

I was. But I was far away by then.

Dr.   Was there anybody on the corner that you could see?

P.P.   Only a civil guard.

Dr.   Didn't he move?

P.P.   He came and went. From the light to the shadow and from the shadow to the light. And that's when his patent leather three-cornered hat shone my way.

Dr.   Did you say anything to him?

P.P.   Not at first, no sir; I didn't let out a peep. That guard looked very young. And I thought to myself: This is probably the first time he's been in a jam like this. He might cringe, and then we'd make a mess of it. So I decided to stay put.

Dr.   You didn't move, then?

P.P.   No sir. It wouldn't have done me any good. Besides, where, I'd like to know, could I have gone? And anyway, I was fine there. After half an hour I didn't notice the smell or anything. I was just fine. You know, things that disgust you are like things that scare you: you get inside them, and after a while you don't even notice them.

Dr.   What did you do all that time?

P.P.   Open my eyes and cock my ears. What else could I do?

Dr.   And?

P.P.   And? Well, sometimes you could hear running and shooting, and sometimes nothing. And one of those times another guard called out to mine: We got him! See what I mean? They'd caught somebody else, and I wondered who it was.

Dr.   Didn't the guard on your corner reply?

P.P.   Yeah, he did. He said, Just two to go.

Dr.   Which two do you think they were?

P.P.   Well, one of them was me, of course.

Dr.   And the other?

P.P.   Don Santiago.

Dr.   Because of the car?

P.P.   You've got a thing about that car!

Dr.   Well, why did you think the other one was Don Santiago?

P.P.   It was only natural, wasn't it? He got away first, and he had a better head than the others.

Dr.   Did the guard stay on the corner once they'd caught the man they were after?

P.P.   Yep. He stayed right there getting snowed on.

Dr.   He'd quieted down?

P.P.   Well, I don't know about *that*.

Dr.   What are you laughing about, Pacífico?

P.P.   Things. Even when you're stuck in the worst way, there's always something funny to laugh about.

Dr.   What was it?

P.P.   It was a cat, see.

Dr.   A cat?

P.P.   Yep. A big black cat that got tangled up in the guard's legs, almost killed him. You should've seen him! It knocked his gun off his shoulder, and it was a miracle he didn't shoot him. He kept saying, You bastard! The scare you gave me! A quarter of an hour fussing about it.

Dr.   I see. And how did it end?

P.P.   The way it had to, Doctor, the way it was meant to be.

Dr.   And how was that?

P.P.   Well, as the sun started to rise, I raised my arms, and I whispered to him.

Dr.   To the guard?

P.P.   Of course, the guard.

Dr.   What did he do?

P.P.   You should've seen him! He turned around, aimed at me, then: Stay where you are, or I'll blow you to bits! I mean shouting, too. So I go: Take it easy. I'm a friend, not a foe. And he goes: Stay where you are, or I'll blow you to bits! And me, I say: Hey, guard, careful with that thing. Let's not do something we'll be sorry about. But he aims at me anyway, won't take the muzzle away from my stomach, and now and then he screams, Sergeant!

Dr.   Didn't you get out of the manure?

P.P.   How could I, Doctor? I stayed right where I was when I'd whispered to him. I didn't dare breathe.

Dr.   And did the guard keep aiming at you in spite of the fact that you had your arms up?

P.P.   The whole time. I mean, every now and then he'd shout at the sergeant and then he'd turn around and say, Don't move, or I'll blow you to bits. He wouldn't turn the gun aside for the life of him. Who knows who he thought I was?

Dr.   Did the sergeant get there?

P.P.   Yes he did. With that business about We'll be off soon.

Dr.   What were his words, exactly?

P.P.   He said, Hey, look what this guy got himself into! That's all. And then I got out of the cart and started to shake something awful.

Dr.   Out of fear?

P.P.   Out of fear and cold, both.

Dr.   What did they do with you?

P.P.   Well, being naked and all the way I was, they stuck me in between four guards and marched me off to prison. It was day by then, and the balconies and streets were packed. It looked like a holiday.

Dr.   Did people watch you go past?

P.P.   Sure.

Dr.   Did they seem compassionate?

P.P.   Compassionate? Why, no sir.

Dr.   Hostile, then?

P.P.   How do I know how they looked at me? Like some weird creature, I guess. Like I wasn't one of them.

Dr.   Did it mortify you to be looked at that way?

P.P.   Well, I guess so. But how did you expect people to look at me? I wasn't suffering any because of it, though. Oh no. I already knew that people in Góyar couldn't stand the sight of the prison.

Dr.   Didn't it please them that it was there?

P.P.   No sir. According to Don Santiago, the authorities had been trying for years to get it moved. I mean, if they'd had their way they would've shot every one of us, understand? When you think about it, nobody likes to have their peace disturbed, Doctor.

Dr.   Well, let's get to the point now. Did you return to your cell?

P.P.   To the hall, you mean?

Dr.   To the hall, yes, excuse me.

P.P.   How were they going to put me in there without covering the hole first?

Dr.   You're right, Pacífico. I don't know what I'm talking about. So what did they do with you?

P.P.   At first they locked me up in a punishment cell.

Dr. Alone?

P.P. Of course. Alone.

Dr. Didn't they interrogate you?

P.P. That came afterward. When I got out of the storeroom.

Dr. Why did they take you there?

P.P. To identify the bodies.

Dr. Who was there?

P.P. The sentry and Vegas, of course.

Dr. And from your group?

P.P. Buque and Capullo, whom I was surprised to see.

Dr. What did you feel when you saw them there?

P.P. Oh, nothing special. I mean, I thought of Catalina and Francisco Rincón, that's for sure. And how it'd all been a waste of time. As for Capullo, well, I thought of Isabelita and his plans for her. And the months he'd thrown away digging in the tunnel with the spoon—all for this.

Dr. Did you pity them?

P.P. Not especially, no sir. I just told myself, That's life, and that's all there is to it.

Dr. You think it's just how life is—to die full of bullets in the open air?

P.P. Don't get me wrong. We live to die. I mean, that's the law, Doctor. How we do it doesn't matter.

Dr. And tell me, were they disfigured?

P.P. No, not really. Buque had two holes about this size next to his left nipple. As for Capullo, he just had one, in his lower stomach, but it was black and blue over his private parts. What a bruise!

Dr. How about the guards?

P.P. Vegas looked like he was sleeping; just the way we'd left him under the cot, except he was stiff. The other guy, though, his head was a mess. I guess Buque must've let him have it with his cast.

Dr. What did you say, that you recognized them?

P.P. Well, yeah. What else was I supposed to say?

Dr. Right there on the spot?

P.P. Well, yeah, at first. Then later on in the office. I mean, I had to repeat it in there. But I guess they hadn't caught Don Santiago yet, and all they did was ask me about him.

Dr. What did you tell them?

P.P.　The truth. That I didn't know any more than they did.

Dr.　Did they believe you?

P.P.　Ask them if you want to know. But from the way they kept badgering me, I don't think they did.

Dr.　What else did they ask you?

P.P.　Everything. Whose idea it was, how we escaped, what we were planning to do, who killed Vegas . . .

Dr.　What was your reply?

P.P.　The truth. You're always best off with the truth.

Dr.　So you told them that Don Santiago was planning to take the train?

P.P.　No sir, not that. But I didn't tell them anything else, either. I mean, I didn't lie. Whatever would've harmed Don Santiago's chances I kept to myself.

Dr.　So you didn't tell them that it was Don Santiago who killed the guard with a fatal blow?

P.P.　Vegas, you mean? No sir, I didn't tell them that, either.

Dr.　And what did they say?

P.P.　They asked me more and more questions.

Dr.　Did they say anything about the fact that the guard's body was under your bed?

P.P.　That was the first thing, sure.

Dr.　What did you allege?

P.P.　What?

Dr.　I mean, what did you answer?

P.P.　The truth. That we put him there as easily as we could've put him somewhere else. In other words, it was the handiest place.

Dr.　And what explanation did you give to justify that you didn't see who killed the guard?

P.P.　That I was in bed, with my bedclothes up to my ears, and that I didn't realize what was happening.

Dr.　Did they accept your explanation?

P.P.　No sir, they didn't like it. That's for sure.

Dr.　Did they insist?

P.P.　Well, they persisted for a while, yes sir; but since they weren't getting anything out of me, they tried another tack.

Dr.　And what did you do?

P.P.   I stayed mum, of course.

Dr.   Since Buque and Capullo were dead, couldn't you have blamed them?

P.P.   But it wouldn't have been true.

Dr.   Would it have made any difference, though?

P.P.   Excuse me. I don't follow you.

Dr.   I mean that since they couldn't do anything to Capullo and Buque, why didn't you blame the guard's death on them, and save the rest of you?

P.P.   That's a nice one! In other words, lying's OK with you where dead men are involved.

Dr.   Well, only as a way out, Pacífico.

P.P.   But hey, it wasn't true.

Dr.   Well, as far as that goes, neither was it true that you were in bed when Don Santiago killed the guard, was it, hmm? Why don't you answer?

P.P.   You know, you're right. I hadn't thought of that.

Dr.   So?

P.P.   Well, if you think about it, I wasn't hurting anybody with that lie. It was the other way around. I mean, if I had said that I saw him but I didn't want to say it, they would have slapped me silly.

Dr.   In other words, whether you lie or not depends on the consequénces it'll have.

P.P.   No sir, it's not like that. I mean, at the trial I'll tell the whole truth, as sure as my name's Pacífico.

Dr.   You won't be that stupid, I hope.

P.P.   Why, what do you mean?

Dr.   Listen, Pacífico. Your case is already complicated enough. Don't make it worse. Since the day you killed Teotista, all you've done is sink lower. We'll talk about this aspect later, if you don't mind. For now, please tell me how the episode ended. Did the sentry's death implicate you too?

P.P.   No sir. From the start they blamed Buque for it. I mean, the bodies were side by side. And they found bits of the cast in the sentry's hair—from Buque's leg, I mean. Clear as day.

Dr.   How did the interrogation end?

P.P.   Well, when I let it all out, the director goes and says: Well, the other guy doesn't agree with your statements. That's how I realized that Patita hadn't gotten it. I mean, that they'd nabbed him too.

Dr. And what did they say Patita said?

P.P. Well, that I'd killed Vegas. Imagine.

Dr. Did you believe them?

P.P. No sir, not in a million years. I could tell what they were up to. And besides, Patita confirmed it later on.

Dr. So you saw Patita again?

P.P. Yes sir, the night they moved us, while we were waiting for the station wagon, just for a moment.

Dr. What did he say?

P.P. Imagine—that he'd had bad luck too.

Dr. Where did they catch him?

P.P. In the forest, near the train tracks.

Dr. Did you agree on what to say at the trial?

P.P. No sir, there wasn't time. All he asked was if it was true that I had said that he killed Vegas. You see how they tried to trick us? Trying to pit us against each other? Patita, poor guy, was done for.

Dr. Did you already know where they were sending you?

P.P. Yes sir. To Navafría, the guard told me so. He said, You're going to see what a first-class sanatorium is like.

Dr. Was he just kidding?

P.P. I guess so. Judge for yourself. If I'm here, it's 'cause I came.

Dr. Fine. The next important point is the trial, Pacífico. Did you speak openly with the lawyer?

P.P. Oh yeah. He does all the talking anyway. What a mouth.

Dr. How about you—what did you say?

P.P. Not much, really. He talks enough for both of us.

Dr. Listen, Pacífico. Are you aware how serious your situation is?

P.P. More or less, Doctor.

Dr. Have you stopped to consider that the next place you may be sent is the executioner's? That you could get the chair?

P.P. I don't think it's that bad, Doctor. You make it sound worse.

Dr. Look, Pacífico, no matter what you say, you haven't realized how serious this case is. I'm almost sure that if you're charged with the guard's death, nobody will be able to save you from punishment. And do you have any idea what capital punishment is like?

P.P.   They hang you, don't they?

Dr.   Worse than that, Pacífico. They break your neck in iron stocks, and then they tighten a screw until it chokes you. They asphyxiate you, that's what they do. But waiting for that to happen day after day, being totally lucid . . . that's an even greater torment, you know?

P.P.   Well, I guess it is . . . I've even broken out in a cold sweat thinking about it.

Dr.   Well, that's what you have to avoid, Pacífico. And to avoid it, the only thing that occurs to me is this: You can say that Don Santiago killed the guard with the bar.

P.P.   Look, I don't want to harm anybody. Not Don Santiago or anybody else.

Dr.   But this way you're hurting yourself, Pacífico. Don't you see? By now Don Santiago has been across the border for five months twiddling his thumbs. What do you think he cares if you say this or that about him here?

P.P.   I won't do that either, Doctor. Life's strange. If they should nab him one day—'cause it could happen—why should he get nailed?

Dr.   And with such a tiny chance, say maybe one in a million, of that happening, are you going to run the risk of getting the chair yourself?

P.P.   If it comes to that, Don Santiago will take care of seeing that an innocent man won't pay for a sinner.

Dr.   Do you really believe what you're saying?

P.P.   Well, it wouldn't be the first time. He's done it before.

Dr.   Honestly now, Pacífico, do you swallow that story Don Santiago gave you about keeping an innocent man from being condemned?

P.P.   Look, Doctor, on something else I might say no. But the local grapevine was pretty dependable. I mean, you can say anything you like, but you can't tell me that Don Santiago didn't offer himself up as a volunteer.

Dr.   In the best of circumstances you'll get thirty years, Pacífico.

P.P.   And is that so bad, Doctor?

Dr.   Well, I guess you'll have to decide that for yourself. Spending one's life behind bars doesn't sound like a very rosy future.

P.P.   It's not so bad, either. I'm fine here. I mean, I'm content.

Dr.   Don't you care about what's going on outside in the world?

P.P.   Oh, I know what's going on outside: everybody's against everybody else.

Dr.   Do you say that because of your war?

P.P.   Oh, come on! Because of mine and everyone else's: the gang from Otero, Candi, Bisa, everybody. Don't you remember what Father said to me once?

Dr.   When? About what?

P.P.   Well, when he was checking the beehives, of course. He said, Pacífico, take or they'll take from you. There's no other way in life. What do you think of that?

Dr.   And do you think you're free from all that in here? What did Don Santiago do except bleed the rest of you to death?

P.P.   Unless you light into Don Santiago, you're just not happy, are you?

Dr.   Listen, Pacífico, until they put us back in our mothers' wombs to be born different, wherever man goes, he's threatened.

P.P.   That's very true, sir.

Dr.   So if we don't like something in life, we shouldn't cringe from it. We should try to change it.

P.P.   Like Don Prócoro and my Uncle Paco? Some stew we'd be in. Look at how many people have put their hands in the fire. Out there, in case you want to know, all they know how to do is compete. And that's not my way, Doctor.

Dr.   But Pacífico, if not for your own good, at least do it so that for once the truth will shine. And the truth is that you didn't want to escape, but then Don Santiago killed the guard and forced you to. He even threatened to kill you if you didn't follow him.

P.P.   That doesn't count, Doctor. I didn't want to, but I left, and that's the honest truth.

Dr.   Don't be obstinate, Pacífico. You took off because they'd threatened you. And the truth is that you didn't kill the guard. At the moment, this is the most important thing.

P.P.   If you stop to think about it, I guess it is: I didn't kill him. But if

I'd been in Don Santiago's shoes I'd have done the same as he did. We're all guilty, don't you think?

Dr. Nobody's asking you that.

P.P. Hey, but I know it. Are you going to tell me that I didn't have it in me to do the same?

Dr. You're very stubborn, Pacífico. The jury tries and condemns you for what you *have* done, not for what you might have done if you'd been in another person's shoes.

P.P. Look, Doctor, I think it's better to let a sleeping dog lie.

Dr. Don't you want to listen to me? Your intentions aren't subject to punishment. In Christian morality they may be, but this isn't a case of that.

P.P. I know what I'm talking about, Doctor.

Dr. Look, Pacífico, I'm only going to ask you one favor . . .

P.P. Go ahead.

Dr. That your lawyer appoint me to speak at the trial. Yours is a medical case.

P.P. Are you going to say I'm nuts, too? Well, I'm not, just in case you want to know.

Dr. Fine, son. But let me warn you about something: being nuts isn't what you think it is. There are shades of it. Man is a very complex machine.

P.P. Some news you're giving me.

Dr. In that case, Pacífico, everything we do to correctly interpret your conduct will be fair, don't you agree?

P.P. I don't know . . . But it seems that what you want is to confuse me.

Dr. Listen, Pacífico, and don't get upset, please. You refuse to let me intervene. Fine, I accept that. But why not speak to your lawyer and have him request a medical examination?

P.P. Another one? Like the other one?

Dr. Exactly. Like the other one.

P.P. And you'll do it, right?

Dr. No, Pacífico. I'll stay out of it, I promise. But aside from the analyses and the tests themselves, you'll authorize me to turn over these tapes and the recorder to the experts, agreed?

P.P. This here gadget?

Dr. That's right.

P.P.   Shit! I'll break it before I allow that.

Dr.   Pacífico, calm down! Let go of the chair!

P.P.   You promised me . . .

Dr.   Calm down, Pacífico, calm down. I promised you that without your authorization I wouldn't make public anything we've said. And a promise is a promise, all right? That's why I requested your authorization. But if you don't give it to me, I won't make a move. What's wrong? Do you feel sick?

P.P.   Never mind, it's nothing, Doctor.

Dr.   Sit down for a minute. Would you like a glass of water?

P.P.   I think I'd better lie down.

Dr.   Wait, don't go yet. Are you feeling better?

P.P.   Yes sir, it's over now.

Dr.   Before leaving, Pacífico, I'd like to ask you a final question. Do you mind?

P.P.   No, not at all.

Dr.   What can I do for you in this difficult situation you've put me in?

P.P.   Nothing, never mind. I mean, just leave me alone.

The prisoner Pacífico Pérez died in the Navafría Penitentiary Sanatorium, where he was serving a sentence, on September 13, 1969. Eight years before, he had been condemned to death by execution with the garrote by the court that judged him, and his sentence was reduced to thirty years of confinement due to the clemency of the chief of state.

On the eleventh of September of the aforementioned year, the prisoner Pacífico Pérez suffered in rapid succession three hemoptyses, for which reason he was admitted to the prison infirmary and underwent emergency treatment. At his request, his father, Don Felicísimo Pérez, and his uncle, Don Francisco Pérez, were informed of the proceedings at meetings attended by the undersigned, at the express will of the deceased party. In the presence of these family members, the aforementioned Pacífico Pérez manifested to the undersigned that, given the time that had transpired, and if such was his wish, the latter was permitted to print the conversations held between the two eight years earlier, a position made official by his signing of the necessary authorization. Thereupon, the prisoner addressed his uncle, Don Francisco Pérez, in a very faint voice, saying in a slightly reproachful tone: "You were wrong, Uncle. We can sink lower than the ground." To this the one alluded to assented, an assent that the prisoner Pacífico Pérez received with a distant smile.

Next, the prisoner addressed his father, Don Felicísimo Pérez, expressing his wish to enter into matrimony with Señorita Cándida Morcillo, these being words that irritated Don Felicísimo, whose literal reply was: "Marry that slut!" To this the prisoner Pacífico Pérez replied that it no longer mattered that he was a cuckold because he was going to die, and the important thing was to give his son a father. Immediately afterward, at his own request, the prisoner made his last confession and received communion totally lucid, entering one hour later into a comatose state. Despite this, Don Anastasio Gómez, the *prison chaplain, as soon as Señorita Cándida Morcillo appeared, blessed them both* in articulo mortis. *Attending the ceremony were the following witnesses: Don Felicísimo Pérez, whose negative response was reiterated; the uncle of the deceased man, Don Francisco Pérez; and the undersigned,*

Francisco de Asís Burgueño
Doctor of Medicine.